VOTE OF intolerance

JOSH

a n d

Vote of

in

MCDOWELL
ED STEWART

tolerance

Tyndale House Publishers, Inc.
WHEATON, ILLINOIS

Library of Congress Cataloging-in-Publication Data

McDowell, Josh.
   Vote of intolerance / Josh McDowell, Ed Stewart.
      p.   cm.
   ISBN 0-8423-3905-1
   I. Stewart, Ed. II. Title.
PS3563.C35935V68   1997
813'.54—dc21   97-11014

ACKNOWLEDGMENTS

We wish to thank the following people for their significant involvement in this novel:

David N. Weiss, for his creative guidance

Kathi Mills, for her skillful editing

Ken Petersen of Tyndale House Publishers, for his vision and input

Dottie McDowell and *Becky Bellis,* for their helpful insights

Dave Bellis,
my (Josh's) Resource Development Coordinator
and agent for twenty years,
for providing oversight and coordination

Josh McDowell
Ed Stewart

spring

1

Friday
March 26

THE NOISY GYM became graveyard silent in an instant. Jon Van Horne had been keeping up with three of his young charges, Ari, Robert, and Jaleen, on easy layups and had just dropped in a nice running hook shot in an effort to pin an *O* on Jaleen during their friendly game of Horse. But now, instead of celebrating Jon's shot with high fives, Jaleen and his two friends were staring past the coach toward the entrance. The other games in the gym had also suddenly slowed to spectator pace. Jon turned to find out why.

There were eight of them, somewhere between the ages of sixteen and twenty, Jon guessed. Characteristic of the current hybrid gangs in L.A., there was a mix of races: three African-

Americans, two Latinos, two Caucasians, and an Asian, all males. They were clad in the latest Valley gang regalia: mismatched military clothing and boots. Although Jon hadn't seen these particular young men before, he was pretty sure they were members of the Valley's own De Soto gang. Even as he silently berated himself for forgetting to lock the door after a kid left ten minutes earlier, he watched one of the gang members lock the door for him, sealing him and the kids inside. Jon felt the icy fingers of a real and present fear touch him inside.

Like many L.A. gangs, the De Sotos patterned themselves after the maverick inner-city militia, which had unofficially occupied four square miles of south-central Los Angeles for over a year. The tyrannized area—called "the dead zone" by the media—was a hellhole of drugs, prostitution, violence, and murder. If you didn't belong there, you didn't dare cross the borders, or you might never get out. Even the Los Angeles Police Department, having lost several officers there, had unofficially conceded the dead zone to the ruthless south-central militia. The De Sotos and other gangs across the sprawling city exploited the reputation of the militia to rule by intimidation wherever they went.

Jon sucked a long, slow breath at the prospect of trouble. The De Sotos were known to terrorize kids for their money and valuables—and sometimes just for amusement. If they couldn't frighten their intended victims into submission, they thought nothing of using a knife or gun to carry out their threats. The rough-looking group who had just invaded the gym were probably packing weapons under their bulky trench coats and bomber jackets.

Jon sneaked a peek at his watch. It was exactly 9:45 P.M. That meant it would be at least fifteen or twenty minutes before parents began arriving to pick up their kids. Jon knew it was up to him as the recreation director to keep the gang docile and preoccupied—and keep the wide-eyed kids behind him safe—until then. Hopefully the adults' arrival would defuse the situation, maybe even scare the intruders off. If not—well, Jon would have to cross that bridge when he came to it. For now, the responsibility rested solely—and heavily—on his shoulders.

As a high school counselor in L.A.'s sprawling, populous San

4

Fernando Valley, Jon spent thirty-seven weeks a year with students. For Jon and most educators, spring break was a jealously guarded respite in the grueling push from Christmas break to summer vacation. Yet here he was, finishing a long spring-break week of supervising youth basketball.

It wasn't that a brief vacation away from the Valley wouldn't have been wonderful, but Jon needed the extra money this year. Besides, it wasn't any fun visiting Mexico or Disney World or even Malibu Beach alone. And this was the second spring break in a row that Jon had found himself without a companion.

Actually, it was kids like Jaleen, Ari, and Robert who were the real reason Jon kept coming back to the rec center during school vacations. In this setting, he wasn't their teacher or counselor. Technically, he was here only to monitor the courts and break up an occasional scuffle between overheated competitors. Yet in Jon's mind, he was here to substitute for the dads who were missing from their lives. He felt sorry for kids like Robert and Jaleen and Kiki who had never met their fathers, and for Ari and Manon whose fathers had recently left home for greener marital pastures.

Jon's sympathy was especially acute this spring break, particularly when it came to the breakup of families. The same personal trauma that had left him without a companion just over a year ago had created an unwanted desert of distance between him and his own two children.

Jon took a deep breath, forcing himself to sound cordial but firm. "May I help you guys?" he asked, slowly approaching the gang members, who stood staring him down from near the entrance. Jon was a muscular six-footer in excellent physical condition, thanks to a regimen of weekly workouts and regular involvement in sports. He was clearly more agile in his shorts and Nike T-shirt than the eight young men in their bulky uniforms. But Jon knew he couldn't take them all on, even if by some miracle they were *not* armed. The thirty or so kids in the gym, now frozen statues of fear, would be of little help and might even be in greater danger if he tried to be a hero.

Then Jon remembered Traci, his part-time aide—a cute college girl—who was dust-mopping the small gym. He hated to think what these guys might try if she wandered into the room. *Wherever you are, Traci,* Jon willed silently, *stay out of sight until these guys leave.*

The reply came from a big African-American kid in a stained, rumpled army trench coat, baggy fatigue pants, green beret, and jackboots. Minus some multiple vulgarities, the kid said, "We're here to play some basketball, dude." Signs prohibiting profanity in the rec center were clearly posted on the walls, so Jon already had cause to dismiss the surprise visitors. But he had learned years ago to pick his battles when dealing with tough kids, especially when he wasn't sure what a kid might do to get his way. Four teachers had been shot in the school district already this year attempting to discipline students for minor misbehavior. It wasn't worth the risk to ignite a major conflict over a minor issue. Jon made a snap decision to let the kid's bad language slide.

"The rec center is only open for a few more minutes," Jon explained, still holding his voice steady. "And as you can see, all our courts are being used." Just as he spoke the final word, Jon heard two or three basketballs drop to the hardwood floor. Jon knew what had happened without looking. The kids behind him had surrendered their basketballs to the invading gang and backed off the courts en masse.

"Looks like a couple courts just opened up, Rashaad," a Latino member said to the leader with a coarse laugh, adding a few vulgarities in Spanish, clearly directed toward Jon.

Anger rivaled fear for supremacy underneath Jon's carefully monitored external calm. Weapons and violence had become commonplace in his school. Jon hated it, but he was becoming less and less shocked at finding a gun on a fourteen-year-old student or breaking through a hysterical crowd to find a kid on a hallway floor spouting blood from a hole the size of a silver dollar in his chest. But it was the impertinence that galled him the most. It leered out at him through the eyes of kids like these who had no respect for authority, no real interest in education and career, and little regard for human life, particularly their own.

Insolence possessed this generation like a demon, Jon had often thought, even slipping its sinister tentacles into his own home and wreaking an unthinkable tragedy, destroying his son and dividing what was left of his family. The demon had outraged Jon to the point of wanting out of teaching. He had written his resignation letter four times over the last four years. But that same outrage had also prevented him from following through with the surrender. If he did not stay to oppose the dragon poised to devour younger kids like Jaleen and the others, even in a seemingly losing battle, who would?

Rashaad, the hulking leader, interrupted Jon's thoughts. "Guess you're right, Chako," he sneered. "Let's play some ball." Six of the eight gang members shed their coats and jackets, leaving any weapons they might be carrying hidden in the inside pockets. The remaining two members, the Asian and the other Latino, kept their coats on, apparently designated to be guards.

As the six new players approached the center court, Jon casually backed away, intent on keeping himself between the gang members and his kids, who were lined against the back wall, silent. He had already detected the odor of alcohol, intensifying his alarm at what the hoods might do. "We don't allow street shoes on our courts," he said with artificial politeness. "Please take your boots off while you play. They scuff up the hardwood floors."

Rashaad, stooping to pick up a basketball with muscular, scarred arms, blew a scornful laugh but said nothing. He tossed the ball to Chako, and the six players began an informal shoot-around, leaving their boots on.

No consideration, no "please may we," only taking. It made Jon seethe inside. Normally a man who looked for the best in people, ready to excuse faults and overlook shortcomings—to a dangerous extreme, according to his ex-wife—Jon found himself wanting to press the issue about the boots, not only because of the gang's insolence but also because he knew it would take him an extra hour to scrub the scuff marks off the court. But this was another battle not worth fighting. *Every minute they're occupied with themselves,* Jon acknowledged silently, *is another minute they aren't harassing me or the kids. Time is on my side. Parents are bound to show up soon and start pounding on the door. And unless these guys are prepared to take on the outside world—and I pray they're not—they'll leave and it will all be over.*

As the players continued to warm up, one of the Caucasian

boys, a hollow-eyed, gaunt kid with tattoos of snakes entwining both arms, caught Jon's attention. The others called him Rattler. He was fairly good at handling the basketball, but he was also drunk. He was especially boisterous and foulmouthed and a little unsteady on his clunky army boots. In between shots, Rattler kept looking past Jon and leering at the line of kids backed up against the far wall. The evil in Rattler's gaze made Jon's skin crawl.

After a minute of practice shots, the six players huddled on the court. Jon glanced over his shoulder and telegraphed his most encouraging look toward the kids behind him. A couple of the younger ones were stifling tears of fear. Jon mouthed the words, "It's all right, it's all right," and prayed that his hopeful encouragement would be rewarded.

The gang members broke their huddle with a raucous laugh. Three of them, including Rattler, threw off their shirts for a typical "shirts versus skins" game. "We need a few more players," Rattler laughed. "Rashaad gets to choose first."

"The shirts take that fat brother over there and that skinny Arab." A quick glance told Jon that the gang leader had singled out Jaleen and Ari, who were petrified with fear. Without turning around, Jon subtly motioned the two boys to stay put.

Before Rashaad could object, Rattler stepped forward, standing a dozen feet in front of Jon. "And the skins take those two tall chicks right there," he said, cackling wickedly as he aimed a tattoo-scarred hand past Jon to the wall.

The small whimper of terror from Kiki and Rachel, two of the five girls locked arm-in-arm against the back wall, was swallowed up by an explosion of mocking laughter and curses from the eight gang members. Rattler's eyes flared with fiendish delight. He began moving unsteadily toward the girls.

Avoiding sudden motion, Jon eased into Rattler's path. He would not compromise with the gang members on this issue. Kiki was barely fourteen—his own daughter's age—and Rachel was only thirteen. They were innocent, fun-loving girls who enjoyed shooting hoops with the boys. Somewhere in his brain Jon knew that he might get shot over this, that some of these kids might get shot, and that one or more of these girls might get raped and even murdered. Things like this were on the news nearly every day in L.A. Rattler's diabolical gaze left no question in Jon's mind that he was capable of such horrors, and his friends looked no better. The fear of death gripped Jon's chest, but he could not let this happen without a fight—on that point he had absolutely no question.

Rattler stopped three feet from Jon. The wicked humor had drained from his face. After blazing a stream of foul breath and curses at Jon, he said, "I want the chicks, man. They're on my team." The other gang members stood by watching the confrontation and egging Rattler on.

Jon kept his hands at his side. Most teachers in Los Angeles were encouraged to take classes on administering physical restraint. Administrators, counselors, and special education staff were *required* to take them. Jon was well-practiced at physically subduing out-of-control students with a minimum amount of inflicted pain, since pain can provoke greater resistance and combativeness. He could subdue Rattler, especially in his inebriated state, and he knew he could hurt the boy and temporarily disable him if restraint was not enough. But how far would the other gang members let him go before they unleashed their hate-filled fury? Jon was afraid he might find out in mere seconds.

"You can play on my court, and you can scuff up my floor," Jon said forcefully but in a reserved tone, meeting Rattler glare for glare. "But you can't mess with my kids. Play your game, but leave these—"

Rattler swung at him, an ill-aimed but potentially vicious blow. Jon stepped back as the fist passed in front of his face. The unsuccessful attack brought a chorus of profane cheers from the squad. Jon had been trained to back away and avoid physical contact whenever possible. In this instance, he also sensed that such a tactic might keep the rest of the gang from getting involved. If it never developed into a fight, they might not feel pressured to join in. But Rattler kept coming at him—swearing, swinging, and fuming, backing Jon closer to the kids he must protect with his life.

Fresh out of evasive options, Jon took the offensive. He snatched the kid's wrist in midswing. In a blur of motion, he spun the kid around. Quickly locking him in a painless but effective bear hug from behind, Jon began to guide the cursing, struggling young drunk back toward the gang.

Before he took two steps, Jon's feet tangled with Rattler's flailing boots and the two of them toppled forward. With the kid's arms locked to his side in Jon's grip, the shirtless gang member hit the hardwood floor face first with his captor's dead weight on his back. The kid howled and cursed in pain. Jon knew it must have looked—and felt—like an intentional, vindictive takedown.

This is it, Jon thought, fighting off a shock of panic. *If the rest of these guys are going to jump me and pound me senseless or shoot me, they're going to do it now. God, help me.* He scrambled quickly to his feet, ready to defend himself.

The other seven thugs were nearly on him when a loud, heavy rap on the gym's main doors stopped them in their tracks. The blur across the far end of the room, Jon realized, was Traci, his aide, sprinting from the small gym to the front doors. She hit the panic bar and pushed open the door, admitting two LAPD officers in short-sleeved navy-blue uniforms and baseball-style caps. Both had their nightsticks in hand.

Blind with pain and rage, Rattler didn't notice the cops. He scrabbled to his feet and lunged for Jon. But Rashaad and Chako, the two largest gang members, grabbed him by the arms and pulled him back. Blood streamed from Rattler's split lip and several loosened teeth in his mouth, running in rivulets through a sparse goatee and down his neck. He hurled vile curses at Jon, spraying the floor between them with crimson droplets. His mates quickly shut him up as the officers approached.

"I saw them come in, and I thought you might need some help," Traci said from a safe distance, her face pale with fright. "So I called 9-1-1."

Jon released an audible sigh, grimacing as a searing pain, caused by his fall, ripped through his right elbow and wrist. "Thanks, Traci," he said, his voice strained from the shock. "Your timing couldn't have been better."

Jon Van Horne lay awake until almost midnight, riding out a massive adrenaline surge and the caffeine-laced pain pills he had taken to dull the throb in his bruised arm. Unable to sleep, he replayed the events of the evening. All had ended well enough, he thought. The two De Soto "guards" were arrested for packing semiautomatic handguns without permits. Jon refused to press charges for the attempted assault. Rattler, whose real name turned out to be Eugene Hackett, was from nearby Canoga Park. He and the others had had no weapons on them. They were released at the scene.

The cops were sure that the two gun-toting boys would also be released before morning. It was almost impossible to make a weapons charge stick in L.A. anymore unless the shooter actually fired at and hit a victim. Someday Rashaad, Chako, and Eugene might go too far and blow someone away with those big guns of theirs, Jon mused somberly. But until they did they were as free to roam the streets of the Valley as he was.

Jaleen, Ari, Kiki, Rachel, and the others had left the rec center a little shaken but able to joke about the scary ten minutes in the gym. Unfortunately, they saw too much of guns and gang violence on their school campuses as it was. Like Jon, they were becoming, if not calloused, at least accustomed to this destructive lifestyle. The parents who picked up the kids had seemed only slightly more disturbed by what happened in the gym.

At the center of Jon's thoughts was his own fourteen-year-old daughter, Shawna. After what could have happened to Kiki and Rachel tonight, he wanted to hold Shawna and never let her go. She was a good girl, but she was naïve and irresponsible, growing up too fast. Jon's ex-wife, Stevie, who he reluctantly acknowledged had been a good single mom since the divorce, lamented that Shawna was watching too much TV and losing interest in church. Jon hoped he could spend some time with Shawna and nine-year-old Collin this weekend. Maybe the three of them could go to church together Sunday morning. Now that he was unable to see his children every day, Jon yearned for their all-too-infrequent visits.

Jon tried to pray for his kids, but as often happened when he tried to pray, his mind wandered. Something terrible could have happened to sweet little Kiki tonight. Horrible stuff happens to good girls, and it could happen to Shawna, too. A knot of worry twisted painfully in Jon's stomach. He finally fell asleep begging God to keep his little girl safe.

Nineteen-year-old Eugene "Rattler" Hackett paced the dark driveway of the run-down house in Canoga Park where he lived with his uncle. Sober now, he had been seething for a couple of hours over being bloodied and humiliated in front of his gang. Eugene vowed to find the guy in the gym, the basketball coach who had taken him down. Rashaad and Chako had told him to let it go, that the dude at the rec center wasn't worth the trouble of getting even. But Eugene wasn't about to let this one go. A man had to take a stand, earn his stripes in front of his brothers. The coach had not only pushed Eugene over the edge but had set himself up as a perfect target.

Rattler took a long drag on the cigarette in his left hand and blew the smoke skyward. Then he lifted his right hand and admired the gleaming, smooth metal object in the dim street light. It was Rattler's equalizer: a military issue .45 automatic he had been clever enough to hide in the car before his squad crashed the gym. He aimed the large gun at a battered trash can beside the house. "Hey, coach," he said softly, adding bitter curses. Then he mimicked firing a lethal burst from the .45 into the can. "You're a dead man."

2

Friday
March 26

SHAWNA GUESSED that she had been lying motionless on her
bunk for nearly forty-five minutes, pretending to be asleep.
One by one her chatty, giggling, teenaged roommates had
fallen asleep, evidenced by the chorus of deep, steady breathing filling the dark cabin. When their female counselor had
finally dropped off, the buzz-saw snore was music to Shawna's
ears.

She quietly slid out of her flannel-lined sleeping bag and
slipped into the clothes she had hidden under her mattress.
She knew the camp leaders would freak out if they saw her in
this outfit. Tight-fitting turtleneck sweaters and microskirts
were not approved attire for a Christian youth camp. Nor was

it an outfit Shawna felt very comfortable wearing—at least not yet. Her mother had often said that a fully developed four-teen-year-old like Shawna was still too young to dress and act like an eighteen-year-old trying to attract boys. But Shawna's friend Destiny had told her what to bring to camp for this spe-cial night, and Destiny was always right about things like this.

Shawna was outside less than three minutes after leaving her bunk. It was chilly in the mountains, even for spring in South California. But the cold air stinging Shawna's bare legs was tame compared to the electric crackle of excitement running up her spine. What she and Destiny were about to do was against the camp rules. But the rules were for kids who needed to be told what and what not to do, "dorks who forgot to pay their brain bills and got the power shut off," as Destiny some-times said. "Trust your own feelings, Shawna," her friend had tutored her. "It's a lot easier than learning tons of rules, and it's a lot more fun." Surveying the dark campground before her, Shawna was suddenly energized at the thought of making her own rules.

Staying out of the moonlight was easy, thanks to the massive shadows cast by bushy evergreens surrounding the camp. Yet Shawna moved cautiously and quietly, not wanting to spoil Destiny's plan through carelessness. Reaching the rendezvous point behind the camp kitchen, she hunkered down behind a large tree trunk and listened. The soft *whish* through the pine branches above her muffled any sounds from the little village of Arrowhead down the road. And the camp, Shawna knew, was sound asleep.

"Destiny," she whispered into the darkness. "Destiny, where are you? It's Shawna." She strained to hear a response, but there was none. She whispered an expletive, a four-letter word most adults considered unbecoming to a girl her age. *I knew you'd fall asleep or chicken out,* she mouthed silently to the girl she imagined was dead out in her bunk. *I'm waiting five min-utes, Destiny; that's it. If you don't show up, I swear I'll . . .*

Shawna couldn't think of what she would do. Tonight had been Destiny's idea all along. Shawna felt suddenly bummed at the prospect of a lost adventure. But for all her eagerness to meet Rik tonight for the first time, Shawna could not shake an inner discomfort about it that urged her to hurry back to her bunk right away.

Before she could act on that urge, Shawna heard footsteps in the pine needles. "Where are you?" came a distinct whisper. Shawna peered around a trunk until she was able to make out a lone figure approaching in the moonlight, a figure she quickly identified as Destiny.

Destiny Fortugno, another fourteen-year-old who could pass for almost twenty, was the worldliest friend Shawna had ever had. The girl was streetwise and experienced in things Shawna had little courage to try. And Destiny wasn't shy about telling what she had done. At first her stories, which she claimed were all true, embarrassed Shawna. But once she got used to Destiny's street-level language and descriptions, Shawna began to look forward to hearing about her friend's adventures, which seemed barely on the edge of sanity. Shawna didn't tell her mother much about Destiny. That would have been the end of the friendship.

Destiny's weird resale-store clothes, flesh-piercing jewelry, hairstyle, and makeup had provoked not-too-subtle criticism in the youth group at church and at camp this week. But it didn't faze her. In fact, Shawna thought Destiny kind of enjoyed it. Shawna admired her friend's who-cares-what-they-think attitude. And her New Age name—Destiny—was perfect. Shawna loved the attention she received just from being around Destiny.

"Destiny, over here," Shawna whispered back, flashing a wave in the moonlight. The girl joined her in the shadow of a pine tree.

"I thought maybe you changed your mind," Shawna said in a subdued voice. In a further attempt to identify with what she saw as her friend's carefree and cool way of talking, Shawna threw in an expletive to emphasize her feigned impatience, then silently scolded herself for feeling the need to apologize for using a word her mother forbade her to utter.

"It was the counselor," Destiny said, adding a curse of her own. "She stayed up reading her Bible till after eleven. Then I could hear her mumbling her prayers. I thought she'd never go to sleep."

"I know what you mean," Shawna commiserated.

"I'm glad *you* showed up," Destiny added. "You're a wicked chick to sneak out of camp."

Shawna appreciated the compliment. She told herself that she didn't care what others thought—of how she dressed or how she talked—except, of course, Destiny. Destiny's opinion of her mattered a lot. Charged with courage, Shawna asked, "Do you have some weed?" Shawna had never smoked marijuana and hadn't planned on trying it tonight. But it seemed cool to ask Destiny about it anyway.

"Yeah," Destiny replied without hesitation, as if she had expected her friend to ask. She dug into the pocket of her tight jeans and pulled something out. Her eyes now accustomed to the dark, Shawna watched the girl slip a dark, skinny cylinder between her lips. Then Destiny cupped her hands around a throwaway butane lighter and sparked a flame.

The aroma of sweet-smelling smoke Destiny exhaled startled Shawna for a second. If they got caught doing a joint, they would be in what Destiny referred to as "bang-dead trouble." But, as Destiny also said—"Who cares?" Once again the excitement of pushing the envelope of independence quickly overpowered the fear of consequences for breaking camp rules. This was her night, Shawna affirmed. No camp rules, no nosy mother or father, and no Bible verses were going to keep her from doing what she wanted to do.

Destiny offered her the smoldering joint. Shawna didn't want to look inexperienced, but neither did she want to burst into a coughing fit trying to look like a pro. Trusting the darkness to cover her ineptness, she took the marijuana cigarette between the tips of her thumb and forefinger and put it to her lips. She cautiously sucked a little smoke into her mouth, held it there as long as she could, and blew it out in Destiny's direction. "Mm, nasty," she hummed, pretending to enjoy it. Shawna liked the *idea* of smoking pot more than she liked smoking it. She told herself that it had to be an acquired taste, one she would work on when she had more time.

"We've got to get going," Destiny urged. Relieved to end the marijuana cigarette charade, Shawna dropped the joint to the dirt and ground it out with the toe of her boot.

Destiny swore. "That was no cheap Camel smoke you just pulverized; that was five bucks' worth of primo weed," she complained. "We could have squeezed it out and lit up again later."

Shawna was glad the darkness covered the flush of embarrassment on her face. "Sorry; that was dumb," she mumbled, doubling up on her slang in an attempt to appease Destiny. "I'll pay you back, I swear."

Destiny didn't reply. Instead, she waved Shawna to follow her to the road.

After they had traversed a couple hundred feet of dark road away from camp, Shawna asked, "How many guys are we meeting in town?" All Destiny had told her was that they were sneaking into town to meet some guys she had introduced to Shawna by E-mail.

"Just Travis and Rik, I think," Destiny answered. "Maybe a couple of their friends are coming too. I don't know." Shawna had not met either guy in person. Travis was Destiny's E-mail boyfriend. At Destiny's urging, Rik had started E-mailing Shawna, and she had replied. Shawna had exchanged pictures with Rik over E-mail, but tonight she was meeting both guys in person for the first time.

"What do you know about Rik?" Shawna asked, trying to brush away the nervousness that nagged her as they walked the dark, narrow road to town.

"Friend of Travis, that's all I know," Destiny said. "I met him in a private chat room on-line. Travis set it all up."

"So Rik is a dorky computer guy?" Shawna advanced. "I really hate keyboard geeks."

"Rik is no geek," Destiny insisted, turning to face Shawna in the darkness. "You've only E-mailed him a couple of times. I've talked to him on the computer. He's an awesome guy, Shawna. You two will blend, I swear."

Shawna pushed away all she didn't know about Rik and clung to the little she thought she knew. Rik had been fun to E-mail. They never talked about anything personal, just favorite movies and cool Web sites they had found and bands they liked. Rik's language was on the crude side, but Shawna didn't let her mother see his letters anyway. She assured herself that Destiny knew about guys. If she said Travis and Rik were OK, they were OK. Tonight was going to be fun, she coached herself. Tonight was going to be exciting.

Destiny resumed walking, and Shawna trekked after her like an obedient puppy. "Rik sent you a scanned picture, right?" Destiny said.

"Yeah."

"So what does *your* guy look like?"

"He's not *my* guy, just *a* guy," Shawna corrected boldly, as Destiny laughed in reply.

Shawna reviewed the picture of Rik in her mind. "He's tall, sandy hair, buffed out." She decided not to tell Destiny that his face was difficult to distinguish, since the picture Rik transmitted was a wide-angle shot of him standing beside his car. She didn't know if she would recognize Rik if she saw him on the street.

"And what picture did *you* send?" Destiny probed.

Shawna giggled self-consciously at the thought. "One from a glamour-photo studio—you know, the bedroom-eyes kind."

Destiny laughed. "You mean a picture of you in a low-cut gown showing lots of skin?"

"No, just lots of lace and feathers. It's hot."

"I'll bet you stoked Rik's furnace, you nasty chick," Destiny cackled.

Shawna blushed again in the darkness.

"Does your mom know about the picture?" Destiny pressed.

Shawna tried another four-letter word to underscore her answer. Again, it seemed to leave a bad taste in her mouth. "Are you numb? She doesn't know a thing about the picture or Rik or anything I do. And she can't get into my E-mail."

Destiny laughed with delight. Shawna smiled to herself at being able to impress her worldly friend.

After a few minutes of silence, Shawna asked, "Where are we supposed to meet them?"

"Coogan's Pub, just outside town. Travis said they would be waiting in his metallic blue Camaro. We'll have a couple of drinks in the pub and—"

"Drinks in the pub?" Shawna exclaimed. "We'll all get carded! We'll get kicked out or busted!"

"Relax, girl," Destiny said with easy confidence. "Travis said he'd take care of it."

"Wait a minute," Shawna said, touching Destiny's arm and slowing the pace. "How old are these guys?"

"Travis is twenty-two, and Rik is probably about the same."

Shawna sucked a long breath of surprise. Rik had never mentioned his age in his E-mail, and Shawna had purposely not revealed hers. She assumed that Destiny's friends were all high school guys. "Twenty-two," she exhaled. "And how old does Travis think *you* are?"

Destiny giggled wickedly. "Travis thinks I'm nineteen, that I'm in cosmetology school in the Valley, and that I drive a red Mazda Miata. And I told him you're the same age."

Shawna sputtered, "But—!"

Destiny cut her off. "Listen, we *look* nineteen, and once they see us tonight they won't care about the other stuff. This is going to be an unforgettable night. You're gonna blend with Rik, I promise."

Shawna could feel Destiny's appraising eyes in the darkness, as if seeking a response. "Unforgettable," Shawna whispered, trying to sound pleased. But she was getting more uncomfortable about this idea with every step toward town.

It was a mile and a half into Arrowhead from the camp, which was situated on a quiet slope of the mountain overlooking Lake Arrowhead. The girls saw no one, and no cars passed them during the half-hour trek down the dark, narrow road.

Shawna and Destiny saw the metallic blue Camaro from two blocks away, angled into the curb in front of Coogan's Pub. "It's party time," Destiny said expectantly as the two girls strode down the sidewalk side-by-side. Shawna subconsciously straightened her posture and tried to assume the mature persona she had portrayed by E-mail to a guy who signed on simply as Rik.

But inside, Shawna's emotions snapped and sparked like live wires. Raw excitement clashed with insistent cautions against unknown dangers. Her parents had sheltered her from some experiences in the name of protecting her from danger, but Shawna was in control now. Headstrong defiance wrestled against deeply anchored rules of behavior, "rules designed to keep you safe," her parents had drummed into her. *Well, the rules didn't keep Dougie safe, did they?* she thought as an unbidden memory of her older brother flitted through her mind. *And they sure didn't help keep our family together. So maybe I have the right to figure out my own rules for a change.* Memories of

19

Dougie were always painful, so she pushed them from her mind and focused on the Camaro ahead.

A man in his early twenties stepped out of the driver's-side door while the girls were still almost a block away on the otherwise deserted street leading into Arrowhead. The guy leaned on the front door like a Levi's model, smoking a cigarette. He wore jeans, a hooded sweatshirt, and a broad, welcoming smile. His hair was jet black and curly. "That's Travis," Destiny whispered. "Isn't he hot?"

"Totally," Shawna said, even as she found herself slowing down slightly.

"Destiny," the guy called out, his smile even broader. At the sound of his voice, another guy stepped out of the passenger's side to watch the girls approach. Shawna thought it could be Rik, but she wasn't sure. She could see another head bobbing for a look out the back window.

Destiny continued to the car and fell into Travis's arms as if they had been going together for months. Shawna slowed her stride and then stopped, leaving a couple of empty parking places between her and the Camaro.

As if sensing Shawna's uncertainty, Travis said, "Rik's up at the cabin getting ready for our little . . . party." He nodded vaguely toward a point up the mountain and behind the pub. "It's just a couple of minutes away. Let's go." He swung the driver's door wide open, inviting the girls in.

Destiny turned to Shawna with a look that communicated, *What's your problem, girl? This is what we came for. Move it before something happens to blow our cover.*

But Shawna couldn't get her feet to move. Warning signs she wanted to ignore flashed wildly in her brain. *Why didn't Rik come himself?* she pondered. *Who are these guys, and why are there at least three of them, four counting Rik—if Rik is really in the cabin, if there really is a cabin?*

"Come in out of the cold," the driver called, waving Shawna toward the Camaro. "There's a place just up the hill where we can all get nice and warm." The car's occupants laughed and hooted at the comment.

"This is what *I* came for, Shawna, a wild party," Destiny said, sounding irritated. "Isn't it what *you* came for?"

Shawna began moving forward, defying the red lights and

warning sirens going off inside her. Destiny had something Shawna wanted: the freedom, the independence to say, "I know what's best for me." *If a party with these guys is good enough for Destiny,* Shawna assured herself, *it's good enough for me.* "Yeah," she said, mustering her confidence. "This is exactly what I came for."

But before she could reach the car's open door, a green Ford Explorer snapped into a quick turn and knifed into the last parking space between Shawna and the Camaro, causing her to jump back in alarm. Painted on the door in large white letters were the words *Lakeside Pines Christian Camp.*

The Explorer's driver, a middle-aged man in a quilted vest, jeans, and baseball cap stepped out and glared at Shawna. She recognized the man immediately: Phil Bledsoe, the director of the camp from which she and Destiny had almost succeeded in escaping. Shawna could hear car doors slam shut on the other side of the Explorer. Then she heard Destiny let fly with a stream of expletives.

The blue Camaro full of guys squealed away from the curb and roared toward the village. Destiny walked dejectedly around the Explorer to face Bledsoe. The camp director's scowl seemed frozen on his face.

"Thanks to you, we're busted," Destiny snapped at Shawna as if the director were not there. "If you'd jumped into that car faster, we'd be out of here free and clear. But no, you stand around and . . ." Her words trailed off on a note of disgust.

Shawna said nothing. She knew Destiny could not begin to understand the sudden sense of relief she felt. She hardly understood it herself.

3
Saturday
March 27

STEVIE'S EYELIDS felt thick and grainy, as if coated with sand. She blinked often, trying to stay focused on the freeway stretched out before her in the predawn light. She could have stayed up all night cleaning house for the amount of rest she got in bed last night. And housecleaning probably would have helped keep her mind occupied. Instead she had thrashed restlessly between the sheets, sorting through a jumble of thoughts and feelings prompted by an unexpected late-night phone call.

Stevie had been asleep when the bedside phone sounded at midnight. "Mrs. Van Horne, this is Phil Bledsoe at Lakeside Pines Camp," the voice said. "I'm sorry to be calling so late."

Startled wide awake with worry, Stevie immediately jumped

to conclusions: "Is Shawna all right? Has she been hurt? Is she ill?"

"No, your daughter is fine. But Shawna violated one of our camp rules tonight. You need to come pick her up."

Stevie's panic turned to slight irritation. "She broke a rule? Can't I deal with this when she gets home on Sunday? It's midnight."

"It was a *serious* rule violation, Mrs. Van Horne. She must be sent home. That's the way we do things at Lakeside Pines."

Stevie's irritation escalated to mild anger at the man's hard-headedness. She couldn't imagine Shawna being sent home in the middle of the night for something like launching peas from her spoon at the dinner table or filling the counselor's sleeping bag with pinecones. "Just how serious was this violation?"

The camp director calmly described where he had found Shawna and her friend, how they were dressed, and what they were doing. Stevie couldn't believe it. Like most teenagers, Shawna had her moments of mischief and rebellion, Stevie acknowledged. But sneaking out of camp after hours wearing "suggestive clothing"—Bledsoe's words—to meet boys at a tavern was beyond anything Shawna would try. She wasn't a boy chaser, and she didn't even own suggestive clothing. Sneaking out was wrong, and Shawna would be disciplined for it. But the camp director was clearly reading more into the incident than was actually there.

"Can't you just ground Shawna until Sunday and let her come home on the bus with the rest of the kids?" Stevie asked. It wasn't that Stevie was trying to humor Shawna by allowing her to ride home with her friends, but a round-trip from the Valley to Lake Arrowhead would take at least four hours and a tank of gas.

"Normally we ask the parents to come immediately," Bledsoe explained. "But since it's so late, if you'll promise to be here before breakfast tomorrow, I'll put Shawna in the nurse's cabin for the rest of the night."

"Before breakfast?" Stevie moaned, more to herself than to Bledsoe.

Stevie knew what the camp director was going to say as soon as he began. "Mrs. Van Horne, if our kids don't face immediate consequences for their misbehavior, they won't learn respect for the rules." Stevie hated it when someone offered unsolicited parenting advice—especially when the advice was right. In fact, she had to admit, it was the exact advice she would have offered if she were in Bledsoe's shoes.

Stevie sighed. She knew she was a good mom. She had been especially attentive to the needs of her fourteen-year-old daughter and nine-year-old son after the horrible crisis with her oldest child two years earlier. But instead of arguing the point with the director, she had agreed to be at the camp by seven-thirty.

Stevie glanced in the rearview mirror and winced. Even in the early morning light she could see the dark circles under her pale blue eyes. She ran her fingers through her short brown hair, glad for the natural curl that kept her from having to spend a lot of time on it in the morning. Taking another gulp of tepid drive-through coffee, she silently urged the caffeine to slap her awake as she guided her white Grand Cherokee through the downtown L.A. interchange and onto the San Bernardino Freeway—eastbound Interstate 10. Mercifully, it was a Saturday and traffic was light. With any luck she would be back in the Valley in time to watch Collin's soccer match at eleven.

A pizza party was scheduled for Collin's team after the match. *Perfect,* Stevie thought. *That will give me a couple hours to run errands and—* She groaned aloud, remembering that Shawna would be at home and seriously grounded this afternoon, meaning that Stevie would be staying close to home with her. *Why is punishment always harder on the parents than on the kids?* she mused.

Stevie drove for several miles, trying not to sulk over the fact that her Saturday morning had been ruined. Actually, she still felt a bit humiliated at being called to retrieve a disobedient daughter. And her stomach was knotted with anxiety over the questions to which she had repeatedly awakened through the short night: Is there more to Shawna's misbehavior than a simple breach of curfew? Is this innocent prank a precursor to more serious rebellion? Is she yielding to pressure from her friends to conform to a lower standard of behavior than she's been taught?

Also gnawing at Stevie was the realization of what could have happened to the two defenseless fourteen-year-old girls during their foolish late-night foray into Lake Arrowhead Village. The fact that Shawna and her friend had survived the experience did not erase the frightening picture from Stevie's thoughts.

Stevie pulled off the freeway in West Covina and drove through a donut shop, hoping a French cruller and more coffee would lift her spirits. The pastry and caffeine only further upset her sour stomach. She slipped a CD of Beethoven symphonies into the dashboard player and turned up the volume, hoping to drown her funk. The melodic allegros and andantes only mocked her sullen mood.

In the middle of the sixth symphony, Stevie tapped off the CD. "OK, Lord, what's going on here?" she said aloud. "I'm not the perfect parent, but I'm certainly not a disinterested, neglectful parent. And I've been doing especially well since Jon left. I've been spending time with the kids—lots of time. I don't work in the evenings anymore and seldom on weekends. I attend their school events as often as I can. I make sure the three of us have dinner together most evenings. I help them with their homework. I read to them and pray with them at bedtime. . . ."

Stevie noticed two children staring at her from a car in the next lane. They appeared fascinated to see someone talking out loud with no one else in the car. She ignored them and continued her impromptu prayer.

"But, Lord, you know I can't go to school with the kids and choose all their friends for them. As hard as I try, I can't monitor everything they read or listen to or watch on TV. I can't get inside their heads and delete the ugly, destructive thoughts the devil plants there. I'm doing everything I know to do. How am I supposed to keep Shawna and Collin from getting swallowed up by the world like Dougie was?"

A vivid snapshot of her eldest child flashed into her mind, derailing her prayer. It was the one picture she most wished could be wiped from her memory: her seventeen-year-old son lying white and lifeless on a gurney as EMTs vainly tried to pound his heart awake. The unbidden scene still brought a lump to Stevie's throat. "Oh, God," Stevie whispered, "please don't let it happen again. Please don't let—"

The car phone sounded, startling Stevie. For an instant she allowed herself to imagine it was God calling to answer her perplexing questions. *If only it were that easy,* she thought wryly. She lifted the receiver from the console and tapped open the line. "Yes?"

The sleepy voice of a nine-year-old mumbled, "Where are you, Mom?"

Alarmed, Stevie asked, "Collin, honey, didn't Mrs. Lopez tell you why she's there?"

"She fell asleep on the couch, and I didn't know why she was here. So I called you."

"Why didn't you ask her, honey?"

"I didn't want to wake her up. Then I saw you weren't in your room, and I got scared. Where are you, Mom?"

Stevie felt awful about causing her son's concern. "I'm on the way to Lake Arrowhead to pick up Shawna."

"Is she sick?" Collin asked, yawning.

"No, she had to—well, she needs to come home today instead of tomorrow." Stevie decided not to go into the details.

"One of those girl things?"

Stevie smiled. Collin had already learned that unpredictable moods and behavior on the part of his sister and mother were often dismissed as "a girl thing you wouldn't understand."

"Yes, it's kind of a girl thing," she answered. "Anyway, I'm halfway to camp now. Shawna and I will be back in time for your soccer game, I promise. Mrs. Lopez can't drive you to the game today, but you can get a ride to the field with Trevor Ishii's parents or with Coach Vasquez. The phone numbers are in the note on the counter."

Collin was silent for a moment. "OK," he said with a hint of disappointment in his tone.

Stevie glanced at the digital clock on the dashboard. "You're up very early for a Saturday, honey. It's only six-thirty."

"I had a sad dream, so I came to get in bed with you."

"Another sad dream about Dougie?" Stevie probed cautiously. She purposely used *sad dream* instead of *bad dream* or *nightmare* with Collin, hoping to diminish his fear. Collin's

27

dreams about his older brother were terrifying. Stevie had been awakened by similar nightmares many times herself.

"Yeah, about Dougie."

Stevie's heart sank. "Oh, Collin, I'm so sorry I wasn't there. Are you all right now?" Her second son was not a baby anymore. But he was still *her* baby, and Stevie hated not being there to console him.

"I'm OK, Mom," Collin said convincingly. "Don't worry about me."

"Why don't you snuggle up in my bed for a while and watch cartoons," she urged. "The clicker is on my nightstand by the clock radio. Get a bowl of cereal and a banana, eat breakfast in my bed, and watch cartoons until it's time to get your uniform on. Good idea?"

"Yeah, Mom," Collin replied, his voice a bit more cheery now. Stevie wondered if it had anything to do with the fact that she had excluded the mention of any chores from her list of instructions.

"And if you need Daddy to come over, or if you just want to talk to him about your dream, his number is in the card file. I'm sure he's home this weekend. OK?"

"Sure, Mom," he answered. "But I don't need to look up Dad's number. I already know it by heart."

Stevie smiled again. "I know you do, honey. I'll see you at the soccer field about eleven. I love you."

Placing the phone in its cradle, Stevie's thoughts were focused on Collin's father—her ex-husband. Even after more than a year she felt uncomfortable thinking of Jon as her "ex." Loving Christian couples with wonderful kids were just not supposed to end up as ex-husband and ex-wife. But then most Christian marriages didn't experience the anguish that she and Jon had suffered with their firstborn, Douglas—sweet Dougie.

There were many things that had happened to her that Stevie never believed could happen to a Christian. The sudden, wrenching loss of a beloved teenaged son to drugs. The oppressive guilt, the cruel insinuations and charges of blame, the growing wedge of cold distance. The blinding, debilitating depression Stevie thought only resulted from mental illness or

28

demon possession. Finally, the willful dissolution of a solemn vow.

Who had initiated the proceedings? Stevie had to admit that she had, under indescribable mental, physical, and emotional stress. But who had actually caused the divorce? Each blamed the other at the time. From her current perspective, however, Stevie could admit that there was no one culprit. The dissolution of their marriage was a regrettable but seemingly unavoidable product of these two people under this kind of pressure.

Again the car phone startled Stevie. She was in San Bernardino, transitioning from I-10 to I-215. Soon she would exit the freeway and begin the climb up to Lake Arrowhead. She answered, expecting to hear Collin's voice again.

The man on the phone clearly had not been awake long. "Steve, this is Jon." Identifying himself was unnecessary; Stevie would know his voice anywhere. Besides, he was the only person in the world who called her Steve.

Without a word of greeting, she asked, "Have you talked to Collin? Is everything all right?"

Jon cleared the sleep from his voice. "Yes, he just called, and he's fine." Then he quickly cut to his concern. "He said you're going after Shawna. What's the deal?"

Stevie pursed her lips and wrinkled her nose. She would have told Jon eventually, after she and Shawna talked, and after she had a better grip on the feelings that taunted her: *Good mothers don't get called to camp to pick up delinquent daughters.* "Oh, she just broke one of the camp rules," Stevie said, attempting to trivialize the incident with her tone. "They're being hard-nosed about sending her home for it."

"Which rule? What did she do?"

Stevie squirmed in her black leather bucket seat. She had to be truthful in her reply, but she didn't feel responsible to be exhaustive. "Shawna was outside her cabin with another girl after lights-out."

Jon's disbelief was obvious. "She's being sent home just for breaking curfew?"

"Like I said, they're kind of hard-nosed about their rules."

Jon was silent for a moment, apparently processing Stevie's explanation. Then he said, "That sounds a little severe to me."

Stevie hummed noncommittally, hoping Jon was satisfied.

Apparently he was. "I'd like to spend some time with the kids this weekend, if that's all right with you."

"What do you have in mind?"

"Maybe pick them up after Collin's soccer game, take them out to dinner and a movie. And I want them to go to church with me in the morning."

"Collin has a pizza party with his team after the game," Stevie said.

Jon sighed audibly at the crimp in his plans. "OK, I'll pick them up after the party—say, three o'clock."

"And Shawna really should be grounded over this camp thing," Stevie continued.

"Geez, Steve, aren't you being as hard-nosed about this as the camp officials? Can't you bend a little for once and come up with a way to punish her without punishing me? I'd really like to spend some time with my daughter this weekend."

Stevie detected the edge of irritation in his voice. Morning was never Jon's best time, she recalled. But she was having to fight some irritation of her own. Why did their conversations so often deteriorate into criticisms of one another's parenting techniques? As usual, Jon was interfering in her attempts to discipline one of their children. At the same time, she had to admit that she hadn't been completely forthright in her disclosure of Shawna's behavior.

Once again Stevie ran her fingers through her hair and sighed. "All right, Jon," she conceded. "I'm too tired to argue with you. I'll think of something else in the way of punishment for Shawna. They'll be ready for you at three."

"And they can spend the night?"

Stevie missed her kids more than she ever let on when they slept at their father's apartment. And she hated being alone at night in the home they had all once shared together. But she was progressing well at working through those feelings and fears. "Sure, they can spend the night," she said.

Jon ended the conversation rather curtly, almost rudely, Stevie thought. *What's your problem, Mr. Van Horne?* she questioned silently as she cradled the phone. Then she guided the Cherokee down the exit to Highway 18, leading up the mountain.

"North Valley Recreation Center. This is Jennifer. May I help you?"

The caller paced as he spoke. A companion slouched in a tattered, overstuffed chair was watching him. "Yeah, there was a guy there last night doin' basketball in the gym with the kids."

"Last night? You mean Jon Van Horne?"

"This guy had short hair, like a buzz job, kind of blond. He was real strong." The caller subconsciously touched his puffy, sore upper lip. Some of his muscles were also sore.

"Crew cut? Yeah, that's Coach Van Horne. But he's off today. In fact, he's off until summer."

"Till summer?"

"Right. He's a teacher, I think. He just works at the Center during school vacations."

"Well, I wanna talk to him—like, about playin' basketball."

"Are you in one of our leagues?"

"No, I don't wanna *play* basketball," the caller said impatiently. "I just wanna talk to the coach—Coach Van Horne. Do you know where I can find him?"

Jennifer paused. "I'm sorry, sir, but I can't give out that kind of information."

"I mean, is he still around the Valley somewhere?"

"Yes, he lives in the Valley."

"How about a phone number then? I just wanna ask him about—"

"It's against the rules to give out addresses or phone numbers of the staff," Jennifer interrupted. "But you can probably find him in the book."

"Van Horne?" the caller probed.

"Right, Jon—J-O-N, no *H.*"

Eugene Hackett snapped off the phone without another word.

"What'd they say, man?" Chako asked.

Eugene didn't respond. Instead he rummaged carelessly through the cabinet underneath the phone until he found what he was looking for: a soiled, dog-eared telephone directory that was four years old. He swept through the pages until he found the section he wanted, then ran his finger down a few columns, stopping below one entry: VAN HORNE, JON AND STEPHANIE. He exulted with a string of epithets.

"You know where Etiwanda Street is in Northridge?" Eugene asked, looking at Chako.

"Hey, Rattler, you're lettin' this guy get to you. He's just dirt on your shoe, man. Let it go."

"Not this one, Chako. This one's mine. This one is gonna wish he'd kept his hands off the De Sotos."

"Rashaad said—"

Rattler cut him off with a bitter curse. "Do you know where this street is or not?"

Chako acquiesced. "Etiwanda? Yeah, over by the college."

Rattler slipped the giant .45 inside his belt and pulled his shirttail over it. "Come on, show me," he snapped, heading for the door.

4

Saturday
March 27

THE DRIVE down the mountain was agony for Stevie. Her
daughter, dressed in denim shorts, oversized sweatshirt, and
hiking boots, slouched against the passenger door, sullen and
brooding. Long, straight brown hair partially covered her face.
Her arms were folded tightly across her chest. It was a classic
pose; Shawna characteristically retreated when caught in a
wrong. Her self-imposed isolation could not have been more
obvious with a neon Keep Out sign flashing in front of her.

Stevie did not intend to let her get away with it. But as she
guided the white Grand Cherokee down Highway 18 toward
San Bernardino, she struggled over how to break through
Shawna's defenses and get to the root of her misbehavior. The

struggle was becoming commonplace for Stevie as Shawna tested the outer barriers of parental control.

The camp director had said little more about the previous night's incident. He seemed in a hurry to have those who violated the rules leave the grounds before the other campers emerged from their cabins.

Stevie never did meet Shawna's "partner in crime," a girl identified to her only by the curious name "Destiny." Mr. Bledsoe had mentioned in private that Shawna appeared to be the accomplice, and Destiny the instigator, in the incident. It didn't matter to Stevie. What Shawna had done was wrong and very dangerous. In spite of her earlier concession to Jon, Stevie would find a way to rein Shawna in where it hurt the most—her freedom—until she saw a change in attitude.

Her headstrong daughter would probably raise a big stink over being grounded. Shawna was getting to be an expert at displaying her displeasure. Stevie would be loving but firm with her daughter, a resolve she had made after Dougie's death. Had she insisted that she and Jon deal more firmly with Dougie, things might have been different. Stevie would not allow her daughter to fall into the abyss that had swallowed her older son. It just was not going to happen again.

Stevie decided to work her way into the issue gradually. "Are you hungry? I could drive through the golden arches." By suggesting McDonald's instead of Shawna's favorite Swedish pancakes at IHOP, Stevie communicated her willingness to fill Shawna's need for food while clearly stating that this was not a pleasure trip.

Just as Stevie expected, Shawna controlled several moments with silence, then muttered, "Not hungry." Stevie decided not to pursue it.

After another two miles of winding mountain highway, Stevie tried the least confrontive approach to the problem she could think of. "Is there anything you want to say about what happened last night?"

Shawna answered more quickly this time. "Nope." Her tone conveyed a message Stevie was hearing more often in her daughter's attitude: *I could say a lot, but I'm not telling you anything.*

Shawna reached out and switched the radio from Stevie's

34

classical FM station to her favorite rock station and turned up the volume. Stevie just as quickly tapped the radio off. Shawna resumed sulking.

After another mile, Stevie said, "Tell me about this girl Destiny." It was a wide-open opportunity for Shawna to finger Destiny as the instigator of the breakout. Stevie wanted to give her that chance.

With a get-off-my-back whine, Shawna replied, "Just a girl in the youth group."

Stevie kept her tone positive as she continued. "And the clothes you wore last night—the sweater and microskirt—did they belong to Destiny?"

Shawna paused, as if considering whether her answer might further incriminate her. "Yeah," she said finally.

"So you let a girl in the youth group talk you into wearing her clothes and doing a very dangerous thing," Stevie clarified.

Shawna's disdainful sigh was the equivalent to her saying, "You don't know anything." Then she said, "Destiny didn't talk me into anything. I wore those clothes because you won't let me wear them at home. And I went into the village because I wanted to."

Stevie could feel her patience and civility eroding. "You could have been kidnapped or raped or murdered, Shawna. Didn't you see the danger of walking into a strange town alone in the middle of the night?"

"I wasn't alone. I was with Destiny," Shawna said.

"You were *both* alone. It's a wonder you weren't grabbed off the street by some maniac. Women—and girls—aren't safe on the streets anywhere, you know. And dressing like prostitutes is simply an invitation to trouble."

"Mom, you make it sound like all guys are perverts," Shawna retorted with the familiar you-don't-know-anything haughtiness in her voice.

Stevie ran her fingers through her hair, reminding herself to stay calm. She glanced over at her daughter, hoping to make eye contact. "So what kind of guys were you planning to meet in town dressed like that?"

Shawna purposely avoided her mother's gaze. "Nobody."

Displeased with Shawna's evasiveness, Stevie bored in.

"Nobody? The camp director told me you were talking with a carload of boys when he found you. Who were they?"

"Just some guys from the village. No big deal."

"Do you know these guys?" Stevie challenged.

"No, but they weren't perverts."

"How can you possibly know that?" Stevie demanded, feeling her face and neck flush warm with indignation.

"I just know, Mom. That's the problem. You don't think I know anything." Then Shawna breathed an expletive. Whether she meant for her mother to hear it or not, Stevie was not sure. But she did hear it.

"What did you say?" Stevie demanded.

Shawna repeated the word, not at a whisper but clearly and defiantly. Then she added, "That's how I feel about always being treated like a baby. I'll bet Dougie felt the same way. No wonder he did what he did."

Slashed by Shawna's words, Stevie could not have said more if she had wanted to. She gripped the steering wheel and focused on the road ahead, hoping Shawna would not choose that particular moment to look at her, because her lip was trembling and her eyes were filling with tears.

Chako turned off of bustling Devonshire Street at the corner of Etiwanda and into a development of well-preserved tract homes built in the sixties. Chako's car was a ten-year-old Chrysler New Yorker four-door. The paint was faded, but the car was clean and ran quietly. Unlike other members of the De Sotos, Chako had spurned the custom wheels, tinted windows, high-decibel sound system, and other accoutrements that attracted police attention on the streets. As such, Chako's car was often the vehicle used to move gang members around the Valley when they didn't want to be noticed.

Eugene Hackett sat silently in the passenger seat, scanning house numbers as Chako drove. It was hazy but warm in L.A. Homeowners busy in their yards with Saturday morning spring gardening paid little attention to the big sedan slowly cruising by. Chako had driven in and out of several neighborhoods looking for the address Eugene had scribbled down from the phone book. With every failed attempt Eugene's already sour attitude worsened. Now that they had found the right section of Etiwanda, his eager eyes darted from yard to yard, looking for the home of the man he had come to hate so thoroughly in less than twelve hours.

"Slower," the passenger directed. Chako eased the speed down to fifteen miles per hour. "There it is," Eugene said, pointing to Chako's side of the street. He was staring at a single-level ranch-style home with beige stucco and chocolate-brown wood shutters and trim. Palms and poplars flanked a lawn of Bermuda grass being overrun by crabgrass. The driveway swept up to a two-car garage attached at a right angle to the house. There were no vehicles in the driveway or at the curb.

Eugene studied the front of the house as they passed it. Next to the garage, which dominated a third of the frontal view, was a large kitchen window, a recessed front entry with a wrought iron security gate, and a large bay window, which Eugene thought might be the living room. A bedroom appeared to be front left, and it also had a window. Eugene was darkly pleased at the number of windows facing the street. It would be impossible, he determined, to pump a full clip from his .45 into the house without hitting someone. Either Jon Van Horne, his wife, Stephanie, or maybe even a kid—it didn't really matter to Rattler. Somebody in this house was going to pay for messing with the De Sotos last night.

"A minivan behind us just turned into the driveway." Chako was looking into the rearview mirror as he spoke. They were three houses past the Van Horne place.

"Go to the end of the block and turn around," Eugene ordered without looking back. "But take it slow." As soon as Chako reached the next cross street he wheeled the big Chrysler through a wide U-turn and headed back toward Devonshire, maintaining the same speed. As he did, his passenger pulled the dull gray Colt .45 automatic out of his belt and checked the clip. Then he gripped the weapon in his right hand between the seat and the door.

Seeing the gun, Chako said, "It's broad daylight, man. There are people on the street. This is bad timing, dude."

"Slow down and be ready to punch it," his passenger said. Chako eased back on the accelerator, dropping the speed to ten miles per hour. Eugene's eyes focused on the beige stucco house coming up on the right. There were people sitting in the minivan, adults in the front and a kid or two in the back. As the Chrysler passed the driveway, Eugene saw what the van was waiting for.

A boy was walking from the house to the driveway. He was about ten, Eugene guessed, wearing baggy blue shorts, a bright orange T-shirt, orange kneesocks, and soccer cleats. The kid was carrying a soccer ball under one arm and a sport bottle in his hand.

It had to be Van Horne's kid, Eugene decided. The young gunman could not ask for a clearer shot: less than fifty feet with no obstructions. A lethal burst from the .45 could be unleashed in two seconds. The kid, who wasn't paying attention to the passing car, wouldn't have a chance. And Jon Van Horne—wherever he was—would wish to God he had never crossed the De Sotos.

But Eugene kept the gun hidden at his side as the Chrysler cruised slowly past the house. Chako's warning made sense. He would do the deed someday soon, but not with the whole neighborhood watching.

Eugene glanced back to see the kid clamber into the van. With his mind focused clearly on the basketball coach who had humiliated him, he thought, *You don't know how lucky you are today, Van Horne.* Then he smiled with ominous satisfaction. *But your luck is going to change soon, and you and your family won't know what hit you.*

Had Shawna objectively assessed the tense exchange of words with her mother since leaving camp, she would have been forced to admit to the series of lies on her part. She had insisted she wasn't hungry. In reality she was *very* hungry, not having eaten since dinner last night. But she wasn't about to give her mother the satisfaction of providing her with an Egg McMuffin. She had turned down toast and cereal from the camp nurse this morning for a similar reason. Now, with a long ride home ahead of her, Shawna wished she had skipped the hunger strike and vented her stubbornness some other way.

Her mother had invited her to talk about what happened last

night, and she had coldly refused. In reality, there was a part of Shawna that yearned to tell her mother everything: her clever escape from the cabin; the halting experiment with marijuana and her stupidity at wasting most of a joint; the approval she felt from Destiny; the raw excitement, the rush of imminent danger, and the ultimate relief she sensed in the space of only a few minutes. These were the things she would tell a trusted friend about last night. Shawna wanted her mom to be a friend with whom she could share her experience without fear of judgment. But she was afraid her mom would look past the experience to deal with the wrong like a mother, not like a friend. So Shawna kept it all inside.

Shawna knew she had also lied about the clothes. They were hers, not Destiny's. And she lied about why she and Destiny sneaked out of camp. She wasn't planning to meet "just some guys" in the village, but, luckily, Bledsoe hadn't found out about Travis and Rik. And Destiny had proven to be a true friend by keeping her mouth shut. For all that didn't go right last night, at least her secret with Rik was still intact.

Pressed to do so, Shawna would reluctantly have agreed that her display of nonchalance over the potential danger of her actions was a snow job as well. She knew what happened to girls when they threw caution to the wind. She had seen the horrific stories on TV: abduction, ritual abuse, rape, mutilation, murder. She had attended the funeral of a classmate who had foolishly decided to walk home from the mall one night instead of calling her parents for a ride. Then, last night, Shawna had sensed the inner warnings and, with Destiny's encouragement, had cavalierly decided to ignore them. Years from now, perhaps, Shawna would tell the story and admit what she suspected was true: that Phil Bledsoe's "untimely" arrival saved her from an unthinkable fate.

Then there was the matter of Destiny. Shawna had denied that the very worldly girl with the uncommon name was any more than "just a girl in the youth group." That was another lie. Destiny had influenced Shawna more than she was ready to admit, even to herself. There was no pretense of righteousness with Destiny, and Shawna found that alluring. Destiny told of experiences that rivaled Shawna's secret fantasies: experiments with booze, boys, and recreational drugs—even titillating dabblings in the occult. Shawna assessed that she was smarter than Destiny, but she envied—even coveted—the girl's worldly wisdom.

Something else Destiny had mentioned during the week occupied Shawna's thoughts now as her mother drove on in silence. Shawna didn't believe Destiny at first. She even scoffed at her implausible statement: "You don't have to take any junk from your parents." Destiny had made that statement to Shawna in private one night during a boring camp flashlight hike. "If they hassle you about grades or going out with guys or staying out late or anything, you just tell them to lay off, that they're harassing you. If they don't leave you alone, you can just leave. And they can't do a thing about it."

"*My* mother would do something about it," Shawna had contested.

"She *can't* do anything about it. You have rights. It's the law now."

Shawna had been skeptical. "I've never heard of a law like that."

"Of course not," Destiny had explained, spicing her words with expletives. "Parents and teachers don't want kids to hear about it."

Shawna had argued with her for most of the hike, but Destiny never gave in. The worldliest girl in camp was either totally nuts or she was on to something. And if she was on to something, Shawna was going to find out about it and take advantage of it.

The white Grand Cherokee swept up the on-ramp to I-15. From the corner of her eye, Shawna had seen her mother furtively brush tears from her cheek. Realizing that she had hurt her mother with her harsh words—actually hurt her to the point of tears—prompted a dull, heavy ache inside Shawna. She ignored it by turning her attention back to what Destiny said.

40

It was going to be a long, silent trip to the Valley, Shawna thought, *but eventually the bomb was going to drop. Mom is majorly ticked, and she's going to ground me for life or take away my TV and phone or harass me in some other way. But if Destiny is right, Mom won't get away with it. If Destiny is right, I'll get the final say on what happens to me. The first thing I have to do when I get home is find out if Destiny is right.*

5

Sunday
March 28

SEVERAL HUNDRED MILES north, a sleek blue-and-white Sport
Nautique raced into the quiet cove at twenty-eight miles per
hour and then angled out toward the lake on a broad arc without decreasing speed. The water-skier utilized the momentum
of the turn to slingshot across the wake and lean into an even
wider, faster turn, producing a wall of water spray that shim-
mered in the late-morning sun. At the precise moment, he
released the handle of the ski rope and veered the single ski
toward the cove. Slowing quickly, the skier settled into chilly
Shasta Lake. The ski, a professional model sculpted for maxi-
mum maneuverability, popped to the surface beside him.

In a dozen easy strokes, pushing the ski ahead of him, he

reached the ladder at the rear of a large and luxurious houseboat anchored in the cove. After lifting the ski to the deck and
sliding it aboard, he pulled himself up the ladder. Then he
unbuckled and shed the life vest. A cool breeze turned his wet,
well-tanned skin to gooseflesh. "Patricia, a towel, please," he
called out.

Six-foot-two-inch Daniel W. Bellardi was a specimen of fitness
and health. His shoulders, pectorals, and limbs were toned and
limber. Only slight sags of skin at the jowls and neck and a modest paunch at the belt altered his physique from that of the university swimming champion he had been forty years earlier. But
a full head of fog-gray hair—which he steadfastly refused to tint,
to the displeasure of his wife and campaign staff—confirmed his
age of sixty-two.

Daniel Bellardi often referred to himself as "the former state
senator from the former state of California." Up until five weeks
ago, Bellardi was in the midst of his third term in the California
state legislature. The popular senator had worked miracles for
the Fourth State Senate District, which occupied the center of
the state from the Oregon border to Solano County, just north
of the San Francisco Bay Area. But on the nineteenth of Febru-
ary, the senator's great dream had finally come true. The resolution he introduced to realign California into two separate states,
approved by the California legislature two years earlier, received
the approval of Congress.

The senator was both proud of his accomplishment and
humbled that God had blessed his efforts. Seventeen times in
the state's history, legislators had tried and failed to reduce
the megastate of California to two or three locally governed
entities. Senator Bellardi had succeeded where all others had
failed. In doing so, he had separated the peaceful, conservative north from the overpopulated, polluted, morally corrupt
south. The people of the new state of North California were
no longer responsible to carry the enormous tax burden of
the extravagant population centers of the south. South
California was on its own, and North California was free.

Only days after the act of Congress, Daniel Bellardi moved
out of his office in Sacramento and returned to his home in
Redding, the capital of the new state. Having rallied support
throughout the state and shepherded the resolution through,

Daniel was clearly the front-runner to become its first elected governor. He already had the support of the interim governor, a man he had promoted for the transitional job. And he enjoyed enormous popularity among the voters of the new state, whom he had liberated from the financial albatross of the south.

For Daniel Bellardi, the seemingly clear path to the governor's office was a rewarding by-product of his tireless, prayerful efforts to establish North California as a political and social haven for decent, God-fearing people throughout his former state. He would spend the months between now and November seeking the office most analysts agreed was his to claim. Though one minor opponent had emerged, the campaign, the senator had been assured, was merely a formality.

A woman two years younger than Daniel opened the sliding glass door at the rear of the houseboat and stepped out. She held a beach towel in one hand. Tall and slender, Patricia Bellardi would have appeared scrawny if not for the grace and bearing acquired during her years as a professional. Her attractively styled hair was more white than gray. Years of expert skin care had kept her thin face smooth and lustrous. Always perfectly dressed, Patricia wore a mint-green belted cotton jumpsuit, floral scarf, and dark green cardigan.

Patricia held out the towel at arm's length to avoid getting splashed by the water dripping from her husband's swimsuit. Daniel received the towel and quickly draped it around his shoulders. "Thank you," he said, smiling appreciatively at his wife. "You should have been out there. You would have loved it. It was marvelous."

Patricia returned his smile. "Maybe next time, dear." It was her stock answer to an invitation to water-ski or take a pleasure ride in the ski boat. She had not been on skis or appeared in public in a swimsuit in twenty-five years. Yet Daniel persisted in tempting his wife to join him in the outdoor life he loved so much.

The ski boat drifted alongside at idle with Matthew Denherder at the helm. Lucy, Matthew's wife and spotter, secured the aft line as Matthew killed the engine. The Denherders were year-round residents and caretakers of Senator and Mrs. Bellardi's prized houseboat and ski boat. Matthew, in his mid-fifties, had been one of Daniel Bellardi's trusted builders prior to the senator's political career. Health problems had forced Matthew out of construction, so Daniel, feeling obligated to provide for his trusted employee, had hired him to maintain his watercraft. It was, after all, the right thing to do for a man who had served him well. And Daniel Bellardi was a man who was known for doing the right thing. On the dozen or so occasions each year when the Bellardis retreated to the lake to rest, transact business, or entertain, Lucy Denherder served as the master shipboard chef.

"How was your ride today, sir?" Matthew called out as he stowed his boss's ski in the bow. Lucy had already scampered aboard to begin lunch preparations for the Bellardis and their guests. Patricia followed her inside.

Daniel continued to towel off. "Excellent, Matthew—thoroughly invigorating. Would you like a tow?" Although some might have interpreted Daniel's offer as condescending, it was actually meant as an expression of kindness. Matthew didn't water-ski, which Daniel knew full well. He also knew the caretaker would decline his offer, which he did—graciously, as always.

"I think it's warm enough for lunch up top today, don't you?" Daniel asked, hanging his life jacket up to dry.

"Yes, sir," Matthew agreed. "I'll set up the round table and rig the canopy right away."

"You're a good man, Matthew. Thank you."

An hour later, Daniel, in blue shorts and a striped polo shirt, stood beside Patricia on the sun-drenched top deck watching Matthew and the Sport Nautique return from the marina with the senator's top staff members. The Bellardis wore sunglasses, and Daniel further shaded his eyes from the glare with a cap bearing the logo of Redwood Development Corporation. Before entering politics, Daniel had grown RDC into a large and lucrative company, assuring the Bellardis' financial future.

One by one, the casually dressed staffers, four men and a woman, climbed the narrow spiral staircase at the rear of the houseboat and joined Daniel and Patricia on deck. Their hosts greeted them cordially and offered chilled California wine or iced sun tea. Hard liquor was never served in the Bellardis' home or aboard their houseboat, nor did the couple approve of staff members who indulged. Substance abuse at the highest levels of government in California had precipitated the legalization of marijuana and accelerated the moral disintegration of the big cities, Bellardi often argued with his inner circle. "We in North California will not only *separate* ourselves from such practices, we will *distance* ourselves from them, and it all begins with us." Staffers joked among themselves that Bellardi's campaign was probably the driest campaign in the history of American politics. Most of them, sharing the Bellardis' views, were proud of that claim.

Lucy Denherder, with the help of her husband, silently served a crisp Caesar salad, followed by baked stuffed salmon and pasta. The distant drone of an occasional powerboat and the quiet lap of small swells against the side of the houseboat were no match for the soothing strains of Vivaldi pouring from the speakers on deck.

Daniel tolerated little small talk at his staff gatherings. No matter what anyone said about his lead in the polls, he was not taking the campaign for granted. Shortly after the entrée was served, conversation at the large round table under the canvas canopy turned to business with Daniel's familiar words, "Robert, get me up to speed."

Robert Johnstone was a tall, solidly built ex-Marine of forty-six whose self-assurance and strictly business demeanor added to his seemingly larger-than-life appearance. With his slate-gray eyes and neatly combed salt-and-pepper hair, he was a striking figure. Daniel first knew Robert Johnstone as a Sacramento lobbyist with unassailable integrity and bulldog tenacity—a rare tandem of qualities in California politics. He brought Johnstone on board during his first term in the state senate and elevated him to direct his second and third campaigns. Now Johnstone, whose wife had died of cancer four years earlier, was locked onto an election victory like a high-tech missile on an enemy munitions store. He would deliver Daniel Bellardi to the governor's chair and take no prisoners in the process.

Johnstone placed his fork on the plate and eyed his colleagues somberly. He had kept his news from the rest of the staff so his chief could hear it with them. "Ms. Dunsmuir has gained a little on us, Senator," he said.

Daniel, with a mouthful of food, gestured with his empty

fork for his chief lieutenant to continue. Everyone else at the table eyed Johnstone and continued eating.

"It's not a large gain; only a couple of points this week, no more than a blip. But it's the first time since the polls began that she's topped 35 percent and dropped us below 60."

All eyes shifted to Daniel Bellardi, awaiting his response. Daniel leaned back in his chair and gazed out at the lake. He would probably ski again later today if the wind didn't come up. "You don't seem worried, Robert."

"No, sir, I'm not worried," Johnstone assured him, then paused. "But I am concerned. A liberal like Juanita Dunsmuir shouldn't be within twenty-five points of us. I think it bears watching."

"What caused the blip? Any ideas?"

Robert responded, "It's hard to tell, sir. People willingly admit which candidates they like in the polls, but they don't always tell us why. Any number of factors may—"

"It's the concerts," Angie Calderone cut in. She was a CPA and a whiz at campaign finances. But the rotund, forty-five-year-old Latino woman was also intuitive and outspoken, and Daniel Bellardi appreciated her insights. "I've said this before and I'll say it again: Juanita Dunsmuir is an entertainer."

"She *was* an entertainer," interjected Mike Bragan, Daniel's appointment secretary. "What she is now is a Hollywood-has-been-turned-marijuana-grower who's running scared that we're going to close down her operation. She knows that the liberal laws of California still apply here until the new legislature changes them. When we reverse the legalization of marijuana, she'll be out of a job."

"She's not making records anymore, Mike, and her voice may sound like a rusty gearbox, but she is still an entertainer," Angie retorted, thumping her finger on the table for emphasis. "She knows how to work a crowd. And that's what she's doing in these seemingly insipid outdoor community concerts of hers. She twangs that guitar and gargles those old freedom songs and protest songs from her gold records. She winks at the men and—"

"As if she's anything to look at," Mike Bragan snorted. "She's fifty-five if she's a day and skinny as a bamboo pole. I'll bet the woman's anorexic."

Angie returned Mike a humorless glance for the interruption, then continued. "And she also sings about women's rights to keep the wives interested. After a few songs the old boomers are weepy with nostalgia and the Generation X-ers are spellbound by the old woman's energy and wit. So when she tells them that Governor Dan Bellardi will drag them back to the archaic values of the fifties and rip off their hard-won freedoms, they get a little agitated. By the end of the concert she has them all holding hands and swaying and singing her campaign tune, 'We need Juanita to keep our state free.'"

"And she's not in this alone," put in Price Whitten, Daniel's media secretary. "Look at the crowd of cronies she's recruited to travel with her. It's a *who's who* from the entertainment industry in the seventies."

Adonislike in appearance, Whitten was a former San Francisco news anchor. He had given up his lucrative TV job a year earlier after his eight-year-old son was abducted, molested, and murdered by a convicted pedophile. The man had been released from prison early and was subsequently acquitted of Gabe's murder due to allegedly contaminated evidence. After the trial, Price and his wife, Teri, sold their elegant Hillsboro, California, home and left the city, which they bitterly termed Sodom-by-the-Bay, and moved to Redding. Price committed himself to help Daniel Bellardi claim North California for decency so that other children might be spared the fate suffered by their precious Gabe.

"Grammy winners and movie stars," Angie Calderone inserted. "Brandon Clay, Sadie Caruso, Trainwreck Thomas—"

"*Old* Grammy winners and movie stars," Mike Bragan corrected. "Sadie hasn't been in front of a camera in fifteen years. And most of Juanita's groupies are drunks or pill heads. Trainwreck has been in and out of detox so often he has a standing reservation for a room."

"But," Price said with a finger in the air, "like Juanita Dunsmuir, Trainwreck and the others are legends—famous people, charismatic people, influential people. I agree with Angie: They can draw a crowd and work a crowd. The mystique of fame has a way of numbing the public to realities such as truth and character. I believe Juanita's so-called Freedom Tour, hokey as it may seem, is making a dent for them. They're rubbing shoulders with, and signing autographs for, thousands of voters around the state. And they're getting media coverage. Let's face it: Soundbites from a concert of rusty old folksingers are more entertaining than soundbites from a political speech or press conference."

Mike took a breath, perhaps to add another disparaging remark about Juanita Dunsmuir or Trainwreck Thomas. But Daniel cut him off, directing a question to Robert. "Do you have any data to support Angie's feelings about the concerts?"

"Again, the numbers gained by the Dunsmuir camp are silent about their precise origin," Johnstone replied. He hadn't picked up his fork since the business discussion began. "Judging from the response along the north coast, the first few concerts may have contributed significantly. But they've also done at least one statewide mailing and a couple of TV spots."

Mike Bragan jumped back into the conversation. "The mass mailings and TV ads reach several million voters," he argued. "But the concerts are only drawing a few thousand each. How can the concerts make much of an impact?"

"The concerts *can* and *do* make an impact," Angie insisted, "because they reach people *deeply*. Folks are mesmerized by Juanita the entertainer. Then she sings about freedom and tolerance and plants the thought in their heads that nobody has the right to determine right and wrong for anyone else. One of her songs goes, 'God gave you a conscience so you can know, when to say yes and when to say no. Say it ain't true, say it ain't so, to those who tell you which way you should go.' By the end of the evening she has people believing that Dan Bellardi plans to turn North California into a forty-five-thousand-square-mile prison camp where the population is told what to believe, what to think, and how to behave. And the people at the concerts tell their friends."

"How many concerts are planned?" Bellardi asked.

Price answered, "I read that they've scheduled two every weekend until the election—up and down 101, up and down the I-5 corridor, Alturas, Susanville, Grass Valley, Yuba City, everywhere."

"And Juanita has the money to make this happen?" Daniel asked.

"Wealthy friends in the entertainment industry have anted up big-time to support one of their own," Angie replied. "And they're passing the hat at the concerts and pulling in even more. Believe me, Juanita is well funded."

Daniel leaned back to process the information. The others around the table used the break to take another bite. Finally, Daniel said, "Well, I guess I'd better get myself a guitar and hit the road." The smile that quickly followed prompted a chuckle around the circle. Daniel's staff was relieved that their chief made light of Juanita Dunsmuir's small gain. Then he turned to Robert Johnstone again. "Do we need to retool our strategy at this point?"

Johnstone, who had resumed eating with the others, put his fork down again. "No, sir, not at this point. I believe we're still on track to reach our goal of victory. I believe the majority of the people of North California will see through Dunsmuir's sensationalism. Nonetheless, the numbers warrant our careful attention. Our greatest error would be to underestimate our opponent."

Daniel nodded. "Very good, Robert; I agree. Thank you for the caution."

Coleman King, Daniel's longtime friend and policy advisor, usually listened more than he spoke at staff meetings. But when he spoke, the wisdom of the balding, sixty-six-year-old retired law professor was clearly evident. "I don't think we need to worry about Juanita Dunsmuir. The majority of the people in North California live up here because they just don't like it in the south. They don't like the pace and pollution and crime of the big cities. They believe in moral values, right and wrong, truth and justice. That's why they backed us to create a new state. If we communicate our vision clearly, patiently, and with dignity—and we all know that Daniel is supremely capable of doing just that—the voters in our new state will support us."

The group was silent for several moments as Coleman King's articulate, reassuring words soaked in. Finally, Daniel placed a hand on his friend's shoulder. "Thank you, Cole. You always bring us back to a proper perspective." Others at the table echoed Daniel's words.

Then Daniel motioned to the Denherders, who stood quietly in the background, awaiting their boss's instructions. "With that encouragement, let's get to the next item of business. Who's ready for more iced tea?"

6

Thursday
April 8

STEVIE LOVED running her own business at home. It brought
her peace of mind knowing she was immediately available to
the children in case of illness or injury at school. And she
accomplished more in one day at home than she could accomplish in two days in an office, where meetings and interrup-
tions were the rule.

    Early in her marriage to Jon, Stevie was a successful advertis-
ing salesperson for a popular L.A. radio station. After taking a
number of years off as a stay-at-home mom, she edged back
into the working world when Collin began preschool. But
instead of returning to KLIQ-FM, she created her own niche in
advertising. She marketed herself to local firms that were too

small to hire a full-time advertising staff but too large not to advertise. As a one-person operation, Stevie did it all: negotiate contracts, write copy, generate graphics, produce radio spots. The income from six to eight steady accounts, along with child-support payments from Jon, was sufficient to cover the bills.

Stevie felt more professional and got more work done when she kept regular office hours at home. Apart from a thirty-minute lunch period, her only breaks were for an occasional trip to the laundry room to move a load from the washer to the dryer.

At this moment Stevie stood in Shawna's room with an armload of her daughter's socks and underwear still warm from the dryer. She glanced around at her daughter's domain and sighed. Besides being perpetually cluttered, the room was plastered with posters of rock groups and bare-chested young "hunks" from the movies and TV. Even the screen-saver images swirling on Shawna's computer monitor glorified the popular music industry.

Stevie much preferred the pictures of horses, puppies, and kittens that had decorated Shawna's room in her preteen years. But Shawna was a teenager now, and the current room decor was much better than what she had first requested: to paint the room black and red and display posters of some of the morally questionable bands and personalities she claimed to like. Stevie felt she had been more than fair in meeting Shawna halfway—and that, of course, only after succumbing to intense "team pressure" from Shawna and Jon, who continually pointed out to Stevie how rigid and legalistic she was in her parenting techniques. Even with Stevie's concessions, however, Shawna continued to complain that she was being treated like a child.

Stevie assured herself often that Shawna was still going through a dark phase over the death of her older brother. The incident of rebellion at Lakeside Pines almost two weeks earlier and Shawna's harsh words and attitude afterward were another expression of it, Stevie was convinced. She could hardly deny her daughter a period of grief and confusion, considering the depression she herself had suffered. But sneaking out of camp in the middle of the night to meet strange boys bordered on self-destruction. And her cutting retorts during the ride home went beyond anything that could be considered "normal" disrespect. Once the children's weekend with their father was over, Stevie had grounded Shawna for a month—except for school, of course—but it had not softened her daughter's surly attitude so far. Glancing around at the worldly images decorating the room, Stevie prayed that Shawna's phase would pass soon, for both their sakes.

In the process of piling the clothes on top of Shawna's dresser to fold, Stevie jostled the desk, causing the computer's mouse to move. In response to motion, the brilliant image on the monitor dissolved, revealing the in-box for the E-mail program. Shawna often exchanged E-mail with her friends before and after school. Stevie had encouraged Shawna in computer skills, and she was proud that her daughter was proficient in word processing, Internet research, and E-mail.

As she matched and folded athletic socks, Stevie surveyed the list of names on the screen. She recognized all of them— Shawna's friends from school or church—except one: someone by the name of Rik. Stevie stopped folding to study the screen. There were several messages from Rik listed in the in-box, including one received this morning at 7:09. Stevie's curiosity quickly turned to concern. *Is this Rik a boy or a girl? Why hasn't Shawna mentioned him or her? Is this someone or something she doesn't want me to know about?*

Stevie had always respected her children's privacy, mostly because Jon had insisted on it. But in Dougie's case, respecting his privacy had been his parents' undoing. It wasn't until after their seventeen-year-old's fatal overdose that they found the paraphernalia hidden in the back of his closet. Stevie was convinced that, had she and Jon been less concerned about Dougie's privacy and more attentive to the subtle danger signs in his behavior, they might have been able to help him, to save him.

The messages to and from Rik were probably as inane and harmless as all the others from Shawna's friends, Stevie thought. Yet as much as she wanted to trust Shawna, the incident at Lakeside Pines had alerted her that the girl was quite capable of deceit. Stevie wasn't about to lose another child through ignorance or neglect. A quick look at a couple of messages would doubtless disarm her fears. She reached for the mouse and clicked on the latest message from Rik.

Stevie was not prepared for what appeared. Several of the words on the screen assaulted her before she even started reading the message. Vile words, unspeakable words. An involuntary groan leaped into her throat, as if someone had rammed a fist into her stomach. Forcing herself, she read the text line by line.

It was a love letter addressed to Shawna, a graphically suggestive love letter. The grammar and spelling were atrocious, but the message was clear. Using the crudest terms of the street, the writer described what he would do to please Shawna sexually and how she could please him. The sender identified himself simply as Rik.

Stevie felt as if she had just witnessed the seduction and rape of her teenaged daughter. And she was enraged that the perpetrator had committed the act in her own home, in Shawna's own room. With trembling fingers she highlighted the text and clicked on DELETE. The letter disappeared from the screen.

She opened another message from Rik, then another, and another. Stevie read every one. They comprised a series of increasingly bold and offensive letters from Rik to Shawna. The earliest entries were playful and flirtatious, typical of romantic banter between a junior high boy and girl. Then Rik became more suggestive and explicit, though markedly juvenile and unoriginal in his sentiments: "I want to hold you, I want to kiss you, I want to be with you all through the night." The last half-dozen messages were as vulgar and sickening as the one that had arrived that morning. Bodily parts and sexual functions were described in ribald slang terms. And Shawna was the unmistakable object of Rik's obscene proposals.

Even worse, every letter from Rik—including the most offensive ones—was followed by a response from Shawna. Shawna's terminology was not as raw as Rik's, but Stevie was appalled at the suggestive words and phrases her daughter had used to stoke the fire in her perverted suitor.

Most disturbing to Stevie was the realization that Rik was not a hormone-driven junior high boy with a command of gutter language. Recent correspondence confirmed that he was in his twenties, that he lived in San Bernardino County, and that he was the one with whom Shawna had intended to rendez-vous in Lake Arrowhead Village two weeks earlier. The dates on the messages revealed that the dirty letters began the week after the camp director had foiled their first date. "I wanted you so bad that night it hurt," Rik's message said.

Having read every word in the folder, Stevie pushed the chair back from the desk. She felt dirty inside and out, violated, as if Rik's blatant overtures had been directed at her. She also felt terrified for Shawna, who was still a naíve child, clueless to the danger of encouraging perverts like Rik. Stevie was stunned by the realization that she had unwittingly facilitated the sordid tryst by encouraging Shawna's computer literacy.

Awash in anger, remorse, and self-condemnation, Stevie reached behind the desk and, with shaking hands, began dis-connecting cables from the computer. In seconds the monitor blinked off and the hum of the CPU was silenced. Then she scooped up the monitor and carried it, cords dangling, to the garage, looking for a safe place to store it until she had more time to consider her next move. For now, she knew only that she had no intention of allowing this disgusting E-mail "romance" to continue.

Still shaking, she turned to see if there might be an empty space on the shelves behind her. As she did, she tripped over one of the dangling cables and stumbled, catching herself before she fell but not in time to keep from dropping the monitor on the hard cement floor, where the screen shattered.

Shocked, Stevie's hands flew to her mouth as she gasped. She had meant to remove Shawna's computer, but certainly not to destroy it. Now what would she do?

Trembling, she made her way back into the house. She was too shaken even to attempt cleaning up the mess in the garage. It would just have to wait until she caught her breath and col-lected her thoughts. Collapsing into a chair in front of the fire-place, Stevie began to weep. The last several minutes had seemed like a bad dream, one from which she wished she could awaken immediately. But having experienced the same feelings countless times after Dougie's death, she knew she could not. This was not a dream; it was real. And the situation was not going to go away. It had to be dealt with—and quickly. Shawna would walk through the doorway in twenty minutes, and Stevie had no idea what she was going to say to her.

Jon Van Horne spent little of the school day in his office, and today was no exception. It had been another harrowing day on campus. He had talked two girls out of slashing each other with razor blades in the hallway between classes. He had called in the cops on another kid who had been suspended but refused to leave the campus. At Foothill High School and other problem schools in the district, an LAPD squad car was assigned to the campus full time. Jon and the other administrators had kept them busy dealing with junior-grade criminals. Still, drugs, weapons, and gang activity on campus injured kids every week. Jon sometimes thought about changing his resumé to read "prison guard" instead of "school counselor."

In between crises, Jon breezed through his office to pick up messages, write referrals, and carefully document each incident on a microcassette. Families occasionally threatened to sue on behalf of their suspended or arrested children, claiming the administration physically or emotionally abused them. Jon had learned early in his career that thorough documentation saved him a ton of hassles in these confrontations.

He was just leaving his office after a brief midafternoon stop when the phone rang. On his way to deal with another minor classroom crisis, he thought about letting his voice mail take the call. But he already had a dozen calls to return before he could leave for the day, so he picked up the phone. "Counseling office, this is Jon."

There was no greeting, just, "I messed up, Jon. I *really* messed up." The familiar female voice sounded on the edge emotionally.

Jon seldom received a call from Stevie, and only rarely did she call him at school. Whenever she did call it was about the children or about his support check being late or about something at the house that did not work. He could not remember the last time Stevie admitted to messing up anything. There was an edge of urgency in her tone, but Jon could not read where she was heading. Was this about messing up the VCR clock again or messing up their marriage? Was she ready to

Josh McDowell and Ed Stewart

broach the untouchable subject of reconciliation, or was she calling to say his April check got shredded by mistake and she needed to deposit a replacement before the bank closed?

Jon was standing over his desk and considered sitting down but did not, unsure if he would be on the phone long enough to bother. "What do you mean, Steve?" he asked.

The answer poured out in a rush. "I found some dirty letters from a guy on Shawna's computer and she's been writing them too so I freaked out and unhooked her computer and took the monitor out to store it in the garage until I could fig-ure out what to do, but I tripped and dropped it and now it's broken and she's going to be home in ten minutes and I don't know what I'm going to tell her when she gets here."

Jon decided maybe he had better sit down after all. "Let's try that again, Steve," he said, easing into the squeaky steno chair behind his desk. "Letters? Computers? What are you trying to tell me?"

His ex-wife, who was clearly upset but thankfully not hysteri-cal, took a breath and filled in the blanks for him. As Stevie summarized Rik's messages, including samples of his vulgarity, Jon felt his skin flush with anger. Self-control was one of his strengths, but Jon realized that this jerk named Rik was lucky not to be alone in the same room with him at that moment.

As Stevie capsulized Shawna's side of the X-rated E-mail correspondence, Jon's anger turned to bitter bile in the pit of his stomach. His disappointment congealed into an impromptu prayer. *Dear Jesus, how could my little girl get involved with a creep like Rik? Where is this foul language coming from? What else does she know about love and sex? What has she actually experienced? She's only fourteen.*

"I'm afraid I overreacted," Stevie concluded, sounding defeated. "I suppose I should have left the computer where it was, but all I could think of at the moment was stopping this filthy correspondence with Rik. I only meant to take the com-puter away from her until we could get this situation resolved. I certainly didn't mean to break it, but now . . ." Her voice trailed off. "Oh, Jon," she whispered, "I just don't know what to do next. If only I'd stayed calm—"

"Steve, you reacted," Jon interrupted, trying to console her.

"It was a natural response. If I'd come across that filth I'd probably have done the same thing—or worse."

"But how am I supposed to deal with this situation? I have to confront Shawna about her involvement with this Rik person, but all she's going to want to talk about is her ruined computer."

"Deal with it just like we taught the kids," Jon said. "'When you mess up, 'fess up and make it right.' That's what we always told them, didn't we? So you apologize for what happened to the computer because of your overreaction, then move on to the real issue."

Stevie responded with a silence that communicated volumes. Jon had been with her enough years to know exactly what she wanted. Finally, he asked, "Do you want me to come over later and talk to her?"

"Yes, please," Stevie said immediately. "This is a big deal, and I'm in over my head emotionally. I think we both need to be involved. Shawna will be home any minute. How soon can you be here?"

Jon glanced at the clock on the wall. "I have parents coming in at three-thirty. I can't get out of here until four at the earliest. But I'll come straight over then if that will help."

"Come as soon as you can," Stevie said, sounding relieved. "I'm sure Shawna will be in her room, either ranting and raving or just being melodramatic and staring despondently at the empty space where her computer monitor once sat." Upon hearing Stevie's lightened tone, Jon smiled in spite of the situation. If their tragic experience with Dougie had done anything for them, it had made them more resilient. Stevie would get through this episode all right, and so would he.

Jon hung up the phone and rubbed his forehead. He could feel a headache coming on. There was more to deal with here than just Shawna. Stevie had turned to him for advice and consolation, something she had done only a few times since the split. Jon could not deny that such expressions of need stirred up the guardian and protector in him. Only fourteen months earlier he had renounced his commitment to occupy those roles in Stevie's life just as vociferously as she had renounced her commitment to him. If those commitments were truly ended, Jon wondered why, at moments like these, there was not more distance between him and his ex-wife.

7

Thursday
April 8

WALKING, EYES FORWARD, past her mother, who sat staring at her from a chair in front of the fireplace, Shawna entered her room at 3:20 and dropped her book bag on the floor. It had been a frustrating day. The teachers were always on her case, nagging her about being late for class, not turning her homework in on time, and a million other nitpicky things. When she had seen her mom sitting in the living room, it was obvious she was waiting for something—or someone. Shawna had a feeling that that someone was probably her, and whatever her mother wanted to discuss with her, Shawna was in no mood to hear about it. She had put up with enough grownups hassling her for one day.

That's when she saw it—the empty space on her desk where her computer monitor should have been. She looked around her room in disbelief. How could something like a computer monitor disappear? Where could it be? How. . . ? What . . . ?

Her mom. It had to have something to do with her mom. That must be what she had been waiting to talk with her about. Shawna reached out and was just about to fling open her door and go charging out to confront her mother when she heard a knock.

"Shawna? May I come in?"

The door opened slightly. "We need to talk," Stevie said, poking her head into her daughter's room.

Shawna's eyes opened wide. She could tell her mother had been crying. But about what? The computer monitor? Had something happened to it? Had it been stolen? Had her mother taken it for some reason? Shawna's breath caught in her throat. Suddenly she knew exactly what had happened to her computer monitor. Her mother had taken it, and Shawna was pretty sure she knew why.

Immediately going on the offensive, Shawna put her hands on her hips and cried, "You took it, didn't you? You took my computer monitor! Where is it? What have you done with it? I want it back!"

Stevie held her hand up. "Hold it," she said, her voice firmer than it had been a moment earlier. "Yes, Shawna, I took your computer monitor. I took it out to the garage to store it for a while, but—"

Shawna pushed past her mother and ran to the garage. When she saw what was left of her monitor, which was lying in pieces on the garage floor, Shawna wailed in feigned disbelief and inno- cence. In reality, she had a very good idea why the monitor had been taken, but she could not imagine her mother going so far as to purposely destroy it. In the midst of her confusion about her mother's actions and her anger at having her monitor destroyed, Shawna felt a slight stab of guilt about her on-line romance with Rik being exposed. But Destiny Fortugno had coached her never to admit to anything in front of her mother. "Do what you want, and don't let her hassle you," her friend had advised. "She's only human. You know she must be hiding stuff from you and from your dad and from her clients and from the IRS. So if she pressures you, scream bloody murder about your rights being violated. And if she doesn't give in, well, you know how to get what you want." Shawna envied Destiny's freedom to do what she wanted at home.

Stomping back to the bedroom where her mother stood waiting, Shawna screamed, "Why did you do this to me?" To her surprise, her mother apologized for "overreacting," then calmly described how she found the "pornographic" correspondence with Rik. Shawna felt stupid for forgetting to password-protect her E-mail program that morning. She could almost hear Destiny mocking her: "What a dork! You fell from the top of the stupid tree and hit every branch on the way down!" What bothered Shawna even more was the look of shock and disappointment in her mother's eyes. But she knew Destiny would really rag on her if she backed down now.

Shawna lashed out at her mother venomously. "You have no right to snoop into my private things. You have no right to steal things out of my room and destroy my belongings. I'm not your slave. I'm a person, and I have rights. You violated my rights!" It took only seconds for her to work up a good cry. Collin, who by now was watching bug-eyed from the doorway, was also tearing up at the conflict.

Shawna was surprised and a little disappointed that her mother was holding together so well. But as soon as she tried to speak, Shawna cut her off. "Get out of my room! Get out of my room and leave me alone," she wailed. Her face was already wet with tears and mucous. She had never ordered her mother out of her room before, but Destiny had urged her to stand up for herself.

"I'm leaving, but you definitely are not," Stevie snapped, squaring her shoulders. "You stay right here until your father arrives."

Shawna slammed the door as her mother left, then threw a few books around the room for effect. But her thoughts quickly turned to her dad. She didn't know how he would respond to the stuff on the computer. Besides, Destiny hadn't said anything about how to handle her dad; Destiny didn't even know who her dad was. *It doesn't matter what Dad says,* Shawna coached herself as she thought Destiny might. *Mom violated my privacy and damaged my personal property. Destiny said that the new law protects teenagers from such things. My school counselor said the same thing. I can live anywhere I choose. I can even live with Rik if I want to—maybe not right away, maybe after I explain everything to him. But I don't have to live here anymore. When Mom thinks I'll leave, she'll let me do what I want.*

Shawna remembered one more thing Destiny told her to do if her mom gave her serious trouble. She felt a little weird about doing it, but Destiny said it was necessary to make sure her mom gave her the space she deserved. She took her phone to a corner where she would not be heard outside her room and made one purposely tearful phone call. Then she sat down on the floor to wait.

About forty minutes later, Shawna heard her dad arrive. Listening through the door, she could hear her parents talking, but their voices were too low for her to get much of the discussion. After ten minutes, there was a soft rap on her door. She immediately recognized her father's voice when he said, "Shawna, it's me."

"Come in," she responded, sniffing loudly to keep up the abused-child act.

Jon entered, dressed in a nice shirt, sport jacket, and slacks, his school counselor clothes. Shawna had always thought her dad dressed well—for an adult. He sat on the edge of the bed with elbows on knees and hands clasped. "Your mom is very upset," he said evenly.

Shawna figured it was best to stay on the offensive. *"She's* upset? What about *me?* Do you know what she did to my computer? Did she tell you she broke it into a million pieces?"

Jon stuck to his point. "Mom and I are upset about the E-mail file she found."

"She had no right to sneak into my personal stuff," Shawna whined, producing another tear.

"Tell me about this Rik guy and the E-mail," Jon said.

Shawna had mentally rehearsed her response before her dad arrived. She looked him in the eye because she knew it was more convincing. "Daddy, it was nothing, just a computer joke, I swear. I've never even met Rik, and I don't intend to. Mom trashed my computer before I had a chance to explain. She's blowing the whole thing out of proportion."

Shawna felt a disquieting pang of guilt invade her before she finished the explanation. *An excuse is the skin of a reason stuffed with a lie,* one of the youth leaders at church had once said. Shawna knew her story was an excuse at best, and she didn't like how it made her feel. Destiny had told her that guilt was just extra baggage from spending too much time in church.

"Mom said Rik is the boy you planned to meet at Arrowhead Village," her dad continued. "It was all in the E-mail."

Shawna knew she was in too deeply. She couldn't quit now. "That's not true. I told you, it was a joke. I never meant to go through with it. Me and Destiny were just having fun. Mom has this all bent out of shape."

For the first time since her father walked in, Shawna saw a shadow of doubt flit across his eyes. *It's my word against Mom's,* she thought, watching him process what she had told him. *That's what you're thinking now, isn't it, Daddy? And you can't really trust the word of an ex-wife.*

Shawna took advantage of the silence. "Mom violated my rights, Daddy. I don't have to take this kind of abuse. I could move out if I wanted, and she couldn't do a thing about it."

Jon cocked his head at her suspiciously. "What are you getting at, Shawna?" The look on his face revealed that he knew exactly what she was getting at.

"You know," she said matter-of-factly. "The Child's Rights Act. I know all about it. You've used it to get kids at Foothill out of bad home situations. Mrs. Wacholtz, my counselor, told me so."

"Shawna, the CRA was designed to protect teenagers from abusive parents," Jon argued. "People who beat or rape or steal from their kids, people who force their kids into performing occult rituals or dealing drugs. It's not an excuse for kids to leave home whenever there's a disagreement or conflict."

"But if a kid's rights have been violated, that's abuse. Mrs. Wacholtz said so."

"Shawna, you know your mother loves you. She would never hurt you. She said she was sorry about the computer monitor; it was an accident. But she was very upset about the E-mail."

Shawna heard the doorbell ring in the entry. Her heartbeat quickened at what was about to happen. She hoped it worked the way Destiny said it would.

"But Mom treats me like a child, Daddy," Shawna said, hoping to coax her eyes full of tears again. "Whether she broke my computer on purpose or not, I don't really know. But she came into my room and took it without my permission, and that's not right. All I want is a life of my own."

The timing could not have been better, Shawna assessed. Her mother appeared at the door of her bedroom. Ashen-faced, she spoke to her ex-husband as if Shawna were invisible. "Jon, the police are here. They say Shawna called them. They want to talk with her."

Jon turned to his daughter. "The police?" he said in disbelief. "Shawna, what are you thinking?"

Shawna was flooded with uncertainty. Had she actually called the police and reported being abused by her mother? It seemed like a dream now, but she had done just that less than an hour ago. Now the police were here. What would she tell them? What would they do to her? What would they do to her mom and dad? She felt Destiny egging her on. "All I want is a life of my own," Shawna repeated as she led her parents out of the room.

The next events progressed so fast that Shawna thought she was in a time warp. She described what she knew about the computer incident to the two navy-clad Los Angeles police officers, both women. Each officer took turns briefly interviewing Shawna and her mother separately, including trips to the garage to inspect the damage. Jon and Collin were politely instructed not to interfere. Collin clung to his father, fighting back tears.

Stevie dabbed her eyes with a tissue during the process, glancing often at her daughter with pained disbelief. Shawna was torn between feelings of sadness for betraying her mother and a dogged insistence to follow through with her plan.

Finally the officers called the family together in the entry. "Based on what we have seen and heard this evening, Mrs. Van Horne," began the senior officer, a stocky Asian with black hair pulled into a short ponytail, "and in compliance with the Child's Rights Act in force in South California, your daughter must find another place to stay until CSD holds a hearing to discuss possible charges."

Stevie turned toward Jon with a despairing, questioning

look. "CSD? A hearing? Possible charges?" she said with voice quavering. "Can they really do this, Jon?"

Jon nodded slowly. "The CRA allows children fourteen and above to leave home if there is evidence of mistreatment. It happens every week at school."

"But that pornography on her computer, it was awful," Stevie argued plaintively. "And I didn't mean to break her monitor, but I had to deal with that . . . that trash in her E-mail."

Jon shrugged to express his helplessness. "It's the law, Steve. I don't like it and I don't agree with it, but it's the law. There's nothing I can do."

Shawna had scarcely breathed since she heard the officer utter the word *charges. Arrest Mom? No, this isn't supposed to happen. The cops are supposed to warn her to cut me some slack and then leave. I don't want Mom in trouble with the law. I don't want to move out. Destiny didn't tell me about this.*

The senior officer addressed Shawna. "Do you have somewhere to stay?"

Her mind was racing. She didn't want to leave home. She didn't want this to happen. But how could she back out now? "I'd like to stay with my dad, if it's all right with him," Shawna said. Ten minutes later, with a small bag of her possessions in hand, Shawna walked out the door with her father. She knew Destiny would be proud of her for hanging in there to the end. But Shawna felt anything but proud of herself.

Eugene Hackett sat in the darkness finishing his third beer of the young evening. He was alone in the house. His uncle had left for Vegas a week earlier with a couple of buddies to drink and carouse and gamble. Since then the electricity and phone had been turned off due to lack of payment. It had happened several times since Eugene had come to live with his uncle. Eugene cursed his uncle's stupidity. If Lyle Hackett got lucky in Vegas, he might return with enough money to get the lights back again. If not, the place would be dark until Lyle turned a couple of good drug deals. In the meantime, there were no lights, no hot water, and no food in the house. Just beer. Lyle always had plenty of beer around.

The inconveniences and the alcohol stoked Eugene's already

sour mood. Sullen idleness always seemed to bring his thoughts back to the night at the rec center. The face of that arrogant coach—Coach Jon Van Horne of Etiwanda Street, he remembered with disdain—leered at him. Every memory of what Van Horne did to him that night demanded vengeance. Eugene had held his anger for nearly two weeks, finding a twisted sense of pleasure in anticipating the moment of payback. Now, with thirty-six ounces of artificial courage goading his anger, he could no longer resist the urge.

Eugene collapsed the empty aluminum can in his hand and threw it across the dark room. Feeling his way to the bedroom, he found the hidden Colt .45 automatic and stuck it in his belt. Then he put on his trench coat and beret and slipped out of the house.

Staying close to the shadows, he walked six blocks to a small home occupied by two Latino families. The fragrance of chorizo and beans met him at the sidewalk, and Eugene was suddenly hungry. A dark-eyed little boy saw Eugene coming and, recognizing him, called Chako in Spanish to the door.

"What's going on, man?" Chako said, stepping outside. The strong, garlicky smell from the house was even stronger on Chako's breath.

The intensity in Eugene's eyes left no doubt about his purpose. "Let's go for a ride, Chako."

Chako studied him. "You really have to do this?"

Eugene nodded. "Tonight, man. I have to do it tonight."

Chako opened the battered screen door. "OK, Rattler. Come in and have something to eat. Then we'll go for a ride and get this out of your system."

After working up her courage to make the call, Stevie was disappointed not to get the minister on the phone. The number at the church, as she expected, connected her to a machine explaining the schedule of services. Dialing the minister's home number, which Stevie accessed through directory assistance, also produced a recording. Callers were politely invited to leave a message and promised a prompt response. But Stevie didn't want to entrust her story to a machine for just anyone to hear. So when the tone sounded, she hung up, making a mental note to try again later.

Having Collin still with her, Stevie could not afford to yield to the shock, disbelief, and grief pummeling her after the afternoon's events. Holding herself together, her first concern was to comfort her nine-year-old, who understood even less than she did about the police coming and Shawna walking out with a suitcase. At Stevie's invitation, Collin piled up on a mound of pillows on her bed to watch a favorite video. Then she locked the doors, armed the alarm system, changed into her pajamas and robe, and went into the kitchen to whip up a batch of popcorn and chocolate milk, Collin's favorites.

Waiting for the air popper to transform the kernels into fluffy white morsels, Stevie ran her fingers through her hair as she replayed the events of the afternoon and evening. It all seemed surreal. But every replay of the events prompted the same very real questions.

What has happened to Shawna? How can a sweet Christian child turn into a lying, conniving, gutter-minded teenager in just two years? And if God loves her, why did he let it happen?

How can a country founded on Christian principles stoop to allowing something like the Child's Rights Act to become law? What will happen to the Christian family if kids can leave whenever they feel slighted? What will become of parental discipline when it can be interpreted as child abuse?

How long will Shawna play out her defiance? Have I lost her forever, just like Dougie? Will she find a way to get together with this Rik character? Is there any way I can protect her from this pervert? Will Jon be able to—

In less than a second, a trio of .45 slugs exploded the windowpanes over the kitchen sink, tore through the curtains, and slammed into the refrigerator.

In the first terrifying instant, Stevie thought the "big one" had finally hit Los Angeles—the killer earthquake seismologists had predicted for decades. But before she could react, she realized that the sudden, roaring danger invading her home came not from the earth beneath but from unknown assailants outside. Angelenos feared random shootings as much as they feared the "big one." In either case, survival depended upon taking cover immediately without pausing to ask questions.

Stevie reacted instinctively. "Collin! Collin! Get down!" she screamed. As glass shards and splinters rained overhead, she dived to the floor and began crawling toward the bedroom. Slugs hitting the walls inside and out sounded like mighty hammer blows. Framed pictures and knickknacks dislodged by the concussion crashed against the furniture on their way to the floor. For six more seconds the deafening barrage continued across the front of the house, round after round piercing walls, spitting chunks of glass, drywall, and wood splinters.

By the time Stevie reached the darkened bedroom, it was over. The windows there had been hit too, and shards of glass littered the bed and carpet. Invading .45 slugs had silenced the TV and blown the bedside lamp to the floor. Through the open window Stevie heard a car speed away, then all was quiet.

Unable to see her son in the near darkness, Stevie cried out, "Collin!" She stayed on all fours searching the room for him, ignoring the cuts she was accumulating from broken glass. She found him lying on the floor on the far side of the bed. Touching his still body, her cry was frantic: "Collin!"

"Mom, there's glass all over me," the boy whimpered. "Whenever I move I get another cut."

Relieved to the point of tears, Stevie said, "Don't move, honey. I'll get the glass off of you in just a minute. I'm so glad you're all right."

Almost immediately, Stevie heard the voices of concerned neighbors approaching the house. The silent alarm, triggered by the shattered window, would bring the police, she knew. Perhaps the same two female officers who had been there earlier were among the contingent rushing to the scene.

The tumble off the bed amidst flying bullets and debris left Collin with cuts on his chin and both hands and a bad case of fright—but no gunshot wounds. Stevie's elbow throbbed from the hard landing, and she had numerous cuts on her hands, knees, and feet. The full weight of what happened—and what *could* have happened—hit her a few minutes later on the front lawn. With the wail of sirens growing louder in the distance, neighbors agreed that eight to ten shots had been fired at Stevie's house. No other homes on the street had been targeted.

Buckling under the emotional weight of her traumatic afternoon and evening, Stevie fell into the arms of a woman from the neighborhood she barely knew and sobbed. Cold reality pummeled her. Dougie was dead and Jon was no longer her husband, confidant, and comfort. Shawna had abandoned her, and Collin could easily have been killed in a hail of gunfire. Floundering to stay afloat in a raging current of *whys*, Stevie was now gripped by a question that threatened to pull her under like a riptide: When would this diabolical assault on her family ever end?

8

*Saturday
May 8*

THE OLD WOODEN grandstand was packed with over forty-five hundred noisy spectators. Another thousand crowded together on blankets and lawn chairs around the large, temporary stage on the field. The outdoor arena had not seen a crowd of over three thousand since the Rev. Bobby Lee Booker's Miracle Crusade in 1959. The scene resembled country-and-western talent night at some backwoods county fair. But the stage, sound system, cameras, and lights trucked in for the event were Hollywood production quality.

The warm-up act, a rowdy rockabilly group flown in from Fresno, got the crowd stomping and clapping. The band exited to reverberating applause. The stage lights dimmed to misty blue, and band members for the feature act took their places, prompting a resurgence of applause. A polished offstage voice boomed through the colossal speakers flanking the stage: "Ladies and gentlemen, Ms. Juanita Dunsmuir and the North California Freedom Band."

The rolling crescendo of cheers and applause obliterated the driving musical intro to the first number. Colored lights deluged the stage with midday brilliance as the star of the show entered. Juanita Dunsmuir, bathed in a white spotlight, strode energetically to the standing mike kicking a long, flowing skirt ahead of her and waving to the crowd. Her trademark braids, now more gray than black, nearly reached her ultra-slender waist. With dark, weathered skin, a belt and splashy earrings of silver and turquoise, and a narrow, decorative headband, she looked like an aging Navajo princess. A broad, worn leather strap slung over her shoulder suspended a very large, blond Martin acoustic guitar in front of her.

Reaching the mike, Juanita joined into the infectious song, first with her rhythmic strumming, then with her piercing voice. She opened all the campaign concerts with a medley of her biggest hits, which brought crowds to their feet cheering and clapping. The first one, "Adios, Tarzan," was her signature tune, typifying her well-documented lifestyle just as "My Way" had for Frank Sinatra. It was an upbeat, irreverent ballad about a woman with many lovers but none who really loved her. Each time she sang the chorus, the audience joined in: "Adios, Tarzan, you ain't good enough for this Jane. I need more than your body, your bucks, and your brain. Your loving ain't love if all I feel is pain. So adios, Tarzan, you ain't good enough for this Jane."

The personality in Juanita's eyes and smile sparkled to the far reaches of the small arena, charming her audience. Tobacco-chewing farmers and pot-smoking students sat side-by-side, enraptured by North California's legendary artist and activist. Roaming video cameras captured the magic and its effect on the crowd for future promotional use.

The eight-minute opening medley concluded with a reprise of "Adios, Tarzan," and the standing ovation rocked the little arena. Juanita bowed as gracefully as she could around her big guitar. As the applause slowly died away, she said, "I came to

Yuba County tonight for three reasons. First, I'm here to show you a good time. Are you having a good time?" The response was loud and long.

"Second, I'm here to celebrate with you one of the most beautiful concepts ever to grace our free country: the virtue of tolerance." Another strong wave of applause swept over the audience. "Tolerance reminds us that every lifestyle, every belief, and every worldview held by every citizen of our great land is of equal value. Tolerance is what America's founding fathers—and mothers—had in mind when they stepped ashore here. Tolerance is the freedom we offer one another to be what we want to be, do what we want to do, and worship whom we want to worship. Tolerance is what Jesus had in mind when he said, 'Judge not that you be not judged.' Tolerance, when allowed to flourish, puts an end to hatred, bigotry, and strife. And isn't that what we want for ourselves and our children in North California?" Another mountain of applause rose and fell.

"Third, I'm here to warn you that not everyone running for governor of our great state believes in the beauty of tolerance." Anticipating her meaning, the crowd began to hoot and clap. "His name is Dan Bellardi, but I think he deserves to be called Dangerous Dan." The crowd roared with approval. "Dangerous Dan doesn't want to be *governor;* he wants to be *warden* with North Californians as his prisoners. His idea of tolerance is counting to three while you decide to believe what he believes, live the way he lives, and worship the way he worships." Laughter exploded around the arena. "I'm here tonight to say, 'Dangerous Dan, the decent people of North California are not going to let that happen.'"

The chant arose from somewhere in the crowd and rippled quickly around the arena. It happened this way at every concert during Juanita's rousing preamble as if it were planned, which many critics insisted it was. In seconds the throng was singing again, this time to Dangerous Dan Bellardi: "Adios, Tarzan, you ain't good enough for this Jane. We need more than your body, your bucks, and your brain. Your loving ain't love if all we feel is pain. So adios, Tarzan, you ain't good enough for this Jane." The band joined in, first percussion, then bass, then guitars, horns, and keyboard. Juanita strummed energetically and lifted her voice. The place was rocking again.

Nearly a hundred miles to the north, Daniel Bellardi campaigned just as fervently, but in surroundings quite different from the Yuba County arena. There were no bright lights or booming speakers, nor was there the lingering odor of beer and smoldering marijuana. Even the ubiquitous cameras and media personnel of a political campaign were unobtrusive.

Crowded into the ballroom of Redding's Red Lion Hotel were almost two hundred church leaders decked out in their banquet best. The senator's staff had invited every denominational leader, pastor, priest, rabbi, elder, and deacon within a hundred miles of Redding to the event, the first in a projected series of "Dinners with Dan" for religious leaders in the state. The gatherings were the brainchild of campaign manager Robert Johnstone and media secretary Price Whitten and were financed by a number of Bellardi's major backers. The strategy was intended to counter the increased popularity of Juanita Dunsmuir, whom the senator's campaign staff had elevated from a mere nuisance to a mild threat to Dan Bellardi's aspirations.

Nor did the program in the ballroom bear a resemblance to the raucous goings-on at the arena. The evening began with an invocation by the pastor of a large Baptist church in Redding. Background music for the complimentary chicken dinner was a selection of light classics performed by a piano instructor from College of the Siskiyous.

As peppermint ice cream was being served, affable Price Whitten thanked everyone for attending and told a couple of preacher jokes, which drew gales of laughter. Then he introduced their host, "a man loved and respected by decent, God-fearing people across our new state, a man who will lead North California in turning our nation back to morality and godly values, Senator—and soon to be Governor—Daniel Bellardi."

Stepping to the lectern, Daniel mirrored pleasure at the enthusiastic ovation from his guests. A few "Bellardi for Governor" placards appeared in the crowd, even though the evening had been promoted as a social event instead of a political rally.

Daniel began his presentation by reading a number of passages from the Bible. The Old Testament texts concerned God's oft-repeated promise of a homeland for Abraham and his progeny. Other verses recalled God's insistence that his people live righteously within the borders of their new land despite the sinful behavior of their pagan neighbors. New Testament texts cited the injunctions of Jesus and St. Paul to spread the light of righteousness and justice in a dark world. Bellardi's lengthy reading was liberally punctuated with murmurs of "yes," "amen," and "praise the Lord" from the audience.

Closing the Bible, the speaker surveyed his guests. Daniel Bellardi's posture and bearing exuded dignity. His smile radiated friendship and trustworthiness. He said, "Ladies and gentlemen, I don't presume to identify the fine state of North California with Israel in these passages. And I certainly don't see myself as a twenty-first century Moses, even though I was privileged to take an active role in the so-called 'parting of the state of California' earlier this year." The laughter was gracious, mixed with a ripple of applause. "But I would be blind to miss the obvious parallels between what I have just read and what we have been called to in this grand new state of ours." Daniel casually but strategically gestured to include himself and his guests in the word *we*.

"Like Canaan of the Old Testament, North California, I am convinced, has been providentially prepared for those of us who believe in truth, morality, law, and order. The approval of the California legislature and Congress was no less miraculous than the parting of the Red Sea. And yet, also like Canaan, our Promised Land will not be possessed and occupied without effort. I'm not talking about a battle of swords and spears, but a clash of ideals between decent people and the undisciplined element in the land—the Philistines, if you will." The analogy got a positive rise out of the crowd.

"The Philistines believe that beautiful, serene North California is no different in nature than our materialistic, self-satisfying sibling to the south from which we have been politically separated. But I believe that North California is destined to be fundamentally different—governed, guided, and populated by those who will no longer tolerate the erosion of America's moral foundation." The audience affirmed the statement with applause and several more *amens*.

Daniel scanned the crowd, hoping to transfuse the passion

of his soul into every listener in the room. "I have a vision for beautiful North California tonight, a vision of freedom. I envision a state where citizens are free to walk the streets at any time of day or night in complete safety. I envision a state where our children are free to go to school, to the mall, or to the community park without being harassed by drug dealers or propositioned by pedophiles. I envision a state where every unborn baby is guaranteed the freedom to come to term and realize the potential for which it was conceived. I envision a state where children grow up in schools and neighborhoods where right and wrong are taught and modeled by adults. I envision a state where parents do not fear the loss of their rebellious children to a ludicrous Child's Rights Act."

Each statement was delivered with a few more ounces of passion than the last. The rapt audience affirmed each with a murmur of approval.

"I envision a state where all are welcome but where all are expected to conduct themselves according to truth, honesty, integrity, purity, and respect for people and property. I envision a state where parents are encouraged to discipline their children, not punished for doing so. I envision a state where individual rights are kept in balance by time-honored community values. Those whose lifestyle and beliefs differ from these norms must be accepted and not persecuted. But to allow these radically divergent views to be propagated as viable alternatives is to invite Goliath and his family to live next door. Our children are too precious for such a risk.

"I envision a North California where the church is separate from the state but not excluded from it. For example, Christmas isn't Christmas without the carols and pageants of the Christ-child. And the Bible and prayer are as much a part of the foundation of our country as the Declaration of Independence. Instead of banning these facets of our religious heritage, we must celebrate them with our children, while respectfully allowing any who believe otherwise to decline participation."

The vigorous applause demonstrated that Daniel Bellardi's audience was solidly on his side. Daniel rode the crest of the wave of approval, concisely delineating a platform of Judeo-Christian values as his passport to leading North California into the twenty-first century. He faced the cameras often, strategically including future viewers in his message. He repeatedly called the God-fearing people of North California to take up his banner and help him conquer the land.

Daniel Bellardi's position had been crystal clear to his rapt listeners before they had arrived for the dinner. Hearing him declare it with conviction and visible passion prompted them to rousing, sustained applause. Several more placards were raised and waved.

Daniel smiled with pleasure. As the noise subsided, he purposely turned his attention to the cameras in the room. "I know there are tens of thousands of people in South California and across America who are fed up with crime and immorality in the streets and disgusted with leaders who refuse to do anything about it. I have one thing to say to these people: Come to North California and help us take the promised land for freedom."

Everyone in the ballroom was on their feet and cheering wildly again. Daniel stepped back from the lectern and silently rejoiced in the reception. He made a mental note to commend Johnstone and Whitten for the idea of the clergy dinners. These were the people who could help him take his message of hope to the people of North California. Only one dark, persistent cloud looming on the horizon shadowed his optimism. Juanita Dunsmuir also had a growing number of North Californians applauding and cheering for her.

9

Sunday
May 9

STEVIE WAS getting nothing out of the sermon. The topic was the priestly ministry of Christ, and people in the pews around her were leafing through their Bibles to find the references and taking notes studiously. Stevie just sat with her hands in her lap wondering why she was there.

It had been this way for several Sundays. Not that Pastor Schofield was a boring or ineffective speaker. To the contrary, he was one of the most insightful and engaging Bible teachers Stevie had ever heard. He was the main reason she and Jon began attending West Valley Bible Church as new Christians hungry to learn about God, faith, and the Bible.

But that was when Dougie and Shawna were small and

Collin's existence was still under discussion. Her favorite Bible verse in those days was Jeremiah 29:11: "'For I know the plans I have for you,' says the Lord. 'They are plans for good and not for disaster, to give you a future and a hope.'" She almost laughed out loud as she thought of those words now. *What future and what hope?* she mused silently. *Is this it, the best I have to look forward to?*

She shook her head to clear her thoughts. Such negativity toward God must surely border on blasphemy. And it wasn't that she didn't believe God's Word, but . . . how was she to reconcile it with what was taking place in her life?

It had been so different in those early years. She and Jon had truly been in love—with God, with each other, with their children, and with life in general. Every sermon had been exciting, every Scripture personal. In fact, Stevie had once thrived on topics like "Six Indisputable Proofs that the Bible Is True" (all beginning with the letter *P,* which Stevie had found fascinating).

The events of the last four years, however, had markedly influenced her view of the church's relevance in her life. All the sermon notes she had scribbled down had not prepared her for Dougie's drug problems and ultimate overdose. And the six *P*'s and the four *S*'s and the rest of Pastor Schofield's cleverly alliterated sermons—not to mention Jeremiah 29:11 and other Scripture promises Stevie had memorized—had not prevented Stevie's two overpowering *D*'s: depression and divorce. Then there was last month's double-barreled emotional jolt. No sermon Stevie could remember had equipped her to deal with her second child's shocking deceit and defection or the unexplained drive-by shooting that could have taken her own life and the life of her third child.

The church promoted parenting seminars occasionally, Stevie recalled, but they were frequently scheduled on weeknights or Saturdays—eating up precious free time for a divorced working mom. Sometimes she would attend a Sunday school class on parenting issues, but they were always taught by other parents, not professionals on the subject. And they were very basic, designed for parents without a clue. Stevie knew the basics. It was the advanced issues with Dougie and Shawna that had stymied her, issues that were apparently too complex for Sunday school and too earthy for a Bible sermon.

As the pastor transitioned into his third point, Stevie considered the irony. *My neighborhood is a war zone, my kids' schools are cesspools of drugs and immorality, my family is falling apart, and I'm supposed to care that the high priest's tunic typifies the purity of Christ.*

What does my church have to do with real life? Guns are in all the schools, and gangs rule the city at night. Marijuana is legal for 21-year-olds, but any junior high kid can get it. Condoms are distributed by teachers in the hallways, and gays and lesbians are free to recruit followers in health classes. Right and wrong are regarded as vulgar and archaic concepts. Tolerance for virtually any value system, lifestyle, or truth-claim—pure or perverted—is backed by the courts. And my daughter can legally call the cops on me and leave home at fourteen because I "abused" her by entering her room and removing her computer monitor without her permission, destroying it in the process.

This is madness. The world is going to blazes around me, and my kids are going down the drain with it. The school and the community only seem to make things worse. Whatever happened to teachers and administrators and legislators who care about their constituents? Why isn't a government commission monitoring E-mail to prevent dirtbags like Rik from electronically molesting girls like Shawna? No wonder Shawna made wrong choices. The moral fabric of the community has been reduced to shreds, and nobody will take responsibility for it.

The litany of social ills and failures nagged at Stevie. She wondered if the nicely dressed saints around her had any idea how angry she felt.

And what is my church doing about the collapse? They're wrapped up in a drive for new pews and choir robes. Where was the youth pastor when Dougie was silently crying out for help? Where were the camp leaders and counselors when Shawna was plotting her escape from Lakeside Pines? And I wonder if Pastor Schofield ever gets out of his library to see what is going on in the world.

Had Collin not come with her to attend Sunday school while she was in the worship service, Stevie would have slipped out during the pastoral prayer and gone home. Unable to do that, she was open game in the foyer after the service. On her way to pick up Collin, Rev. Roger Schofield was suddenly in her path.

"Stephanie, it's good to see you today," he said with unimpeachable sincerity. His hand was extended, so she shook it.

"Thank you, Pastor. Wonderful message this morning." It *was* a wonderful message, she rationalized to herself, a fine specimen of oratory, just irrelevant to her.

The pastor lowered his volume discreetly. "How is Shawna doing?"

Stevie didn't want to get into it. She was sorry she had mentioned Shawna's E-mail problem and departure to the pastor when it happened. When she'd first called him to tell him about it and got the answering machine, she should have left it at that. Instead she had called back later, requesting prayer for the situation. Now he knew, and she could not very well avoid the subject. She answered in as general terms as possible: "All right, I guess. She's with Jon—probably driving him crazy." Had she spoken her true feelings at the moment, Stevie might have said, "My daughter doesn't want to live with me and I'm very upset about it. So far I've lost a husband, a son, and a daughter while attending your church. Perhaps I'd better leave while I still have Collin."

"And how about you?" Pastor Schofield asked. He had seen her at her worst during and after the divorce. Stevie couldn't help but interpret his question as, "You're not slipping back into depression, are you?"

"Really good, thank you, Pastor," she said, trying to sound upbeat.

Another parishioner begged for the pastor's attention, but before turning away he gripped her shoulder and said, "We're praying for you, Stephanie." Coming from anyone else, the words might have sounded condescending. But Stevie was convinced that Schofield meant it. She just wasn't sure that it was doing any good.

That afternoon, Stevie ironed clothes in the family room, where it was cool and quiet. It had reached the high eighties in the Valley. Collin and a friend from his soccer team were in the backyard taking turns being goalie for the other's shots against the cinder-block wall. Ben, a handyman from the neighborhood, was in the front yard finishing repairs to the stucco and woodwork where .45 caliber slugs had penetrated a month earlier. The kind neighbor had also replaced the shattered windows for the cost of materials and a modest labor charge.

Enjoying the minutes of relative tranquility while completing a mindless task, Stevie drifted back to Pastor Schofield's parting comment: "We're praying for you, Stephanie." Only people in the outer circle of her relationships called her Stephanie. Roger Schofield clearly saw himself as her pastor, not her friend— which was fine, because Stevie was uncomfortable calling him anything but Pastor Schofield. But his statement, and the conviction with which he had delivered it, was that of a caring friend.

A few other friends at church were praying for her too, Stevie knew. And despite her doubts and frequently flagging spirits, Stevie had not stopped praying herself. But prayers seldom progressed beyond the topic of her own needs and disappointments, and that bothered her.

As she ironed, she analyzed what all this praying might have accomplished. One huge answer to prayer was obvious: CSD had decided not to press charges against her for abusing Shawna's rights and destroying her property. The state court system was so choked with serious child-abuse cases—abandonment, assault, rape, murder—that Stevie had been let off with a stern reprimand and an order to compensate Shawna for her losses.

Reflecting on the E-mail fiasco, Stevie had to admit that her daughter's relationship with Rik might have been discovered as a result of prayer. The curious impulse to open Shawna's E-mail, though it precipitated Shawna's departure and a storm with the CSD, allowed Stevie to nip in the bud her daughter's relationship with a potential sex criminal. Yet Shawna was still gone, choosing to live with her father, something neither she nor Jon wanted. Stevie agonized daily that worldly influences and temptations might lead her daughter farther and farther away.

The fact that she and Collin had escaped death at the hands of an unknown gunman was clearly an answer to prayer. And someone must have been praying for her afterward, too. Unable to work for days due to the trauma, Stevie had considered moving out of the Valley. But she kept returning to the same question: *Where can we find immunity from such savagery? It pervades the entire greater Los Angeles area.* So she consoled herself with the improbable odds that she could be a random target more than once. Just to be safe, she moved her bedroom furniture into Shawna's room next to Collin's room at the back of the house and beefed up the alarm system.

Stevie slipped a freshly pressed shirt onto a hanger and buttoned the top button. She stretched a kink out of her back and took a long drink of cranberry iced tea from the glass on the counter. Then she returned to her pile of ironing.

Consciously accepting that prayer sometimes worked for her, Stevie was even more acutely aware of God's silence in response to the major petitions of her life. For all she prayed that her children would be protected from a worldly lifestyle, Stevie was worried that Shawna was being sucked right into it. Why had this prayer not been answered? There were times when Stevie had even begun to hope and pray that her family might be together again. But Shawna seemed headed in the opposite direction, and Jon was keeping his distance. Stevie could not really fault her ex-husband after the way she had blamed what she saw as his permissive parenting philosophy for Dougie's death. But even after all that, was God not powerful enough to soften his heart in response to her prayer?

Then there was the disheartening issue of the moral climate in which her struggles were being played out. For years Stevie had prayed for godly civic leaders and tougher laws in Los Angeles County, only to see things get increasingly worse. Anarchy had already gained a foothold in south-central L.A.; even the police unofficially avoided some parts of it. Marijuana was legal for adults. A measure legalizing "brothel zones" in the county would be on the November ballot, an attempt to regulate prostitution and curb the spread of sexually transmitted diseases. The latest polls revealed that the well-financed measure had a good chance of passing.

The city school district had sold out to values-neutral education, setting kids adrift without a moral compass. Cheating had evolved into a science, justified and practiced at some level by most students. Junior high health classes stressed safe sex for kids instead of no sex. Teachers regularly had students role-play sexual situations and practice putting condoms on bananas. Kids today seemed just as embarrassed at being labeled virgins as Stevie's generation had been at being labeled promiscuous.

Stevie believed in prayer. But for all her praying, this mountain—the godless culture in which she struggled to raise godly kids—was getting larger instead of smaller. The world had already reeled in her Dougie, and the hook apparently was set in Shawna's jaw. If God didn't give her some answers soon, Stevie held little hope that Collin would survive. *God, if my baby is taken away from me too . . .* Stevie lamented silently as a tide of despair ebbed nearer.

Not pleased with where her thoughts were headed, Stevie decided to take a break. She grabbed the glass of iced tea and began searching for the TV remote. She found it between the sofa cushions, right where Collin often left it. Stevie hoped a dose of decorating tips from the home-and-garden channel would change her frame of mind. She dropped into the sofa and snapped on the TV across the room.

Before Stevie could switch channels, the caption on the screen caught her attention: THE GROWING BATTLE FOR NORTH CALIFORNIA. It was a story segment on one of the Sunday afternoon news talk shows she never watched. Stevie had followed only casually the debates in the California assembly and senate about dividing into two states. She was in favor of it because she thought it might somehow help decongest the Los Angeles area.

Once the measure was approved by Congress, Stevie seldom gave another thought to the small new state to the north. She certainly didn't know anyone was interested in fighting over a state with no large cities, no amusement parks, and no movie or television studios. Curious, she pulled up the volume to listen.

The host was introducing the topic. A guest sat on either side of him. All wore business suits of blue or gray.

"—that there would be a contest to govern a population largely made up of conservatives who have no use for places like L.A. or San Francisco. By an act of sleight of hand, Dan Bellardi and his band of magicians made North California magically appear. And it seemed that his magic in the north would continue until the voters woke up on November second to discover that Bellardi was the state's first governor.

"But apparently, long-time activist and folksinger Juanita Dunsmuir has conjured up a way to break Bellardi's spell. Her decision to run for governor was viewed by many in politics and the entertainment industry as a joke, a publicity stunt. Though active in politics throughout her career, Dunsmuir has never sought or held elective office. Many thought her decision to run against the framer of the North California resolution was a move to resuscitate her career and record sales. That she had no chance of toppling Bellardi, the charismatic leader of the North California movement. No chance, that is, until she hit the road with her Freedom Tour."

A video clip showed Juanita Dunsmuir on stage flailing her guitar and belting out one of her old hit songs. She exuded the energy of a woman half her age. Stevie knew little more about Juanita Dunsmuir than what she saw in the media. The singer lived hard, fast, and loose, she had heard. And Dunsmuir always seemed to align herself with political candidates Stevie opposed. But she made good music. The song she was singing now had been a favorite of Stevie's when she was pregnant with Shawna.

Like most everyone, Stevie had never regarded Juanita Dunsmuir as a serious candidate for governor of North California. The commentator's hint that Dunsmuir's campaign was gaining support intrigued her. She leaned forward to watch and listen.

As the Dunsmuir clip rolled, the program host described the concert tour and remarked at its success. Next came footage of Daniel Bellardi addressing a group of religious leaders. The senator looked quite professional and distinguished in contrast to Juanita Dunsmuir's braids, headband, and country/folk/rock music. Stevie found it hard to believe that the singer was any threat to an established political leader like Bellardi.

The host ended his introduction with a question to his two guests: "So what do you make of the battle for North California?"

"You're absolutely right, Sid, when you say it's a battle," answered the more portly of the two male political analysts. "But instead of a war of missiles and smart bombs, it's more like the redcoats versus the colonists. Dan Bellardi expected to march into the governor's office without a threat from the unconventional and inexperienced Dunsmuir troops. But like the ragtag revolutionary colonists, Juanita Dunsmuir pops out of the bushes with her funky concerts all over the state and starts taking potshots at Bellardi. And the senator is taking some hits in the polls."

"Good analogy, Edgar," the second analyst chimed in, a man the others called David. "And we need to remember that the combatants in the battle for North California really do regard the conflict as a revolution. In this case, Dan Bellardi is the revolutionary. He's the one out to change things in a big way. The two states are under the same laws now. But if Bellardi and conservative legislators are swept into power, four years from now the laws of North California won't look anything like the laws on the books today."

"Ironically, Juanita Dunsmuir, who has been something of a rebel all her life, represents the establishment in this war. She is battling to retain the status quo for her home state: tolerance, legalized marijuana, gay rights, children's rights, abortion rights, clear separation between church and state. Bellardi is out to change all that. He wants to take North California back to the morals of the 1950s."

Stevie listened with piqued interest. This was something she had not heard before, or if she had heard it, it hadn't registered. Her take on Daniel Bellardi was that he had been a little fish in a big pond: a rural, strongly conservative state senator in the populous, increasingly liberal state of California. But this little fish wanted to be a big fish, and he also happened to be wealthy. So, from what Stevie gathered, Bellardi shrewdly exchanged his money for influence, magically transformed his influence into public support, and bought himself a small pond: the new state of North California. It was an ego trip, Stevie had heard on TV. But the commentators on the screen right now were talking about a different agenda for Bellardi, an agenda that Stevie suddenly wanted to know more about.

"You mentioned tolerance, David," Sid, the host, cut in. "Would you agree with many analysts who say that the issue of tolerance is the battle cry for both sides in North California?"

"Absolutely, Sid. Dan Bellardi strongly believes that tolerance as our culture defines it does away with absolutes, standards, convictions, and conscience. He is banking on a hope that the people who helped him establish North California will help him create an outpost of Judeo-Christian values where—"

A sudden shriek launched Stevie to her feet and turned her attention to the backyard. Before she reached the sliding glass door, Collin had pushed it open from the outside. His eight-year-old soccer teammate stood beside him wailing. The boy's hand was pressed over his forehead, and blood seeped between his fingers and streamed down the side of his face.

"Mom, Perry hit the block wall with his head," Collin blurted with concern. "He's bleeding all over the place."

Stevie sprang into action. She grabbed a dish towel from the kitchen, doused it with water, and applied the compress to the bleeding gash. "It's OK, Perry," she said to the boy, who was crying more from the sight of his own blood than from pain. "You may need a couple of stitches, so let me run you home. We'll call your mother on the way."

Hustling the boys toward the front door, Stevie paused to turn off the iron. Then she glanced at the TV screen. North California gubernatorial candidate Daniel Bellardi was explaining his vision for the new state based not on tolerance but on love, respect, moral values, and truth. Stevie determined to find out more about this man. She wished he were running for governor of *South* California.

10

Wednesday
May 12

"IT'S THE CINCHIEST thing you've ever done." Destiny was in Shawna's face, trying to keep her voice down. The hallway was noisy with kids jabbering, slamming lockers, and scurrying for the buses. It was ten minutes past three.

"Mr. Nguyen will be out on the baseball field until four-thirty. Make sure his room is empty, then go inside and lock the door behind you. The cabinet is right behind his desk. Unlock it with this." Destiny made sure no one was watching, then she pressed a small key into her friend's palm.

Shawna hoped Destiny did not notice how sweaty her hand was. She had not been this nervous since the night they sneaked out of Lakeside Pines. "Where'd you get this?" she asked, quickly jamming the key into the pocket of her jeans. She was awed that Destiny could get ahold of the key to a teacher's filing cabinet.

"Tara Marshall, Nguyen's TA this semester, and another Lindley Belle," Destiny said proudly. Then she glanced around again. "The Belles do anything for each other. They swear it. If you want to be a Belle, you do what we say—no questions. Got it?"

The Belles comprised a secret sorority of handpicked eighth and ninth graders at Lindley Junior High. Shawna did not know who the Belles were or exactly what they did—that really *was* a big secret. She did know that there were no adult advisors, and that the administration discouraged students from involvement with such organizations. But all the girls at Lindley knew that being invited to pledge the Belles was the ultimate in cool. Shawna was not positive she wanted to be a Belle, and she knew her dad would be upset if he found out she was still spending time with Destiny. But Destiny Fortugno wanted Shawna to be a Belle, and Shawna could hardly resist the magnetism of this popular, fearless classmate.

"Got it," Shawna answered. "No questions."

Destiny moved even closer to Shawna as a cluster of boys swept by them. "Open the top drawer and find the biology section. Get the Unit Four exam, make a copy of it on Nguyen's machine, then put the original back and lock the cabinet. Bring the copy and the key to me before four-fifteen. I'll be in the quad."

"Isn't that stealing?" Shawna offered weakly.

Destiny scowled at Shawna. "No questions, remember?"

"Sorry, I forgot," Shawna said quickly.

Destiny ignored the apology and answered the question anyway. "You're *borrowing* Nguyen's exam for ten seconds to copy, you little dork, then you're putting it right back. A couple of Belles in Nguyen's class need to ace this test. When I tell them you got the test for them, they'll vote you right in."

"They could get busted for cheating."

Destiny laid a hand on Shawna's shoulder and shook it as if to waken her friend. "Hey, it's only cheating if they see the *answers*. You're only borrowing the *questions* for them. They still have to study for the exam. Does that sound like cheating to you?"

Destiny had a way of making everything sound so logical. "Guess not," Shawna said.

Before Shawna could voice any more doubts, Destiny said, "OK, get going. I'll see you in the quad in less than an hour. Don't be late." Then she merged with the river of students coursing toward the exit.

By the time Shawna found her way to room S210, the halls were empty except for a custodian dust-mopping classroom floors. A glance through the door proved to Shawna that Mr. Nguyen's classroom was deserted. But the custodian was cleaning S206 on his way to S220. So Shawna kept walking past S210 to the end of the hall where she sat down on the floor, opened her book bag, and pretended to be studying algebra.

As she waited, Shawna's stomach flip-flopped nervously. This was a crazy thing to do. This was a dangerous thing to do. But thinking of Destiny and the other Belles who had proved themselves in similar ways, it was also a thrilling thing to do. *Destiny's right,* Shawna assured herself. *I'm borrowing, not stealing. And even if the girls who study from the test are cheating—and I still think they are—at least I'm not cheating. And in just a few minutes, it will all be over and I'll be a Lindley Belle.* A sense of importance and acceptance charged Shawna with excitement.

The custodian seemed to be moving in slow motion. By the time he finished cleaning S210, it was almost four o'clock. Shawna could imagine Destiny pacing the quad right now, cursing at her for being so slow. As soon as the custodian rolled his cart into S212, Shawna got moving. Sneaking by S212, she slipped into Mr. Nguyen's open room and locked it behind her. The lights were off, but the afternoon sun flooding in from the windows made Shawna feel as if she were in a spotlight.

Light-headed with excitement, Shawna walked straight to the copy machine in the corner of the room and switched it on to warm up. Digging the key out of her pocket, she unlocked the cabinet and found the exam right where Destiny said it would be. It was a four-pager, two sides to each page. *Eight copies to make,* she thought in mild panic. *Hurry, Shawna, hurry!*

The copy machine was even slower than the custodian. But

as each warm page spewed out, Shawna's excitement mounted. It was going to happen like Destiny said, cinchy as pie. Nobody would ever know about this except the Belles. And she would be a Belle before the semester ended.

Shawna snapped off the copier and shoved the pages into her book bag. Returning the original to the folder marked Unit Four, she quietly closed the drawer, locked it, and pocketed the key. She was halfway to the door when she heard the handle rattle. Someone was trying the locked door. She sucked in a breath, and it froze in her chest.

She flattened herself against the inside wall, out of sight from the door. It rattled again and again, then stopped. Shawna slowly released her breath as seconds of silence passed. *It was only a kid fooling around, maybe even one of the Belles sent to freak me out,* Shawna told herself. *Or it was the custodian checking the door.*

Then a new sound paralyzed her with fear: a key slipping into the lock and turning. *This was a stupid idea, Shawna,* she thought with alarm. *Why did you listen to Destiny again?* When the athletic Vietnamese-American science teacher entered the room, Shawna had nowhere to hide. Mr. Nguyen's surprise quickly dissolved to suspicion. "What's going on?" he asked, his eyes locking on hers.

Doing her best to return his stare, Shawna grabbed at a straw. "M-my friend, uh . . . Tara Marshall thought she left her jacket in here," she stammered. It sounded stupid as soon as she said it. She felt a lump of remorse rolling up her throat but she steeled herself against the hot tears that were already beginning to sting her eyelids. She did not think Belles ever cried about something like this.

The teacher studied her as intently as he would a slide under a microscope. Shawna knew he could see through her flimsy excuse. Finally Mr. Nguyen extended his hand. "Let me see your book bag, Miss Van Horne," he said sternly. Before she could get the bag off her shoulder, Shawna dropped her gaze and began to cry.

Jon Van Horne hung up the kitchen phone, but he remained at the breakfast bar for several minutes, dejected. It was almost four-thirty. He had been home from school only a few minutes before his counterpart at Lindley Junior High School had called. Jon and Curt Holgate were friends, having taught and coached together at Balboa Junior High before moving to different Valley schools. But Curt had called as a vice principal today, not a friend. He somberly explained that Shawna had been caught in the act of stealing biology exams from the teacher's files. She was in his office now and still crying pretty hard.

Jon was immediately aware of the consequence for such misbehavior, which was automatic in the district. Curt had even apologized when announcing that Shawna would be expelled for the rest of the term. Jon said he would be at the school in twenty minutes to take her home.

Jon rubbed his forehead. *It's been going so well with Shawna, and now this,* he lamented silently. *She was actually talking to me a little about the camp problem and Rik and getting along with her mother. We worked on homework together. She even cooked dinner for me a couple of times. She seemed like my sweet little girl again. What is going on in her brain that causes her to steal biology exams? She's not even taking biology. And why is she crying? Because she's sorry for what she did or because she got caught?*

As he drove his Ranger pickup to the junior high school, Jon considered the ramifications of his daughter's expulsion. She was done with school for the year, meaning he would have to find someplace for her to stay or something for her to do during the remaining five weeks of school. Maybe he could talk her into going back with her mother at least until summer. Lindley might take her back in the fall. If not, he would have to enroll her in another school, probably the alternative school in Chatsworth. That would mean providing daily transportation for her.

Jon released a disconsolate sigh. He felt miles away from the life he had planned for himself, for his children, for his family. Pangs of guilt and sadness, which were never far from him, troubled Jon again. He missed Dougie terribly. His older son would have been nineteen this summer, finishing his sophomore year at Cal State on a basketball scholarship—Jon's goal for him—or an academic scholarship—Stevie's hope. *How did he slip away?*

Where did we lose our grip on him? The questions still taunted him.

Divorce from Stevie had not been in Jon's plans either. He had entered marriage expecting a lifelong magic carpet ride of passion, sexual fulfillment, and camping trips. Love with Stevie was special—automatic, he had thought, not something he had to guard, nurture, and work at. Had their love not grown subtly anemic through years of passivity, and had they somehow found common ground when it came to parenting techniques rather than constantly opposing each other over rules and regulations, Jon and Stevie might have prevented or at least survived Dougie's drug overdose. But instead of melting them together, the tragedy and subsequent bitterness, suspicion, and blaming drove them to opposite poles. Out of necessity, he had learned to communicate with his ex-wife from this distance over issues related to the kids. And months of solitude and reflection had caused him to wonder at times if he had been too hasty about allowing the marriage to dissolve. But the oceans of perceived distance they had created seemed immense and impassable.

Thinking of Stevie, Jon knew he had to call her right away. He was not eager to break the bad news, particularly since Stevie might implicate him as a cause. After all, this incident happened on his watch, not hers, and she had always accused him of running too loose a ship when it came to their kids. But she would be even more upset if he delayed telling her. Still five minutes from the school, Jon picked up the cell phone and tapped in his ex-wife's number.

Sitting in the hall outside the vice-principal's office, Shawna felt like a piece of old furniture just waiting to be hauled off and discarded. Women from the school office staff walked by her on their way home as if she were not there. Having called Shawna's father, Mr. Holgate was busy in his office talking to another parent. Even Mr. Nguyen had walked away without a glance after delivering Shawna and the "evidence" to the vice principal. Having been expelled for the semester, Shawna was not their responsibility anymore, and it showed. She could have left the building and disappeared for all the attention given her.

Shawna's pockets were stuffed with used tissues, and her nose was still running. She felt awful. She had never been suspended from school before. Her friends would talk about her for days, she knew. "I can't believe Shawna would steal an exam; she goes to church and everything," they would say.

Destiny and Tara would have a good laugh over Shawna's ineptness—until tomorrow when Mr. Holgate called them out of class. Shawna felt badly about that too; she had not intended to nark on the Belles. But Mr. Nguyen had asked her point-blank, "Did you get this key from Tara Marshall?" Shawna fumbled her lie and finally nodded. She had the same experience when the vice principal asked her if Destiny Fortugno was part of the scheme. Tara and Destiny would probably get suspended, and neither one of them would ever speak to her again. Shawna knew she could never be a Belle now. She wished she had never tried in the first place.

Then there was the matter of facing her parents. Shawna guessed they already considered her a borderline juvenile delinquent after Lakeside Pines and the E-mail to Rik. And her mother must despise her after she called the cops on her and moved out—another dumb idea inspired by Destiny Fortugno. Now she had further embarrassed her parents, especially her dad. The news about Jon Van Horne's expelled daughter would surely heat up the gossip lines in the Valley schools. Her mom and dad were not perfect, Shawna knew. But she would agree with anyone who said they did not deserve the kind of stress their daughter had brought to them over the last two months.

Shawna pulled out a used Kleenex and took another swipe at her nose. So why had she done it? she pondered painfully. Why did she do stuff she really did not want to do, stuff she wished she had not done almost as soon as she did it? Why did she keep listening to Destiny Fortugno when it always seemed to get her into trouble? Why had she encouraged Rik and kept the gross stuff he sent her? And why, after all she had done to hurt her mother, could she not admit her stupidity and ask to move back to her own room? Dad was kind and fun, but Shawna had missed Mom and Collin since the first night she so pridefully walked out.

Shawna found herself thinking about a devotional the youth minister had given during a youth group all-nighter. He had talked about Peter or Paul or John who said something like, "I don't do the things I should do; instead, I do the things I shouldn't do, things I don't even want to do. Living like this is the pits!" Shawna was sure that Brian gave an answer to the apostle's dilemma from the Bible, but she had been passing notes to Destiny at the time. She wished now she had been listening.

The door at the end of the hall opened, and Shawna saw her father's athletic frame silhouetted against the late afternoon sunlight flooding the doorway. Another wave of remorse swept over her, but she determined not to cry again.

When her dad reached the chair where she was seated, he just looked at her. Shawna could not force herself to return the gaze. Then he touched her shoulder, not an angry touch, more of a friendly pat. Shawna finally looked at him.

"I just talked to your mother," he said. Surprisingly to Shawna, his tone was no more angry than his touch. "She wants to see us—both. She's fixing some dinner. Said she has something important to tell us."

"Something important?" Shawna said, sounding like she had a cold. Her nose was still a little stuffed up.

Jon shrugged. "She didn't say what it was."

Shawna and her father left the building in silence. Going to the house sounded much better to her than going back to Dad's apartment. But it still seemed strange that the four of them would be there for dinner. They had not eaten dinner together since the divorce.

11

Wednesday
May 12

STEVIE DECIDED to fix cubed chicken breast and fresh vegetables over linguine for dinner. It was quick and easy, and the groceries were already on hand. Her hands flew through preparations while she braced herself mentally and emotionally for the arrival of Jon and Shawna.

Jon's phone call thirty minutes earlier had shifted her already active thoughts into high gear. An outrageous plan had been fomenting in her brain over the last three days—and a good portion of three nights. It was a proactive plan to take control of her life and surroundings again, a way to protect Collin and hopefully Shawna from the encroaching, destructive world, a way to do something right for herself and her kids instead of always trying to ward off the wrong. All she needed was the impetus to make the difficult decision.

The latest incident with Shawna was like a sign, an answer to prayer. As soon as Jon told her the news, Stevie quietly and firmly made her decision. All that remained was to explain it to Jon and Shawna, and then weather the storm that was sure to follow.

When she saw Jon's truck pull up to the curb, Stevie took a deep breath, ran her fingers through her hair, and went out to meet them. News of Shawna's misbehavior and expulsion had stunned and saddened her. But as Stevie watched her daughter trudge up the driveway, she felt more compassion than disappointment for the sad-faced girl. Where once Stevie would have been ready to ground her daughter for life, she now noted that her decision only thirty minutes earlier had already positively affected her attitude.

Stevie offered Shawna a gentle embrace on the front porch. Surprisingly, Shawna accepted it. "Honey, a pan of water is boiling on the range," Stevie said. "Will you put the linguine in and watch it, please? I need to talk to your dad alone for a minute." Shawna nodded and disappeared inside. "And tell Collin to set the table," Stevie called after her. "He's playing video games in his room."

Stevie motioned Jon to follow her out to the sidewalk. The sun had dipped below the hills at the west end of the Valley, but it was still in the upper sixties. Sufficiently away from the house, Stevie turned and faced her ex-husband to deliver the news. "Jon, I've decided to move to Redding."

Jon's jaw slacked in surprise. *"Move? To Redding?"* He appeared equally dumbfounded at both concepts. "When? Why?"

"As soon as the semester ends, maybe sooner. Why? Because I'm sick to death of what L.A. has done to our kids—and to me. I want Collin to grow up in a better place. I know this is the right thing to do."

Stevie easily read the shock in Jon's expression, which she had expected. But she also saw the disappointment in his eyes. For three days she had wrestled with the reality that acting on her plan would separate Jon from his surviving son. Having evaluated her motives, she was confident that she was not acting to hurt Jon. In the end, Collin's best interest was her responsibility. Even though it disappointed Jon, she had to do what she deemed best for their son.

Stevie continued building her case. "We lost Dougie here in the Valley. I don't want it to happen to Collin. I think he has a much better chance if we move to North California."

Jon looked wistfully toward the sunset. Stevie let him process. Finally he said, "Why Redding? Is there . . . someone. . . ? I mean, are you . . . involved. . . ?" He seemed unable to verbalize the rest of his obvious thought.

"No, no," Stevie interjected quickly. "Nothing like that."

"Then why so far away? I mean, you could move to Barstow or Bakersfield to get out of the city, and I could still see Collin occasionally. Redding is over five hundred miles away."

Stevie slowly shook her head. "It has to be Redding. North California is going to be different. Bellardi is going to—"

"You really believe that stuff? You think that Daniel Bellardi— if he even wins the election—can make North California a moral Disney World: no drive-by shootings, no drugs, no abortions?"

Stevie stiffened defensively. "Jon, I am not foolish enough to believe it's going to be a perfect world up there. But I have been researching Senator Bellardi and the North California movement on the Internet this week. I believe in what the man is trying to do. You know as well as I do that South California is falling apart at the seams morally. It's getting worse instead of better, and I've had it. At least up north somebody is trying to do something about all this junk in our culture, and I want to be part of it. I believe Collin has a better chance there."

"Steve, you know how politicians make promises just to get—"

Stevie reacted to the lecture tone and cut him off. "The man is running on a platform of moral standards, not campaign promises. Senator Bellardi believes in everything we believe in. He is a godly man who wants to establish a godly state. This is the answer to my prayers."

"There's still going to be crime and conflict."

"I know that. But at least someone is doing something about it there. It's going to make a difference for Collin, I just know it."

"But—"

"My mind is made up. I'm going whether you agree with me or not."

Jon turned and walked a few steps away, huffing. Then he turned back. "You know I could contest this in court, Steve. Collin is still my son, and you can't move him out of state without my permission."

Stevie had been hoping this issue would not come up. She knew Jon was right, but she was praying silently that he would not push it that far. "I know," she answered. "But I'm asking you not to do that. It would only make it harder on Collin, especially if he had to be involved in the mediation part of it."

Jon didn't answer, but Stevie could see his jawline tense. She held her breath.

"And just how do you plan to make a living in Redding?" he asked finally.

Stevie exhaled, relieved that he was no longer pursuing the legal issue, but annoyed at the lack of confidence she detected in his tone. Still, she knew he had taken the first step in accepting her move, so she swallowed her irritation. "Doing just what I do now," she answered. "Freelance advertising. They have radio and television and newspapers up there too, you know. I've already checked with a few firms in Redding, and I'm sure I can find plenty of work."

Anticipating more objections, Stevie pushed ahead. "You can have the house for the time being. It will be cheaper for you than living in the apartment. I'll rent something smaller up there, so I won't need all the furniture."

Offering the house and much of the furniture to Jon was a calculated concession to prepare him for what Stevie planned to say next. She took a step toward him. "One more thing. I'm going to ask Shawna to come with me."

As he had earlier when he received the phone call from Shawna's school, Jon rubbed his forehead. Stevie recognized the habit as his reaction to stressful situations or unpleasant news. She remained silent as he dealt with the possibility of both children moving away. Finally he said, "She won't leave, Steve. And because of her age, you can't make her go with you."

Stevie heard the disappointment in his voice. She responded more considerately. "You're right, I can't make her go. But I feel I have to give her the option. I know if I can get her to North California, she has a better chance of turning around."

Jon continued to rub his head absently. "I don't know. Both kids living in another state. You're making it really hard for me to be a father."

"My purpose is not to make things hard for you, believe me," Stevie said with sincerity. "Can't you see? This is the answer. This is the way to isolate our kids from the culture. If there were any other way, don't you think God would have shown it to us by now?"

Shawna did not believe anyone at the table really wanted to be there. Mom's chicken-and-vegetable linguine was always good, but no one seemed eager to eat tonight, including her. Collin still looked confused. While setting the table together, he had asked Shawna repeatedly why their dad was there for dinner. But she had no more of a clue than Collin did about why Mom had set up this contrived scene of family unity. Usually a chatterbox at mealtimes, Collin had said nothing.

Shawna decided to keep her head down and remain quiet too. Sooner or later one of her parents was going to drop the bomb about the biology exam incident. Neither of them had seemed upset so far; her mother even surprised her with a hug. But Shawna was sure they had been talking about her punishment outside while she was cooking the linguine. She still felt foolish for getting involved in Destiny's plot. She would never admit it to her parents, but whatever form of punishment they had agreed upon, Shawna knew she deserved it.

Her parents tried to fill the awkward silence at the dinner table with small talk that did not even sound like a real conversation to Shawna. Any questions they directed to her or Collin were met with one- or two-word answers. *Let's get to the point of this stupid meeting,* Shawna urged silently.

Finally, her mother put down her fork and said, "Kids, just before dinner I told your father about an important decision I've made. Now I want to tell you about it."

Collin quickly blurted out, "What kind of decision?" Shawna watched his eyes flit between his mother and father, unable to disguise his hope that the announcement might be about his parents getting back together. Shawna was pretty sure he would be disappointed. But unable to quell her own curiosity, she looked up at her mother.

Stevie was focused on Collin. She delivered her news with as much enthusiasm as she could muster. "Collin, you and I are moving to Redding in the new state of North California."

Collin wrinkled his nose. "Can I still play soccer with my team?"

"Only a few more Saturdays, honey," Stevie explained. "Redding is about five hundred miles from here. But I'm sure they have soccer leagues and baseball leagues up there."

"What about you, Dad?" Collin said. "Are you moving to Redding too? You can be a counselor in one of their high schools."

"No, I can't leave my job here, son," Jon said without emotion. "But I'll come up to see you as often as I can. Maybe during the summer I can stay a couple of weeks."

Shawna felt her heart sinking. The announcement and the discussion clearly excluded her. She had been exploring ways to get closer to her mother again. The surprising hug on the front porch was a hopeful step in the right direction. Now she felt suddenly abandoned. Was this the punishment her parents had decided upon: her mother and brother leaving her behind and moving to another state?

Before Collin could voice another concern about the move, Shawna spoke, carefully screening disappointment from her voice. "Why are you moving to Redding?"

Stevie gave Shawna her full attention. "Because I think it's the best place for Collin to grow up. I'm tired of the crime and drugs down here. I'm tired of the negative influences in the schools. I want to live where we don't have to worry about shootings and drug pushers on every corner. The new governor up there is going to make it a wonderful place for families."

"*Candidate* for governor," Jon corrected.

"Candidate, yes," Stevie said. "But I'm sure he's going to win, especially if the decent people of the state get to work."

Stevie continued to itemize the evils of the culture, but the words passed through Shawna without sticking. All she could think about was the distance between herself and her mother increasing instead of decreasing with this move. It had been her own doing, Shawna knew. She had stubbornly lashed out at her mother instead of owning up to her own bad choices. She had foolishly called the police and made an issue over the Child's Rights Act. She had pridefully refused to back down and avoid moving out of her own room. No wonder her mother was leaving the state without her. Shawna had conveyed in a number of ways that she did not want to be around her.

Stevie's next words changed everything. Still looking at Shawna, she said, "Honey, I'd like you to consider going with us. I know we haven't hit it off too well lately. And I know you have your own problems to deal with. If you decide to stay with Dad, it's OK. But I think a move like this could give you a new start. It could give *us* a new start. I hope you'll think about it."

That was it—no tears, no begging, no threats, no promises. Just an invitation with monstrous implications: leave her friends, her familiar surroundings, her problems, and her dad to move to some town she had barely heard of and where she knew no one.

Collin let fly with another barrage of questions about the move. He wanted to know how soon. Within the month, Stevie said. The benefit of quitting school early seemed to counterbalance Collin's disappointment at leaving his friends. He wanted to know if Redding had a baseball team like the Dodgers or the Astros. Learning that they would be less than half an hour from a huge lake more than compensated Collin for the knowledge that the nearest major league team was the Oakland A's, four hours to the south.

Shawna was glad the focus had shifted to her brother. Having been invited to go along, Shawna did not know what to think. A part of her wanted to cry out immediately, "Please don't leave without me, Mom. I want to go with you." Another part of her resisted the thought of walking away from her friends, particularly the addictive acceptance and affection she had tasted being around people like Destiny and Rik. At this moment Shawna was not sure a new start with her mother could adequately fill her craving for excitement. She was glad she had a little time to think about it.

103

🌐

Stevie did not get back to loading the dishwasher until almost ten-thirty. Jon and Shawna had gone home right after dinner, but Collin was wired with excitement and full of questions until his bedtime. Stevie had pored over an old map of California with him, locating Redding and tracing the route of their impending move. Then Collin wanted to research Shasta Lake and Mount Shasta in the computer's CD-ROM encyclopedia. With every new discovery came another round of questions. *Where will we live? Where will I go to school? Are there gangs in Redding? Do they have malls and batting cages and video games and McDonald's there? Can we buy a boat for the lake? Will Dad take me fishing when he comes up?* Stevie was pleasantly surprised that her nine-year-old had only a few negatives about the move. She had to laugh when her serious-faced son offered to stay up late and start packing his things.

As she rinsed the forks and spoons and loaded them in the silverware basket, Stevie still felt surprisingly good about the move herself. Enough time had passed for her to realize a number of the pluses she was leaving behind: supportive friends and neighbors, a pastor who seemed to care about her, an excellent client base, the conveniences of a large city. And, of course, there was Jon. Legally, except for obtaining his permission to move their son out of state, she was no longer dependent on him. Emotionally, not all the lines had been severed. In ways she did not fully understand, it would also be difficult to leave Los Angeles without him.

But every loss was overshadowed by one all-consuming gain: Collin would be saved from the influences that had been so detrimental to Dougie and Shawna. Having made the momentous decision after only a few days of thought, Stevie was remarkably free of misgivings. She was almost as excited to leave as Collin was.

One major loose end remained: Shawna. Stevie had not been able to read her daughter's response, either to the move itself or to the invitation to go along. She had prayed throughout the evening that Shawna would choose to move to Redding. Had she thought it might help, Stevie would have been more persuasive. Instead, she had purposely backed off and given her daughter plenty of room. In the meantime, since Shawna still lived with Jon, he would bear the brunt of disciplining her for the biology exam caper.

Stevie had barely finished kitchen cleanup when Shawna

called. Fighting off the urge to probe, Stevie held her breath and listened.

"Dad and I have been talking. It was a hard decision, but I've decided to go with you, if you still want me to."

With difficulty, Stevie kept the sudden surge of joy inside. "Yes, honey, I want very much to have you with us in Redding. But, as I said earlier, it's your decision. Is that what you really want?"

"I'm going to miss Dad a lot, and some of my friends. But like you said tonight, a new start in a new place might be a good thing. So I want to go. And would it be OK if I moved home until we leave? I can help you pack."

"Of course you can come home, honey," Stevie said, barely holding herself together. "I'll come get you tomorrow morning if you like."

Shawna said little more before saying good-bye. Hanging up the phone, Stevie's eyes flooded with tears at the joyous news. *I knew this was the right thing to do. Thank you, God, for directing me. We're a family again, and life is going to be wonderful for us in Redding.*

Stevie brushed the tears from her cheek and set out for the garage to find a cardboard box. She was too excited to sleep. She had to pack at least one box tonight.

summer

12

Friday
July 2

MIKE BRAGAN pulled to the curb in front of the small airport
and parked. He stayed at the wheel of the big Olds sedan with
the air-conditioning running until he saw the arriving passenger emerge from the terminal. Stepping out of the car, Mike
was engulfed in the stifling 102-degree heat typical of Redding
in the summer. His wavy, rust-colored hair turned to Day-Glo
orange in the brilliant midday sun.

"Wes!" Mike called out, waving a hand. The young man
with shaggy dark hair had already spotted his ride and was
headed Mike's way. Wes's faded tan shorts and rumpled T-shirt
looked too big on his skinny frame. A leather fanny pack was
cinched around his narrow waist. Loose-fitting leather sandals

flapped against the young man's bare heels as he walked. A large duffel bag and a smaller canvas laptop computer case were slung over the same shoulder.

Mike met him at the curb with an outstretched hand. "Wes, I'm Mike Bragan, your father's appointment secretary—the walking, talking Bellardi calendar," he said, adding a laugh at his own description.

"Right, I think we've met before," Wes said, shaking Mike's hand. "But I recognized the 'uniform' first. I'll bet you guys are the only people in North Cal not wearing shorts today."

Mike laughed again, glancing down at his slacks, white shirt, and tie, standard office attire for the men on Daniel Bellardi's campaign staff. "'Look sharp, feel sharp, be sharp,' the senator always says," Mike responded, loading the young man's luggage into the trunk. "And you'll be putting on the uniform yourself soon, right?"

"Yeah, that's what it looks like," Wes said, sliding into the air-conditioned Olds. Mike hurriedly jumped into the driver's seat and gunned the big sedan away from the curb. He always acted like he was late for a meeting.

Had Mike Bragan not kept stoking the conversation, young Daniel Weston Bellardi, Jr., might have remained silent all the way into town. But Mike was a people person, so he kept the questions and comments flowing. "You're at Berkeley, aren't you, Wes?"

"Yeah, just finished my second year."

"California Golden Bears. Great school. I'm an Oregon grad myself. Fighting Ducks, you know." Mike laughed. "The senator is a Cal Bear too, as I recall."

"Yeah. Mom, too. They met in school."

"Following in their footsteps at the old alma mater. Can't blame you. I'd like my kids to attend Oregon, carry on the family tradition, you know."

"That's the way my father planned it, I guess," Wes said, gazing at the arid landscape absently.

"You must be a business major all the way, just like your father," Mike continued.

"American literature," Wes said. "My father encouraged me toward business, but numbers aren't my thing. I'm a words-and-pictures type. A right-brainer like my mother, I guess."

Mike allowed a mile of country highway to pass under the wheels without speaking, but he could not stand the silence. "So you're going to work with us in the campaign for the summer."

Wes paused as if deciding whether or not he wanted to continue the conversation. "Actually, I'm scheduled to be here through the election. Dad asked me to take the fall term off and help him through the big push. It's hard to say no to a future governor, especially when he's paying the tuition."

Mike glanced over to see a wry smile on Wes's face. He laughed at the young man's dry humor.

"So what does the senator have in mind for you to do?" Mike probed.

"Don't know," Wes said distantly. He was participating in the chat, but didn't seem very interested.

"Angie Calderone in Finance has been swamped. She's always begging for help."

Wes gazed straight ahead, as if the ribbon of asphalt had hypnotized him. "I don't think Dad wants me in Finance," he said. "My checkbook hasn't balanced since I left home two years ago. Like I said, I'm not a numbers person."

Mike kept talking. "Our media guy has been charging like a racehorse to keep up with the ads and TV spots and press conferences. And then there's the debate team getting ready for the discussions with Juanita in September." Mike whistled. "Plenty to do around here. *Always* plenty to do."

Wes was silent long enough to make Mike think he was no longer listening. Finally the young man said, "Well, I'm home for the next five months. I may be kissing babies, I may be licking stamps, I may be taking out the trash. Whatever Dad needs, that's what I'll do."

"You haven't been home in a while, is that right?" Mike said. He glanced over at Wes. The young man's eyelids were at half-mast.

Wes nodded. "Not since Christmas. My studies and my job keep me close to the Bay Area."

"What kind of job?"

"I run a little campus newspaper."

"You run the Cal newspaper?" Mike echoed, sounding impressed.

"Not *the* campus newspaper," Wes said, shrugging away the job's importance. "Just a desktop rag, kind of an underground thing. But it keeps me close to the campus. Besides, it hasn't been much fun coming home this last year. The folks have been pretty busy."

"Tell me about it," Mike said. "Between getting North California on the map and gearing up for the campaign, none of us is taking much time off. And it's only going to get worse. Your father's appointment book is in fifteen-minute increments, and there aren't too many spaces open between now and November second."

The next time Mike glanced over, his passenger's eyes were closed. Apart from a few obvious physical traits, Wes Bellardi bore little resemblance to his hardworking, cause-passionate father. Mike wondered if the kid had enough energy to dive into a political campaign that seemed to set a new record for pressure every day.

Stevie Van Horne guided her Grand Cherokee through a maze of multiunit apartment buildings that seemed like a small city. The sprawling Shasta Commons development was more expensive than many of the complexes in Redding, but the extra cost was worth it to Stevie. Her three-bedroom, two-bath apartment was spacious and relatively quiet. Shawna and Collin loved to pass the hot summer days in and around the large swimming pool and spa. The video game room in the Commons rec center was heaven on earth to a nine-year-old boy. And an hour a day in the well-equipped workout room made Stevie feel better about spending the summer in shorts, tank tops, and a swimsuit.

Pulling into the carport, Stevie gathered up her attaché case and three sacks of drive-through lunch she had acquired on the way home. She hurried to the apartment and quickly changed from lightweight business attire into a swimsuit and cover-up. Left to herself, she preferred to stay indoors during the heat of the day. Besides, she had work to do. Her appointments that morning would likely result in at least one new client. She knew she should spend a couple of hours at her desk lining up calls for the next week.

Yet the kids were expecting her—and the feast from Mucho Burrito she had promised them—at poolside. Besides, it was the start of Independence Day weekend. Stevie had worked hard since arriving in Redding five weeks earlier. She and the kids deserved a long weekend together. So Stevie headed for the pool, loaded down with lunch and a straw bag containing beach towel, hat, sunscreen, sunglasses, and the latest *Reader's Digest* condensed book.

At the sight of his mother arriving, Collin flew out of the pool and dived into a bag of tacos and nachos without even toweling off. Shawna had a more civil approach, but she was just as eager to eat. "Thanks, Mom," they mumbled between mouthfuls.

"You're welcome, my little water babies," Stevie acknowledged with a smile. Then she slipped out of her cover-up, donned her hat and sunglasses, and waded into the pool to cool off before starting on her chicken taco salad.

Hunkering down neck deep in the cool water, Stevie watched her children and marveled. Even with the protective lotion she insisted Shawna and Collin wear when exposed to the hot Redding sun, both glistened golden brown from days at poolside. Collin, with his wavy blond hair and blue eyes, was in a growth spurt, stretching out toward his adolescent height while still very much an energetic little boy. And Shawna's appearance was nothing short of striking. This summer her sun-bleached hair looked more blonde than its natural brown, and she had chosen to change her formerly long straight style to a short, brushed back look, which fully revealed her lustrous skin and her father's large green eyes. Even in the modest one-piece swimsuits her mother insisted upon, the statuesque fourteen-year-old had attracted the eyes of the college-aged male residents at Shasta Commons. Though the attention caused Stevie some concern, it also confirmed her notion that Ms. Shawna Van Horne was beautiful beyond her years.

Stevie was also pleased that Shawna's and Collin's transition to North California was proceeding well. All three of them were teary that Saturday morning in late May as they loaded the Cherokee and said their farewells to friends, soccer teammates, and neighbors. Jon only made things worse when he broke down while hugging his children good-bye. But soon after Stevie pointed the car north on Interstate 5, leaving the Los Angeles basin behind, the kids were playing the license plate game and arguing about where they wanted to stop for lunch. Most of the conversation during the ten-hour trip to Redding concerned not what they had left behind but what lay ahead.

During the first weeks in their new state, Stevie involved the kids in the major decisions. They had a choice of two apartments in the Shasta Commons complex. Stevie secretly wanted the one with a nice view of Mt. Shasta, but she yielded to the kids' choice: the unit nearer the swimming pool. They also voted on where to go to church. Surprisingly, Shawna and Collin opted for a small neighborhood church over one of the larger churches in town boasting impressive youth programs. Much to the kids' amazement, Stevie went with their choice. She was pleased that her concerted efforts to acclimate them to their new surroundings were paying off.

Thankfully, Shawna seemed to have left her problems behind in South California. Stevie had resisted the temptation to squeeze every possible moral lesson out of the incidents. But whenever Lakeside Pines or the Rik E-mail incident or the biology exam came up, Shawna was sober and contrite. It pleased Stevie that her daughter apparently did regard the move north as a new start in her life.

After a few minutes in the pool, Stevie stepped out and patted herself dry. She was subtly aware and quietly pleased that a couple of the men lounging around the pool—men closer to her age than to college age—apparently found her pleasant to look at. In the two years following her divorce, Stevie had no interest in dating, nor did she believe her children would have approved, with their father still nearby. But having launched a brand-new life in North California, Stevie had wondered if men—more particularly, one special man—might come back into focus in her life. She still chilled at the prospect of being asked out, but at least she found it possible to think about it.

"Are there more tacos, Mom?" Collin asked, wiping salsa off his chin with the back of his hand.

An irritated Shawna cut in with the answer, making sure

Stevie heard. "No, you little garbage disposal, because you already ate your two tacos and one of mine and all the nachos."

Collin feigned innocence. "I didn't know you wanted any nachos. And it's not nice to call me a garbage can."

"I didn't call you a garbage *can.* I called you a garbage *disposal.*"

"Same thing," Collin insisted.

"No it isn't," Shawna argued.

"All right, that's enough," Stevie said as she retrieved her taco salad from the bag and sat down under a patio umbrella to eat it. She assessed that the juvenile exchange between Shawna and her brother was a dead giveaway to any college guys watching that this beautiful young woman was still just a girl.

Collin hovered over his mother at the table. "Can I have your salad, Mom?" he begged with affection.

"Too bad, so sad," Stevie said without sympathy. "If you're still hungry, there's fruit—"

Collin didn't stay around to hear it. Having lost the battle, he took three running steps and threw himself into the pool with a shriek of delight. Shawna followed him in, leaving Stevie in peace.

After eating, Stevie slathered her front side with sunscreen and stretched out on a chaise lounge for a few minutes. The searing blanket of rays wrapping her body felt therapeutic. She imagined the heat coaxing toxins from her pores with the perspiration and injecting new life into her system with the penetrating warmth. These cleansing moments in the sun each day capsulized what the move north had been for her: a sloughing off of the past and an energizing for the future. Pulling up stakes and transplanting her family had not been easy, but Stevie was convinced it had been right. Work was good, the children were adjusting well, and for the first time in months she felt happy and safe. By all accounts, North California was well on its way to becoming the haven Senator Dan Bellardi had promised.

Leisurely baking in the early afternoon sun, Stevie turned her thoughts to the reason she had moved to Redding in the first place. Amidst the hassle of moving in and getting her advertising business off the ground, Stevie had had little time to follow the campaign of her new hero, gubernatorial candidate Bellardi. News reports showed the state senator still leading in the polls by 20 percentage points. But challenger Juanita Dunsmuir continued to pare away at his margin with her high-visibility tour. Political analysts on the local news estimated that, if the trend continued, the two candidates could be sprinting for the finish line neck and neck by November. The remote possibility was disturbing to Stevie.

Stevie had never worked in a political campaign in her life. Considering the candidates in Los Angeles and South California to be only varying degrees of bad and worse, she had little motivation to vote, let alone jump on anyone's political bandwagon. But Bellardi was different. Here was someone she could not only support at the polls but campaign for.

But how could a rank amateur in politics hope to help a major candidate like Bellardi? Lick stamps and stuff envelopes? Run errands? Stevie intended to find out this Sunday afternoon at Caldwell Park. She and her children would be there for a picnic with their new church and to watch the fireworks display after dark. Senator Bellardi would also be at the park Sunday for a campaign rally and Independence Day address. Stevie was eager to hear the senator in person. Sunday would also be the perfect time to ask a staff member if there was some small way she could help Dan Bellardi succeed in his drive for the governor's seat. After all, she had not turned her family's world upside-down to see the moral utopia of North California evaporate before her eyes.

13
Friday
July 2

PATRICIA BELLARDI crossed the large den to greet her son. "Weston," she said, arms outstretched, "I'm sorry we're so late, dear."

Wes tapped the remote to mute the eleven o'clock news on the forty-inch monitor, then stood from the plush leather chair where he had been watching TV most of the evening. "Hello, Mom," he said, welcoming her embrace.

Daniel Bellardi followed his wife across the room and thrust out his hand. "Welcome home, Son," he said with a broad smile.

Slipping out of Patricia's arms, Wes grasped his father's hand. "Thanks."

"I addressed a North California Fruit Growers Association meeting in Red Bluff this evening," Daniel explained, shedding the jacket of his light gray suit. "It went later than I expected. They had a lot of questions."

"And I couldn't let your father face those growers alone, you know," Patricia put in with a chuckle. "But we're sorry we weren't here when you arrived."

"It's OK," Wes said, dropping back into the leather chair. "I had a nice swim this afternoon and took a little nap. Then Elena fed me a wonderful dinner." The Bellardis' Honduran cook and housekeeper had long since retired to her quarters, but the faint fragrance of one of her native specialty dishes, a favorite of Wes's, lingered in the den, which adjoined the dining room. "Since then I've been catching up on some of the television I missed this year."

Wes and his parents exchanged a few minutes of surface conversation: How was your flight? Did Mike Bragan pick you up at the airport on time? What has the weather been like in the Bay Area? Then Patricia said, "You'll have some popcorn with us, won't you, dear?" She was already heading for the kitchen to microwave the Bellardis' standard late-night snack. "I want to hear all about your last term."

"It wouldn't be home without popcorn, Mom," Wes called to her with a laugh. "That's what I've been waiting up for."

Daniel loosened his tie and unbuttoned his collar, then lowered himself to the sofa with a sigh of fatigue. "What are they saying about us tonight?" he said, motioning to the muted TV screen.

Wes threw a leg over the broad arm of the chair. He was still dressed in a maroon swimsuit, having shed his T-shirt and sandals early in the afternoon. "Depending on whose poll you like, you're ahead by nineteen to twenty-two points. And depending on the analyst, you'll win the election by five to ten points or lose by one or two." Wes knew his father was anxious to hear the news, so he yielded control of the TV by tossing the remote to the sofa.

118

"You know we don't use the 'L-word' around here, Weston," Daniel retorted, his tone only half joking. He tapped the sound on. The local station was doing the weather report. Most of inland North California had hit triple digits on the thermometer that day.

"I didn't use the 'L-word,' Dad," Wes said. "The analysts did."

Daniel did not seem to hear him. He was flipping through the channels looking for more news. The local stations were into sports and weather now, and the cable news stations were on to national stories. Daniel kept rolling through the channels anyway.

"Did anyone talk about the debates tonight?" Daniel asked, still watching the screen.

"Krueger, the guy on KRED, was building them up like the final rounds of a winner-take-all heavyweight title fight," Wes responded, watching his father surf the channels.

"Not a bad analogy," Daniel said, more to himself than to his son.

"Krueger said it doesn't matter who's leading in the polls in September. Whoever wins the debates will win the fight by a knockout. He said the topic of tolerance will be the deciding factor. Whoever has the best barrage of punches on that issue will win the fight."

Daniel nodded, still glued to the monitor. "Should the race be close in September, he's probably right. However, we don't intend to let Juanita Dunsmuir close enough to land a blow. And if she tries to take a wild swing at us during the debates, we'll just have to deck her."

Wes whistled in surprise. "Geez, Dad, that sounds brutal."

Daniel grinned mischievously. "It's Brad Krueger's analogy, Weston, not mine. I'm just telling you how it's going to play out."

Daniel resumed his channel hopping as a crescendo of muffled pops from the kitchen announced that the first bag of microwave popcorn was nearly ready. Still watching his father, Wes inquired, "Dunsmuir is that vulnerable on the tolerance issue? I mean, she doesn't stand a chance?"

Daniel turned to Wes again, this time shaking his head. "First, she won't be close enough in the polls for the debates to make a difference. Second, her argument that tolerance is the greatest and most maligned virtue in America today just won't fly in this state. By making tolerance the issue of the campaign and pressing it in the debates, Juanita Dunsmuir is committing political suicide."

"So why is she gaining in the polls?" Wes challenged.

Daniel cocked his head and flashed a queer smile. "Weston, whose side are you on?"

Dismissing his father's curious suspicion with a laugh, Wes answered, "Your side, Dad, of course. But if I'm going to work in your campaign, I need to know the answers to these questions. If Dunsmuir is already dead meat, why does she continue to gain on you? What fatal flaw do you see that her supporters can't see?"

Daniel turned off the TV but continued to stare at the blank screen for several moments, formulating his thoughts. Then he gave Wes his full attention. "In a nutshell, Son, Juanita Dunsmuir's campaign will crumble because it is founded on, at best, a partial truth and, at worst, a blatant untruth. The virtue of tolerance she so vehemently promotes is no virtue at all." Daniel paused, obviously wanting to allow time for his statement to sink in.

After a few seconds, Wes asked, "What do you mean?"

Daniel's response was strong, even passionate. "The tolerance movement insists that all value systems, worldviews, and truth-claims are equal. Every individual is free to decide what is right for him or her, and no one has the right to say, 'My way is better than yours.' To people like Dunsmuir, tolerance means more than *accepting* the values of others. It means *affirming* those values—even *praising* them—and never *criticizing* them. Right and wrong is not the issue. The most important tenet of tolerance is an open mind, because an open mind cannot hate.

"In other words, no matter how lovingly you say it, you can't say to a woman seeking an abortion, 'I believe in your right to privacy, but I don't agree with your choice to terminate the life of your unborn child.' Neither can you say to a homosexual, 'I respect you and accept you as a person, but I don't agree with your lifestyle.' That's being intolerant. Instead we're supposed to say, 'I applaud your choice to kill unborn babies' or 'Your homosexual relationship has my approval and blessing' or 'If pedophilia is your thing, that's fine with me.' To the tolerance crowd, everyone has the right to believe and live the way they choose."

Daniel's eyes were locked into his son's, as if waiting for Wes to voice his agreement. Wes only offered a slight nod and said, "Yeah, that's what I've heard."

Daniel sat up straight, leaned closer, and lifted his index finger for emphasis. "Now let me ask you something about those who preach tolerance: Are they tolerant of those they consider *in*tolerant?" The senator continued without allowing his son a chance to answer. "No! That's where all the love and acceptance and open-mindedness falls apart. They are tolerant of the *tolerant,* but they are intolerant of the *intolerant.* Anyone who accepts moral absolutes is branded as intolerant. If you say to a homosexual, 'I accept you as a person, but I don't agree with your lifestyle,' then your value system—which the tolerance-mongers claim is as valid as any other—is suddenly worth nothing. But it doesn't cut both ways. It's either tolerance for all or bigotry. That's the fatal flaw in Dunsmuir's argument. And I believe the people of North California will see right through it."

Wes took a breath to respond, but Patricia broke into the conversation with a heaping bowl of hot popcorn and a glass of lemonade for each of the men. "That's quite enough business, you two," she said. "You have all day tomorrow to talk politics and the campaign. This is family time. I want to hear about your last term, Weston."

The senator and his son acquiesced. But as Patricia retreated to the kitchen for her bowl of popcorn, Wes advanced one more question. "If you expect to be so far ahead in September, why challenge Dunsmuir to a debate at all? If Krueger is right, you may risk a big loss only weeks before the election."

Daniel filled his mouth with a handful of popcorn and sat back into the sofa to chew it. "Two things," he said as he ate. "First, *they* challenged *us.* Refusing to respond to such a major plank in their platform might be perceived by the people as weakness. Second, the people of North California must understand tolerance for what it is: total disregard for moral absolutes and family values. When they understand how the concept of tolerance undermines traditional values, they'll be ready to help us outlaw wrongs like abortion and special rights for gays and lesbians. They'll help us make North California a state that welcomes all people who live within the time-honored guidelines of moral decency.

"No matter where we are in the polls come September, Weston, the debates will bring out the truth on the issue of tolerance. And the truth always wins out."

Patricia's return to the den ended the exchange. She settled into a maple rocker with her popcorn. "All right, Weston," she said with pleasant eagerness. "Start at the beginning of spring term, and don't leave anything out."

Jon Van Horne tossed the half-eaten third slice of gourmet veggie pizza into the box. It was a large, deep-dish pizza, enough to feed a family of four. Jon always bought a large one and saved two-thirds of it for microwave lunches. But sitting in an empty house staring at a family-sized pizza with no one around to enjoy it with him stirred up Jon's feelings of loneliness. The fact that this was a holiday weekend only made things worse.

Moving back into the house on Etiwanda Street had been both a blessing and a curse for Jon. Paying down a mortgage was certainly more satisfying than investing in rent receipts, and the house was more of a real home to him than his old apartment, which he had regarded merely as a hotel room rented by the month. But at times, living in this spacious home without his kids was worse than living in that sterile apartment. Of what value is the space if there are no people to fill it? Why dust, vacuum, wash windows, or rearrange furniture if there is no one to appreciate it? Why even come home after work if only to eat in silence and stare at the walls? Tonight Jon was fresh out of satisfactory answers.

It had been over five weeks since Shawna and Collin rode away in Stevie's white Cherokee. The weekly phone calls to Redding only seemed to make Jon's loneliness more acute. He not only missed his daughter and son, he even missed his ex-wife. The dissolution of their marriage on the heels of losing their oldest son had been excruciating. Piercing resentment and cutting accusation had slashed them both deeply. Well over a year later, the emotional wounds were not healed, only sufficiently anesthetized and bandaged. The scar tissue would likely never completely disappear. The reconciliation hinted at by well-meaning friends was out of the question after what Jon and Stevie had put each other through. But sometimes, when the pain seemed far away, Jon yearned for the oneness that once characterized his life with Stevie.

Jon cleaned off the kitchen table and wedged the pizza box into the refrigerator. He shut down the house for the night, then headed for the bedroom to catch the midnight news. On the way, he found himself in Shawna's dark, empty room. Standing still and silent for a few seconds, he relived his daughter's infancy and childhood in a flash of unbidden memories. It happened in Collin's room also. The nostalgia materialized as a swollen knot of emotion in Jon's throat. He missed his kids terribly.

Jon paused at the door of Dougie's old room, not daring to enter and risk an emotional breakdown. He had long since emerged from the black cloud of self-condemnation that had dogged him after Dougie's death. He had stoically acknowledged his part in allowing his older son to drift unchallenged into questionable relationships and the drugs that eventually claimed his life. As a result, Jon resolved to remain active in the lives of his other two children. But tonight he felt intense frustration prompted by five-hundred-plus miles of the Californias standing between him and the objects of his resolve.

Jon had not yet been to Redding, nor would he be able to go until the break between sessions at the recreation center. He was already planning to spend nine days up north with the kids, and Stevie had approved the visit. But that was still three weeks off, and Jon was getting crazy to see his daughter and son. *If only I could cook Saturday morning breakfast for them again,* he thought as he closed the drapes in his bedroom. *If I could take them to church and maybe to the park—*

A sudden thought froze Jon at the window. Without taking a breath, he processed it. *Sunday is the Fourth, and I get Monday off. Why didn't I think of this before?* After only seconds he released a breath and glanced at his watch: 11:49 P.M. "I won't be there in time for breakfast, but if I leave right now I can make it for lunch," he said aloud. "And I don't have to head home until Monday afternoon." Jon slapped his hands together triumphantly. "Yes!"

Fifteen minutes later Jon threw a small bag behind the seat of his blue Ranger pickup and drove to the all-night Chevron station on Devonshire. After filling the tank and washing the windshield, he bought a twenty-ounce cup of hot coffee and headed for Interstate 5. Reaching the freeway, he turned north for the ten-hour trek to Redding. As he gunned the Ranger up the on-ramp, Jon turned on the radio and started singing country-and-western songs at the top of his lungs.

14

Saturday
July 3

"SHAWNA. Shawna, wake up."

Her mother's voice grew louder and more insistent with each word. Shawna felt Stevie nudge the bed, then groaned as her mother flipped on the light switch.

Light penetrated her eyelids. "What time is it?" she mumbled.

"Quarter to nine. Terilyn is on the phone. She wants to know about your plans today."

"What about today?" Shawna said, unraveling the cocoon of bed linens around her. Squinting in the harsh brightness of morning, she saw the cordless phone thrust out to her.

Her mother, sounding a little impatient, said, "Here, just

talk to her." Then she dropped the phone on the bed and left the room.

Shawna picked up the phone and tapped TALK with her thumb. She started to speak, then stopped to clear the sleep out of her throat. "What about today, Terilyn?"

Shawna had met Terilyn Spradlin and her two friends, Josie and Alexis, at the Commons pool. They were all fifteen or sixteen, soon to be juniors in high school. But they had taken in the lowly sophomore like she was family. These girls were obviously not Lindley Belle material—no cheerleaders, class leaders, guy chasers. They were kind of plain, the way Shawna had expected farm girls around Redding to be. But Terilyn, Josie, and Alexis were smart and witty, and they really knew how to laugh and have a good time. Shawna found them to be uncomplicated and fun.

Most important of all, Terilyn, Josie, and Alexis were not anything like Destiny Fortugno. The longer Shawna was away from L.A., the more she realized she was better off without Destiny around. Even though her new friends were not overtly religious, in that they and their families did not seem to be involved with church regularly, there did seem to be a spiritual element about them, and they certainly were not trouble magnets like Destiny. Thanks to her three new friends, Shawna's life in North California was off to a good start.

Stevie had expressed concern to Shawna that these girls from the Commons did not attend church. In fact, her mother had urged Shawna to invite them to church services and the church picnic at Caldwell Park on Sunday. But Shawna did not want to scare away her new friends by coming on like a Bible-thumper. She promised she would invite them to church eventually, when she felt "right" about it—and she meant it. In the meantime, Shawna secretly liked the idea of having friends who did not expect her to behave like a nice Christian girl.

Terilyn said, "A day at the lake, Snow White, that's what." Shawna was taller than her new friends, so Terilyn dubbed the quartet of friends Snow White and the three dwarfs. "Josie's uncle has a big powerboat," Terilyn continued. "We're going to ski and tube and get sunburned to a crisp. Do you want to go?"

Shawna hesitated. She only knew these girls from around the pool. They were fun, and she was flattered by the invitation. But she wasn't sure she wanted to lock herself into a full day with them. If she did, she would be stuck at Shasta Lake whether she was having a good time or not.

"Who's going?" she asked, buying time to think.

Terilyn laughed. "The three dwarfs, and maybe a couple more short girls. Don't worry; you can still be Snow White, the fairest on the lake."

"Any guys?"

Terilyn laughed louder and longer. She had a great laugh, full of fun, free of cynicism and superiority. "No handsome princes today, Snowy. Just Uncle Jack. He's ancient, and he is definitely more of a toad than a prince. Besides, the current Mrs. Toad will be there, so Uncle Jack will be a good boy."

Girlfriends were great, Shawna noted, but some of the single guys lounging around the Commons pool were real hunks. Did she really want to give them up for a day to be with only females and a toady old man?

"The food is all taken care of," Terilyn continued. "All you need is your suit, a towel, and plenty of sunblock. Everybody wants you to come. We're leaving in a half hour. What do you say?"

Before Shawna could respond, a tone in the receiver announced an incoming call. She was grateful for a few more seconds to make up her mind. "Hold on for a sec, Terilyn. Call waiting." Then she switched lines with the tap of her thumb. "Hello?"

"Good morning, sunshine. You're up early for a Saturday."

Shawna smiled at the voice and sat up in bed. "Hi, Dad," she responded. "Actually I'm *not* up yet. The phone woke me."

"I'm sorry, honey."

"Oh, it wasn't you. It was my friend. She's on the other line. Just a second, I'll tell her good-bye." Shawna switched back to Terilyn. "It's my dad calling from L.A. Can I call you back in a few minutes?"

"Sure, but do you want to go to the lake or not?"

Shawna made a snap decision, although she knew she still had to talk her mom into it. "Yeah, I guess so."

"Super. I'll be over in about twenty minutes. See you." Terilyn hung up and Shawna switched lines. "OK, I'm back."

Shawna did not regret moving to North California with her

mother, but she missed her father. She found it easy to talk to him. He was always so upbeat and positive. Sometimes Mom seemed more interested in what Shawna did—or did not do—than in who she was. Dad made her feel like a real person, not just a kid.

"So is it hot in the Valley this morning?" she asked, lying back for a conversation. "It's already eighty degrees here, maybe ninety by now."

There was a hint of mischief in her dad's voice as he answered, "I don't know. I'm not in the Valley."

"You're not? Where are you?"

"I'm at a gas station in Willows. I'll be in Redding in about an hour and a half. Where would you and Collin like to go for lunch?"

Shawna bolted upright in bed again. "Daddy! You're in North California?"

"Just down the freeway, honey," Jon said, chuckling at her excited response. "I couldn't stand it any longer. I had to come see you guys." He explained that he would get a motel room in Redding and stay until Monday. Then he asked Shawna to put her mother on so he could clear the visit with her.

Tapping HOLD, Shawna flew out of her room and excitedly announced the good news. Collin was ecstatic. Her mother even seemed guardedly pleased. Shawna returned to her room to get dressed. As soon as the phone was free, she would call Terilyn and cancel out on the lake trip. She deeply hoped that the three dwarfs would invite her again. Even though she was thrilled at the prospect of spending the day with her father, she liked being Snow White to somebody besides him.

Daniel Bellardi was dressed in summer slacks, shirt, and tie before breakfast. He was on his third cup of coffee and second newspaper by the time Wes finally shuffled into the dining room at almost nine o'clock. Daniel just about succeeded in keeping the impatience out of his voice. Peering over the top of the business section of the *Sacramento Bee,* he said, "Your mother and I would like you to travel with us today, Son." Then he clamped his mouth shut to keep from commenting on Wes's appearance, one Daniel felt was totally inappropriate for the dining table.

Wes scratched his head through a disheveled mop of long, dark hair. His eyelids drooped, and his cheeks were shadowed with stubble. He was still wearing the baggy maroon swimsuit he had on the night before. Elena met him at the table with a steaming mug of coffee. He nodded his thanks and sat down, then looked over at his father. "Where to?"

"Just a normal day," Daniel answered. "Brief staff meeting at the office at ten-thirty. Luncheon with the North California Senior Coalition at the marina. Three o'clock, tape a couple of TV spots at the studio. Dinner with a small group of financial backers aboard the houseboat at sunset. Back home around midnight." Daniel flashed a smile, hoping to draw at least a flicker of excitement from his son. "How does that sound to you?"

Wes's eyes were closed as he sipped coffee slowly, the steam drifting up to caress his face. "You're the boss," he said, lifting his eyelids. "And I assume the wardrobe hanging in my closet constitutes the duty uniform."

Daniel folded the paper and placed it on the table. "That's right, Son. Slacks, shirt, and tie every day, jacket during public appearances. It's all lightweight summer wear, very cool, comfortable, and professional. Like I tell the staff, 'look sharp—"

"—feel sharp, be sharp,'" Wes finished for him. "I know. Your walking calendar told me yesterday. By the way, Mike asked me what my job was in the campaign. I had no answer. What do you want me to do, boss?"

"We can talk about that through the day," Daniel said, standing. "Basically, I would like to utilize your gift with words. How would you like to write for me: press releases, responses to personal letters—?"

"Speeches?" Wes questioned.

After a pause, Daniel shook his head. "Probably not, Son. Price Whitten has a couple of professional writers on retainer for me. I need volunteers like you to pick up the slack to grind out the day-to-day stuff."

Wes nodded and sipped.

Daniel glanced at the antique grandfather clock tick-tocking quietly in the corner. He said, "Right now you have to get moving. Shave, shower, shampoo, and shine. I'm leaving for the office. You and your mother leave at nine-forty-five sharp."

Wes raised his eyebrows. "It's only fifteen minutes to the office. What's my hurry?"

Daniel slipped into his suit coat and edged toward the front door. "You have an appointment with Norman at ten. Your mother will drive you in. I'll see you at the office as soon as you're done."

"Norman?"

"You remember Norman," Daniel said, smiling. "He's been my barber for twenty-five years. He cut your hair when you were a kid."

Wes nodded and smiled. "Part of the uniform."

"Look sharp, feel sharp, be sharp," Daniel said.

Wes took a final gulp of coffee as he stood. "Whatever you say, boss."

Daniel stopped in his tracks. "Please, Weston. We'll be working together, but call me *Dad,* or call me *Senator* in public if you like. But not *boss.* OK?"

Wes's face blanched with chagrin. "Sorry, Dad."

Mike Bragan and the big Olds were waiting near the front door of the sprawling Bellardi ranch when Daniel stepped outside. "How was your visit with young Mr. Bellardi?" Mike asked as he guided the sedan down the long entrance road toward the security gate and the highway into town.

The senator passed over the question and spoke the thought on his mind. "He means well, but I just hope Daniel Weston, Jr., has what it takes to make it all the way to November."

While the outdoor temperature hovered at 103 degrees, Stevie spent the afternoon puttering around the apartment and working on advertising proposals. Jon's surprise visit to the children had resulted in a delightfully quiet day for her. Her ex-husband had arrived around ten-thirty, bleary-eyed from lack of sleep but eager to spend time with Shawna and Collin. They quickly made big plans: a trip to the batting cages, lunch at the barbecue place Shawna had been wanting to try, an early afternoon movie at the mall—which Jon would no doubt sleep through— and a drive to the lake. Stevie had been so pleased at the prospect of a day to herself that she gave Jon the Grand Cherokee to use. She did not expect them back until dark.

During the day, Stevie turned on TV only once, to watch a "docu-mercial" on the gubernatorial campaign of Senator Daniel Bellardi. The one-hour presentation offered a captivating behind-the-scenes look at the candidate—devoted husband and father, successful businessman, respected and effective former state legislator, aspirant to the governor's seat in the state he helped create. The program clearly outlined Bellardi's platform of moral responsibility and traditional family values. Stevie was greatly impressed by what she saw, in both the content and quality of the presentation. She was even more eager to see and hear Senator Bellardi at Caldwell Park the next day. She hoped she would have the opportunity after the rally to shake his hand and encourage him in his endeavors.

With Jon in town, Sunday as well as Saturday had opened up for Stevie. Before Jon and the kids left for the day, Stevie and her ex-husband had compromised on the Sunday schedule. Stevie wanted the kids to attend church with her. Jon conceded, admitting that he would probably sleep in Sunday morning to recover from the all-night drive. Jon wanted Shawna and Collin after church through the fireworks display at the park on the Sacramento River. Stevie agreed, aware that the kids were dragging their feet over attending the picnic and rally in the park anyway. The plan also allowed Stevie the freedom to talk to Senator Bellardi's people if she had the opportunity.

Apart from the delightful free time she gained from "Daddy weekend," Stevie was of two minds about Jon's surprise visit. The kids were obviously pleased to see him, and they needed to be with him. But Stevie felt Jon should have given her more time to plan and prepare—at least a few days. She would kindly but firmly insist that he avoid last-minute drop-ins in the future.

She also found herself a little uncomfortable with the greeting Jon received. Did the kids have to be so excited to see him, so eager to leave her at home alone? They acted as if they had received a weekend pass from the Redding jail. Stevie did not enjoy feeling like a jailer.

Most disturbing of all was the subtle, nagging fear that

Shawna and Collin might prefer their father to her. This was the pitfall of the "Disneyland father" syndrome. Daddy breezes in, spends wads of money on the children, lets them eat anything they want, never says no, never lifts a hand of discipline. Then he disappears, and Mom is left to restore order. The kids soon get the skewed idea that being around Dad is more fun. Stevie hoped this weekend did not leave her kids yearning to return to Los Angeles with Jon. The strategic move to ideal North California would be neutralized if Shawna and Collin were not there to benefit from it. And the dark prospect of being completely alone was too disturbing even to consider.

By seven o'clock the punishing heat was retreating from Shasta Lake as noticeably as the setting sun. The accommodating breeze had allowed topside dining to be not only bearable but enjoyable. An elegant dinner for fifteen aboard the houseboat—even a spacious houseboat like the Bellardis'—was a sizable challenge. But Lucy Denherder, with the expert help of her husband, Matthew, managed to pull it off. And, of course, Daniel Bellardi, even if he neglected to acknowledge or thank them publicly for their extra work, generously compensated them, as always. The guests, all very wealthy and accustomed to exquisite cuisine, were pleasantly surprised by Lucy's feast of tender, marinated venison chops and classic, cold ratatouille.

The ambiance was so pleasant and the accommodations so near perfection that even the perpetually task-focused Daniel Bellardi took notice. Yet nothing was more pleasantly conspicuous to him than the appearance and behavior of his son. During the evening's entertainment—a dramatic recitation of the wisdom of Abraham Lincoln performed by an actor in costume— Daniel had expressed his wonder to Patricia. Their hushed conversation at the rear of the top deck went unnoticed by the guests.

"Weston has been marvelous this evening," Daniel whispered. "Did you notice how pleasantly he greeted everyone as we introduced him, and how easily he made conversation?"

Patricia hummed agreement. "And jumping in to help

Matthew serve the wine and hors d'oeuvres without being asked. I couldn't be more proud."

"The haircut and the clothes made the difference," Daniel insisted. "I knew they would."

They watched their son, who sat at a table with a communications entrepreneur, the CEO of a national health care provider, and their wives. The new wardrobe and the visit to Norman's salon had transformed Wes's image from scruffy-looking college kid to young executive.

"He looks as if he just stepped out of *Esquire*," Patricia breathed with admiration.

Daniel nodded. "And it's affected his attitude. Weston was a different person when he arrived at the office this morning. I think even *he* was surprised at the change."

The Abe Lincoln look-alike had captivated his audience. The senator and his wife turned their attention back to the performance, watching and listening in silence for several minutes. Then Daniel leaned close to Patricia to continue the whispered conversation. "To be honest, I've been worried about Weston, how he would fit in, if he would even be interested in working with us."

"Yes, I know."

Daniel added, "But I certainly feel better about it tonight than I did when I left the house this morning."

Patricia patted her husband's hand reassuringly. "Weston will be just fine, dear," she said. "He's an individual—his own person, just the way we raised him to be. But first and last, he is a Bellardi. He has his father's blood coursing through his veins. Next to me, no one will be more proud of your victory in this campaign than Weston. And I'm certain that your son will make you just as proud of him."

Daniel squeezed Patricia's hand. She always seemed to speak the words he needed to hear.

15

Sunday
July 4

Jon surprised himself by sleeping until almost nine. The window-mounted air conditioner in his tiny room at the Quiet-Nite Motel was anything but quiet, but it worked to his advantage. Its steady, monotonous drone masked most of the noise of the morning's departing guests, allowing Jon to sleep in.

As he shaved and showered, Jon reviewed the previous day in his thoughts. He acknowledged that being with Shawna and Collin had been well worth the grueling, sleepless drive and the marathon day of activities in the oppressive heat. Sure, the childish nit-picking and bickering between the kids got on his nerves a few times, but he endured it. He had not been foolish enough to think they had become saints in the last five weeks. All in all, the day of fun and conversation had been everything he had hoped it would be.

With a good night's sleep behind him, he was ready to do it again. But Stevie and the kids were in church, so Jon had a couple of hours to kill. Worship for Jon that morning consisted of halfheartedly watching a church service on TV while he dressed. It was an Independence Day program with flags and patriotic songs. Jon wondered wryly if the service was in worship of God or democracy and freedom.

Wearing shorts and a polo shirt from the Foothill High School athletic department, Jon walked one block to Denny's and bought a local Sunday paper from the rack outside. The only seat open was a stool at the counter, which several other customers had intentionally passed over. The reason was obvious. Sitting next to the empty stool was a vagrant seemingly spending his last half-dollar on a cup of coffee. Jon plopped down on the stool and ordered coffee and a ham scramble with sourdough toast. As he sipped coffee and waited for breakfast, Jon started through the paper. He kept his elbows in and folded the paper to the size of a tabloid so as not to bother the unkempt man sitting next to him, who was huddled over his mug of coffee.

Jon was struck by the amount of space in the newspaper devoted to the campaign for governor. The election was still four months off, yet the coverage in the *Redding Mirror* was extensive: news stories, feature articles, photos, columns, advertisements. Jon assessed that close to half the articles in the front section related to the campaign and/or the two candidates. By contrast, the print media in South California had relegated the Bellardi-Dunsmuir contest to inside pages opposite department store ads.

"We got us a real horse race goin' here, ain't we?" A tobacco-stained finger was aimed at photos of Juanita Dunsmuir and Senator Daniel Bellardi on page three.

Jon turned to appraise his neighbor, who was unashamedly reading over his shoulder. The man's matted hair and beard, leathery skin, and threadbare clothes seemed encased in a veneer of oily grime. The odor had assaulted Jon even before he sat down.

"I'm just visiting North Cal this weekend," Jon returned

with a smile. "I don't know too much about the candidates."
Jon was not offended or intimidated by down-and-outers.
Instead, he regarded them as intriguing individuals with layers
of mysterious history. For some reason Jon was able to engage
the person behind the sometimes offensive exterior. Before his
family breakup, Jon had been active on a church commission
formed to assist the homeless.

"If you ain't from here, where you from?" the man asked.

"South Los Angeles."

"I'm from the south too. But then I'm also from the north
and east and west. Like my kinfolk used to say, 'Mac is from all
over in general and nowhere in particular.'" Mac allowed himself a quiet chuckle, which revealed a mouth full of stained,
crooked teeth.

Jon laid the newspaper down. "But you know something
about the election, so you must spend a bit of time in North
California."

"Yes, sir, I do," Mac said emphatically. "I like to be here
when it's hot, real hot, like June, July, and August. The heat
helps purify the soul of many evils, if you know what I mean."

Jon nodded even though he could only guess at what Mac
meant. The waitress skated by with coffee refills. Mac busied
himself by emptying four packets of sugar into his mug.

Hoping to keep the conversation alive, Jon asked, "So who's
going to win this horse race?" He gestured toward the newspaper as he spoke.

Mac stirred his coffee, seemingly deep in thought. At last
he said, "I know it don't look like it now, but I think that
folksinger lady is gonna catch that politician and whup him
by a whisker. Serves him right, too—tryin' to take over and
make his own rules like he was the king of right and wrong.
This here's the home of the free. People don't need to be told
what they can and can't do. We all got our God-given brains,
you know."

"So you're not a big fan of law and order," Jon said, primarily to see how the man would react.

"Of course I believe in law and order," Mac snapped a little
too loudly. "You gotta have rules, but there's a difference
between rules and meddlin'."

"What's the difference, as you see it?"

The searching look in Mac's eyes caused Jon to think that his answer would be strictly from the hip, something the transient had not processed before. "Well, of course, er . . . well, rules is like tellin' a kid he's got to brush his teeth. Meddlin' is saying he can't do it with a red toothbrush, because red toothbrushes is evil or somethin'."

Jon stifled a laugh at the man's surprising analogy. It did not appear that dental hygiene was a topic with which Mac was very familiar.

Mac continued, trying to make his point. "And them homosexuals, they shouldn't be foolin' around and gettin' married and the like. Men should be with women, everybody knows that. That's the rules of nature. But tellin' a homosexual, 'You can't live in our state because you're too weird' or 'You can't live on Pine Street where we live because you dress funny,' that there is meddlin'." Having completed the thought, Mac looked rather proud of himself.

Jon acknowledged that the man had a point. There were rules and there was meddling. Jon admired Daniel Bellardi for taking a stand on the moral issues plaguing both ends of the former state of California. But was the former state senator pushing his convictions too far? In his attempt to establish a morally sound environment in North California, had he, as Mac so simply illustrated, crossed the line between enforcing rules and meddling?

Apparently Stevie did not think so, Jon noted. Following through with her surprising decision to move north and radically change her lifestyle assured Jon that his ex-wife thought Bellardi was on the right track. Jon had not studied the issues thoroughly enough to make a decision about Senator Bellardi. But then, not being a resident of North California, Jon did not have a say in the matter either way. He just hoped Stevie did not get swept up in something she would later regret.

A platter heaped with diced ham and eggs with toast was placed in front of Jon. From the corner of his eye, he saw Mac adoring the feast. Jon made it a practice not to give money to panhandlers, but he rarely turned down an opportunity to provide food or clothing to someone in obvious need. "If you haven't eaten yet, Mac, I'd be happy to treat you to breakfast," he said to his neighbor.

Mac cleared his throat. "Well, I usually don't eat breakfast this early, but since you offered . . ." Jon knew it was a line. Mac probably worked the summer crowd on motel row for at least one hot meal a day. But from the vagrant's appearance, it still did not look like enough. Early on as a Christian, Jon had internalized a truth that had guided him in his responses to people like Mac: Each disadvantaged individual is a person for whom Christ died, someone to whom the love of Christ must be displayed in practical ways. In most circumstances, Jon had little trouble buying a meal for, or simply taking a few minutes to be friendly to, someone like Mac. Besides, this morning Jon had time to burn.

Jon's eyebrows raised only slightly when Mac ordered steak and eggs with a short stack on the side and a large glass of orange juice. "So, Mac," he said, consciously reminding himself of the man's intrinsic value to God, "tell me about your travels."

The church picnic was boring and poorly attended for a church of two hundred. Shawna and Collin would have groaned in pain had Stevie insisted they come with her. She rather envied them driving to the redwoods with their father.

Not even the pastor had attended the picnic, and Stevie thought she knew why. The potluck lunch was unimaginative: fried chicken by the bucket and box; four Crock-Pots of baked beans—two with sliced wieners mixed in; seven versions of potato salad—three of them store-bought; enough watermelons for an army; and generic red punch. Church members passed by Stevie's fresh spinach-and-orange salad as if something so different violated church bylaws. She later wondered if people mistook the poppy seeds in the dressing for dead fruit flies.

After lunch, there were no games for the kids, no horseshoes or table games for the adults. Church members just sat around tables in the shade in a reserved corner of Caldwell Park and talked. Being a newcomer, Stevie was on the outside of the conversation. And being alone, she felt like a fifth wheel among so many couples and longtime friends. It was not that anyone was overtly standoffish, but Stevie could not help imagining that the words *newcomer* and *divorcée* were tattooed across her

139

forehead. It would take some time to break into this "loving" group of Christians, she assessed.

Stevie drifted away from the picnic early, taking her salad bowl and table service to the car. Then she strolled through the crowded park alongside the Sacramento River, watching children play at the water's edge. The small amphitheater at the west end of the park was decked out in red, white, and blue bunting, streamers, and balloons in preparation for the rally at four.

When Stevie arrived, it was barely three-fifteen. Nearly half of the rented metal folding chairs were now in the shade of a phalanx of massive eucalyptus trees. A few people were scattered among the chairs watching the sound crew finish preparations on stage. Stevie moved close to the front on the shady side and sat down. For her, the highlight of the day was hearing Senator Bellardi, so she was happy about securing a good seat early.

A young man appeared from behind the stage, conspicuous in his business attire. Amidst a park full of citizens dressed in shorts, including Stevie, he wore a beige summer suit, pale blue shirt, and maroon and blue patterned tie. Stevie guessed him to be about twenty. His face was flushed red from the heat, and his stylishly trimmed hair was glued to his scalp with moisture. He carried a large stack of brochures in the crook of one arm. Starting at the front, he began placing one brochure on each empty chair. He appeared lost in thought.

Stevie just couldn't sit still and watch the kid melt before her eyes. Meeting him in the middle of the first row, she smiled and said, "I don't mean to sound like your mother, but you're going to have heatstroke if you don't get out of that jacket and loosen your tie."

Startled by the woman's sudden appearance, the young man snapped up straight.

"Here, let me hold those, and you take off that jacket," Stevie insisted, reaching out to take the stack of brochures from him.

"I'm fine, really," he said defensively, even as he allowed her to relieve him of the brochures.

Stevie laughed. "That's what they all say, right before they keel over in a dead faint. If you take off your jacket, I'll help you deliver the rest of these folders. I'd rather do that than administer CPR." Stevie glanced at the brochure. A full-color picture of Daniel Bellardi dominated the front page. The caption read, "Let's do it right for North California. Senator Dan Bellardi for Governor."

The kid looked behind him as if a surveillance camera were trained on him. Then he sheepishly slipped out of his jacket and draped it over a chair as ordered.

"Now the collar button," Stevie said. She felt no compunction about ordering the kid around. Someone with as little sense as to wear a jacket and tie on a day like today needed to be confrontively mothered.

"I'm really OK," he countered.

Stevie stuck by her guns. "Your neck is bulging. You'll feel much better if you undo your collar button. And so will I."

The young man reluctantly loosened his tie, released the collar button, then snugged the tie back into place. It looked hokey, but Stevie let it pass. Handing him half of the brochures, she said, "You're with the Bellardi campaign, I take it."

"Yeah." The kid resumed his duty with the brochures, avoiding Stevie's eyes. She knew the response well. Her own children had always reacted the same way when corrected in public.

Stevie stayed with him, passing out folders in the second row. "Volunteer?"

A few seconds of silence, then, "Sort of."

"How long have you been working on the campaign?"

The young man paused before answering. "About twenty-four hours."

Stevie laughed. "No wonder you're dressed to the nines. Trying to make a good impression, right?"

The kid shook his head. "No. Everyone on the campaign dresses up. It's important to the senator."

"Well, I'm all for looking professional and dressing for success," Stevie said. "But isn't a Fourth of July picnic a little different from nine-to-five at the office?"

The young man placed a few more brochures before he responded. "Not to the senator."

Stevie allowed two rows to go by, hoping the young volunteer would take some responsibility for the conversation. He remained silent. Finally she said, "So what do you do when you're not working on the campaign?"

"I'm a student."

"Where?"

"Cal Berkeley."

"Studying—?"

"American literature."

"Faulkner, Hemingway—Danielle Steele?"

Stevie was relieved to see a smile crack the young man's serious face. But he still did not look at her. "Right," he said.

Four more rows passed in silence. Stevie tried again. "Are you a writer yourself?"

The kid made a sound, something like a sigh mixed with a laugh. "Not really. Theses, critiques, book reviews, stuff like that."

"You don't have a novel or an epic poem churning inside you, something other than what you write for a grade?"

"I'm editor of a small newspaper. Actually, I'm editor, publisher, and staff writer of a *very* small newspaper. I suppose that's my main creative outlet."

This time the young man looked at Stevie briefly. She was quietly pleased that he was opening up. Her patient mothering was paying off. She continued to nurse the conversation until their task was completed. The chairs were beginning to fill with people, and Stevie was anxious to get back up front and claim hers.

Receiving the unused brochures from Stevie, the young man actually smiled and thanked her.

"You're welcome," she responded, sticking out her hand. "I'm Stephanie Van Horne. My friends call me Stevie."

The kid shook her hand timidly. "My name is Weston, er, Wes."

"Weston Wes?"

"No, just Wes."

"By the way, Wes, if I had a little time to give to the campaign—you know, stuff envelopes or do phone canvassing—who should I talk to?"

Wes looked away. "Well, I . . . I'm not sure. I've only been on the job one day. Maybe if you call the campaign office . . ."

142

He left the sentence uncompleted, appearing eager to get back to work.

"Call the office. That's what I'll do. Thank you."

Wes nodded and quickly retreated.

Sitting in the third row awaiting the start of the rally, Stevie could not push the young man named Wes from her mind. What was it about the campaign volunteer that stimulated her maternal emotions? She did not realize it until the brass band, playing the obligatory Sousa march, led a processional of dignitaries down the center aisle and onto the elevated platform. There was Wes in his jacket and tie, collar buttoned again, walking among a cadre of smartly dressed staffers ahead of Senator and Mrs. Bellardi. Wes smiled and waved to the cheering crowd with his fellow campaigners, but Stevie read the adolescent awkwardness in his bearing. Wes seemed to be an intelligent, artistic, timid young man who was uncomfortable in the limelight.

Wes reminded Stevie of Douglas Van Horne. Dougie would be close to Wes's age if he were still alive, she guessed. Her son had also been introspective and shy—"socially challenged," Jon used to joke. And Dougie had a love for words, preferring a book to a ball game or a party, given to writing an occasional poem. Throughout Dougie's childhood, Stevie had encouraged his reading and writing. He could very well be studying literature at Cal Berkeley or UCLA now, she thought wistfully, had his life not taken such a tragic turn. Wes even looked a little like her son: slight frame but not too skinny, narrow face, dark eyes. No wonder she had leaped into action when she saw him in need of some mothering.

Once Bellardi's large entourage arrived on the platform, the band played on to the delight of the audience, which was now on its feet. The blaring patriotic music charged Stevie with excitement, which she knew was the precise response the rally's organizers had anticipated. Advertising is advertising no matter what the product, she thought.

Stevie's eyes flitted between the smiling candidate and his wife, standing front and center, and Wes, the young volunteer, buried three rows back in the platform crowd. She eagerly awaited the senator's address, aware that her hope for her children had grown because of this man and his mission in North

California. Suddenly Jeremiah 29:11 flashed through her mind: *"For I know the plans I have for you," says the Lord. "They are plans for good and not for disaster, to give you a future and a hope."* For the first time in a long time, that verse seemed to come alive in Stevie's heart. *Plans for good and not for disaster, to give you a future and a hope.*

Yes, thought Stevie, *a future and a hope. . . .*

Yet even as she allowed herself to hope for a brighter future, each glance at Wes prompted a sad nostalgia. She found herself wishing that Dougie were here to share this hope and future with her.

16

Sunday
July 4

SHAWNA TAPPED in the number and then flopped onto her bed with the phone.

"Hello?"

"Terilyn, this is Shawna."

"Snow White! You must be back from the dead," Terilyn said with a laugh. "I left a gazillion messages since yesterday."

Shawna smiled at the exaggeration. "It was four, actually."

"All right, so I left *four* gazillion messages since yesterday. Where have you been, girl?"

"I told you: My dad came up from L.A. Me and my little brother have been with him the whole weekend."

Terilyn snorted a laugh. "Doing what? I mean, what can you

do with a dad for forty-eight hours straight?" Terilyn was not fond of dads in general, Shawna had learned. Both her real father and her stepfather had run out on her and her mother.

"Went to the batting cages and a movie," Shawna answered. "Then ate barbecue and watched fireworks at the lake. Today we drove to the redwood forest. Just got back."

"All the way to the redwoods and back in one day? Yuck."

"Yeah, being on that windy road to the coast was like driving forever. At least we had my mom's Cherokee instead of my dad's pickup. I slept halfway home in the backseat."

"Your mom let your dad drive her car?" Disbelief marked Terilyn's tone.

"Of course," Shawna answered. "And she used his pickup. What's wrong with that?"

"Too bizarre," Terilyn said. "If my mom loaned a car to my dad or stepdad, it would have a bomb planted in it. And me and her would fight over the remote control to see who got to make the car go boom."

Shawna wrinkled her nose. "That's sick."

"Not if you knew Charlie or Gil." Terilyn spat the names more than spoke them. Shawna felt badly about her own parents being divorced, but at least her dad and mom could talk to each other. She felt a little sorry for Terilyn.

Shawna quickly changed the subject. "So how was the lake yesterday with Uncle What's-his-nose?"

"It was fantastic, Snowy!" Terilyn exclaimed, obviously happy to be talking about something else. "We skied and tubed our brains out. Uncle Jack loved showing off his big powerboat to his new plaything, Sweet Charlotte. You have to go next time."

"I'll be there," Shawna said, envious of Terilyn's fun. Being with her dad was good, and Shawna enjoyed it. But missing out on so much fun with her new friends almost made her wish her dad had not come—at least not this weekend.

Terilyn went on excitedly. "We brought sandwiches and stuff, but Captain Macho sprang for a big lunch at the marina. And he had a cooler full of cold brewskis for everybody."

"Brewskis?" Shawna repeated. "You mean, beer?"

"Yes, in the native tongue of the North California lake

people, brewski means beer," Terilyn said in a funny voice. "What do the refugees from South Cal call it? Kool-Aid?"

"Are you telling me that your uncle let you drink beer?"

"No, he practically *forced* us to drink it," Terilyn said, giggling. "That's all he had in the cooler. Ain't it a shame?"

Shawna had not taken Terilyn, Alexis, and Josie for the beer-drinking kind. She asked, "What about the sheriff? You could have been picked up."

"Snowy, Snowy, Snowy, think about it," Terilyn said condescendingly. "Shasta Lake is like forty miles long, and there are coves everywhere. You can go all day without seeing the sheriff's boat. In fact, you can get back in one of those long arms of the lake and not see *anybody* all day. That's where we went skinny-dipping."

Shawna couldn't disguise her shock. "What?"

Terilyn hooted with laughter. "Yes, Miss Snow-White-never-done-anything-wrong. Skinny-dipping."

"In broad daylight, all of you, even Uncle Jack?"

"No, silly," Terilyn said, still laughing. "It was just the three of us girls. Uncle Jack dropped us off, then he took Sweet Charlotte to find their own private little cove."

Shawna was somewhat relieved to know it had been only the girls. Still . . . She lowered her voice to make sure her mother couldn't hear. "You didn't tell me you were going skinny-dipping."

"We didn't *plan* to go skinny-dipping. It just kind of happened. Josie dared us. We dared her back. Nobody chickened out. It was so much fun. You would have loved it. It was actually a very spiritual experience, a great way to get in touch with your inner self."

I would not *have loved it,* Shawna objected silently. *And I don't think I want to be in touch with any "inner self" that would think of something like skinny-dipping as a "spiritual experience." How embarrassing. I don't care if the cove was deserted. I don't want anybody to see me naked, not even other girls. What a dumb dare. I'm so glad I didn't go.*

As if reading Shawna's thoughts, Terilyn said, "Are you freaked, Snowy?"

"Somebody could have seen you," Shawna argued weakly.

Terilyn's answer shocked Shawna again. "So what if somebody saw us? So what if a perverted old fisherman out in the middle of the lake with a telescope got an eyeful? That makes it even more exciting. I hope he enjoyed it. We sure did."

Shawna was stunned to silence. Terilyn continued almost apologetically, "It was just us girls having some fun, Snowy. It's not like there were guys there or anything. It was something different, something spontaneous and exciting and, like I said, spiritual. You've probably noticed by now that it's not L.A. up here. We don't have Disneyland, Knott's Berry Farm, Six Flags, or Sea World. There aren't that many exciting places to go. So me and the girls make our own fun. We never know what we're going to do next. And we all want you to come next time."

Shawna felt torn. For her money, meeting Terilyn, Josie, and Alexis was the best thing so far about moving to Redding. The last five weeks would have been completely boring had she not hooked up with Terilyn and her friends at the Commons pool. Having been so quickly accepted by them, Shawna felt she belonged—a feeling that did not come over her often.

And the "dwarfs," as Terilyn liked to call them, were so nutty and uninhibited. They were so into having fun together that they did not have much time to be boy-crazy. Of course, they were interested in boys; they had all noticed the hunks at the pool and had commented and giggled about them more than once. But they were not obsessed with them the way Destiny had been. Shawna was glad for that.

Still, there was a daring edge to the dwarfs' outlook on life, something Shawna just could not put her finger on. Nor could she explain the inner attraction she felt to such excitement. In fact, she was not even consciously aware of it. She knew only that she wanted to stay close to the zany girls who called her Snow White and transformed otherwise boring summer days at the pool into wild fun.

But here was a new side to Terilyn and her friends. Underage drinking, apparently condoned—more like encouraged—by a so-called responsible adult. Shawna knew it happened all the time, even among good kids like her new friends. But if her mother ever found out, it would be the end of Snow White and the three dwarfs. Shawna flashed on a mental picture of her and the beer-drinking dwarfs being caught on the lake by the sheriff. Anticipation of the consequences made her shudder. And who knew where else Terilyn, Josie, and Alexis might push the envelope on the law and drag their innocent friend into it?

Shawna did not want to dampen the positive side of the friendship while sorting through the scary side. "Yeah, maybe next time," she said as cheerfully as she could. "But I've got to hang up now." For once she was grateful for the time limit her mother set on phone conversations.

"See you at the pool tomorrow?" Terilyn asked.

"Maybe in the afternoon. My dad doesn't leave until after lunch."

"OK. Bye."

Shawna tapped off the phone, her mind drifting to another friend—former friend, actually—who had pushed her to the edge and gotten her into a lot of trouble. For all the excitement Destiny brought into her life, Shawna was glad to be separated from her by five hundred miles. Terilyn Spradlin was not Destiny Fortugno by a wide stretch, but Shawna sensed in her new friend the same magnetism to the outer limits. *Why is there always someone around trying to turn me the wrong way?* she asked herself.

Jon sank into the steaming outdoor spa until one of the powerful water jets pummeled the small of his back. Exhausted after a day of driving to the redwoods and back, he tried not to think about the next day's long journey back to L.A. He had enjoyed being with the kids this weekend, but it had been anything but restful. After a late breakfast with them tomorrow, he would head south. Jon thought it might take him all week to recover from the whirlwind trip and strength-sapping heat.

It was after eleven, but the sound of an occasional cherry bomb or Roman candle could still be heard in the distance. There were four other motel guests in the large tank with him. Conversation between them was sporadic and superficial. Jon just sat and soaked in the churning hot water.

He thought about grimy old Mac, his last-minute breakfast guest at Denny's that morning, and smiled. The man loved to eat and talk, and he had no trouble doing both at the same time. As Mac droned on about the "horse race" for governor, Jon had reminded himself to look more thoroughly into the two candidates, whom Mac referred to as "Dangerous Dan" and "Juanita, the sweet angel of freedom."

As a resident of South California, Jon had no stake—and only a passing interest—in the contest between the dignified state senator and the flamboyant entertainer/activist. But Stevie's drastic relocation to the "promised land" proved that she had a substantial emotional and financial stake in a Bellardi victory. Jon could not shake a growing sense of urgency to know exactly what she was getting involved in. Bellardi, though a Christian, seemed too narrow and idealistic for Jon's taste. Yet Dunsmuir was an avowed pro-choice, pro-gay, pro-death-with-dignity marijuana grower. He would thoroughly study the candidates before his next visit to Redding, both to satisfy his curiosity and to convince himself that Stevie was in good hands with the senator. He acknowledged that the old habits of being protective were still in place.

Jon climbed out of the spa and dove into the adjoining swimming pool. The sudden change in water temperature revived him. He swam two slow laps, then settled into the spa again.

He thought about Shawna. The physical transformation from little girl to young woman was complete, and she had blossomed into a beauty. Jon had noted with fatherly suspicion the furtive double takes and sustained glances she attracted from young men almost twice her age. But emotionally, Shawna was still a young adolescent: frivolous, naive, self-absorbed. It concerned Jon that his daughter's mature appearance might unwittingly gain her entrance into situations her immature mind and emotions could not handle. There might not be as many temptations in North California, he acknowledged, but it takes only one to ruin a defenseless girl's life. The disturbing memory of a pervert named Rik was still fresh in his mind.

From his veiled questions and her equally veiled responses, Jon was confident that Shawna had turned a corner behaviorally after the move. The description of her new friends did not remind him of Shawna's trouble-seeking sidekick, Destiny, and Shawna apparently was not using E-mail on her new computer. Jon hoped that Shawna's rebellious period was behind her.

Jon thought about Collin, his "little buddy." It grieved him that weeks of his son's childhood were slipping by and he was not involved. Jon resolved to call more often to show a greater interest in Collin's activities.

And Jon thought about Stevie. The divorce had been final for eighteen months now. When would the news reach his emotions? Seeing her again briefly while picking up and delivering the kids alerted him that he had not totally let her go. He reminded himself that flashes of sexual desire for his ex-wife tended to momentarily dull his memory of the differences and pain that ended their marriage. He looked forward to the day when he would be able to look at Stevie without recalling the exhilarating physical intimacy they once shared.

Jon returned to his room and showered to rinse away the chlorine smell. Drowsy from the prolonged soak in the spa, he climbed into bed. Before turning out the light, he dialed his home number from the bedside phone to check his messages.

There was a call from his mother in San Luis Obispo, wondering where he was spending the holiday. The only other message caused him to sit up and search out a pad and pen to take notes.

"Mr. Van Horne, this is Leta Huntsinger with the Los Angeles County District Attorney's office. I'm sorry to disturb you on a Sunday, but I thought you would be interested to know that the Los Angeles police have taken into custody a suspect in the drive-by shooting incident at your residence in Northridge on April eighth. The young man was apprehended during a gang incident in the Valley. Slugs from his weapon match the slugs removed from your property in April. The gun could have changed hands several times since then, but one of the suspect's 'homeys' slipped up and implicated him in the shooting.

"The suspect will be arraigned on Tuesday morning at eleven. I'd like to talk to you before that time to discuss the procedures. We also need to determine your intentions about pressing charges. If possible, please call my pager on Monday and I'll get in touch with you." The woman left a number and signed off.

Jon's first reaction was surprise that a suspect had materialized. Drive-bys were conducted by phantoms; few were ever apprehended. Jon never expected the police to turn up a clue.

Jon's second reaction was directed at the suspect, and he had to get up and pace the room to deal with it. Dormant feelings of anger roused within Jon toward the faceless individual who had jeopardized the lives of his ex-wife and son. The image of a burst of deadly fire crashing into his home and barely missing Stevie and Collin turned his blood cold. Of course he would press charges. This maniac deserved to be punished to the full extent of the law. But even that prospect did not satisfy Jon at the moment.

Kid, he thought, *you should thank God above that I'm not the one in charge of your punishment.*

17

Friday
July 23

"STEPHANIE, I'm Eden Hunter-Upshaw. Thank you for coming in."

The African-American woman approaching with smile unfurled and hand extended impressed Stevie at first glance. Dressed in a stylish, tailored suit of dusty rose, Ms. Hunter-Upshaw looked every bit as professional as she had sounded over the phone. Stevie had dressed up for the meeting, but she suddenly felt underdressed. Standing to shake hands, she reminded herself that she was not interviewing for a job, simply offering a couple of hours a week as a campaign volunteer.

"Good to meet you in person, Mrs. Hunter-Upshaw," Stevie said, shaking hands and returning the smile.

"Come on back, Stephanie. And please, call me Eden."

Following Eden through the old downtown department store in central Redding that had been converted into Daniel Bellardi's campaign headquarters, Stevie was again impressed. She halfway expected to find a noisy campaign "sweatshop": rows of tables crowded with assembly-line envelope stuffers, banks of phones manned by volunteers doing "vote for Bellardi" cold calls. Instead, the main floor was a maze of office cubicles containing desks, computers, phones, and well-dressed volunteers quietly going about their work. Judging from its appearance, the office could be the nerve center of a thriving insurance, mortgage, or advertising business.

Stevie had wondered if she would run into the young man named Wes while in campaign headquarters, but she saw only a few faces bob above the cubicle walls and Wes's was not among them. Remembering how out of place the kid had seemed at the Fourth of July rally, Stevie would not have been surprised if he was long gone by now.

Comfortably seated in Eden's small, modestly adorned office on the building's mezzanine level, Stevie accepted a cup of decaf from Carolyn Carter, Eden's assistant. Carolyn was the first person Stevie talked to when she called the office on Wednesday. Eden rolled her chair to Stevie's side of the desk and sat down with her own cup of coffee. After several minutes of conversation, mostly about Stevie's family and the recent move to the north, Eden asked, "How would you like to become involved in Senator Bellardi's campaign, Stephanie?"

Stevie felt a little awkward. "Well, Mrs. Hunter-Upshaw—"

"Eden, remember?" She flashed Stevie a warm smile. "'Mrs. Hunter-Upshaw' is just too much name to say comfortably."

Stevie returned the smile. "Eden, yes. And please, call me Stevie. Anyway, not having been what you might call 'politically active' in the past, I'm not really sure how to answer your question. I'll be happy to do anything in the trenches: lick stamps, telephone voters, empty the trash, make coffee. I believe in what Senator Bellardi is trying to do, and I just want to help."

Eden smiled. "Like many people I talk to, you may be surprised to learn that very little 'trench work' is done by our volunteers. Mailings these days are totally automated. The printing and shipping are all done in Sacramento by a company that services hundreds of campaigns annually. The days of hand-stuffing envelopes are in the past, at least at this level of politics. And our phone work is farmed out to telemarketing professionals. In fact, the ideal campaign volunteer is not a retiree with time on her hands. We need professionals, people who offer specific skills."

Stevie suddenly felt a little out of her depth. "I'm not sure where that leaves me. My skills—"

Eden did not wait for Stevie to explain. "Carolyn tells me you've done some writing."

Stevie paused. "Well, I don't consider myself a professional writer, but, yes, I do quite a bit of copy writing in my advertising business."

Eden nodded. "Frankly, Steph—Stevie—that's the reason I asked you to come in today. The senator has a great need for capable communicators, particularly in the print medium. There are a number of projects underway in this office that require the skills you utilize in your business, particularly copy writing. I wonder if you would consider helping out in our communications division—as your schedule permits, of course."

"Can you give me a few examples of the kinds of projects you're working on?"

Eden nodded, sipped her coffee, then responded. "On the first of August we're initiating a weekly, one-page bulletin from the senator to be delivered by fax and E-mail to several thousand supporters in the state. It will have an insiders' update feel to it. We're planning a similar electronic bulletin to ministers—kind of a prayer letter format. These bulletins will be pithy, poignant, informational, and motivational."

"Like a magazine ad or a radio spot," Stevie interjected.

"Exactly. Grab their attention, hit them hard and fast with the hottest topics, leave them with something to think about. That's what your work is all about, am I correct?"

"It's what I do for a living," Stevie replied confidently.

"That's why I think you could help us here," Eden continued. "We have a staff person in communications who will get the bulletins off the ground. But she needs someone like you— a writer who knows how to present the product well—to carry on the work." Eden leaned a little closer. "Senator Bellardi told me personally that these weekly 'reach out and touch someone' bulletins will greatly assist him in disseminating his vision to the people of North California. Does this sound like something you could sink your teeth into?"

Stevie felt a flash of excitement at the prospect of using her skills in such a vital area of the campaign. But she also sensed the damp, gray cloud of inadequacy hovering over her. She tried to be positive in her response. "It does sound attractive to me, but I have to tell you that I don't know very much about the senator yet. I'm not very politically aware."

Eden set her cup on the desk and locked onto Stevie's eyes. "A prospective client calls you and says, 'I want you to put together an ad campaign for Acme Widgets.' Would you say, 'I'm sorry, I can't help you because I don't know the first thing about widgets'? Of course not! You'd say, 'Tell me what the world needs to know about Acme Widgets, and I'll get your message across.' Am I correct?"

The point was clear, and Stevie nodded, wondering why she had not seen it that way.

Eden pounded the point home. "We can use you here not because of what you know but because you can help us communicate what *we* know. Part of the process, of course, will be your 'indoctrination,' if you will, on the subject of Senator Daniel Bellardi and his platform. In fact, you'll probably learn more about us than you ever wanted to know. But in the meantime, you'll be part of the team that puts a godly leader in the governor's chair of our nation's fifty-first state. Would you like to help us do that, Stevie?"

Stevie guessed that in "real life" Eden must be a successful corporate headhunter. She was convincing and to the point without being abrasive. Stevie liked her. Already awash with a sense of team spirit, she said, "I'm willing to try, Eden."

In the last five minutes of the interview, Eden informed Stevie that she must submit to a thorough police background check—routine for all campaign workers. She explained that in a highly charged emotional campaign the possibility of infiltration and even sabotage must be guarded against. Stevie almost laughed at the idea, until she saw that Eden was not joking. She could not believe that competition over the little state of North California could become so serious.

Eden also requested that Stevie serve at least four hours a week, and more if possible. Flushed with anticipation, Stevie quickly agreed. Eden set up an appointment for Monday, when she would introduce Stevie to the small communications staff. Then the office manager warmly thanked her for volunteering to serve and escorted her to the door.

Driving home, Stevie wrestled with the ramifications of signing on with Senator Bellardi's volunteer army. The opportunity Eden Hunter-Upshaw had offered to her could not have been more appealing. The prospect of applying her creativity and writing skills to the senator's campaign seemed like a great honor instead of a task—and it sure beat stuffing envelopes.

But, realistically, four hours a week was going to encroach upon her work and her time with Shawna and Collin; anything more would be a painful tax on her schedule. But she had committed to at least four hours, and she would follow through with her commitment. It would be a sacrifice to the cause of establishing the ideals of Senator Daniel Bellardi in the new state of North California. And with Juanita Dunsmuir slowly but steadily narrowing the gap in the polls, Stevie had to do her part for the sake of her children. Her work would survive the challenge, and once the election was over and their new state was securely under Bellardi's wise leadership, normal family life would resume. And someday Shawna and Collin would thank their mother for investing her time in the secure and peaceful future of their new home state.

Momentarily at peace with the stretching commitment, Stevie turned her thoughts to another pressing challenge. Jon would be driving up the next day for a nine-day visit with the children. He had promised to take the kids up the Pacific coast into Oregon and Washington for several days. In a weak moment, she had offered her car for the trip, even though she disliked the idea of being stuck at home with Jon's pickup. She was also uncomfortable with the thought of the kids being alone with their father for such a long period of time. Over the last few days, rekindled fears taunted her that Shawna and Collin might choose Jon over her. Stevie dreaded what might happen to her children if they returned to what she considered hell on earth: South California.

Shawna popped out of the water on her fourth try. The skis were wobbly and she clung to the handle of the towrope for dear life, but she was up and skiing. Terilyn and Charlotte cheered and applauded her from the boat. Shawna could not hear them above the roar of the engine and the rush of water under her skis, but she grinned broadly and released a whoop of joy at her accomplishment.

Shawna bounced along unsteadily for several hundred yards before losing her balance and taking a dive. Uncle Jack circled around her in the boat until she found the rope handle, and soon she was up on the skis again. With every successful pull out of the water she exulted in her good fortune to be out on the lake having so much fun. She reaffirmed her belief that, if she had not met Terilyn, Josie, and Alexis, summer in Redding would have been completely boring. But over the last three weeks, wherever the trio went, whatever they did, they always invited Shawna to come along. When her mother allowed her to go, Shawna went and had more fun than she'd ever had with friends in South California.

They had been to the lake twice with Jack and Charlotte. Shawna loved it when all four girls were bouncing across the waves on big tubes behind Jack's powerful boat. With the three dwarfs around, there was always plenty of joking and ache-in-the-side laughter, and Shawna had learned to dish out her share of the mischief. Best of all, nobody had even mentioned skinny-dipping or offered her a beer during these lake trips, nor had they hassled her about her surprised reaction to these topics. Shawna found it unthinkable that Terilyn, Josie, and Alexis would lead her into trouble the way Destiny had done so often. She had begun to believe she had finally found some friends she could trust and be herself with.

After half an hour of being pulled out of the water, fighting the skis and the mild swells, and falling, Shawna's sinuses sloshed with lake water and she was exhausted. They were near the shore, and she was ready to be out of the water. As the boat idled around her after her latest tumble from the skis, she said, "I'm thrashed, Terilyn. Your turn."

"Here, let me pull you in," Terilyn said, extending a hand from the rear platform.

Shawna shook her head. "I'm going to paddle to the beach and walk back to the cove. You can take off from right here."

Charlotte looked at her questioningly. "Are you sure? We can jet you back to the cove in a few seconds."

"Thanks," Shawna said as she lifted the beginner skis up to Terilyn's waiting hands. "But I can walk from here. No problem."

"Keep your vest on while you're in the water," Jack admonished.

"OK," Shawna sputtered through a mouthful of water from a swell that caught her off guard.

Terilyn snapped on her vest, dropped her slalom ski into the water, and jumped in after it. "Great skiing, Snowy," she said as she slipped her right foot into the ski. "You looked fantastic out there."

"Thanks. I just wish I could zip around on a solo ski like you."

"Stick with me," Terilyn said with a wink, "and you'll be slaloming before the end of the summer. In fact, I have a lot of fun things for you to try before summer's over."

In position behind the boat with the ski rope taut, Terilyn yelled, "Hit it!" Jack shoved the accelerator forward, transforming the motor's purring idle into a ferocious roar. Terilyn popped out of the water and skied away with a cry of triumph.

Shawna floated to the shore and stood up on rubbery legs. Remembering the sandwiches and cans of soda waiting in the cove just around the point, she was suddenly famished. But the shoreline was strewn with rocks, so she moved her bare feet along cautiously.

The scorching midday sun evaporated the water from Shawna's deeply tanned skin almost instantly. The warmth felt good, and for this moment, at least, she loved living in North California. The hot weather suited her just fine—as long as she was near the pool or the lake. And, as her mother had repeatedly told her, the people here really seemed different—more pleasant, not as weird and wacky and paranoid as people in the south. Shawna had to agree that Redding really was a good place to make a new start away from people like Destiny. And thanks to Terilyn, Josie, and Alexis, she was having a good time doing it.

As she followed the water's edge back into the small cove, she spotted the blankets, towels, and large sun umbrella of their site in the distance. This was Terilyn's favorite beach because it was well away from the main lake, too small to accommodate houseboats or waterskiing, and rarely visited by fishermen. Shawna liked it too. It was like being on a deserted island, especially when Jack and Charlotte took the big noisy boat out onto the lake for a long ride.

Josie and Alexis were not under the umbrella or anywhere around the blankets. Shading her eyes in order to follow the waterline, Shawna spotted the two girls on the other side of the quiet cove. Shawna stopped at what she saw. It was Josie and Alexis, all right; she recognized their swimsuits. But what were they doing? They seemed to be facing each other. And they were sitting on the sand, cross-legged, their hands positioned strangely on their knees. They were too far away for Shawna to see their expressions or hear their voices, but they seemed totally engrossed in whatever it was they were doing.

Shawna tried calling to them, but there was no response. She was sure they were close enough to at least hear her yell, even if they could not understand what she said. But they did not even move.

Oh well, she thought, *at least they're not doing something weird like skinny-dipping again.* She sighed as her empty stomach reminded her to keep moving toward the cooler. *I'll have to remember to ask them about it later. Who knows? Maybe there's more to life in North Cal than I first thought.*

18

Friday
July 23

DRIVING INTO the city, Jon alternately railed on himself and
commended himself for what he was about to do. He was
bummed about delaying this task until he had to take an
afternoon off work to complete it. On the up side, he was
pleased about doing the right thing, even though he had
procrastinated to the last minute. It had taken almost two
weeks to get his head straight about this, but at least it was
happening.

And it really *was* the last minute as far as Jon was concerned.
He would leave tomorrow morning for a nine-day visit with
the children, and he was not about to put off seeing Shawna
and Collin. He knew if he waited until returning from Redding

to come downtown, he might come up with an excuse to let himself off the hook. It was now or never.

The Los Angeles County Jail in the heart of downtown is an imposing structure, housing more inmates than many state prisons. Jon was ushered through several levels of security, including a pat-down search, by khaki-clad county sheriff's deputies. His attorney had paved the way for this visit, but Jon still felt the suspicious gaze of guards who were trained not to trust any civilian inside the jail's walls.

Having cleared security, Jon was admitted to the visitors' area. Directed to an unoccupied cubicle, he sat down at the metal counter on a folding chair. On the other side of the bulletproof glass was another counter and a metal stool, which appeared bolted to the floor.

Waiting for the appearance of the prisoner, Jon marveled at the turnaround in attitude that had brought him here. Nearly three weeks earlier, when he learned that a twenty-year-old kid had been arrested in the drive-by shooting on Etiwanda Street, Jon was incensed at the nameless suspect. Drive-bys happened every day in L.A., and Jon admitted that he was rather desensitized to the carnage reported in the news. But this shooting happened in the Valley, on his street, in his home. Worst of all, it could have killed Stevie and Collin.

During that long drive from Redding to L.A., Jon's anger had escalated to a boil. Arriving home, he contacted Ms. Huntsinger of the D.A.'s office and demanded that the county throw the book at the kid. He stated that he intended to file a civil suit as well.

When Ms. Huntsinger mentioned the suspect's name— Eugene Hackett—Jon thought it sounded a little familiar. He wondered about the name again a few days later when he saw it in a sheaf of reports mailed to him from the county. Having been exposed to thousands of students in the school district over the years, including many Eugenes and Hacketts, Jon was not sure he ever knew a Eugene Hackett. But he could not shake the ringing familiarity of the name.

Then he came across Hackett's photograph in a days-old issue of the Valley newspaper. In the photo, the kid was being arrested for attempted robbery of a Stop-N-Go convenience store on Roscoe Boulevard, an arrest that produced the

162

weapon used in the shooting on Etiwanda. Jon recognized the snake tattoos entwining bare arms, the gaunt face, the hard eyes. His homeys had called him Rattler, but his name, stated by the police officers on the scene, was Eugene Hackett.

In that instant of recognition, the frightening spring break encounter at the rec center was suddenly fresh in Jon's memory. He remembered Hackett's vile taunts, his threatening behavior, the scuffle and fall that had bloodied the kid's face. In the next instant, Jon knew his home had not been a random target for the shooting. Somehow Hackett had tracked down his address, obviously thinking Jon still lived in the house on Etiwanda Street. Hackett's assault with the .45 was premeditated payback, an act of retaliation by a gang member who had been "dissed" in front of his homeys. In Hackett's sick mind, shooting up Jon's house and blowing away anyone inside was somehow justified because of the humiliation he had suffered in the gym at the hands of the recreation director.

Hovering over the newspaper that day, Jon no longer wanted the county to prosecute Eugene Hackett to the full extent of the law. Whatever the court system did to him would be too little and far too late. Jon wanted to take care of Hackett himself. It took a few days for the primal, vengeful urge to cool and give way to rational thoughts and decisions. Waiting now in front of the bulletproof glass, Jon wondered if those hostile feelings would flare up when he looked into Rattler's eyes for the first time since that night in the gym.

When Eugene Hackett sat down on the other side of the glass and appraised the visitor, his face showed no sense of recognition. He looked up at the guard who brought him in as if to say, "Why did you bring me here? I don't know this guy." At the same time, Jon almost did not recognize Hackett. With a short haircut and generic, faded orange jail clothes, the kid did not much fit the mental snapshot Jon carried from the night in the gym. But the tattoos on his scrawny arms were a dead giveaway.

"What do you want?" Hackett asked with a sneer, glaring at Jon, jaw pushed out. His voice sounded tinny coming through the speaker. He sat tentatively, as if ready to return to his cell if the answer failed to suit him.

Jon could almost feel the cold defiance directed at him

through the glass. A small ember of hatred flared within him. For an instant he was tempted to blister the kid with the diatribe he had rehearsed several times over the last three weeks. But he curbed his emotion and spoke with control. "My name is Jon Van Horne." He waited for the kid to process the information.

Jon had imagined a number of ways Eugene Hackett might respond to his surprise visit, from broken contrition (which Jon considered remote) to cold indifference to renewed rage. The kid's response was immaterial to his purpose for being here, Jon knew, but with the hostility blazing at him from beyond the glass, Jon had to keep reminding himself of that fact.

Hackett telegraphed a glimmer of recognition. The jaw thrust out again. "Yeah?" he challenged in a *so-what* tone.

A sudden flash of vengeance within Jon begged for expression. This arrogant, unconscionable jerk had come within inches of killing a nine-year-old boy and his mother. Hackett's only regret, he had boasted during a confession to police, was that he had not wasted someone in the process of shooting up the house. *You are an incorrigible young thug who should be locked up and forgotten,* Jon wanted to say. *But I sure would enjoy knocking some of that attitude off your face before they throw away the key.*

Again he corralled his hostility and forced himself back to the point of his visit. Delivering these words was even more difficult for Jon than formulating them. But he knew he had to do it.

"Eugene, I have a couple of things I need to get off my chest. First, I want you to know that I was very angry and upset by what happened to my wife and son on April eighth." Jon had decided not to complicate the matter by trying to explain the divorce. "We felt traumatized and—"

Hackett cursed and moved to stand. The husky, middle-aged deputy standing nearby placed a firm hand on his shoulder and forced him back into his seat. "Sit down and listen," he said. Hackett remained seated, jerking his shoulder out of the deputy's grasp. He refused to look at his visitor.

Jon nodded his thanks to the deputy and continued. "We felt traumatized and violated. The injuries to my family, and the mental and emotional pain I suffered because of it, were completely uncalled for. And the realization that they could have been more severely hurt or killed is a—"

"So sue me," Hackett spat, adding vile epithets directed at Jon.

Jon saw the deputy flinch, then noticed his nostrils flare and his face redden with anger. Had Eugene Hackett not been visible to so many civilians on the other side of the glass, Jon thought, he might have been the victim of a quick outburst of police brutality. Jon could hardly blame the deputy, and he admired his restraint.

Again Hackett tried to get up, and again the deputy pushed him back to the stool. "I said, sit down and shut up," the man in uniform commanded. Hackett complied, but his smirk of contempt was obvious.

Jon's determination was wearing thin. He decided to finish his business before his emotions got the best of him. "Eugene, you need to know that I wholeheartedly support the criminal justice system and the consequences it may impose for your— I mean, for such—behavior." Jon understood the importance of employing *I* messages, but he found it difficult to confront Eugene Hackett without reverting to accusative *you* messages. Hackett was doing a good job of acting out his disinterest. He sat sideways on the stool and stared at the floor.

Jon drew a long, silent breath in preparation for the most difficult part of his prepared speech. "The second thing I want you to know is that I forgive you for what happened. I don't hold anything against you personally. In fact, I hope and pray that you come out of this experience a better person. That's all I wanted to say."

The surprise on the deputy's face was as obvious as his anger had been moments earlier. He glanced at Jon as if to say, "Are you crazy? A worthless scumbag like him doesn't deserve forgiveness." In the meantime, Eugene Hackett continued to stare at the floor as if catatonic. Still, his response was not Jon's primary concern. Eugene had not asked for forgiveness, nor did Jon expect the perpetrator to receive it graciously, if at all. Jon had come to the jail today to resolve his side of the forgiveness issue. If his action made a difference to Eugene Hackett—and he doubted that it would—all the better.

Jon stood to leave. Eugene turned to him with a leer. "What if I didn't miss? What if I snuffed them? You still say that?"

The question was clearly not intended to test the depth of Jon's mercy. It was a taunt, a cruel jab aimed at an open wound.

Jon felt the pain of the verbal blow. He saw the devil in Eugene's eyes. The temptation to retaliate verbally rose like bile in Jon's throat, but he swallowed it. In the last three weeks he had awakened to something about people like Eugene Hackett: people who break the rules, push the envelope of decency, inflict pain, ignore convention, law, and sanctity. It was something he had known all along but failed to apply generally.

People might be unkind, misguided, disadvantaged, or evil in any number of ways, but they were still people—individuals created in the image of God. Appropriate consequences must be meted out for misbehavior, but those who misbehave must still be treated with respect. *Hate the sin but love the sinner.* How many times had he heard Pastor Schofield and others make that statement? By his own evaluation, Jon had done well at looking past personality and performance to see the real person. Mac, the transient at Denny's in Redding, was Exhibit A in his most recent self-evaluation. *Didn't I engage him in conversation and buy him a hot meal while everyone else in the restaurant ignored him? Didn't I show the love of Christ to him without judging his lifestyle? Haven't I done this repeatedly for people like Mac?*

Jon's conscience was clear regarding down-and-outers like Mac. But in the last couple of weeks Jon had realized something: Unconscionable thugs like Eugene Hackett made it difficult to look past the sin to love the sinner. Jon's attitude toward the Eugenes of the world was anything but respectful. But in less than three weeks' time, Jon had experienced a transformation that had brought him here to the county jail.

Jon countered Eugene's evil glare with a smile. He said, "Thank God you *did* miss, Eugene. Good-bye and good luck." Then he left the jail.

166

Driving back to the Valley to pack, he wondered how Stevie would respond when he told her what happened at the jail. Would she be impressed at his Christian attitude? Or would she berate him for befriending the man who had almost killed her and Collin? Unsure of the answer, Jon thought it best, at least for the time being, not to say anything to her about Eugene Hackett.

19

Saturday
July 24

IT WAS AN awkward situation, but Stevie had decided she could endure it for one night. It seemed ridiculous for Jon to get a motel room in Redding when he and the kids would be leaving early the next day for their vacation. So Stevie had offered him the sofa bed in the living room for the night. Jon's initial hesitancy revealed his own sense of awkwardness, but he finally accepted, saying thanks by treating the family to dinner out at the Burger Barn.

After dinner, Stevie stayed inside the air-conditioned apartment while the kids played in the pool and Jon soaked his travel-weary back in the spa. She felt a little sorry for her ex-husband, who faced another long drive the following day after sitting behind the wheel of the Ranger pickup for nearly ten hours that day. While they were married, she had nagged him about over-taxing his endurance like that. Even now she was tempted to say something, but Jon was no longer her responsibility. If he wanted to take off for Oregon with kinks in his back, that was his choice. Besides, in spite of her nagging concern that the kids might end up choosing Jon over her, she was rather looking for-ward to the solitude of the next several days.

The most awkward part of the evening came at about nine o'clock. Shawna excused herself to go say good-bye to her friends, who lived in the Cascade unit of Shasta Commons. Collin slipped away to his bedroom to take a shot at 100,000 avenger points in Stealth Fighter, his favorite video game. Stevie and Jon were alone in the living room. After bringing him up to date on everything the kids were doing, Stevie expected the conversation to fall off to an uncomfortable silence.

Instead, Jon picked up the slack, asking about her work. Stevie talked briefly about the advertising accounts she had secured since arriving in Redding. Jon bored in inquisitively for details. He was not asking nosy questions, she recognized, but questions that reflected an interest in her success. As she talked, he made them cups of tea, obviously remembering that her favorite was lemon spice with an extra splash of bottled lemon juice. Moving back and forth from the kitchen as if he were the host, Jon continued to listen and draw out her thoughts and feelings about the new business.

Stevie found herself warming to Jon's attention and interest. She asked about his summer at the rec center, and he consider-ately talked about the people he worked with, not just the job. This was Jon Van Horne at his best, she acknowledged. Before the impassable desert formed between them over the issue of their first son's death, Jon had been better than the average male at sustained conversation. They had not talked like this since before the divorce, and it reminded Stevie how starved she was for adult conversation. Talking with Jon also drew Stevie's thoughts to the emotional and physical intimacy they once shared, alerting her to a quietly persistent hunger in this area also.

Returning to the living room with tea refills for both of

them, Jon said, "Tell me about your involvement with Daniel Bellardi."

The change of topic surprised Stevie for two reasons. Judging from their limited discussions about North California politics to date, she did not think Jon was interested in hearing about her fascination with Daniel Bellardi. Rather, Stevie assumed that Jon regarded her as something of an idealistic right-wing fanatic for moving up here. Also surprising was the fact that Jon seemed as genuinely interested in listening now as he had been when asking about her work.

"Nothing much to tell, really," Stevie said, setting her tea aside and deciding not to go into too much detail. "I volunteered to work in the office, but I don't know exactly what I'll be doing. As for Senator Bellardi, I haven't even seen him since the Fourth of July in the park."

"But you still feel good about where he's headed, should he get elected?"

"Oh, absolutely," Stevie answered with conviction. "This is a wise, godly man. Can you imagine a state governed by someone who is committed to biblical values? I mean, think of the situation at your school as an example: drugs sold and used in the rest rooms, gay kids holding hands and kissing in the halls, condoms distributed in health classes, kids practicing with them on bananas. That's not going to happen here. Think of how a morally positive environment will benefit our kids. And Senator Bellardi *will* win the election, Jon. There's just too much prayer and good work going on here for it not to happen."

"I've read that Juanita Dunsmuir continues to gain in the polls. Some writers think she'll eventually overtake the senator."

Stevie shook her head. "She's still almost 15 percentage points behind with a little over three months to go. After the debates in September, the margin will widen again—perhaps to twenty or thirty points."

"You really think it will?" Jon pressed.

"I have no doubt. When the people of this state see Senator Bellardi and Juanita Dunsmuir side by side, it won't even be a contest. During the debates, she won't have her loud music and famous friends along to charm the audience. Her liberal views will sound ridiculous next to the senator's high ideals

169

for this state. I think the election in November will be a mere formality."

Jon nodded slightly. Then he alternately stared into his tea and cautiously sipped it. A Corelli trumpet sonata wafted softly from the stereo speakers. The muffled sounds of supersonic fighter jets and exploding nuclear warheads could be heard from Collin's room down the hall.

Stevie watched Jon furtively for a response. In the past, when she expressed an opinion to Jon, pleasant conversations sometimes deteriorated into arguments, especially if Jon did not fully share her view. Stevie no longer needed 100-percent agreement from Jon to feel good about herself. Yet she still valued his approval more than she cared to let on.

After several moments, Stevie filled the silence: "I believe I did what God wants me to do for the kids by moving up here, Jon. Remember how we prayed together for Dougie and Shawna and Collin when we first became Christians? We used to sneak into their rooms every night while they were asleep. We laid our hands on them and asked God to protect them from the 'nasty old world.' Remember?" She waited for a response.

Jon looked up. "Yeah, I remember," he said, nodding. "At least we did something right back then, didn't we?"

"Well, I now believe our prayers were only the beginning of what we should have done. I think we should have been more responsible about protecting our kids from the evil in the world. I can almost hear God trying to answer us back then: 'Hey, I'm doing my part. But why do you think I put those kids in your hands? Use the brains and resources I gave you to protect them from the evil world.'

"It's like Sodom and Gomorrah, Jon. God didn't send the angels there to *pray* for Lot and his family. He sent them to *remove* those people from that vile environment. That's what Daniel Bellardi wants to do in North California: provide a positive moral environment for kids like ours. Praying for Dougie, Shawna, and Collin was important, but it wasn't enough. We should have pulled them out of L.A. and become involved with political leaders like Senator Bellardi a long time ago. If we had, maybe our Dougie . . ." Stevie did not need to complete the thought to convey her meaning.

Jon studied his tea again. Stevie knew her strong comment had implicated him as a failure with their children. Watching him process her words, she could not read his response.

Finally he resumed eye contact. "How does Daniel Bellardi intend to keep North California 'morally positive'? People are people, Stevie. You can take them out of Sodom and Gomorrah, but you can't make them moral."

The change in Jon's tone might have been imperceptible to someone who did not know him, but it was obvious to Stevie. It signaled that there was a point behind his question about Senator Bellardi, and his point was probably in conflict with the conviction she had just expressed. His question could be the first subtle step in the transition from conversation to argument. Stevie did not want their pleasant discussion to end with harsh words. Neither did she want Jon to leave thinking that Daniel Bellardi was just another hotheaded, doomsaying religious conservative. Nor did she want Jon to think that about her.

"Legislation, Jon," Stevie answered, purposely avoiding an argumentative tone. "Every law imported from California will expire here within the next three years. It's part of the resolution. The new North California legislature is responsible for reinstating, replacing, or abolishing each of them. Senator Bellardi will use his political clout to put laws on the books that will encourage moral behavior and discourage immoral behavior. Once the laws are in place, the people who push drugs and abortion and homosexuality and assisted suicide and the like won't want to be here. Shawna and Collin will have the benefit of growing up in a world with a minimum of violence and immorality."

"Legislated morality," Jon summarized.

"For lack of a better term, yes," Stevie said.

"Toe the line in North California or suffer the consequences," Jon added. Stevie detected a slightly sharper edge to his voice.

"It worked with the Ten Commandments, Jon. Right and wrong were black and white, not a matter of personal preference or public opinion. You have to lay down the law and make it stick. That's Senator Bellardi's vision for the state. If people don't like it, they can leave."

"And these laws won't be challenged in the courts? It

sounds like Bellardi's proposed legislation could be interpreted as unconstitutional and discriminatory."

Stevie rolled her eyes. "Yeah, I've heard talk about that. There most certainly will be challenges by the ACLU and such, but there's a lot of interest in Congress to see if this will work. Even prominent judges and lawyers have cautiously voiced support of the laws if they can stem the tide of crime and take the strain off of the prison system. Constitutional interpretation could see a radical change of direction if the quality of life in North California improves. The laws would be here to stay."

Jon took a generous sip of tea. "All right, so let's say there's a physician in Redding—Dr. Smith or something. One of his elderly patients—Fred—has terminal cancer. Fred is in horrific pain, which will only worsen until he dies. He has no family, his insurance has run out, and he wants to die with dignity. So Fred summons Dr. Smith to administer the painless fatal injection. But a new law in North California makes mercy deaths illegal—the senator does intend to abolish mercy deaths, doesn't he?"

"Yes," Stevie said firmly. "Taking a human life is wrong. Isn't that what you believe?"

Jon paused thoughtfully then nodded, adding, "At least I *think* that's what I believe. But let me finish. Dr. Smith is a good doctor. He really cares for old Fred, and he agrees that nothing can reverse the disease or permanently relieve the pain. What should he do?"

Stevie answered immediately. "Refuse to administer the injection, because it's wrong."

"But Fred is in great pain."

"Give him drugs, sedate him."

Jon flashed an impish grin. "Fred has no more insurance. That means the state will have to pay for his drugs and hospital care until he dies. Not only for Fred, but for others like him. Your taxes will go through the roof. Will you pay to keep these people alive?"

Was Jon sparring playfully or arguing seriously about Senator Bellardi's platform? At this moment, Stevie could not tell. She gave him the benefit of the doubt. "You can't put a price on human life," she said, returning the grin. "I'll pay the taxes."

Jon pressed on. "But Fred doesn't want the drugs. He wants

to die. He demands that Dr. Smith transfer him to a clinic in San Francisco where mercy killing is still legal. If you're the doctor, do you let him go?"

"No, that's the same as killing him."

"But in South Cal mercy killing is legal, it's not wrong," Jon insisted.

Stevie argued, "It may be legal, but it's still morally wrong to take a human life."

Jon nodded. Then after a silent moment, he continued. "OK, now Fred says that if you won't help him die, he'll kill himself. Will you turn your back and let him slash his wrists?"

"Of course not. I'd be assisting in his suicide by default."

Jon leaned forward in his chair. "Steve, are you telling me that you'll keep this man in North Cal against his will, dope him up against his will, and physically restrain him if necessary, all in the name of doing the right thing? Isn't that just as wrong as letting the man die if he wants to?"

Stevie did not know what to say. Her mind was scrambling for an answer. She felt as if she were being backed into a corner. Thankfully, Jon didn't seem to be aiming for the jugular. He was sparring, not arguing. He was trying to make a point, and he seemed rather passionate about it.

Finally Stevie said, "Maybe Dr. Smith would be better off in a state that supported assisted suicide."

"No," Jon answered with animation. "Dr. Smith is just like you. He's a good person, maybe even a Christian. He wants his kids to grow up in a morally positive environment. But he also wants to be merciful to people like Fred."

"Well, it's a highly hypothetical situation, so—"

"OK, forget Fred and Dr. Smith for a minute," Jon cut in. "Here's another scenario. For the sake of discussion, let's say that in three years Bellardi's legislation is in place. Collin comes home from middle school one day and tells you that his science teacher, Mr. Jones, stated in class that he's gay. You check it out, and it's true: Mr. Jones is living with another man. What happens to Mr. Jones under the Bellardi regime?"

Stevie felt more confident about this answer. "Senator Bellardi doesn't believe homosexuals should occupy positions of influence over our children. And I wouldn't want Collin in his classroom. So I would hope the teacher would be removed."

"But Mr. Jones didn't try to influence anyone. He simply stated his sexual preference. He believes an individual's sexual orientation is personal."

Stevie shook her head. "But he *is* influencing his students—by example. Teachers are role models whether they intend to be or not. I want positive role models for our kids, and so does Senator Bellardi."

"So poor old Jones gets fired for being gay," Jon summarized.

"I have no sympathy for 'poor old Jones,'" Stevie retorted. "His lifestyle and his career are both his choice. He can teach school if he wants; he just can't do it in North California."

"Unless he changes his lifestyle," Jon said.

Stevie thought for a moment, then said, "Yes, if he changed his lifestyle—*really* changed—he might be able to keep his job."

Jon smiled confidently. Stevie suspected he was ready to spring another trap on her. He said, "Then what about Ms. Brown, Collin's English teacher?"

"OK, I'll bite. What *about* Ms. Brown?"

"Ms. Brown is single and straight, but she lives with her boyfriend. Does she also get fired as an undesirable role model? Or is adultery a more tolerable form of immorality in North California?"

Even though Jon was being kind about it, Stevie was tired of being baited. "I don't know, Jon, but I'm sure that Senator Bellardi does. He's a good man, a God-fearing, Bible-believing man. And he wants what's right for the people of North California."

Jon spoke before she could continue. "I'm not trying to hassle you or confuse you—really, I'm not. I just want you to know what you're getting into. I hope Dan Bellardi is everything you say he is, and I hope he can do some good up here. But right and wrong isn't always so black and white, Steve. You can't categorically say that all homosexuals and abortion doctors and marijuana growers ought to be arrested or shipped south. I just don't want you to go into this campaign with blinders on."

Stevie looked askance at him. "You sound like someone campaigning for Juanita Dunsmuir."

Jon was silent for a few seconds, as if trying to decide whether or not to speak his mind. Then he said, "I've been

174

reading a lot about the campaign since my last visit, and I don't doubt Bellardi's sincerity. But, to be honest, Steve, if I lived here, I might have to vote for Dunsmuir."

Jon's words pierced Stevie like an icy lance. It was worse than being disagreed with; it was betrayal. Stevie knew the difference. All the squabbles and arguments she and Jon experienced through their marriage could be categorized as disagreements. But being blamed by him for Dougie's death—no matter how much happened to be the truth and in spite of the fact that she too had blamed him—was betrayal. With this statement about Juanita Dunsmuir, no matter how well he meant it, Jon again took the adversary's position. How dare he accept her hospitality and then side with the opposition.

Stevie knew that Jon intended to explain himself, but she did not want to listen. Before he spoke again, she stood and said, "You're entitled to your opinion, but I don't think one more vote will help Juanita Dunsmuir. Now, if you'll excuse me, I have some reading to do. The linens for the Hide-A-Bed are in the hall closet." Then Stevie went to her room.

The four girls laughed until their sides ached and their faces were wet with tears. The clip from the video Terilyn had cued up for them was not even intended to be funny. Rather, it was a long, steamy love scene. Terilyn started giggling at the beginning of the scene. "This cracks me up," she said. "Can you believe it? Guys actually get turned on watching this stuff. Look at them. They're like a couple of animals flopping around in heat. Can you imagine doing something like that?" Soon Terilyn, Josie, Alexis, and Shawna were hanging on each other and howling with laughter.

Shawna's hilarity was greatly exaggerated by pangs of guilt and embarrassment. No way would she admit to her mother that she watched this stuff. And Shawna doubted that Terilyn's mother, if she had been home, would have allowed the girls to watch it. Shawna could hardly believe what she was seeing. It was raunchy, the stuff you had to rent from the back room of the video store. But she was not about to be a goody-goody in front of her new friends, who were so fun to be with. And at least they were in agreement with her that they would not want to be involved in the sort of behavior they were witnessing on the screen. Shawna was especially relieved about that, particularly after Terilyn's comments about skinny-dipping being a "spiritual experience." *I'm so glad my new friends aren't like Destiny or Rik,* Shawna told herself. *The stuff in this video is the type of thing they used to talk about all the time.* So Shawna allowed herself to become swept up in the infectious, irreverent craziness until the wild scene in the video clip was over.

"I've got to go," Shawna said as the hilarity subsided. "My mom thinks I only came to say good-bye."

"Oh, don't go on that lame vacation with your dad, Snowy," Terilyn pleaded comically. "It won't be any fun around here without you."

"Yeah," Josie agreed. "You can't take off without us. The three dwarfs don't know what to do without the princess around."

Shawna smiled at her three friends. "I'll miss you guys too," she said honestly. "But it's only a week. I'll be back next weekend."

"Well, stay out of trouble while you're gone, Snowy," Alexis warned with a laugh. "And especially stay away from guys like we just saw on that video."

"That's for sure," Josie added. "They're animals. Save yourself for someone special—someone *wise* and *mature* who can *guide* you into a more meaningful life."

Josie's emphasis on certain words seemed to send all three of the dwarfs into another fit of laughter, one Shawna did not understand and joined only halfheartedly.

"Don't worry," she said. "I have no intention of getting involved with any guys like we just saw. Besides, I'll be with my dad, remember? Any guy who wants to date me when he's around would have to submit to fingerprinting and a background check."

The girls laughed again. "We'll be thinking of you while you're gone," Terilyn said, still smiling. "You do the same, OK?" She glanced over at the other girls, then back at Shawna. "We can stay *connected* in our thoughts, you know."

There was that word emphasis again, something the dwarfs all seemed to understand but that went right past Shawna. "Sure," she answered. "I'll be thinking of you."

176

Walking back to her apartment in the warm night air, Shawna frowned. Had she just imagined it, or was there some hidden meaning to the words they had emphasized: *wise, mature, guide, connected?* She sighed and shook her head, even as she remembered the scene on the beach the previous day. She had asked Josie and Alexis what they were doing and why they had not responded when she called them, but their answer was vague—something about meditating—and they had changed the subject before Shawna could pursue it. She could not help but wonder if their unexplained behavior at the lake was somehow tied in with today's emphasized words and their periodic references to "spiritual experiences." Somehow Shawna was sure the spiritual experiences Terilyn and the other two dwarfs referred to had little or nothing to do with what she had been taught in church, but she could not imagine what else they might mean.

Shawna sighed again. It seemed the more she knew of her new friends, the more amazed she was at how different they were. Destiny and the Lindley Belles were obsessed with boys. The three dwarfs, even though they did talk and act a little weird sometimes, just wanted to hang out with her and have fun. Overall, she felt a lot safer with them than she had with Destiny or Rik, in spite of the dwarfs' occasional ventures on the wild side, like skinny-dipping, beer drinking, or watching raunchy videos.

Shawna decided to keep her questions about her new friends to herself. Her mother certainly did not need to know about the video, and the less she knew about Terilyn, Josie, and Alexis, the freer Shawna would be to find out on her own what made them tick. She tingled with a reckless sense of adventure about her closeness to her Shasta Commons friends. She had felt this way before that night at Lakeside Pines and during other adventures with Destiny Fortugno. But at least now she was smart enough to keep herself out of trouble.

20

Monday
July 26

STEVIE WOKE herself up crying. It was barely light outside, so she tried to go back to sleep. It was no use. Vivid images from another dream about Dougie were burned into her consciousness. Rarely a month went by that Stevie didn't dream about her firstborn child. No matter what else was portrayed, her dreams always concluded with the scene in the emergency room at Northridge Hospital: A limp, seventeen-year-old body stripped to the waist, pasty white tinged with blue; ER staff dejectedly backing away from the table after a frantic but futile attempt at resuscitation; lifesaving appliances still attached but useless.

As during the real event almost three years earlier, in her

dreams Stevie struggled to reach Dougie's side. If she could just touch him gently and kiss him on the forehead, he would awaken for her as he had so many mornings of his brief life. But Stevie had been restrained in near hysteria outside the ER on that dark day. In her fitful dream again this morning, she could not reach her son. The doctor's solemn announcement always stirred her awake: "We did everything we could. I'm sorry."

This morning, in the first few moments of consciousness, Stevie dabbed her eyes and nose with a tissue and ruminated on those words. *I know the doctors did everything they could. But did I do everything I could before he reached the hospital?* Stevie knew better than to evaluate her parenting at a vulnerable moment like this. Even minor flaws and failures appeared monstrous to her. But she could not completely quell recurrent yearnings for a second chance with her son. Other parents made much worse mistakes and their children survived. She knew she could do better if only she had another opportunity.

A hot shower, a cup of coffee, and several minutes reading her Bible and praying always helped clear Stevie's head after a rough night. At the top of her prayer list this morning were Shawna and Collin, who were in Newport, Oregon, with their father. Stevie welcomed a week to be alone and get some work done, but her maternal concern for Shawna and Collin had risen a notch since Jon's disturbing statement about Juanita Dunsmuir. Stevie prayed that the kids' minds would be protected from any kooky ideas their father might try to plant.

Stevie was dressed for the day and writing ad copy by seven. Shortly after nine she was on the phone to a couple of prospective clients. Even with the early start, she left a few tasks unfinished to keep her ten-thirty appointment with Eden Hunter-Upshaw at Senator Bellardi's campaign headquarters. Stevie was anxious to meet the communications staff and zero in on a task. She hoped that anything she could do to further the senator's campaign would also help mitigate the fresh pangs of guilt over not doing enough to keep Dougie from being captured by the evil culture.

Ms. Hunter-Upshaw announced with a beaming smile that a weekend background check had cleared Stevie to go to work on the campaign. After a few minutes of conversation on the mezzanine, the office manager led the new recruit downstairs to a cluster of cubicles in the back corner of the first floor. A large painted sign high on the back wall identified the area as the sleep shop of the former department store.

"A misnomer if I've ever seen one," Eden said with a small laugh, pointing to the sign. "Communications is one of the busiest corners of this building."

She introduced Stevie to Rhoda Carrier, the head of the department. Stevie was immediately distracted from the woman's roly-poly figure by a very flattering, tailored suit and an engaging smile. Rhoda said, "As soon as you complete the tour, I want to show you what we do here in the 'Sleep Shop.'" Then she returned to a phone call she had put on hold.

Stevie met a few more "key volunteers," as Eden termed them, in the communications area. They were as impeccably and professionally dressed as Eden and Rhoda, prompting Stevie to consider shopping for a new outfit or two for the campaign.

On her way back to Rhoda's office, Stevie passed a cubicle that had not been included in the tour. A quick glance inside caused her to stop at the doorway. A young man sat hunched over a small desk, turned away from the entrance and attacking the computer keyboard with his index fingers. He seemed completely oblivious to his surroundings and absorbed in his work. The likeness to Dougie was again apparent to her.

"Hello, Wes," she said. The kid did not flinch. Then Stevie noticed the tiny white cords running from ear buds in his ears to a jack in the mini-tower next to the CD slot. She stepped up behind the young man and tapped his shoulder. He snapped around wide-eyed as if touched by a live wire. Seeing Stevie, he smiled weakly, flipped off the CD player, popped the buds out of his ears, and politely stood.

"Hello, Wes," she repeated.

"Ah, hello. You look familiar, but I don't—"

"Stephanie Van Horne," she said, offering her hand. "Stevie. We met at the rally at Caldwell Park on the Fourth. Actually, it was before the rally."

Recognition dawned in the young man's eyes. "Oh, yeah.

You helped me with the folders and probably saved me from heatstroke." He took her hand barely long enough to qualify for a handshake. Then both his hands retreated to the pockets of his pleated gray slacks.

"So you didn't melt away after that scorching day in the park," Stevie said. "You're still with the campaign."

Wes shifted his feet and smiled self-consciously. "Yes, I'm still here."

"Well, I've signed on myself," Stevie said. "I'm going to help out in the communications department. So I guess we'll be coworkers."

"That's nice, that's—good," Wes said, as if hoping it was the appropriate response. Stevie again detected the lost-little-boy look in the way he avoided eye contact. She remembered the trait from the day in the park. *So like Dougie.*

She also recalled Wes being rather backward at maintaining a conversation. She picked up the slack. "So what do you do in the communications department?"

"I write letters."

"Letters?"

"Yeah. The senator receives stacks of mail—including E-mail and faxes—from people all over the country."

"Like fan mail?"

"Fan mail, hate mail, questions, applications for employment— you name it. The senator sends a personal reply to every one of them."

"You write all those letters?" Stevie asked, astonished.

"Not exactly. You see, I have a file of about four dozen form letters generated by the senator. For each letter he receives, I select the appropriate response, personalize it to the sender, and send it—letter for letter, E-mail for E-mail, fax for fax."

"Fascinating!" Stevie exclaimed.

"It's a no-brainer, really," Wes said, matter-of-factly. "Not much of a writing challenge."

"Oh yes, I remember now. You're a university lit major and newspaperman. I admire you for applying your talents to such a mundane task. You must be very committed to Senator Bellardi and his mission."

Eden appeared at the entrance to the cubicle. "So, you've already met our celebrity volunteer."

"Celebrity?" Stevie said, appraising the young man standing in front of her. Wes seemed uncomfortable with the added attention.

"He doesn't like us to make a big deal about it," Eden answered, "but you're talking to Daniel Weston Bellardi, Jr., the senator's son."

Stevie was speechless for several seconds. Wes looked suddenly disconsolate, like a little boy who had just dropped his double-scoop ice-cream cone on the sidewalk. Feeling the young man's embarrassment at being labeled the boss's son, Stevie ignored her own surprise and said for his benefit, "Well, no matter whose son he is, Eden, Wes impresses me as a fine young man and a dedicated volunteer."

Wes flashed a weak smile. In that instant Stevie sensed that she had made a friend.

Stevie knew she should be out making calls, but she stayed home all afternoon. She had a good excuse, she thought. It was nearly one hundred degrees outside, and the air-conditioning in Jon's Ranger did not work very well. Besides, visiting a client or prospective client in a pickup truck seemed inappropriate. But Stevie really rescheduled her calls because, after three stimulating hours at Senator Bellardi's headquarters, she could not keep her mind on her work.

She was impressed after another glimpse into the efficiency and professionalism of the senator's campaign. She was also excited at the prospect of working under the direction of Rhoda Carrier to publish the weekly *Prayer Fax* for clergy and *Fax-O-Gram* for the senator's supporters. Rhoda had outlined the goals for both pieces and solicited Stevie's suggestions. Together they produced several prospective layouts in less than an hour. Rhoda would help Stevie with the first few issues of *Prayer Fax,* and she promised to turn the weekly project over to Stevie as soon as she felt ready. The *Fax-O-Gram* would remain with Rhoda for the time being, but Stevie was free to contribute as she was able. Rhoda and Stevie even prayed together before their time together was over.

Stevie was especially anxious to get into her "homework." Eden and Rhoda had given her reams of material to study:

booklets published by Senator Bellardi, position papers, speeches, transcripts of interviews on *Face the Nation* and *Newsmakers*. Sitting at the computer ostensibly to prepare advertising proposals, she found herself leafing through the stack of Bellardi papers on her desk. She longed to curl up with a glass of iced tea and immerse herself in the information about the senator and his platform.

Chief among Stevie's distractions from work were her thoughts about the unassuming, enigmatic young man, Wes Bellardi. She was still in mild shock from discovering his true identity. No wonder he was on the platform at the Independence Day rally even though he looked so terribly at loose ends. He was first a conscript—not a trained volunteer—in his father's campaign, though he appeared to be a *willing* conscript. No wonder Wes was closemouthed about his relationship to the senator. Few kids his age welcome the pressures and notoriety of being the son of the leading candidate in a controversial campaign, especially if those kids—like Wes—are less gregarious.

Stevie's esteem for the young man had risen sharply over the last few hours. What an advantage to have been raised in the home of such godly parents. Here was a kid who grew up under the positive moral guidelines Stevie so desperately wanted to inculcate in her own two children. Here was a kid who was rescued from Sodom and Gomorrah before it was too late. Indeed, Wes Bellardi was the kind of kid Dougie Van Horne would be today had she and Jon—Stevie had abruptly terminated the thought at that point several times during the afternoon.

It was uncanny to her that Wes Bellardi resembled Dougie in so many ways. The senator's son was twenty; her son would have been nineteen. There was the faint physical resemblance: blow-away-in-a-stiff-wind physique, faraway eyes. Both young men were quiet, bookworm types, deep thinkers but apparently not deep talkers. Both had a yen for literature and a bent to write. Yet for whatever reason in God's abstruse wisdom, Wes was alive and Dougie was dead. Daniel and Patricia Bellardi had done their work well, and Wes was their reward. Stevie and Jon had done the best they knew how at the time and failed, and Dougie was their albatross.

184

Ruminating on this contrast again, Stevie was gripped by a new thought that launched her to her feet. The arresting concept burgeoned with a hope that, at first, Stevie found difficult to accept. Yet after pacing the quiet apartment for several minutes, she cautiously began to explore the premise that had arrested her.

Wes Bellardi was her second chance. She had failed with Dougie, but she was clearly doing the right thing for Shawna and Collin. She had uprooted the family and fled immoral Los Angeles to give them a better life. Wes Bellardi was confirmation from God that she was on the right track. Like Dougie, Wes had writing talent in need of cultivation. She could provide a measure of encouragement and guidance in that area as she would have with Dougie. What other reason could there be for the chance meeting at the rally, for the maternal instincts he awakened in her, and for the fact that they would be working together in the same department of the campaign?

This was not a parenting task, Stevie knew. By the looks of it, Senator and Mrs. Bellardi had that role well in hand. They were the kind of parents Stevie only hoped she could become for Shawna and Collin. Rather, she could be a kind of mentor to Wes in this one area, as she would have been to Dougie. She relished the possibility of contributing to this young man's life, not only to encourage him but to thank his parents for their contribution to her life and to thank God for the second chance.

Stevie returned to the computer and shut it down. She had not done all she needed to do, but her brain was done thinking about work. Tomorrow was another day.

It was dinnertime and Stevie was hungry. But she could not wait to get started on the intriguing pile of reading material from the campaign office. Grabbing a handful of cold carrot sticks from the refrigerator, she kicked off her shoes and settled into the sofa, launching into the stack of documents with anticipation, as if beginning a gripping novel.

21

Friday
July 30

"DAD, WHY DOES Mom want us to live in North California anyway? Why don't you move up here too? Then you could
marry Mom and we could be a family again. Wouldn't that
be great?" The words belonged to Collin, sitting in the front
passenger's seat of the Grand Cherokee while his father
drove. Shawna was in the backseat with a magazine.

Jon was stunned at the sudden barrage of knotty questions
seemingly out of the blue. He wondered if his nine-year-old had
been saving them up during their week-long tour of Oregon and
Washington. Today certainly was a good day for a long talk.
Moments ago, Jon, Shawna, and Collin had set out from Seattle
for a five-hour drive down Interstate 5 to Eugene, Oregon,

where they would spend the night with Jon's aunt and uncle. It was the first leg of their return trip to North California. Jon would have the children back in Redding by the next evening, then drive home to L.A. on Sunday.

"Which question first?" Jon responded, buying time to think about his answers. He noticed in the rearview mirror that Shawna was listening. Perhaps she had put her little brother up to asking the questions.

"The last one, about you and Mom," Collin said.

"Yeah, that one," Shawna chimed in eagerly from the backseat.

Jon would rather have chatted with the kids about the highlights of their trip. It would not take much to get Collin started on the topic of the Mariners game they attended in Seattle and how he almost caught a foul ball. And Shawna had been very excited about visiting a couple of outlet malls along the way and finding sandals, shorts, and a swimsuit on sale. All he had to do to get her started was mention that they would pass another outlet mall about halfway to Portland.

But Jon knew this was the perfect opportunity to talk with the kids, especially since they had broached the topics. Yet it was as difficult for him to talk about these issues as he expected it was for the kids to bring them up. "Sorry, but I have to start with the easiest question," Jon said, buying time to think about how to answer Collin's inquiry about reconciliation.

"In answer to why your mom wants to live in North California, the answer is *Ask your mom.*"

Shawna groaned, and Collin said, "Come on, Dad, we already know what Mom says."

Jon silenced them with an upraised hand. "OK, OK, I'll tell you why I think she moved to Redding. She loves you two so much that she wants you to grow up in the safest, healthiest possible environment. Big cities like Los Angeles and San Francisco and Seattle are centers for crime and pollution. North California is a much better place to live. Isn't that what she says?"

"Yeah, that's what she says," Shawna answered for both of them. "But what do *you* say?"

Jon searched for a diplomatic answer. "I think she has a good point. It is safer and healthier in North Cal."

"But Redding doesn't have a baseball team like the Dodgers or the Mariners," Collin interjected disappointedly.

"Or a Nordstrom's," Shawna added from the backseat.

"Everything has a downside, kids," Jon said. "Your mom is more concerned about protecting you from gang violence, drug pushers, and other criminals." He wondered if his children were driving toward asking permission to go back to L.A. with him.

Shawna said, "The new governor is going to make so many laws that nobody will want to live in North California. That's what my friend Terilyn says."

Jon recalled his conversation with Stevie on the topic of legislated morality. He admired Daniel Bellardi's goals for the new state; he wanted Shawna and Collin to grow up secure and happy just as much as Stevie did. But Jon still wrestled with the candidate's proposed hard-line policies. At the same time, he knew he had already offended Stevie with his thoughtless crack about voting for Juanita Dunsmuir. Expressing his doubts in front of the kids would likely get him into deeper trouble with their mother, and Jon did not want that.

"I'm sure Senator Bellardi has the state's best interests at heart, Shawna," Jon said, thinking he sounded like a politician himself. "It's impossible to please everyone. He's doing the best he can for the most people."

"Terilyn says he's Adolf Hitler reincarnated, trying to get rid of everyone he doesn't like," Shawna said.

"What do *you* think?" Jon asked.

Shawna was silent, flipping through her magazine. Finally she said, "I don't think he's Adolf Hitler. He doesn't have a mustache."

Jon chuckled at her dry humor.

Collin pressed on with his questions. "So why don't you move up here, Dad? If South California is so bad, you'd be safer here with us."

"Ah, question number two." Jon said nothing more until he had changed lanes to get around a knot of freeway traffic. They were just north of Tacoma now. "I've thought a lot about moving to North Cal. I love you kids very much, and I hate being so far away."

"We miss you too, Dad," Collin said. Shawna was silent.

"But I can't move, at least not yet."

"Why not? It's easy. You just put your stuff in a truck and drive it up here like we did."

Jon smiled at Collin's childish simplicity. "Mainly, Son, there's my job. I know I could find a job in one of the school districts in Redding or Red Bluff. But I'd probably take a serious cut in pay and lose a hunk of my retirement from the L.A. school district."

"Because you have ten years, right, Dad?" Collin put in.

"Tenure, dork, not *ten years,"* Shawna corrected, laughing.

Collin laughed too. "Oh yeah, *tenure,"* he said.

Jon smiled again and continued. "I don't want you kids to think this is only about job security and money, because it isn't, although I do have to consider such things in my decision making. It's also about *why* I work at Foothill High School. The kids on my campus have a lot of problems, serious problems. I'm trying to make things better for as many of those kids as I can. I think God put me there to be a positive influence. I can't just walk away from that."

"If you go, maybe God will put somebody else there," Collin suggested.

"That's true, Son. But I can't leave if God wants *me* to be that person. So, even though I'd rather be near you kids, I just don't feel it's the right time to move."

There were at least three more roadblocks between himself and North California, Jon knew, but he dare not share them with his children. These were more personal reasons they might not understand.

First, Jon did not *want* to move away. He had grown up in what used to be called Southern California, and the Valley had been his home since he left college. Despite its well-documented crime, pollution, and immorality, L.A. was not the "Sin City" so many people made it out to be. There was much about the area that was positive and worth preserving.

Second, there was Stevie. North California was her turf. Jon did not want her to feel that he was spying on her to make sure she was being an adequate single mother or competing with her for the affections of the children. No, it was better for all concerned if he stayed out of the way and let Stevie do her own thing in North California.

Third, Jon did not want to move because he hoped that Stevie might reconsider and bring the children back to Los Angeles. She might find that she missed the city. The kids might clamor for their old neighborhood and friends. Senator Bellardi might lose the election; or if he won, he might not fill Stevie's elevated expectations. It was ludicrous for Jon to move north only to pass Stevie on Interstate 5 in a U-Haul truck heading south.

Jon hoped Collin had forgotten about the third question. But as soon as the Tacoma Dome was out of sight, his son brought up the issue again in a slightly different way. "When you get married to Mom again, you'll *have* to move to Redding, won't you, Dad?"

This is why divorce is so traumatic, Jon thought. *Kids are incapable of understanding all the ramifications of a relationship gone sour. All they know is that it doesn't feel right when their parents no longer live together.* Jon had been through this before with the kids; he knew the dialogue by heart: *Mom and I still love each other, but in a different way; divorce means we no longer live together, that we lead separate lives; even though divorce is final, we both still love you and want the best for you.*

The discussion was always difficult for Jon. He struggled to explain himself well, but his attempts never seemed to fully satisfy Shawna and Collin, especially innocent Collin. But Jon knew he could not ignore the topic, so he drew a long, silent breath and began another run at it.

That's when Shawna tuned her dad out. Why listen to his attempt at an explanation again? There would be no remarriage, she knew. Her mother had made it clear by moving five hundred miles away, and her father had confirmed it by stating that he was not about to follow her. With the family dissolved for good, why try to make something positive out of it? If Collin needed to hear it again, fine. She did not.

Setting her magazine aside, Shawna retrieved a spiral-bound notepad and pen from her book bag. She browsed through several filled pages, letters she had written to Terilyn during the week. Shawna missed her wacky new friends much more than she thought she would. Why was she attracted to Terilyn, Josie, and Alexis? The three dwarfs were certainly nowhere near the center of Redding's social universe. In fact, Shawna did not think they had many other friends. If they did, she had never met them and the dwarfs never mentioned them. Shawna was also aware that her friends put little effort into selecting their clothes and fixing their hair, and none of them seemed to have discovered makeup yet. These were nice-looking, well-developed girls. With just a little more attention to style, the guys would be hanging all over them. But their interest in boys seemed to take a backseat to their interest in being together. To some extent Shawna was glad for that, but she still found it a little hard to understand.

Yet Terilyn, Josie, and Alexis were very bright, very funny, and very friendly—qualities that seemed to be missing from Destiny Fortugno and other Lindley Belles. True, they were not Christians, which their occasional daring behavior sometimes confirmed. But they obviously had some sort of interest in spiritual things or Terilyn wouldn't use the term so often. Surely that must be a point in their favor.

Shawna found a blank page in the notebook to enter her most recent thoughts to Terilyn. The weeklong letter—which she had kept secret from Collin and her father—chronicled not only the events of the vacation but her growing interest in knowing more about her new friends and what it was that made them different. *Not really different,* she corrected herself. *But special and unique. I really like that about the dwarfs.*

As her father in the front seat droned on about the finality of divorce, Shawna began her new entry:

Dear Terilyn: What you said last weekend is beginning to make sense. We really can stay connected in our thoughts. I have a feeling you're thinking about me right now, even while I'm writing to you. Is that what you mean sometimes when you talk about spiritual experiences? I'm not sure I understand, but I think I'd like to. Maybe you can be my guide. Let's talk about it when I get home.

22

Friday
July 30

STEVIE RETRIEVED the first dummy copy of *Prayer Fax* from the printer as soon as it emerged and inspected it proudly. Although she had only been associated with the campaign four days, her sense of ownership for the *Prayer Fax* project was practically maternal.

The content for the page—key moral issues at stake in the gubernatorial race—had been provided by Rhoda Carrier, who admittedly was not a skilled writer. At her supervisor's direction, Stevie had transformed the raw material into pithy, punchy, bulleted blurbs designed to evoke sympathy and prayerful support from Christian leaders. Sensing that her first attempt would be under close scrutiny by Rhoda and others, she had meticulously reworked and fine-tuned the page. She also inserted a couple of salient Bellardi quotes discovered during her week of self-directed indoctrination. When the page turned out to be a few lines short, she added a prayer request for the debates coming up in September.

Finally, Stevie had formatted the document with eye-catching graphics—including an impressive photo of the candidate—on the Master Publisher program. Gazing at the sheet now, she could not keep a smile of satisfaction from her face.

It was almost noon, at which time Stevie was expected to deliver a copy of *Prayer Fax* to Rhoda for approval. After making corrections, Rhoda would fax or E-mail the page to Price Whitten, the senator's media secretary, whom Stevie had yet to meet. Whitten would make the final call on the content. Once Rhoda returned the page to her, Stevie had until two o'clock to fold in all the corrections and broadcast-fax the page directly from the computer to nearly a thousand clergy and lay leaders throughout the state. Content from *Prayer Fax* would also be reformatted to an E-mail document and electronically dispatched to several thousand more Bellardi supporters and sympathizers in churches around the country.

Greatly pleased with her work, Stevie walked to Rhoda's cubicle and placed the sheet in her in-basket by the entrance. Rhoda, who was on the phone, acknowledged Stevie with a wave and a wink.

Returning to her tiny workspace, Stevie had nothing to do but wait. Having skipped breakfast to be in the office early, she was starving. She recognized that her stomach was churning as much from anxiety as from hunger. She had poured several hours into *Prayer Fax,* and she felt very good about what she had done. But would anyone else? Strictly from an advertising standpoint, *Prayer Fax* clicked. It looked sharp, it communicated concisely and clearly, it called for a response. Was her "secular" approach appropriate to the "spiritual" purpose of the piece? She would know in two hours or less.

Eager to eat something but not eager to eat alone, Stevie acted on an impulse. She slipped another copy of *Prayer Fax* in her handbag and made her way to a nearby cubicle. "Can you break away for a sandwich—my treat?"

Wes Bellardi, wearing the office uniform of slacks, shirt, and tie, swiveled his chair from the computer to face her. It took a few seconds for him to process the invitation. Stevie had only interacted with Wes on a few occasions since they were formally introduced by Eden, but she was already getting used to his thoughtful pauses. The quiet, sober young man apparently had a lot on his mind.

"Really?" Wes said at last, mirroring disbelief.

Stevie laughed. "Yes, I will really buy you lunch; that is, if you don't mind eating with someone old enough to be your mother."

After another pause, Wes shrugged and answered without emotion, "OK." Stevie smiled, wondering if he ever got excited about anything.

On their way out of the building, Stevie explained, "Actually, I have an ulterior motive. When we sit down, there's something I want you to look at—as a writer and as someone who knows the senator well."

Wes was silent until the pair stepped outside and simultaneously slipped on their sunglasses against the summer glare. "Then it's true what they say."

"Who is *they,* and what do they say?" Stevie asked.

"There's no such thing as a free lunch." Wes smiled from behind his shades, as if the sunshine had suddenly warmed him to being social. Stevie encouraged his humor with a good laugh.

They walked three blocks to Hoppy's, a hole-in-the-wall sandwich place on Market Street where Stevie had eaten with Rhoda on Wednesday. As they walked, Stevie probed Wes with generic how's-the-work-going type questions. She had stopped by his cubicle a few times during the week to say hello and encourage a stage-one friendship. But so far it was her questions and comments that kept their conversations alive. Stevie did not begrudge the effort; it had been like pulling teeth to get Dougie to talk as well.

Since discovering that Wes was Senator and Mrs. Bellardi's son and only child, Stevie yearned to ask more personal questions: What was it like to grow up in the home of such an influential leader? How have your parents' strong convictions shaped your own perspective of life? When did your Christian faith take root and blossom? Do you see yourself following the senator into politics at some point? Then there was another level of questions, which she attributed just to being a mother: Are you eating and resting well? Are you attending church and fostering spiritual growth? Do you have a girlfriend? But it was too soon to get so personal. Stevie did not want to jeopardize the relationship by being too curious.

"For what it's worth, I think this is very good," Wes said between bites of his Reuben. The *Prayer Fax* he had been reading was on the table between them.

Stevie teased him. "The sandwich or the prayer letter?"

"The sandwich is good, too, but I mean the prayer letter."

"Do the bulleted points clearly represent your father's position on these key issues?"

Wes glanced at the sheet again as he nibbled on a dill-pickle spear. "I'm not the world's greatest authority on Dad's platform. I've been away at school, you know—a little out of the North California mainstream. I'm still getting up to speed myself. But it sounds like him."

"From one editor to another, how about the language? Does it grab you? Motivate you? Anything you'd change for clarity or emphasis?"

Wes leaned away slightly and frowned. "Are you kidding? It looks perfect to me. Besides, you're the professional. I should be asking *your* advice about *my* writing."

Stevie exulted inside. *Yes! I would be happy to talk with you about your writing, Wes,* she responded silently. *Dougie and I had some wonderful conversations about what he was reading and writing. I see some of him in you, a creative mind struggling within the restraints of a mundane existence. Captured by the evil culture around him, Dougie never found his way out. But you can, Wes, and I can help you.*

Stevie restrained herself and probed gently. "What do you like to write?" she asked. Wes seemed engrossed in rearranging the potato chips into a design on his plate, so she supplied some options for him. "Poetry? Fiction? Essay? Satire?"

After eating one of the chips that didn't fit the design, he said, "Poetry mostly. A few short stories."

"What kind of themes?"

"Just . . . life, I guess."

"I'd like to see your writing someday," she said casually.

Wes waved away the request. "It wouldn't interest you. It's very amateurish."

"I'm not a writing critic, Wes. I don't want to edit it or correct it. I'd just like to see it. Is that OK?"

Wes took a large bite of his sandwich, conveniently unable to answer her for a minute. She waited for him to chew and swallow. Finally he said, "I don't think so. At least not now. Maybe—someday."

"Fine, no pressure, whenever," Stevie said. Then she occupied herself with a forkful of tuna salad. Dougie had also been very defensive about his writing, and she had respected his privacy. In Dougie's case, however, she wished she had been more inquisitive; it might have prevented a tragedy. But Stevie had no cause to intrude on Wes's privacy.

After two minutes of silence, Stevie tried a different tack. "Once I have the *Prayer Fax* project running smoothly, they might want me to take on the *Fax-O-Gram*—you know, the weekly bulletin for key constituents and supporters. I don't think I can handle them both. Would you be interested in getting involved in something like that?"

Wes studied his plate and ate potato chips as Stevie continued. "There would be more room for creativity than you have cranking out form letters." Wes looked at her as if ready to speak, then his eyes retreated to the plate. Stevie filled the void again. "Of course, I'm assuming that you have the freedom to try other things, this being your father's campaign."

"Yeah, Dad cuts me a little slack once in a while," Wes said without looking up. "But I don't think he'd turn over to me something as important as a *Fax-O-Gram*."

"I'm not talking about your taking over. I'm talking about the two of us working together on it for the rest of the summer, until you go back to school. It would be a great experience for you."

Wes shrugged slightly. "I won't be going back to school, at least not until winter term."

"Why not?"

"Dad wants me to stay on through the election."

It was Stevie's turn to pause and ponder. "How do you feel about that?"

Wes shrugged again. "OK, I guess. It's something Dad and Mom need me to do."

Stevie's esteem for the shy young man rose another notch. "Wes, that's wonderful of you to postpone college to help with the campaign." Characteristically, Wes had no response. Stevie smiled and asked again, "So will you at least think about working on the *Fax-O-Gram* with me?"

Wes nodded slowly. "Yeah, I'll think about it."

Stevie paid the bill and they headed back to the office. They strolled in silence until Wes asked, "Why do you want *me* to work on the *Fax-O-Gram*? There are other volunteers around with more writing experience."

Stevie considered her answer. It seemed too soon in their relationship to tell Wes about his uncanny resemblance to Dougie. And she certainly wasn't going to say anything about the crazy maternal urge that resemblance provoked in her. Wes already had a wonderful mother; he did not need another one. Nor did she want him to think her interest was even remotely romantic, because it most assuredly was not. So what was left to tell him that was completely true?

At last she said, "In junior high school, I discovered that I was pretty good in composition, while being poor in grammar. I never did get the hang of diagramming a sentence, and I still can't tell you what a gerund is. But I loved to write stories, and my English teacher, Mr. Jager, recognized that I had a gift for writing. He said I was like a pianist who played beautifully by ear but couldn't read a note.

"So Mr. Jager offered me a challenge. He said he'd give me extra credit for every original story I read in class. I was in heaven! I tortured my classmates with at least one new story a week. By the end of the year, my extra-credit points in composition more than made up for my poor grades in grammar and I got an A in the class. Thanks to Mr. Jager's encouragement, I've been writing ever since."

They stopped outside the main entrance to Bellardi headquarters. The digital readout on the bank at the corner read ninety-seven degrees. Stevie concluded her explanation with what she hoped would convince Wes to join her on the project. "I guess I've always wanted to give something back, to be

198

an encouragement to other young writers where I have the opportunity."

Without a word, Wes opened the glass door and they stepped into the cool building. As Stevie excused herself to go to the rest room, he finally said, "Thanks."

"You're welcome," Stevie said pleasantly. She could not tell if he was thanking her for lunch, for the chat, for offering him a job on the *Fax-O-Gram,* for trying to encourage him as a writer, or what. But any kind of a positive response from Wes Bellardi was a victory, she decided.

Returning to her desk, Stevie noticed the flashing light on the phone alerting her to voice mail—her first message as a volunteer. She lifted the receiver and tapped in the code to retrieve it.

"Stephanie, this is Price Whitten, Senator Bellardi's media secretary. I just received a copy of *Prayer Fax* from Rhoda Carrier, and she tells me that you're largely responsible for this week's issue. I'm very impressed. This is excellent work. I don't see how it could be any better. I'm so pleased to have you on our team, and I look forward to meeting you the next time we're both in the office. Keep up the good work."

Stevie felt a surge of exhilaration that nearly lifted her off the chair. Had Price Whitten asked her to quit her advertising job and work on the campaign full-time, she might have been tempted to do it.

23

Monday
September 6

"I READ your letter."

The announcement caught Shawna by surprise and she flinched, startled at the interruption to the silence the two friends had shared for the past several minutes. She and Terilyn sat on separate straw beach mats at the water's edge, gazing blankly at the shimmering lake and baking in the afternoon heat. Their deeply bronzed bodies and faded swimsuits were silent testimony to a summer spent in the sun. It was Labor Day, and even mammoth Shasta Lake seemed overcrowded with boxy, meandering houseboats and noisy ski boats. Alexis and Josie were out on the lake with Jack and Charlotte. As Shawna focused her eyes and panned the horizon, she could see them on giant tubes in the middle of the lake, bounding over the choppy surface behind Uncle Jack's boat.

"I figured you did," she answered. Terilyn had not mentioned the letter Shawna sent while she was on vacation, and she did not want to bring it up in case Terilyn thought she was a complete loser. She tried to look relaxed and confident, stretching lazily and turning over to lie on her stomach. Terilyn joined her.

"I'm glad you're starting to see things more clearly," Terilyn said.

Shawna frowned but did not raise her head. "What do you mean?"

"I mean," Terilyn answered, "you're starting to realize that what you've been taught all your life isn't necessarily the only truth—and may not even be the truth at all."

Now Shawna was really confused. She raised up on her elbows and looked at her friend. Terilyn's head was resting on her arms, but her eyes were open and fixed on Shawna. "What are you talking about?" Shawna asked. "How can there be more than one truth, and how do you know what I've been taught?"

Terilyn smiled at her friend. "Don't get all freaked out," she said. "What I'm trying to tell you is, I think you're breaking out of your shell, sort of expanding your horizons; know what I mean?"

Shawna did not know what Terilyn meant. "No, I don't," she answered. "I don't have a clue what you're trying to say."

Terilyn lifted her head, her smile gone now as she looked at Shawna with an obvious intensity. "What I'm trying to say, Snowy, is that you're starting to think for yourself—and that's good. There's a lot more to life than just what we can see and feel and touch, although those things are important and can be used to lead us into something deeper. But we've got to take the next step if we're ever going to realize our potential."

Shawna's frown deepened. She was intrigued by what Terilyn was saying, but still confused. "I don't get it," she admitted. "I'm trying to follow you, really. But it's just not working."

Terilyn's smile returned. "It takes a while," she said. "Alexis and Josie and I are just starting to figure things out ourselves, and we've been experimenting for a year or so now."

"Experimenting? In what?"

"Spirituality," Terilyn answered, her warm brown eyes taking on a faraway look. "The *real* world. Eternal things." Her eyes came back into focus. "That's where we fulfill our potential, Snowy, because that's where the power is. Now do you follow me?"

Shawna wasn't sure if she was following her exactly, but at least she was getting a better idea of what wavelength Terilyn was on. "Eternal things," she said. "Yeah, I guess I do know what you mean . . . sort of. But . . . I didn't think you were into going to church or—"

Terilyn interrupted her with a laugh. "No way," she said. "I never set foot in the place, unless my mother drags me to a funeral or a wedding or something." She leaned closer. "I'm not talking about religion the way your mom thinks of it, or the way she's tried to brainwash you into believing that hers is the only way and anyone who doesn't believe like her is wrong. I'm talking about real spirituality and power and connecting with a spirit guide—"

Shawna was on her feet before Terilyn could finish. "I don't care what kind of spirituality you're talking about," she said. "I don't like you saying my mom's trying to brainwash me. Just because she takes me to church doesn't mean she's brainwashing me."

Terilyn sat up and raised her eyebrows. "Oh, I suppose you go by choice?"

Shawna squirmed. "Well, not exactly," she admitted. "But the people there are really nice and—"

"And I'm not?" Terilyn asked.

"I didn't say that."

"I know you didn't," Terilyn said. "But think about it. If you go to a church that says only people who believe a certain way are right, what does that say about the rest of us?" She stood and looked into Shawna's eyes. "It's not a very tolerant attitude, Snowy. One way or no way. One truth or no truth. Do you really believe that? Or can't you admit that maybe— just maybe—there's more than one truth, and that each of us has a right to choose what that is?"

Shawna felt trapped. She sensed there was something wrong with Terilyn's logic, but she couldn't put her finger on it. "I . . . I guess so," she mumbled, suddenly wanting to get far away from Terilyn and her discussions on spirituality and truth. But for some reason she just could not get her legs to move.

Terilyn smiled. "You're starting to see it, aren't you—the bigger picture?" Shawna didn't respond. "That's OK," Terilyn went on. "You just keep thinking about what I said and it'll start making sense to you. And when you're ready, the four of us can talk about it."

"The four of us?" Shawna's green eyes were open wide. "You mean . . . Alexis and Josie feel the same as you about . . . truth?"

Terilyn laughed. "Of course they do. In fact, most people do. You've been listening to your mom and that Hitler-Bellardi guy too long. Like that lady candidate, Juanita, says, 'You gotta learn a little tolerance.' It's the only way, Snowy. Trust me."

Shawna wasn't sure she was ready to trust Terilyn—yet. But even as she tried to think of some argument—or even a Bible verse—to counter her friend's words, Terilyn's logic was beginning to make more sense all the time.

"I . . . I gotta go," Shawna said. "Really. I'm going to take a walk and I'll . . . I'll talk to you later."

"No problem, Snowy," Terilyn said. "Just let me know when you're ready."

"I want to go to the carnival!" Collin had been pestering Stevie incessantly for the last hour. His irritating whine was escalating to a mild tantrum. Mother and son trudged along in a jostling stream of spectators departing from the recently completed downtown Labor Day parade.

Having battled the crowd and the heat for two hours so Collin could watch the parade, Stevie was in no mood to argue, so she laid down the law. "Collin, no carnival. I have work to do in the office, and you're coming with me."

"Why do I have to go to the office? I hate the office."

"I already told you: Because Shawna is at the lake, and there's no one to stay with you."

"It's boring at the office. There's nothing to do."

"I want you out of the heat and resting for a while," Stevie said, grasping for an excuse. "You can play with the video games you brought."

"It's a holiday, Mom. Other people don't have to work today."

"It's only for a couple of hours, Collin. Then we'll go to the Manns for a barbecue and swimming."

"I don't want to go to the Manns. I want to go to the carnival."

"Collin, not another word!" Stevie snapped, shaking him by the shoulder. She felt herself beginning to unravel. She hated making Collin hang out at the office, but until school started she had no choice. Stevie had saddled Shawna with baby-sitting her brother an average of twenty hours a week since beginning her volunteer work for Senator Bellardi. Her daughter deserved a day at the lake with her friends. But Stevie didn't have time to waste at the carnival. The advertising work was piling up at home, and clients were getting antsy. Stevie had a full week of calls starting tomorrow. So to get a head start on this week's critically important editions of *Prayer Fax* and *Fax-O-Gram,* she had to start today. Collin would just have to tough it out. After all, she was doing all this for his benefit.

Evie Mann, another campaign volunteer, and her eleven-year-old son, Brett, bumped into Stevie and Collin near the entrance to the Bellardi building. "You don't have to work today, do you, Stevie?" Evie asked.

"Just for a couple of hours," Stevie answered, hoping she could keep Collin occupied that long. "But we're still planning to come over later for the barbecue."

Evie turned to Collin. "And what are you going to do while your mother works?"

Collin turned to Stevie with a pained expression as if to say, "This is your fault, so you have to tell her."

Stevie said, "He's going to stay with me. He brought his video games."

Brett piped up, "We're going to the carnival. They have the Corkscrew this year. It's the coolest."

Evie addressed Collin again. "Wouldn't you rather go to the carnival with Brett and me?" Before the boy could answer, Evie turned to Stevie. "We'd be happy to have him along. Then we'll go back to the house and the boys can swim. You can join us for the barbecue when you're finished."

Stevie opened her mouth to refuse the offer, but Collin

halted her, his eyes pleading desperately for clemency. Stevie yielded. "As long as it's no trouble, Evie."

"No trouble in the least. Brett will have someone to enjoy the rides with."

Opening her wallet, Stevie handed Evie a twenty-dollar bill to cover her son's expenses. Collin thanked his mother with a big hug and kiss, then Evie and the boys disappeared into the crowd flowing toward the carnival at the end of the street.

Bellardi staffers needed both a key and a security card to enter the first set of glass doors when the office was closed. Then each individual had to submit to a retina scan in the lobby in order to use key and card on the second set of doors. At first Stevie thought the expensive, high-tech system was a little much. Then she began to hear more about threats on the senator received by mail and phone—threats that were kept from the general public as much as possible. Others on the staff had quietly reminded her that the issues in the campaign were highly volatile, not only in North California but throughout the country. Strong forces were at work to thwart Bellardi's successful candidacy. Some of those forces were capable of employing violence to achieve their goals.

Although most threats were considered a hoax, Senator Bellardi's security was not taken lightly. He had two full-time bodyguards: a former Secret Service officer and a former local cop. The CHP was also present in force wherever he traveled. A small, private security force, paid by the senator, was stationed at the ranch on rotating shifts. Volunteers were solemnly briefed about the possible dangers of being associated with the campaign, and a few of them had decided to leave the office. Others, like Stevie, strengthened their resolve to serve in view of the high stakes of securing North California for decency. She was in this for her kids, and she was not about to bail out now and forfeit their future to invisible troublemakers.

Stevie had learned a lot during her first month in Senator Bellardi's campaign headquarters. The honeymoon was definitely over, and the romance of working for a nationally recognized political leader had long since been replaced by the cold reality of weekly deadlines, tension among coworkers, and budget crunches. But Stevie had not been dissuaded.

Indeed, *Prayer Fax* and *Fax-O-Gram* had become her passion; and coaching her apprentice, Wes Bellardi, was a delight.

The advertising business had deteriorated to a mundane but necessary intrusion into what she really wanted to do. Between Stevie's two major commitments, time with Shawna and Collin had been at a premium. Yet Stevie had paid the price, trying to compensate for the lack of quantity time with the kids by providing quality time. They might not understand her restricted availability to them now, she reasoned, but in years to come they would understand—and thank her for it.

Passing through the security system successfully, Stevie entered the quiet building. The office was officially closed for the holiday, but a few casually dressed volunteers—like Stevie—had stopped by to put in a few hours.

Even though the office was practically deserted, the state-wide campaign was in high gear. Senator and Mrs. Bellardi were stumping the North California coast from Ukiah to Arcata this weekend with a string of picnics, parades, and speeches at shopping center rallies. The eight-person debate team was holed up in a suite at the Red Lion hammering out arguments and rebuttals for the first in a series of televised clashes between the two candidates. Hundreds of grassroots volunteers, from Christian elementary school students to the Senior Saints from the Baptist church, were marching door-to-door and farm-to-farm across the state passing out free bumper stickers and ballpoint pens. Stevie appreciated the efforts of all involved, but she had far too much on her own plate to think much about what was going on outside *Prayer Fax* and *Fax-O-Gram*.

Stevie glanced into Wes's dark cubbyhole on her way to her office, knowing he was not in town. Wes had accompanied his parents to the coast at their request, although he had confided to Stevie that he disliked being in the fishbowl. She found her shy young friend's transparency refreshing. Had she not been told who he was, Stevie would never have guessed Wes to be the son of the dynamic, self-confident senator.

Stevie snapped on a desk lamp and booted up the computer. As the machine hummed through its warm-up cycle, she retrieved a thick file of data on the key debate issues. For the rest of the month, both fax bulletins would focus on these issues. She felt a large weight of responsibility for heightening public sentiment in support of the traditional values of morality, voluntary prayer in schools, no-parole sentences for convicted drug dealers and sex offenders, and mandatory capital punishment for convicted first-degree murderers. She also hoped to raise public ire against legalized marijuana, abortion, euthanasia, minority rights for homosexuals, and pornography in the print and broadcast media. Stevie's goal for this afternoon was to grind out the rough drafts for both sheets so she could spend the week shoring up her advertising business.

"Good afternoon, Stephanie."

Poised over the keyboard and intent on beginning her task, Stevie was startled by the surprise greeting. Her eyes snapped up to find the senator's campaign manager, Robert Johnstone, standing at the entrance to her cubicle. Hoping to cover her surprise and embarrassment over her less-than-professional apparel, she said, "Mr. Johnstone, I didn't expect to find you here today."

In reality, Robert Johnstone was seldom in the office. On the days when he was present, he was in meetings with his lieutenants and all but oblivious to campaign foot soldiers like Stevie. She understood. As Senator Bellardi's warlord, Johnstone was consumed with the large picture and totally committed to getting things done through chain of command. With the senator's lead over Juanita Dunsmuir continuing to erode, Johnstone had no time to stroll through the cubicles encouraging the troops. He had a battle to wage, and he was intent on waging it successfully. Consequently, Stevie had spoken with him only briefly on two occasions. She was mildly surprised that he even remembered her name.

"I'm not here, really," he explained with a soft smile. Stevie had not seen him smile before. She liked what it did to his gray eyes. "I'm on my way to the chopper. Meeting the senator in Arcata for the rally." Robert Johnstone's concession to the holiday and the heat was a mist green dress shirt instead of the customary starched white, and a floral print tie instead of the standard business check pattern. He carried his suit coat neatly folded over one arm.

Stevie grasped for something to say. "I . . . I hope it goes well, Mr. Johnstone."

"I'm sure it will," he said. "And please, call me Robert. Mr. Johnstone is OK most of the time, but with you, it just makes me feel old."

He smiled again and Stevie flushed. "I . . . certainly didn't mean to make you feel old," she said, adding a smile of her own. "And I'll make it a point to call you Robert from now on, if you'll call me Stevie."

Robert raised an eyebrow. "Stevie," he repeated pensively, then shook his head. "No, I don't think I can do that."

Stevie's eyes opened wide. "Why not?"

"It just doesn't fit you," Robert explained. "You're classy, professional. You're . . . Stephanie. Would you mind terribly if I stick to calling you Stephanie?"

Stevie flushed again, wondering how anyone could think she looked classy or professional in the casual attire she wore today. "Well, no, of course not. Stephanie is . . . fine."

"Thank you."

Not only was Stevie a bit uncomfortable about their exchange, she was also surprised that he had stayed to talk as long as he had. She had never seen this side of Robert Johnstone, nor had she heard anyone else in the office speak of him in this way. He always seemed to be on a tight schedule, and she had fully expected him to rush away as quickly as he had appeared. But even now he remained standing at the entrance to her small office. "Stephanie, the senator and I appreciate very much your contribution to the campaign," he said, switching the conversation back to a more professional note, for which Stevie was grateful. "The fax bulletins are excellent—very professional and very effective. Your good work is critical to the success of the senator's campaign."

Stevie flushed with pride. "Thank you. I'm just happy to help in some small way."

"Your role is anything but small, Stephanie," Robert said. "Do you realize how many people you touch with your work? You may send fewer than ten thousand faxes each week, but the individuals who receive them influence hundreds of thousands of voters. Communications is the nerve center of this campaign."

"Thank you . . . Robert."

Resting his shoulder against the corner of the upholstered

panel, he slipped a hand into the pocket of his slacks. It appeared he was settling in for a long stay.

"So, how are your children adapting to North California?" he asked.

"You know my children?" Stevie said, surprised at the personal question and flattered by his concern.

"I know *about* your children. Rhoda says they're great kids. A boy and a girl, right?"

"Right." Stevie could not believe she was talking family with Senator Bellardi's right-hand man.

"And they like North California?"

"Yes, mostly. They miss some things about L.A., but they're settling in. Getting into school and meeting some new friends will help."

"I'm sure that's true." Robert smiled again as he returned to his upright posture, obviously getting ready to leave. "Well, I have a helicopter to catch, but I do have one more question, if you don't mind."

"Of course not," Stevie answered, trying not to get lost in his captivating smile.

"May I ask you to dinner sometime, Stephanie?"

Stevie hadn't seen it coming. Totally blindsided, she was stunned speechless. The facts were immediately evident. Robert Johnstone had learned about the children from Rhoda. The communications supervisor must also have mentioned that Stevie was single. Johnstone was a widower, she had heard, having lost his wife to cancer. Was he in the habit of dating women in the office, women he barely knew? She had no clue. Had he been watching her, asking people about her? As flattered as she was by his attention, she did not want to think about it.

Silent seconds passed. Robert did not prolong the agony. "You're busy now," he said softly. "And I'm afraid I caught you off guard. Forgive me. We can talk about this later. Keep up the good work, Stephanie." Then he was gone.

Stevie held her head in both hands for a full two minutes. Several more minutes rolled by as she tried to refocus on the blank monitor awaiting her keystrokes. She rewrote the same sentence six times, then finally deleted it. She paced the tiny office, trying to clear her head. She should be grinding out copy right now, but her concentration had been shattered. She berated herself for acting like a schoolgirl. Then she dropped her head into her hands again, trying to block out the memory of that warm smile and those gorgeous gray eyes. *Dear God,* she prayed, *I don't need this, not now, not from him. What are you doing to me?*

24
Wednesday
September 8

A LONE FIGURE moved silently along the storefronts in the
night shadows. The bars were closed, and their bleary-eyed
patrons had long since gone home. Central Redding was
asleep. The seemingly invisible visitor had only to be alert to
the infrequent appearance of a patrol car on graveyard shift.

Nearing his destination, he hunkered down in a dark doorway to make preparations. Slipping a heavy work glove on his
right hand, he pulled from a gym bag two quart-sized vodka
bottles wrapped in old towels. Quickly removing the lid from
one bottle, he sprinkled two strips of cloth with the liquid contents. He recapped the bottle and tied a cloth strip tightly
around the neck of each bottle. Then he slipped a bottle in

each of the two deep pockets of a threadbare, thrift-store sport jacket. The air in the recessed doorway reeked of kerosene.

Checking the empty street once more, he sprang into action. He lifted a large hammer from the gym bag and moved to one of two large display windows at the front of the adjoining building. A huge banner across the face of the building read "Bellardi for Governor." Shielding his eyes with his left arm, he plunged the hammer and gloved hand into the glass, creating a shower of shards and splinters and leaving a gaping, jagged hole. The blow tripped the noisy alarm bell.

Grasping one bottle in his gloved hand, he ignited the wick with a butane lighter, then lobbed the bottle deep into the maze of office cubicles. It landed with a crash and a burst of flame. The second bottle was catapulted to another area of the office, where it also exploded into a fireball.

Pausing only a second to appreciate the spreading flames, the culprit scooped up his bag and hammer and sprinted down the sidewalk. Ducking unseen into a passageway between buildings, he disappeared into the darkness before the sound of the first siren reached his ears.

Stevie's plan for a couple of quiet, crack-of-dawn hours at her headquarters computer evaporated as soon as she saw the fire trucks, police cars, and television vehicles. Fire personnel were in the early stages of mop-up, and spectators rimmed the scene as if expecting more excitement. It was only six-thirty, and the temperature was already in the low seventies.

Approaching the building cautiously over broken glass and a tangle of fire hoses, Stevie gasped with each new discovery. The large display windows on either side of the entrance were completely broken out. Charred pieces of office furniture and computer equipment littered the front sidewalk. Peering through the cavernous openings, Stevie saw that the fire damage seemed contained to two large circles of office space on the main floor. Anything that survived the fire had surely been ruined by water. She was heartsick at the destruction and wondered about the cause.

"Stevie, over here." Stevie followed the voice to a knot of onlookers standing near a yellow pump truck. Rhoda Carrier was beckoning her. Several other Bellardi volunteers were there, two of them grieving to the point of tears. Stevie's coworkers had obviously dressed in a hurry to reach the scene. They wore jeans or shorts, T-shirts, and caps to cover their hair. Most were without makeup or jewelry. Having dressed for a long work day, Stevie felt conspicuously overdressed in an off-white business suit and low heels.

"It happened about three-thirty," Rhoda began, her round face drawn with disbelief. "Arson, they said. Somebody smashed the window and threw in a couple of firebombs."

"Firebombs? Arson?" Stevie exclaimed. "Was anyone hurt?" The warnings to the staff about the dangers of the campaign were suddenly well founded.

"No one was hurt, thank God," Rhoda said. "The main floor looks like a total loss. The mezzanine has a little smoke and water damage."

"It could have been a lot worse," said a slight, middle-aged woman Stevie didn't recognize. She was leaning against a man, thin and not much taller than herself, who Stevie guessed must have been her husband. His arm was around her shoulders. He was nodding in agreement.

"The automatic sprinklers never went on," he said, frowning. "The whole building could have gone up in smoke. But the fire department got here before the fire spread very far."

Stevie nodded. So much for the security of automatic sprinkler systems. Stevie was about to introduce herself to the couple when Rhoda spoke up.

"And thank God for backup files," she said. "I'm glad Eden insisted we back up our work and take it home."

Stevie was similarly relieved, so much so that she forgot the middle-aged couple who had turned and were beginning to move away into the crowd. Stevie always backed up her work, and she always carried backup disks in her briefcase.

"Does Senator Bellardi know about the fire?" Stevie wondered aloud.

"The senator and his wife were in Sacramento last night. Mr. Johnstone called their hotel about an hour and a half ago. He's meeting them at the helicopter and driving them out. The TV people are circling like vultures to get his reaction to the damage. He must be terribly upset. He doesn't need something like this just two weeks before the debates."

After commiserating over the tragedy for several minutes, Rhoda and Stevie agreed to meet at the city library later in the morning to discuss backup plans for the two fax bulletins. Rhoda promised to come with some ideas on rental equipment and temporary office space. Other departments in campaign headquarters would make similar arrangements to keep working under these conditions.

As the discussion concluded, Stevie turned to see Wes Bellardi standing alone in the street, staring at the fire-damaged building. Like others who had hurried to the scene, Wes looked to be just a few minutes out of bed. His shorts and tank top were rumpled, and the laces on his faded canvas deck shoes were untied. He had not shaved or run a comb through his hair. It was the first time Stevie had seen him without a dress shirt and tie. At last he looked like a university sophomore.

"Did you just hear the news?" Stevie asked, approaching him.

"The cop at the house woke me up about twenty minutes ago," Wes answered.

"Are you OK with . . . all of this?" she asked cautiously, motioning toward the fire-damaged building.

"You mean, am I concerned for my dad?"

"Yes, exactly."

Wes shrugged. "Sure. But I suppose I don't need to be. He always seems to land on his feet somehow."

"Will he be discouraged, angry . . . ?"

Wes raked his hair with his fingers, then jammed his hands in his pockets. "I don't know how he'll take it. Nothing quite like this has ever happened before."

They stood watching firefighters remove charred office panels from the building. The senator's insurance agent and the owner of the building were already on the scene itemizing the damage.

"I guess this means no faxing on Friday," Wes said.

Stevie had already contemplated the implications of the fire on their work. "Not necessarily. Everything is on disk. We can set up shop anywhere we can plug in a rented computer and a modem. It may be inconvenient, but it's doable." She smiled reassuringly. "We're not going to let some amateur pyromaniac derail the Bellardi Express."

"Amateur?"

"Of course. If the guy really wanted to burn the place down, he—or she—would have used something more potent than a couple of Molotov cocktails. If the sprinklers had come on like they were supposed to, the damage might have been limited to a couple of large holes in the carpet."

Wes seemed surprised. "The sprinklers didn't come on?" he asked. "Who told you that?"

Stevie thought for a moment before she remembered. "A middle-aged couple," she answered, scanning the crowd. "I didn't recognize them and I don't see them now, but—oh, there they are, over there, across the street."

Wes looked in the direction Stevie had gestured. "Oh, sure," he said. "The Denherders, Matthew and Lucy. They live out at the lake and take care of my dad's boats." Then he frowned. "But I wonder what they're doing here? I mean, I wonder how they heard about this?" He shrugged again. "Oh well, it doesn't really matter."

Together they turned their attention away from the Denherders and back to the fire-damaged building. They watched again in silence until Wes said, "Well, since everything's been backed up on disk, I guess this means we don't get the week off due to fire damage."

Stevie saw the crooked smile on Wes's face and was relieved that he seemed able to joke in the face of what could have been a real tragedy. "On the contrary," she assured him. "We get overtime."

Stevie spoke the words as lightly and with as much optimism as she could muster. But underneath the facade she was fighting a mild case of panic, even as she knew Wes must be. For Wes, the attack might seem a personal one. Although that was not true in her case, her already busy schedule did not allow for spending overtime on the campaign. She was already behind on client calls. The only soft spot in her schedule was the time she had promised to the kids. She might have to negotiate with them on that.

Stevie pulled her thoughts back to Wes. He looked so discouraged. "Hey, partner," she smiled, punching him playfully on the arm. "We'll get it done. Where's your pioneering spirit?"

Characteristically stoic, Wes answered, "I'm not sure I have any. My father does all the pioneering in our family. Mom and I just ride in the wagon and hope for the best."

Senator Bellardi's burgundy Town Car arrived moments later. Reporters and camera operators swarmed to it like hummingbirds to a succulent blossom. Emerging from the front doors were Robert Johnstone, his aide, who did the driving, and one of the senator's bodyguards. The other bodyguard was first out of the back door, followed by Mrs. Bellardi and the senator. The men were dressed in stylish summer suits, and Patricia was resplendent in a pastel silk blouse and flowing skirt. Stevie joined the growing throng of onlookers moving toward the car, trying not to focus too intently on Robert's good looks while, at the same time, congratulating herself for having the foresight to dress up for the day.

With Johnstone and one bodyguard clearing a path and the other two men taking the flank, Senator and Mrs. Bellardi moved slowly in the direction of campaign headquarters. A bevy of mikes and cameras were trained on the senator. Stevie looked around to see if Wes was still with her, but he had disappeared. She guessed that he did not want his parents to see him out of uniform. That's when she noticed Senator Bellardi's caretakers—the Denherders, was it?—hurrying away from the senator's car, seemingly trying to disappear into the crowd. *Strange,* she thought. *You'd think they'd want to stick around and see how their employer is dealing with all this.* Then she turned her attention back to the reporters and leaned in close to listen to the questions.

"Senator, what was your first reaction when you heard about the bombing?" a reporter asked.

"Very thankful that no one was hurt," the senator answered, typically congenial.

"Do you have any idea who might have done this?" asked the local anchor of the CBS affiliate.

Bellardi shook his head. "No idea at all, Roberta. I'm very interested to see what the police turn up in their investigation. We will find the perpetrators eventually and prosecute to the full extent of the law."

"Do you think Juanita Dunsmuir is behind the bombing?"

Bellardi scowled at the young man addressing him, a new reporter in town. "Absolutely not. Ms. Dunsmuir called me moments ago to express her outrage at the attack. She is just as appalled about this as I am."

Stevie applauded the senator's noble defense of his opponent, but wondered if he really believed his own words. The mobile, impromptu interview approached the front sidewalk, where the fire chief waited to brief the senator on the damage.

"Will the bombing hinder your campaign for governor, sir?"

Bellardi answered, "As you know, Greg, I have a marvelous staff, from Robert Johnstone here to the hundreds of volunteers who work tirelessly to do what's right for North California. These people are the heartbeat of my campaign. Computers and office furniture can easily be replaced. No, Greg, this won't slow us down at all."

Bellardi's bodyguards politely but firmly kept the media at bay as the fire chief described the damage to the senator and his wife. Cameras continued to roll and local TV anchors taped segments for the noon news. Stevie was about to leave when Robert caught her eye and summoned her with a polite wave of the hand. A knot formed instantly in her stomach. She had not fully recovered from their brief encounter less than forty-eight hours earlier. He had leaped the gap from business relationship to social relationship much too quickly for her comfort. More disconcerting, however, were her feelings of anticipation at talking with him again.

Since their last encounter, however, Stevie had reasoned that, if and when she was ready to welcome male companionship again, she might be agreeable to having dinner with Robert Johnstone. He was intelligent and attractive, and his goals in life certainly paralleled hers at this point. But Stevie was sure she was not ready to date yet. As she crossed the pavement to meet him, she prayed that he would not press her again on the issue. She promised herself she would turn him down if he did.

"The senator wants to meet you, Stephanie," Robert said as Stevie reached him.

Again his words took her by surprise. "Me?" she said.

"As I said, he's very impressed with your work. Can you stand by until he's finished here?"

Stevie was torn. Since she obviously was not going to be able to get the work done that she had planned, she should go home and surprise Shawna and Collin with a nice breakfast. Then a grueling day of calls awaited her. But how often would she have the opportunity to speak to the man who had prompted her move to North California, especially at his request? She was flattered and excited at the prospect. "All right, I'll wait," she said.

The round of interviews, discussions with city officials, and impromptu statements at the site of the fire seemed interminable to Stevie. She checked her watch often as she paced the sidewalk. Thankfully, Robert was as involved as the senator, so Stevie did not have to worry about passing the time with him.

Just before eight, Robert summoned her again. "Where's your car?" he asked.

"Around the corner, on the street," Stevie answered, deeply curious about where he was headed this time.

"It should be OK there for a couple of hours. We can take my car. Senator and Mrs. Bellardi have invited us out to the ranch for breakfast. Are you free?"

Stevie silently commanded herself to wake up. So far, the morning seemed more like a dream than reality. Firebombs seriously damage campaign headquarters. Robert Johnstone, an untimely suitor, invites her to meet the senator. Then the meeting suddenly turns into breakfast at the Bellardi ranch, via Robert Johnstone's car. "What's this all about?" she asked, intrigued by the invitation but suspicious that Robert might have another shock for her up his sleeve.

Robert glanced around, hinting that he was about to speak candidly. Then he looked down at her, his eyes warm but serious as he spoke. "The senator is very organized and methodical. He works through channels and lets us make the decisions in our areas. But occasionally, he gets an idea and runs with it. Usually, it's a good idea, so we run with it too."

More and more, Stevie was seeing a new side of Robert Johnstone: coworker and confidant instead of the all-business superior. Which side portrayed the real Robert? Stevie did not know. She was obviously more attracted by the former. She would find it easier to date a coworker than a superior.

"Here's his latest idea—only about two minutes old," he continued. "You're not supposed to know this yet, but Senator Bellardi has decided to add a skilled writer to the debate team. He wants you to be that writer."

fall

25

Thursday
September 23

THE VANDAL struck Bellardi campaign headquarters again thirteen days later. This time the culprit used a high-powered hunting rifle, shattering the front windows and perforating new computers and office furniture with a dozen well-placed shots. By the time police arrived on the scene, the shooter was long gone without a trace. Detectives later determined that the shots had been fired from a rooftop two blocks away in the dead of night, probably with the aid of night-vision opticals.

The attacker signed all his communications to Senator Bellardi—including the ones taking credit for the firebombing and the shooting—"AntiCrist," thought to be a novice's attempt at "antichrist." The pithy, untraceable faxed notes had actually begun to appear several weeks before the firebomb incident, but they were not taken any more or any less seriously than the others. They were among a handful of hostile, profane, and usually anonymous messages received weekly telling Daniel Bellardi just what he could do with his bigoted, fascist, homophobic campaign.

Notes from AntiCrist were as poor in grammar as they were in spelling. The content was mild compared to other messages the office received. They briefly and straightforwardly urged the senator to pull out of the race and leave North California alone. But none of Bellardi's other enemies had actually done anything. Following the firebombing, AntiCrist had claimed full responsibility, referring to the "firey vile of judgement" he had been forced to "unlesh" on the "senitor." However, due to the amateurish nature of the attack by the seemingly simpleminded attacker, authorities had not been overly concerned. Graveyard patrol of the building increased, but experts predicted that the klutz would get himself caught, if indeed he even tried something again.

After the building was riddled with bullets early Tuesday morning, followed by AntiCrist's note identifying the size of the shell and number of rounds fired, the police changed their tune. A high-powered rifle with night-vision scope was a significantly more lethal and sophisticated implement of terrorism than a bottle filled with kerosene, especially in the hands of someone with questionable mental capacity. Although no mention of a personal attack on Bellardi was found in AntiCrist's notes, the possibility of a sniper attack was suddenly quite real. That reality provoked serious concern inside the Bellardi-for-Governor camp.

The strongest reaction to AntiCrist's two attacks came from Patricia Bellardi. Though the general public and most of the campaign staff never learned about it, the senator's usually serene and confident wife suffered a mild breakdown in the face of such overt violence directed at her husband. Patricia was visibly shaken after the firebombing, so the senator's aides strategically kept her out of public view. The shooting two weeks later pushed her even farther over the edge. She begged Daniel to pull out of the race. The governor's office was not worth the risk of Daniel's assassination and her early widowhood, she had said, trembling.

The senator had listened and understood, but he did not yield. Every security precaution would be employed, he assured her, but he could not turn back now. Patricia was not pleased. Top level staff were considering sending her to visit her aged and ailing mother in Redwood City for the remainder of the campaign.

Stevie sat at her computer, distracted by the events of the past two weeks and wishing she did not know so much. The goings-on at the Bellardi ranch and in the senator's strategy chamber had been carefully withheld from volunteers as a matter of course—except for her. Stevie considered that she also would be blissfully ignorant if not for her close working relationship with Bellardi's campaign manager, Robert Johnstone.

As a recent addition to the campaign debate team, Stevie found herself under Robert's direct supervision—therefore, often in his company. To date, though, even during the ride to and from the senator's ranch for breakfast, he had not veered in his conversation from professional and business topics.

Greatly flattered at being invited to breakfast with Senator Bellardi the morning of the firebombing, Stevie had accepted the role of debate team writer the moment it was offered. Later she remonstrated with herself for jumping at the position without being more inquisitive about the senator's expectations. She had discovered almost immediately that her "promotion" came with a significant amount of baggage she had not foreseen.

For openers, the senator expected Stevie to continue to supervise *Prayer Fax* and *Fax-O-Gram,* with Wes taking over more of the writing. Apart from the pressure of added responsibility, Stevie was pleased to retain oversight of the bulletins and her young protégé. Wes was finally warming up to his current responsibilities—as much as he warmed up to anything. But he was slow and error prone. He would need additional mentoring, which Stevie yearned to supply.

Time commitment was another huge burden. Stevie's two roles in the campaign—debate team and communications—would require at least thirty hours a week until the conclusion of the debate series on October ninth. On top of her campaign work, she would have to burn the midnight oil almost every night just to keep her advertising business afloat. Client meetings would have to be sandwiched into her already busy daily schedule. She would have to make every minute count to get everything done.

Additionally, Senator Bellardi wanted Stevie on site for all three debate series. She would be away from home a total of three weekends in September and October, holed up with the debate team during each of the sessions to be televised from Red Bluff, Ukiah, and Eureka. Shawna and Collin were already on her case for being gone so much. With the kids back in school, weekends were family time, at least the hours Stevie could spare from her other commitments. They were going to give her a hard time about these weekend trips, especially since she could not take them along.

Shawna would sleep over at Terilyn's each weekend. It was not the best arrangement, in Stevie's judgment, since she knew very little about Shawna's friend and her mother. But Shawna flatly refused to stay anywhere else, and Stevie was fresh out of bargaining chips. Stevie resolved to invite Arlene Spradlin over for tea and a mom-to-mom chat some morning—probably after the elections. She felt OK about Collin staying with his friend Brett Mann, but she still agonized over the time she would be away from him and Shawna. She consoled herself repeatedly with the words, *I'm only doing this for their good. I'll make it up to them when Senator Bellardi is safely in the governor's mansion.*

Another large challenge accompanying the promotion was working under Robert. Just being in the same room with the self-assured, affable ex-Marine addled her emotions. He was her boss, but the man had already revealed that he saw her as something other than just another volunteer. So far, Robert had not revisited the invitation to dinner since he surprised her with it two weeks earlier. Half of her wished he would, because she was on edge waiting for the other shoe to drop. Half of her prayed that he would not, because she was afraid she might say yes. And whenever she thought about Robert, she sensed Jon glowering at her disapprovingly, even though she chided herself for even being concerned with what Jon might think. *After all,* she reminded herself, *he's no longer my husband. Other than the children, we have no ties. I'm free to go on with my life and date whomever I please.* Sometimes that reminder helped; most of the time it didn't.

Since Stevie had agreed to serve as a debate-team writer, Robert treated her like a member of the campaign's inner circle. He had confided in her about the notes from AntiCrist, police investigations of the firebombing and shooting, and Patricia's shocking breakdown. Though flattered by Robert's trust, Stevie realized that privileged status brought added emotional pressure. She was more distracted than impressed by the behind-the-scenes information, especially that which tarnished her vision of what Senator Daniel Bellardi strived to accomplish for North California. She did not really need to know the inner workings of the campaign; she just wanted to do her part to keep it rolling toward a victory in November. The health and safety of her children depended on it.

"Do you want anything from the coffee shop?" Rhoda Carrier asked, summoning Stevie from her wandering thoughts. "It's break time." The communications department was confined to a suite at the Red Lion for at least another week following the rifle attack on headquarters. Hoping to boost morale among her volunteers, rotund Rhoda made a trip down to the hotel restaurant every midmorning for bran muffins and coffee.

"Sure," Stevie said, reaching for her change purse. "A large iced tea, please—with extra lemon slices."

Rhoda waved off Stevie's offer to pay. "You're into the hard stuff pretty early in the day, aren't you?" she said with a laugh.

"I need the hard stuff to keep me going, Rhoda," Stevie said, forcing a smile. "In fact, you'd better bring me an *extra* large iced tea. I have a mountain of work to climb this morning."

With Rhoda on her way, Stevie returned to the keyboard. The first debate would take place the following night, and Robert was counting on her to streamline and polish the senator's opening remarks in time for him to memorize them. The debate team had hammered out the basic concepts; Stevie's responsibility was to make the message sing, convict, and captivate. Unlike her previous assignments, she had a large personal stake in the copy writing she did for the senator. She had two very dear reasons to make it the best work of her career.

Ladies and gentlemen of North California, the unconscionable act of terminating the life of a human fetus is dead wrong. Abortion is dead wrong physically because it stops a human heart. Abortion is dead wrong morally because it violates a person's right to live. Abortion is dead wrong spiritually because it usurps God's authority over life and death. As your governor, I will do what is right for North California. I will oppose every movement, every law, and every individual that supports abortion, because abortion is dead wrong.

Stevie scanned the completed paragraph with satisfaction. "Dead wrong" had been her contribution to the brainstorm on the abortion plank. Robert, along with the senator's policy adviser, Coleman King, and the debate team loved it. The phrase had shock value, between-the-eyes punch, they said. Stevie had also hinted that dissecting and attacking the abortion issue on three levels—physically, morally, and spiritually—would generate emotional momentum. Again the team agreed. The paragraph before her was snappy and solid. She was awed that Senator Bellardi would be delivering these words as his own tomorrow night. North California and much of the nation would be listening.

Stevie crafted several more paragraphs addressing the key planks of the senator's platform. The debate team had mined the raw ore on these issues during weeks of grueling skull sessions, many of which were attended by Senator Bellardi. In the days before Stevie joined the team, Johnstone, King, and the others had hacked away much of the slag, exposing the key concepts like uncut stones. Applying her skills, Stevie had transformed the rough-hewn ideas and words into dazzling, convincing gems of truth for the senator to present to the citizens of North California. Stevie was convinced that Juanita Dunsmuir's argument would pale in comparison, like cheap costume jewelry.

Someone entered the suite; Stevie assumed it was Rhoda returning with her iced tea. She looked up from the monitor to find Robert standing over her, holding a thirty-two-ounce cup and a straw in one hand, a small cup of coffee in the other. "I ran into Rhoda in the coffee shop," he said. "She sent this up for you. Extra large with lemon." The man's slacks, shirt, and tie were perfectly coordinated—as always—and his expression was winsome and friendly. Sometimes Stevie wished he weren't quite so perfect.

"Thanks," Stevie said, receiving the drink. Robert smiled and sat down in the desk-side chair with his cup of coffee. The now familiar knot returned to her stomach. Stevie did not really have time for a coffee-break chat; she had work to do. Besides, she did not want to get into a conversation that might lead to a dinner invitation. But Robert was her boss, she reminded herself, and he had every right to sit at her desk if he wanted to. Stevie poked the straw into her tea and swiveled toward him.

His stock opening line—"How's it going today?"—gave Stevie the opportunity to control the conversation. She took it. She read several paragraphs from the monitor, briefly explaining her reasoning. Robert suggested a couple of minor adjustments, giving evidence that he was listening carefully. When Stevie had reported on everything she could think of, Robert smiled warmly, thanked her, then stood and walked away. Turning back to the keyboard, she could not decide if she was disappointed or relieved.

Suddenly he was beside her desk again. Stevie sensed his presence even before she looked up.

"Yes?" she said, hoping he couldn't hear the loud thumping of her heart as she gazed up into his questioning eyes.

"Stephanie," he said, "I know I came on a little strong and my timing wasn't the best when I asked you out to dinner before, but I was hoping you'd give me another chance. Is this a better time?"

Her throat felt frozen. She knew, if she opened her mouth, not one word would come out. But how long could she sit there, speechless, while he waited for an answer?

It was his little-boy look that did it. Obviously interpreting her hesitancy as a rejection, Robert's usual confidence seemed to disappear before Stevie's eyes. That such a handsome, powerful, self-assured man could feel insecure in her presence was just too much to resist.

"Yes," she said, nodding her head in affirmation. "Yes, this is a much better time."

Robert's relief was evident. "Wonderful," he said, smiling broadly. "So, how about tonight?"

"Tonight?"

"Tonight," Robert repeated. "For dinner. We could combine business with pleasure, get to know each other while we finalize those statements before delivering them to the senator." He paused, then raised an eyebrow questioningly. "Please?"

The proper response came to mind immediately: *Thank you, Robert, but this is my last night at home before leaving for the weekend. I need to do laundry and pack. Maybe some other time.* It was a direct, kind, and reasonable refusal. But when she opened her mouth, those were not the words that came out.

"I'd like that," she heard herself say.

Robert's smile was even broader. "Great! We'll make it early, say around six? I promise to get you home before nine. I know you have a very busy schedule, not to mention two kids who probably don't appreciate your being gone all the time."

Stevie was not only excited about the prospect of going out on an actual date, even if it was a combination business and pleasure date, but she was also impressed by Robert's consideration of her personal and family time.

"Six would be fine."

"I'm looking forward to it," Robert said, his eyes locking into hers briefly before he turned and walked out the door.

So am I, Stevie thought. *I think.*

Robert had no more than walked out the door when Stevie inadvertently knocked her cup over with her elbow, spilling iced tea across her desk. As she wiped it up with tissues from her top drawer, she hoped she'd be a bit less clumsy tonight.

26

Thursday
September 23

JON AND BEN stood at the sink. Ben peeled and sliced cucumbers while Jon opened the package of refrigerated pasta to boil. The thought never ceased to amaze Jon: His houseguest had come into his life as a result—indirectly, at least—of the incident six months earlier, when Eugene Hackett had physically attacked him at the rec center and then peppered the front of his house with a .45. When Jon had spoken to Hackett at the Los Angeles County Jail, he had assumed that confrontation would be the end of it. The shooting was in the past, and the attacker had been summarily forgiven by the victim. Jon's involvement with Eugene Hackett and people like him was over.

God, however, seemed to have other plans. In mid-August,

Jon was officially notified by the county that Eugene Hackett
was being released, having served forty-five days of a sixty-day
sentence. The notice was a standard courtesy to victims, in
effect to say, "Ready or not, we're letting him out." The letter
also stated that Eugene's uncle, Lyle Hackett, was presently
incarcerated, and his home, where Eugene had lived prior to
his arrest, had been foreclosed upon. However, a citizen sponsor had been found, a sort of big brother "to assist Mr. Hackett
in returning to the community as a productive citizen."
Citizen sponsors, the letter explained, provided safe, positive
living environments as well as mature guidance and companionship. Although a citizen sponsor had been found for Mr.
Hackett, the program was always in need of new volunteers.
The letter closed with an invitation for Jon to let them know
of anyone who might be interested in becoming involved in
the program.

Jon had argued with God about it for several days. "I've
already traveled beyond the second mile for Eugene Hackett
by visiting him in jail and extending my forgiveness," Jon con-
tended one sleepless night. "The last thing I need to do is take
on someone else just like him as a rehab project. I work with
juveniles all day at Foothill; coming home to a severely emotionally disturbed junior high dropout every day will send me
over the edge."

But his resistance was short-lived in the face of such an obviously God-ordained opportunity. Apart from the intervention of
a caring adult, Eugene Hackett would likely be an L.A. gang fatal-
ity in a matter of a few years if not months. How many other
Eugenes were there, in desperate need of a second chance before
it was too late? Jon knew that mercy and compassion were every
bit as important to God as justice. Once justice had been served,
it was time to exercise love. So Jon had volunteered to become a
citizen sponsor.

The appointment was not automatic. The motivations of a
former crime victim volunteering to serve as a citizen sponsor
had to be carefully examined. However, Jon's background
check was squeaky clean and, with a serious dearth of citizen
sponsors in the county, his application was processed quickly
and approved.

Before accepting Ben into his home and care, Jon had

learned what he could about the young man. Benito "Ben" Hernandez—formerly known as *Flaco* ("skinny") to his fellow gang members—had never known his father. His fifteen-year-old mother had died of a drug overdose soon after his birth, and he had been raised by his maternal grandmother until she too died just as he was entering his teens. With no other immediate relatives to take him in, Ben yielded to the pressure to join a local gang, glad for the homeys who became his family and protected him from the dangers of growing up alone in the barrio. His formal education did not extend beyond the eighth grade, but his street-smarts were extensive, as was his rap sheet.

Ben also had some say-so in whether or not he came to live with Jon. However, that say-so was greatly influenced by the ultimatum given him by the courts: Accept the placement with Mr. Van Horne and cooperate, or we will assign you to a work farm in Castaic. Ben quickly accepted the placement, and Jon picked him up at county jail on August twentieth.

"Make your slices a little thinner, Ben," Jon said, watching the kid hack the cucumber into large chunks. "You should get at least a dozen slices out of one small cucumber." Ben grunted. He was not used to cooking dinner or taking orders.

Jon tried to encourage conversation. Sometimes it was a major chore. "How was class today?"

"OK," Ben answered without enthusiasm.

"What are you working on these days?"

"Acetylene."

Shortly after Ben moved in, Jon had shepherded him through vocational testing. The kid had shown aptitude and interest in metalworking and welding, so he was enrolled in a welding program at Los Angeles Pierce College at county expense. Jon dropped him off every morning on his way to work and picked him up on the way home at four. Ben was cooperative but kept his feelings about the experience to himself.

"Do you like working with the torch?"

"Yeah. It's OK."

The response was not enthusiastic, but Jon interpreted Ben's double affirmative as a burst of emotion in contrast to his usual non-committal grunts.

It had occurred to Jon a few times over the last month that

Ben was a little like Dougie. Getting Dougie to talk to him had been a major chore. Stevie always seemed to have more patience and persistence with their reclusive older son than did Jon, who often gave up when Dougie clammed up. Jon thought Stevie might be proud of how well he was doing with the equally defensive and aloof Benito Hernandez. Jon knew he would eventually have to tell his ex-wife all about Ben and how he had met him as a result of having gone to the jail to visit the young man who had tried to kill her and their son. But so far he had told Stevie nothing.

Shawna stood at the front door, packed and ready to leave for the weekend with Terilyn. It really bugged her that her mother picked the last minute to interrogate her about weekend plans. Collin had already been picked up by Brett Mann and his mother. Shawna was eager to get out the door, but Mom was snooping about her activities again. Shawna found herself easily irritated at her these days.

"When are you leaving for this conference thing with Terilyn?" Stevie was fluffing her hair as she spoke, rearranging the short curls to frame her face.

"Ms. Carmona picks us up at seven tomorrow morning," Shawna said with an impatient sigh.

"And when do you get home?"

"It's a three-day conference. We'll be back Sunday evening about six."

"And what is this conference exactly?"

Shawna had told her about the conference before, but not "exactly"—for obvious reasons. Had Shawna told everything, her mother would have freaked out and quickly slammed the door on the weekend. "Young Women's Leadership Conference at the Hilton in San Francisco," she recited. "Terilyn says its the best way to get into student government at Reagan High School. The student council advisor is taking ten girls from Reagan, and Terilyn got me in."

It was all true. Shawna had emphasized the student leadership aspect of the conference because her mother had often encouraged her to seek student office. What Shawna was *not* telling her mother was that a major unit planned for the young women's conference was tolerance, that she would attend an unofficial small group session on the benefits of ancient religious beliefs and practices directed by Reagan's student government advisor Lisa Carmona, and that Ms. Carmona was considered an expert at reading and interpreting horoscopes.

"And you have an excused absence from school tomorrow?"

"Of course. This is a school trip."

Apparently satisfied with the explanation, Shawna's mother turned from prying to nagging. "Did you leave the number for the Hilton?"

"Yes, Mom, it's on the kitchen counter."

"Do you have my number in Red Bluff, at Best Western?"

"In my bag."

"Do you have a sweater? It gets chilly by the bay."

"Yes, Mom," Shawna said, becoming more irritated by the minute. "I have warm clothes."

Her mother seemed reluctant to see her go, Shawna sensed, as if there was something more she needed to say. Shawna turned to leave but her mother followed her to the front door.

"Honey," she said, her eye contact less than direct, "I'm having dinner with one of the men I work with at the office this evening. It's no big deal, not even a date really. But I wanted you to know. Are you OK with that?"

"Which man?" Shawna said, keeping a grip on her surprise.

"Robert Johnstone, Senator Bellardi's campaign director—I don't think you've met him. He's a widower, no children, a very nice Christian man." Her mother paused, obviously awaiting Shawna's response.

"Sure. Why not?" she said, not sure how she should answer.

"I know this is rather sudden. I don't want you to think I'm shopping for a husband or something."

"Something" meaning a stepfather, I suppose, Shawna commented silently. *It's all right, Mom. You can use that word around me. I've heard it before. Just don't expect me to get excited about having a stepfather, because I don't plan to be a daughter to anybody but you and Dad.*

"No problem," was all she said.

Her mother paused again, as if seeking greater assurance. Shawna decided she had said all she was going to say on the topic.

235

Finally Stevie said, "Well, honey, I hope you enjoy the conference. I'm so glad you have a good friend to do things with."

"We'll have fun, Mom. Don't worry about me."

Finally, Stevie embraced her, kissed her on the cheek, and said she loved her, then Shawna was out the door. Walking to Terilyn's apartment, she wrinkled her nose at the prospect of her mother going on a date. *First your new advertising business, then your stupid fax bulletins, then your lame debate team, now this,* she thought with a smirk. *Just one more thing to keep you busy.* Then she swore under her breath, something she had not done in several weeks. *Wake up, Mom. North California was supposed to be a fresh new start for us. That's why I came up here in the first place. Why do you keep stuffing things in between us?* Shawna was glad to be gone for the weekend. She did not want to see this Johnstone guy or even hear about her mother's date.

27

Friday
September 24

STEVIE EASED the speedometer up to sixty-five and activated the Cherokee's cruise control for the thirty-minute drive to Red Bluff. It was only one o'clock, and the big meeting did not start until four. But she wanted to get settled into the Best Western and try to gather her wits before the debate activities began. Several people from the office had offered her a ride to the opening night of the series, but she had turned them all down. She hated to be stuck in a hotel away from home without a car. Stevie realized that she might appear independent to the point of stubbornness about this, but she didn't care. She needed to feel mobile and free.

Robert had been among those who suggested a carpool

arrangement. Had she accepted a ride from anyone, it likely would have been him. Any fears that the campaign director was gearing up for a romantic rush at her had been allayed last night at D'Marco's Restaurant. Their dinner together had been exactly what Robert had promised: a combination of business and pleasure. They talked about the campaign in general, the debates in particular, and a little about their personal lives. The most enjoyable part of the evening for Stevie had been discovering how natural and comfortable it had felt to talk with Robert. He was an interesting conversationalist but also a great listener, drawing her out and putting her at ease. He had been a perfect gentleman, insisting on paying for the meal, but not pressing Stevie for another date or trying to flatter her with sweet talk. Stevie was impressed.

Actually, she was more than impressed. Stevie found Robert's warm, gentlemanly manner much more attractive than if he had come on to her romantically. Still, she reminded herself, she didn't need another distraction at this hectic juncture in her life. It was better that she had not accepted a ride from Robert today. She could not allow herself to entertain further involvement with him, at least until the end of the debate series. Even then she would have to untangle her feelings for Robert from questions about remarriage for a Christian.

Stevie dialed Wes Bellaidl's desk on her cellular phone. "Communications," Wes answered.

"Are they on the way?" Stevie asked, hoping she didn't sound too pushy. Keeping Wes on task with the two fax bulletins had been a stiff challenge.

"Almost."

Stevie glanced at the digital clock on the dash. Wes was notorious for cheating the deadline by several minutes every Friday. Today's bulletins, hyping the opening of the debates, were critical. "When do you hope to send?"

"Two at the latest."

Translated into real time, that meant two-thirty at the earliest. "What's the holdup?" Stevie asked.

"Rhoda brought me a dozen new names to add to the database. And Mr. Whitten was late sending in his corrections. I'm working on them right now."

"Keep up the good work, partner," she said in her most

encouraging tone. "Give me a call when you tap the send button, OK?"

"Sure."

Stevie heard something that concerned her. "You sound a little stuffed up, Wes."

"Yeah, I think I picked up a flu bug or cold or something."

"So are you coming down for the debate tonight?" Stevie knew that Wes had been waffling on the idea of attending the opening round of the debates at the Red Bluff High School auditorium. With Patricia living in Redwood City for the time being, the senator wanted Wes on the platform to assure a family presence. Characteristically, Wes had dragged his heels. Now he apparently had a valid excuse to ditch the appearance.

Wes sniffed, obviously to underscore his condition. "I think I'd better stay home and watch it on TV."

Stevie tended to agree with him. She could not afford for Wes to get seriously ill at this stage of the campaign. Her maternal instincts kicked into gear. "Drink plenty of fluids and get lots of sleep. If you lay low for the weekend, maybe you can beat this thing before it gets worse."

"That's what I figured," Wes said, adding a slight cough. "I hope Dad will understand."

"I'm sure he will," Stevie said. Then she voiced another concern that had grown with the bold attacks of the person known as AntiCrist. "The security people will be at the ranch this weekend, right?"

"Sure. They stick to me like black sticks to tar."

"Good. You know it's important to let them do their jobs."

Wes sighed. "Yeah, I know. But these guys are a nuisance sometimes. They'd sleep in my bedroom if I let them."

"It's all for the best."

"I suppose."

Satisfied that she had performed her motherly duty, Stevie put a smile in her voice and said, "All right, back to the salt mines. Call me when you send." Wes agreed and hung up.

The next call was to her business voice mail. The only message was brief and sobering. "Ms. Van Horne, this is Andy Fletcher at Cody's Foods. We've decided to go a different direction with our advertising. Sorry we couldn't get together with you on something."

The small Cody grocery chain was not dropping her, Stevie knew; she had dropped Cody's Foods. *Fumbled* was probably a better word. Andy Fletcher could not "get together" with Stevie because, in her busyness with the campaign, she had twice failed to return his calls on time. Her carelessness was as inexcusable in sleepy North California as it was in the high-pressure sales world of Los Angeles. Her commitment to Senator Bellardi had finally cost her in a very tangible way: something in the neighborhood of a seventy-five-hundred dollar contract.

Fortunately for Stevie, the campaign was entering the homestretch. What she was doing for North California and her own family was critically important, but somehow she had to pay closer attention to her business commitments. She still had to feed her children after she delivered to them a godly governor.

The four o'clock meeting in Senator Bellardi's suite at the Best Western was like a high-level military briefing prior to a critical battle that was destined to turn the war. All of the senator's key people were there: Robert Johnstone and the debate team, policy advisor Coleman King, media secretary Price Whitten, and a few men Stevie had never seen before—media consultants, someone called them. Then there were the security people: Senator Bellardi's personal bodyguards and two plainclothes officers from the California Highway Patrol. CHP officers in the north would be invited to fill the ranks of the soon-to-be-formed North California State Police.

Everyone in the room seemed on edge. In the center of the maelstrom was Senator Daniel Bellardi, looking more nervous than Stevie had seen him before. In the first minutes of the gathering she found out why: Polls released today showed the senator to be only five points ahead of Juanita Dunsmuir, with up to 11 percent of the population yet undecided. Still, Stevie could not identify with the concern that crackled in the room like static electricity. She was confident that the debates would turn the war solidly in Bellardi's favor.

Stevie was the only woman admitted to the room, and from the onset of the meeting she felt like the odd person out. She did not have an official task during the debates. She was "support staff," politely asked to stay out of the way until she was needed. She felt like an on-site seamstress, standing by with a sewing kit in case the senator lost a button or split a seam. Actually, Stevie was the on-site wordsmith, a walking dictionary, thesaurus, and grammarian. She would be called upon if the debate team needed to clarify a key statement.

The media had compared the Bellardi-Dunsmuir debates to an odd boxing match in which only one candidate at a time was allowed to throw punches while his or her opponent stood there passively and got pounded. Each candidate would have several opportunities to verbally deck the other. The debates were scheduled for two hours on both Friday and Saturday nights for the next three weeks.

On the Friday sessions, candidates would be allotted fifteen minutes each for opening statements—in effect to state why they should be elected governor and why their opponent should be tarred, feathered, and run out of the state. Opening statements would contain an overview of campaign issues and general statements on positions. No opportunity would be given for rebuttal of opening statements.

Stevie had played a significant role in the crafting of Senator Bellardi's opening statements. They were powerful and airtight, she knew. Delivered with the senator's characteristic passion, this fifteen-minute address would doubtless send the Dunsmuir camp reeling. Truth and righteousness would prevail. It would be a first-round knockout.

The rest of the Friday and Saturday evening sessions would focus on nine specific issues: abortion, assisted suicide, gay rights, legalized drugs, crime and punishment—including capital punishment—church and state, values in education, pornography, and tolerance. Three issues were scheduled each evening, allowing for statements and rebuttals by each candidate. Stevie had helped the debate team polish each position statement and each rebuttal to Juanita Dunsmuir's anticipated arguments. During rebuttal, Senator Bellardi would be free to use the prepared materials or speak from his own thoughts. Either way, Stevie was confident that he would blow the opposition away.

As Stevie watched and listened, Senator Bellardi's brain trust reviewed the plan of attack for that night's issues: abortion, assisted suicide, and gay rights. Last-minute minor adjustments were made to the position statements. Dunsmuir's anticipated arguments were tossed randomly at the senator to test his response. He parried each thrust with aplomb and confidence. Senator Daniel Bellardi was ready for battle.

The senator usually acknowledged Stevie with a personal greeting and a word of thanks whenever he saw her. But not this time. He was intensely focused on the battle ahead. Stevie did not feel slighted. Sitting in the room virtually unnoticed, she quietly warmed with pride, relishing her role in the upcoming triumph.

Shawna really did not feel like eating pizza, but the Reagan High delegation had split up for dinner and the group she wanted to be with had voted for pizza. So the six of them, including Shawna and Terilyn, had left the downtown San Francisco Hilton and walked four blocks to an upscale pizza place. The five other girls had opted to snack out of the vending machines and play in the indoor pool until the evening session began.

Ms. Lisa Carmona, the faculty advisor and chaperone, was the main reason Shawna wanted to be with this group. She was enthralled by the woman's strong personality, self-confidence, and worldly wisdom. Shawna and Terilyn had guessed that Ms. Carmona was somewhere between thirty and forty years old. Her long black hair was swept up neatly in a French roll, her silver and onyx jewelry was very stylish, and her makeup was impeccable. She was a beautiful woman, the girls had decided, whether wearing a dress, a suit, or jeans and a T-shirt. Shawna agreed with the assessment Terilyn once offered her privately: "Ms. Carmona is one classy, spiritual lady."

While helping her young disciples make a deep-dish gourmet veggie deluxe disappear, Ms. Carmona took advantage of a teachable moment. They were discussing the topics of the conference listed in the program, one of which was tolerance. Annette, a sophomore Shawna had met in the van on the drive down, commented that she was confused when she heard people talking about tolerance. It seemed to have two different meanings, she said. Shawna was glad Annette had brought up the topic. She had wondered about it too, especially when she heard her mother use the term. She leaned in close to listen.

"Tolerance is the highest of all virtues," Ms. Carmona instructed her charges around the table. "And it is quite often misunderstood. It is the highest virtue because it acknowledges and celebrates the personal rights and values of every individual. It is misunderstood because fundamentalists and bigots in our culture have improperly defined it."

"So what's the right definition?" Annette pressed.

Ms. Carmona sipped her soda thoughtfully, twirling the straw with her manicured nails, then answered, "The virtue of tolerance is based on the reality that everyone is equal in value. Nobody at this table is any better than anyone else, right?" The girls nodded on cue. "That's right. We're different from each other in a lot of ways, but we're all equal in value."

Shawna could not argue with Ms. Carmona so far. She had heard the same thing in Sunday school and youth group for years: *Jesus loves the little children, all the children of the world. Red and yellow, black and white, they are precious in his sight. Jesus loves the little children of the world.*

The teacher continued. "If all persons are equal, then all lifestyles are equal. You are a person of value, so however you choose to live your life is OK. Nobody can tell you what's right for you or what's wrong for you. That's something everyone must decide for herself. Whatever you decide is right for you is right. Whatever you decide is wrong for you is wrong." She paused, and her dark eyes scanned each face briefly. "Of course," she said, "if you have trouble deciding just what's right for you and what isn't, there are higher powers available to help us in those decisions."

Shawna wondered if it was mere coincidence that Ms. Carmona's gaze seemed to rest longer on her than on the others. Was Ms. Carmona trying to convey something to her—to "connect," as the dwarfs called it? Shawna sensed an electricity in that brief moment of eye contact, and the sudden warm flash reminded her of Destiny Fortugno and some of their escapades together.

Ridiculous, she told herself. *Ms. Carmona and Destiny Fortugno are not at all alike. They have absolutely nothing in common. Destiny was always trying to lead me into trouble. Ms. Carmona only wants to help me, to teach me how to understand myself better and how to be more tolerant of others. What could be wrong with that?*

The teacher's explanation that all people and lifestyles are equal sounded reasonable to Shawna and yet, no matter how hard she tried to convince herself otherwise, something about it nagged at her. Although she had learned in church that all individuals have great worth because they are made in the image of God, the church did not teach that all lifestyles are equal and, therefore, acceptable. Rather, Shawna had been taught that right and wrong are determined by God and expressed in the Bible. However, she found it hard to argue with the logic that every individual is special and has the right to do what is best for himself or herself. In spite of her doubts, Shawna was eager to hear more.

"In its purest sense," Ms. Carmona continued, "tolerance is simply the kindness to accept and to praise people for the life-styles they have chosen. Tolerance says, 'I'm OK with what I believe and how I live, and you're OK with what you believe and how you live.' That's just where the narrow-minded bigots screw things up. They say, 'I'm OK, but I'm not so sure about you.' They say, 'I accept you as a person, but I can't accept your lifestyle.' What right does anyone have to question your lifestyle? None, because everyone is created equal. Anyone who says, 'My truth is right and yours is wrong' is setting up a hierarchy of truth. But there is no hierarchy of truth, because all beliefs, values, and lifestyles are equal. The most loving thing your friends, teachers, and parents can do for you is to praise your lifestyle. If they don't, they are intolerant. And no one is more selfish or arrogant than someone who is intolerant."

The words popped out of Shawna's mouth before she could stop them. "But how can *everybody's* beliefs be right? I mean, what about Adolf Hitler?"

Ms. Carmona and two of the other girls at the table laughed lightly at Shawna's obvious naiveté. She felt her face flush warm.

"That's just the point, Shawna," the teacher responded. "Adolf Hitler had the right to believe whatever he wanted. But by imposing his beliefs on others, he displayed his intolerance and paid for it with his life. Decent people saw through the

German dictator's intolerance and put an end to it—and to him—by defeating his country in the second world war." The other girls at the table nodded knowingly.

Another question popped into Shawna's head. It seemed odd to her that the beliefs of Adolf Hitler—whom Terilyn equated with Daniel Bellardi—qualified as intolerance while the beliefs of the "decent people" who defeated him were seen as right. *If all truths and beliefs and lifestyles are equal, why were we right and the Nazis wrong? The things Hitler did were wrong, but our side also killed a lot of people in the name of what we believed. What's the difference?* But this time Shawna kept her lips zipped. She already felt stupid for exposing her ignorance. *Ms. Carmona obviously knows what she's talking about, so there must be a logical explanation. All I need to do is keep quiet and listen. It will all make sense to me eventually—especially if I find out more about these "higher powers" that Ms. Carmona says can help me.*

28
Friday
September 24

"WHAT ARE YOU going to do to Ms. X, Senator Bellardi? Arrest her for having an abortion? Take her to trial? Throw the book at her? Put her in prison and throw away the key? Send her to the gas chamber?" Juanita Dunsmuir's defiant questions opened her rebuttal and iced the auditorium crowd to sudden silence. Stevie's eyes widened in amazement at the woman's cutting words and tone. Dunsmuir had unleashed the first brutal blow of the debates.

Senator Bellardi's opening statement had been nothing short of eloquent, swelling Stevie with pride. He poured the foundation for his argument by stating his intent to do only what was right for North California. Then he hammered each of the platform planks firmly into place on the issues to be covered in the debates. Finally he enumerated proposed guidelines for transitioning North California from the "abyss of moral relativism into a safe, secure, and peaceful haven of traditional values."

Ms. Dunsmuir's fifteen-minute opening address had also been delivered with polish and persuasion, punctuated by her stunning physical appearance. Gone were the trademark braids, boots, and buckskin. Gone was the cowboy twang from her voice. The senator's opponent wore a gray-green summer wool suit. Her long hair was wound into an attractive chignon at her collar. Streaks of gray, which made her look old for a singer, gave her a distinguished appearance as a politician. It was a look she had begun to cultivate in her television ads several weeks earlier. Stevie assessed that Juanita Dunsmuir had spent a bundle on image and packaging, just as she knew the senator had.

During the opening statements, the two candidates, like wary boxers, had circled each other in the ring, tapping gloves respectfully, sizing each other up without attempting any hard punches. Both knew that playing the role of the aggressor too early in the bout might give one the appearance of a bully to the live audience and hundreds of thousands of voters watching by television. Better to come on confident and positive than to start swinging from the heels at the opening bell and encourage sympathy for the underdog.

The pattern continued into round two: Senator Bellardi's presentation on the topic of abortion. The senator argued with the issue, not with his opponent. He cited convincing data supporting the viability of the fetus at all stages of development. He introduced a hypothetical example, the unwed and pregnant "Ms. X," at the crossroads of a decision between a convenience abortion and the responsibility of bringing the child to term and offering it for adoption to a loving, childless couple. "The right thing for North California is to do the only right thing for Baby X," Bellardi declared. "Let this defenseless little person live, and stand against anyone who would take from it the precious gift of life."

Using a poignant, true-to-life example in the presentation

had been Stevie's suggestion. She marveled at the strength of the story and its application as Senator Bellardi delivered it.

Juanita Dunsmuir's response quickly changed the complexion of the debate, as a boxing match would change if one combatant pulled off the gloves and began swinging fists armed with brass knuckles. Dunsmuir was not reacting emotionally, Stevie knew. Her tack of biting, rhetorical questions was carefully calculated to solicit support for her liberal position. Stevie held her breath as the challenger turned her eyes from the senator to the cameras and continued.

"Ladies and gentlemen, the Ms. X Senator Bellardi introduced to you does not exist. No one in North California goes by such an impersonal name. But there are numbers of young women in our state named Jenny and Sarah and Jessica and Patty and Elizabeth. They are your coworkers, your neighbors, your nieces, and your daughters. These girls are troubled, frightened, and embarrassed. They have one thing in common: unplanned or unwanted pregnancy.

"Sixteen-year-old Jenny over in Windsor was talked into a night of intimacy by her twenty-year-old boyfriend. When Jenny confessed that she was pregnant, her boyfriend disappeared and her alcoholic mother threw her out of the house. Feeling abandoned and scared about the future, she hastily sought an abortion, a decision she now regrets."

Stevie marveled at how Juanita Dunsmuir was subtly turning the senator's presentation to her favor. Transforming the impersonal Ms. X into a "Jenny" was a stroke of genius. Stevie wished she had thought of it earlier, even though she knew there was no real Jenny in Windsor, North California. By stating Jenny's "regret" at having an abortion, Dunsmuir had purposely introduced a small margin of doubt about the firmness of her formerly unyielding pro-choice position. She was cutting the senator some slack in an attempt to make a few friends in his camp.

Stevie silently acknowledged that the Dunsmuir brain trust had done its homework. While appreciating their effort from a professional standpoint, Stevie's faith in the senator's ability to deal with the clever ploy remained firm.

Juanita Dunsmuir continued her rebuttal. "Elizabeth, an upstanding Christian student at College of the Siskiyous, was

abducted at knifepoint and raped. Discovering she was pregnant from the attack, Elizabeth decided to risk the embarrassment of her condition and the misunderstanding of her family
and friends in order to bear the child for the sake of adoption.
But when the rapist was apprehended, he tested positive for
HIV. In order to spare an innocent child the horrors of AIDS,
Elizabeth mercifully terminated the pregnancy."

Clever strategy, Stevie thought, *for a New Age atheist like
Dunsmuir to introduce Elizabeth as a Christian and intimate that
her abortion was an act of mercy. She is as persistent as she is
resourceful at poking holes in the stained-glass curtain between
her and Senator Bellardi.*

Juanita played to the heartstrings of the crowd with two
more brief scenarios. The stories were carefully framed to
make each girl's choice for abortion appear logical and even
moral. "Legislation proposed by Senator Bellardi," she concluded, "would brand as criminals the Jennys and Sarahs and
Elizabeths of our new state. Can you imagine your teenaged
neighbor being handcuffed and hauled off in a police car just
for protecting an innocent child from a brief, painful life and
a horrible death? Can you imagine your own niece being
arrested and imprisoned simply because she made a hasty,
emotional decision that will punish her with regret for the
rest of her life?

"That's what Senator Daniel Bellardi will do to these
unfortunate girls. 'Abortion is a crime, abortion is murder—
period,' he says. 'Do the crime and you do the time. It's the
right thing for North California.' Fellow North Californians,
Jenny and Elizabeth need guidance, counseling, encouragement, understanding, and love to turn their lives around—a
little tolerance and compassion, if you will. Contempt and
incarceration are not right for these girls. And if it's not right
for them, then it's wrong for North California.

"Remember, a vote for Dan Bellardi is a vote of intolerance."

Placards, demonstrations, and overt campaigning were
strictly prohibited in the auditorium, which was supposed to
be a neutral site. But Dunsmuir supporters in the crowd of
eight hundred spectators were notable by their enthusiastic
applause as their candidate returned to her chair. Senator
Bellardi had three minutes to respond to Ms. Dunsmuir's

rebuttal before the challenger presented her own case on abortion. Even though she did not know what the senator would say, Stevie anxiously and confidently awaited his reply.

"Ms. Dunsmuir has done well to remind us of the heart-rending stories of girls like Jenny." Senator Bellardi exhibited no ill effects from his opponent's barbed rebuttal. His poise at the lectern seemed unflappable. "And although a sanctity of life standard must be upheld in all cases, my quarrel is not primarily with women who submit to abortion during a momentary lapse of conscience or good judgment. Thankfully, these occurrences are in the minority. Rather, the pro-life legislation I propose is aimed at multiplied thousands of women who think nothing of terminating new life simply because pregnancy or motherhood is incompatible with their lifestyle." A soft murmur of affirmation from the audience confirmed that the senator's supporters were also present in force.

"I refer to these women impersonally as Ms. X because their unconscionable acts are inhumane. Animals sometimes kill their young, but sane and sensible people made in the image of a loving God do not. We cannot tolerate careless, thoughtless, heartless women and their male partners whose devotion to convenience, career, and the good life leads them to kill their young in the womb. Convenience abortion is not right anywhere at any time. If that is intolerance, so be it. As governor of North California, I will make sure that the rights of the unborn are protected by law."

Stevie marveled at Senator Bellardi's self-control. Were she at the lectern instead of him, she would be worked into a fire-breathing frenzy right now defending the senator's cause in the face of the challenger's impudence. Yet Bellardi remained self-assured and winsome as he calmly deflected the challenger's verbal assault. And he always seemed to know which camera was trained on him, holding both the on-site audience and the television audience with his steady gaze.

Ms. Dunsmuir's prepared fifteen-minute presentation on the topic of abortion would be next. The senator would be allowed a ten-minute rebuttal, which would be followed by Dunsmuir's three-minute response. Thus would end round two of the debate. The folksinger-turned-politician had launched an impressive mid-round offensive, Stevie thought. But the former state senator from California had minimized the threat and turned it to his advantage. Stevie did not know much about boxing, but she would have to give rounds one and two to Senator Bellardi. She could not wait until tomorrow night. She could smell a knockout coming.

Ernesto "Ernie" Cruz was a California Highway Patrol officer stationed in Redding while Dan Bellardi was making his mark and his millions as a land developer. The two had been classmates in high school, competing together on the swim team. About the time Dan entered California politics, Ernie took an early retirement from the CHP and formed a security patrol company specializing in commercial properties and large private estates. Ernie and his wife, Carmen, were long-time supporters of Bellardi's North California movement and his bid for governor.

The Bellardi ranch in the Palo Cedro area east of Redding had been one of Ernie's accounts since Bellardi's second term in the California State Senate, yet Ernie had never patrolled the property personally until AntiCrist emerged as a serious danger. Still fit and muscular at sixty-one, Ernie had personally commanded the detachment of four security cops at the ranch every night since Bellardi campaign headquarters was fire-bombed more than two weeks earlier. The fact that the senator was in Red Bluff for the debates did not diminish in Ernie's mind the potential for some kind of attack on the house. He remained vigilant as if guarding the life of his old teammate and friend.

"Midnight check," Ernie said into his radio. He sat in his pickup, which was parked in the Bellardi's driveway just outside the arc of the bright security lamps mounted on the garage. The pickup's windows were down, but not a breath of wind stirred the night air. All was quiet.

His four armed officers were stationed unobtrusively in the darkness around the house, far enough out in the field or beyond the corral to surprise an intruder sneaking in from the road or the creek, yet near enough to be inside the house in little more than a minute if needed.

The men replied one by one on their portable radios.

"Number two. All quiet."

"Four check. Dead as a possum on the freeway out here."

"One. I think I saw a satellite go over. Nothing else moving out here."

"Three is ready to march."

"OK, let's rotate, guys," Ernie said with a sigh. Once every two hours—not exactly on the hour, so as not to be predictable—the four men picked up their camp stools and surveyed their quadrant of the area around the house. Then they rotated to new positions. At the same time, Ernie walked around the house with a flashlight, checking windows and assuring that all doors to the outside were locked. Then he walked the length of the quarter-mile driveway to the road in the dark just to work the kinks out of his legs. Every night had been as quiet and uneventful as tonight. Like most ex-cops, Ernie missed the action of being on the road. But in the security business, a quiet night is a successful night.

Ernie was halfway out to the road when he heard Gary Ragsdale's expletive through the ear bud of his portable radio. Ernie whirled as his number two officer spoke again. "Fire, Ernie!" Gary said. Ernie could tell the man was running. "Part of the back of the house just lit up like a torch."

An orange glow and the first traces of smoke appeared over the peak of the sprawling one-level house. Ernie Cruz changed frequencies on his radio and called the county fire district as he ran back toward the house. Then he was back on with his men. "Who's back there, Gary? Did you see anybody?"

"Negative. I didn't see nobody." Ragsdale was panting as he spoke. "I was about a hundred yards back of the house. One second it's all dark, the next second—*whoosh!*—a section of the wall is on fire."

Ernie was puffing a little himself as he ran. "County is rolling. You guys look for some garden hoses. I'm going inside to get the kid and the housekeeper out."

Ernie had two urgent concerns. First, he had to make sure the occupants of the house got out safely. Mrs. Bellardi was still visiting her mother in Redwood City; only Wes and Elena were at home that night. The fire had just started, the tile roof was resistant to sparks, and there was no wind to fuel the

253

flames, so Ernie knew that no one was in immediate danger. Wes Bellardi was sick with a cold, Ernie had been told, and had gone to bed early. Judging from the glow behind the house, Wes's room was closest to the flames. Elena's quarters were in the west wing, away from the growing blaze. The kind Honduran woman had been cordial toward Ernie and his men, serving them coffee and treats almost every evening. Ernie would get the boy first and then Elena.

His second concern was the cause of the blaze. Was this the work of the crazy amateur terrorist called AntiCrist? If so, how did he get to the house, and where was he now? Or did the sudden fire spring from a less menacing source, such as an electrical failure or a long-smoldering cigarette? Either way, Ernie had to get the residents to safety before he could concentrate fully on the cause.

Using the key he had been given, Ernie hurried through the front door and began calling Wes's name as he raced toward the bedrooms. There was only a trace of smoke in the house, but Ernie moved as quickly as he could.

Dan's kid was asleep in his bed, wearing maroon pajamas. The room reeked of cold medicine. Ernie shook the young man, who seemed drugged. "There's a fire, Wes," he said, pulling the young man out of bed. Ernie helped the mumbling and stumbling kid out the front door. Then he took off for the housekeeper's quarters yelling, "Fire, Elena! Fire! Fire!"

The housekeeper, wearing a nightgown and robe, met him in the dimly lit hall, whimpering with fear. "It's a fire, but you're all right," he assured her, then ushered her quickly out the front door to the driveway where Wes sat stunned on the cement. Ernie's four colleagues were already valiantly battling the blaze with garden hoses, as sirens from the county fire rigs wailed in the distance. Thanks to the men's quick work and the fact that there were no dry weeds or brush immediately surrounding the house, the Bellardi home would be saved and the fire damage would be minimal. Ernie was most relieved that no one was injured.

During the fire crew's mop-up, Ernie Cruz toured the perimeter of the house as he had twice earlier in the evening. He checked the windows and doors away from the fire damaged area. Everything was secure except the door from the backyard to the attached garage. It was closed but not locked as it had been during the ten-fifteen walk-around. Perhaps one of the firefighters needed a tool or something, Ernie thought.

The county fire chief told him off the record that arson was a strong possibility, which meant that someone had penetrated Ernie's security perimeter undetected, something he could hardly believe. Wes and Elena had seen no one. Ernie and his four coworkers had seen no one. So how did the mystery arsonist get in and out unseen? Ernie was baffled and embarrassed. How would he explain this to Dan Bellardi?

Two o'clock in the morning and all was dark and quiet at Bellardi headquarters. A single sheet of paper rested in the tray of the fax machine, having emerged almost three hours earlier. The bold letters of the brief message read: "The fire was no accident. Belardi must quit north Calfornia. Next time somone you love will get hurt. AntiCrist."

29

Sunday
September 26

ARRIVING HOME from Red Bluff at nearly one in the morning, Stevie had crawled into bed and given herself permission to sleep late the next day. Shawna would not be home from the leadership conference until midafternoon or early evening. Collin was going to church with the Manns, the family who had taken him in for the weekend. Stevie had arranged to meet them after the service to pick up her son, opting to miss church again this week because she was exhausted. She knew it was a bad habit she would have to correct after the campaign.

It had been a grueling weekend for Stevie in Red Bluff, not so much physically as emotionally. Though very little of her time had been required by Senator Bellardi and the debate team, Stevie had spent the last forty-eight hours wound tight, ready at a moment's notice to help out as needed. Then for two hours each evening she was on the edge of her chair emotionally during the Bellardi-Dunsmuir debates. Stevie had the sense that each question, each comment, each word uttered on the platform in front of the television cameras bore directly on her future in North California. Every Bellardi gain was a personal gain for Stevie and her children. Every glimmer of a Dunsmuir success felt like a personal defeat.

All in all, Stevie had been pleased with the outcome of the first weekend clash. Political observers in the media offered mixed reviews. Juanita Dunsmuir's seemingly compassionate approach on the abortion issue had won her some points with her detractors. In fact, she had done so well that one analyst declared her the weekend winner simply for not losing as badly as many people expected. But most pundits predicted that Daniel Bellardi's lead in the polls would widen slightly as a result of his rock-solid presentations and composure under fire. Stevie liked to think she had a hand in every point the senator gained that week.

Being so close to Robert Johnstone all weekend had also taken an emotional toll on Stevie. Although they had not spent any time alone together, Stevie was constantly aware of his presence. Each time their eyes met across the room, her stomach tightened and she scolded herself for reacting so childishly. At the same time, she found herself counting the days until November—not just so the pressures of the campaign would be behind them, but so that she and Robert could finally begin spending personal time together without the distractions of deadlines and statistics.

Even more taxing to Stevie's emotions this weekend had been the frightening event at the Bellardi ranch. She did not hear about the fire until early Saturday morning at staff breakfast. Senator Bellardi had been driven home in the middle of the night to view the damage and talk with his security staff. The note from AntiCrist was discovered early Saturday morning before the senator returned to Red Bluff. News of another attack, especially one that could have destroyed the senator's home and killed his son and housekeeper, sobered Stevie. Hearing of AntiCrist's threat to purposely hurt someone—particularly someone the senator loved—gripped her with fear.

Even though Robert had made it a point to assure her that Wes had escaped the blaze unharmed, Stevie still had felt moved to call him. When she finally reached him late Saturday morning, her protégé was as noncommunicative as ever, but Stevie was relieved just hearing his foggy voice. She wanted to implore Wes to quit the campaign and fly back to the university. Whoever AntiCrist was, he was crazy enough and crafty enough to make good on his threats—and Wes might very well be a target. But it was not her place to boss him around—except perhaps about the fax bulletins. So she just urged him to be careful. Every thought of harm coming to Wes reminded her of the tragedy that befell her own Dougie.

During a press conference at noon on Saturday, Senator Bellardi had made clear his intention to continue the campaign. He was so adamant about not giving up, Stevie had noted while listening, that he seemed to mock the peril facing him and his loved ones. She had never seen such resolve blaze from his eyes before. It had caused her to wonder about the balance of his commitment to family and career. He seemed intent on pushing through to victory at all costs. His goals for North California were important, but were they worth the loss of a wife or a son?

During the Saturday evening debates on the topics of crime in general and legalized drugs in particular, Senator Bellardi was his confident, articulate self again, as if the fire had never happened. He took his characteristic black-and-white hard line on crime issues and adequately defended his position against Juanita Dunsmuir, who pressed him on the gray areas as she had during the abortion discussion. It was not a resounding victory, Stevie had assessed, but she was confident that the senator was inching farther ahead of his challenger in the debates, just as she had hoped. A victory party until midnight had drained the last ounces of Stevie's energy. She fell asleep grateful for a Sunday morning with no responsibilities.

Stevie was so deeply asleep at seven-thirty that she only heard the last of the telephone's four rings before her answering machine kicked in. "We can't take your call right now, but if you leave your name, number, and a brief message at the tone, we'll get back to you as soon as possible. Have a great day!"

Stevie remained still, with her eyes closed. She decided not to pick up unless it was one of the kids. But when she heard the concern on the other end of the line, she began to waffle on her decision. "Steve, this is Jon. Maybe you're still in Red Bluff. I just had to call and check in with you. I got worried when I heard about the Bellardi fire on CNN. Just wanted to make sure you're all right. It sounds like the campaign is getting a little nasty. I hope you're taking care of yourself. I'll call you again later today and—"

Stevie picked up. "Hello, Jon," she said, her voice husky from sleep. Stevie knew she would have to talk to him eventually. Now was as good a time as any.

"I thought you might be there listening. Thanks for picking up."

"It's been a killer weekend," Stevie said over a yawn, wincing at the poor choice of adjectives. "I didn't get to bed until one."

"Sorry. I can call later."

"It's all right. I'm awake now. . . . I think."

"It sounds like a war zone up there," Jon said. "I've been a little concerned about the kids' safety—and yours, too, of course. This AntiCrist is a real nut, a loose cannon. Somebody could get hurt."

Stevie was all too familiar with the weight of concern Jon had expressed. "Senator Bellardi is taking every precaution," she said, stretching the truth a little to placate him.

"I'm not so sure," Jon retorted. "Bellardi had five security cops around his house, and it still got torched."

"No one was hurt," Stevie said.

"Somebody could have been. And from the note, this guy *intends* to hurt someone."

"He's a crackpot, an amateur. He can't even spell *antichrist.*"

"Then why haven't the cops found him? Why can't they turn a clue about who he is? This guy is smarter than you think, Steve. Just because he can't spell doesn't mean he can't blow away your candidate or one of his family members."

Jon's words prompted a frightening mental picture of a gunman wielding an assault rifle, spraying a crowded platform with bullets. In the split-second image, Stevie saw Senator and

Mrs. Bellardi, their son, Wes, and a half-dozen others fall mortally wounded. She rolled over in bed to escape the picture.

"The senator has bodyguards," she rationalized aloud.

"I hope they're more efficient than the Keystone Kops guarding his ranch," Jon shot back.

Stevie felt a rush of anger. Jon's cynicism always pushed the wrong buttons with her. "What an awful thing to say," she remonstrated.

After a moment of silence, Jon agreed. "You're right. That was bad. I'm sorry. My point is, they can't protect Bellardi completely. Look at the Kennedys, Martin Luther King, Rabin. They were protected too. If a terrorist wants to get to somebody badly enough, Steve, he can always find a way, no matter how much security is in place."

"I know about assassinations, Jon," Stevie said, her patience beginning to erode.

Jon stumbled over his words trying to start his next sentence. Stevie perceived that he was a little self-conscious about what he was about to say. Finally he took a long breath and spoke slowly and deliberately. "Steve, my concern is, if AntiCrist can get to Bellardi, he can get to you too. I mean, the nut may blow up campaign headquarters or a hotel or an auditorium trying to hurt Bellardi, and you could get hurt or killed—and maybe the kids too. I just don't like it. That's all I have to say."

Stevie was flattered at her ex-husband's concern and rather surprised to hear him express it so pointedly. "It's not like I travel with the senator all the time, Jon. And the kids aren't even involved in the campaign."

"I know, but you travel with him *some* of the time. And you work in the same office. It only takes one time."

It occurred to Stevie that no one else she knew had voiced concern for her safety in the wake of AntiCrist's attacks. Shawna and Collin seemed oblivious to the extent of her involvement in the campaign itself, let alone aware of the possible dangers. Robert Johnstone and the others Stevie worked with in the office were clearly preoccupied with Senator Bellardi's safety and the success of the campaign. Even Wes Bellardi, her secret project, seemed unconcerned. Hearing someone say with sincerity, "I'm worried about you," warmed her inside. The fact that these words came from her ex-husband—someone who was no longer required to care—made her appreciate them more.

"It's not your job to worry about me, Jon," she said, only halfheartedly trying to persuade him to stop.

"I know. It's just that—well, I . . . I had to call and find out what was going on. I mean . . ."

After a few seconds Stevie realized that Jon had given up trying to finish his bumbling sentence. During the worst days before and after the divorce, she gloated over any ineptitude Jon displayed. Every negative quirk, every failure further validated in her mind their decision to end the marriage. Right now, she did not feel that way about the man's clumsy defense of his concern for her. Instead, she felt a surge of appreciation and respect for him, a feeling that had attended some of their best days together.

"Thank you," she said at last.

After a ragged silence, Jon continued as if they had not digressed into the personal area. "So, what about Bellardi's wife and kid? Who's taking care of them?"

"Patricia is with her mother in Redwood City until the elections," Stevie explained.

Jon hummed, adding, "I read about that. Trouble in paradise?"

"No, just stress," Stevie explained, parroting the party line—which was mostly true. "And she has bodyguards too—I'm pretty sure."

"And the boy?"

"He's a young man, really; twenty years old. Lives at the ranch. I think they assigned a security cop to him yesterday." Stevie was momentarily revisited by her maternal feelings for the boy—he seemed more boy than man to her also—who reminded her so much of Dougie. She decided not to say any more about Wes. She would tell Jon about her project someday, perhaps when she had a little more to show for her effort.

After a pause, Jon spoke again with hesitation in his voice. "Steve, there's something else I've been meaning to talk to you about, if you have another minute."

"Sure," she answered. "What is it?"

"I should have mentioned this before. It's not fair to keep you in the dark, especially since this sort of involves you. But you've had a lot on your mind the last couple of months.

Besides, I didn't exactly know how to explain it or how you would react."

Stevie sat up in her bed. From a distant dark corner of her mind, one thought rushed to the front of her brain. *Jon has a girlfriend. He's going to tell me he's dating someone. Why else would he sound so tentative about something he's been meaning to talk to me about? He has a lot of nerve saying he's so worried about me and then popping this kind of a surprise on me.*

"What is it?" she repeated.

Listening to her ex-husband tell about Ben Hernandez and all that had led up to his moving in with Jon, Stevie rolled through a kaleidoscope of feelings. Her initial reaction was that she was glad she had not blurted out something like, "So you're dating again, is that it?" Then she was shocked to learn that Jon had actually gone to jail and visited Eugene Hackett, the young thug who had been involved in both the assault on Jon and the drive-by shooting—indeed, the two events were morbidly connected.

Stevie's anger about the shooting flared anew at the identification of a culprit. She was incensed that the kid had been let off so easily after what she regarded as two counts of attempted murder. She was also miffed at Jon for withholding from her for almost three months information about Hackett's arrest and incarceration.

More than anything, however, Stevie was astounded to the point of disbelief that Jon had confronted the young hoodlum at County jail and forgiven him to his face. *You weren't there,* she challenged Jon silently as he told his story, *when those bullets exploded through the kitchen window. You didn't crawl over shattered glass in panic to find out if our little boy was alive or dead. Had you been there, Jon, and felt the terror I felt, you might not be so quick to get chummy with the sociopath who tried to kill Collin and me. If anything you should have protested such a short jail sentence.*

The final part of the story left Stevie numb and speechless. Jon had volunteered to serve as a citizen sponsor to someone with a rap sheet frighteningly similar to Eugene's. And now that kid was actually living in the house—*her* house—with Jon. He slept in one of her beds, ate at her table. It was as if Jon had invited the devil to be his roommate.

263

The only word she could utter at the end of the story was, "Why?"

"Because he needs a sponsor and there wasn't anyone else available."

Stevie sat in silence pondering the imponderable. There had to be more to it than that.

Seemingly trying to sell her on the idea, Jon added, "Because the guy needs a break, and I think I can help him. Actually, I think God wants me to help him."

More silence as Stevie remained unconvinced.

"OK," Jon said, as if playing his trump card, "I'm also doing it because Ben reminds me a little of Dougie. I know that sounds funny since they seem to have little in common other than their age and their slight builds. But there's something . . . I don't know, maybe I'm reliving an opportunity I missed."

Stevie felt the temptation to gloat rise within her. *So you have a Dougie project too, Jon,* she thought, knowing she would never say it aloud. *But when we finally compare notes on these two young men, you'll discover that a young writer and governor's son has far greater potential for success than a dropout gang member.*

30
Sunday
September 26

"DAD, I really don't need a bodyguard." Wes was pacing the family room at the ranch as he spoke. His voice was still hoarse from a chest cold.

Daniel Bellardi sat at the dining room table hastily finishing a sandwich. "Of course you do, Weston. This crazy man may try something again. I don't want anything to happen to you." The senator was dressed in jeans, boots, and a western shirt. His appointment secretary, Mike Bragan, stood impatiently in the living room near the front door, ready to whisk him off to another campaign appearance: a fishing derby at Whiskeytown Reservoir.

The Bellardi ranch was still functional after the fire. Two

rooms at the back of the house, including Wes's bedroom, experienced minor smoke and water damage. But, thanks to the quick action of county fire crews, the place would be livable during repairs.

"Then maybe I should just go back to school," Wes conceded. "At least I'd be out of the way."

The senator shook his head. "No, Son, that wouldn't do any good. If this AntiCrist person decides he wants to come after you, he can track you down there easily enough. Besides, I need you here. We're in the homestretch now. There's work to be done, and we need to maintain a positive family image, especially with your mother . . . gone for a while."

Wes's jaw line twitched as he pressed his lips together. "I'm worried about her," he said softly. "Do you think she'll be all right?"

Daniel reprimanded his son with a sharp gaze. "Your mother will be fine. She'll be home in a couple of weeks. She just needed some time away. Campaigning is very hard on her." Wes knew there was more to Patricia's absence than campaign pressure, but he also knew that, with Mike Bragan in the room, his father did not want to pursue the subject. Returning to their original topic of conversation, he said, "I'm very uncomfortable with someone shadowing me everywhere I go, Dad."

Daniel wiped his mouth with a napkin and stood. Elena appeared from the kitchen on cue to carry away his plate and utensils. "And I'm very uncomfortable with your being alone. Ernie is a good man. He won't be a burden to you, and knowing he's with you eases my mind when I'm gone."

Daniel walked into the living room to Mike, who held out a bulletproof vest disguised as a sleeveless fishing jacket. "You should be going out to the lake with us, Weston," Daniel called over his shoulder as he slipped into the vest.

Wes tagged behind him. "I told you, Dad, I don't feel up to it yet. My head's clogged up, and I may still have a fever."

Daniel raised a doubtful eyebrow. "Fine," he said. "But I will see you at the dinner in Weed, won't I?"

Wes nodded. "I'll rest this afternoon and be there tonight."

"Ernie will drive you up," Daniel said as Mike opened the door for him. "Do what he says. I'm paying him well to take care of you."

Wes nodded again. His father stepped out the door without another word. Mike Bragan followed close behind.

Before the door closed, another man entered, a muscular Latino with shocks of gray dominating once jet-black hair and bushy mustache. Ernie Cruz looked uncomfortable in the suit and tie he was required to wear for his new assignment. He carried a brown paper sack in one hand.

"Hello, Wes," he said, holding out the sack as he approached. "Carmen sent some of her famous tamales for you. She remembered how much you like them."

Wes smiled as he received the gift. "Thanks, Ernie. And you're right. Your wife's tamales are my favorite. I'm just not sure I'm quite up to eating them yet, but they'll be a great incentive to get well quickly. Please thank Carmen for me."

Ernie returned the smile. In Wes's preteen years, Ernie and Carmen Cruz had been like an uncle and aunt to him. With the emergence of Daniel's political career, Wes occasionally stayed with the Cruz family while his parents were on the campaign trail. Robby Cruz, close to Wes's age, had been like a brother. Ernie used to take both boys fishing and rifle shooting out in the hills.

Wes led Ernie into the family room, where he slipped out of his jacket, revealing a .357 Magnum holstered at the belt. Elena appeared and greeted the visitor, received his order for a cold beer—nonalcoholic—and then took the tamales to the refrigerator.

Ernie eased into the large leather chair. "The Forty-Niners are on in a few minutes. Playing the Seahawks. Should be a good game."

Wes did not sit down. "Help yourself, Ernie. I still feel kind of lousy. I'm going to crash in the guest room if you don't mind. Got to be ready for tonight. It's a command performance—for both of us, I'm afraid." Wes sighed. "Sorry. I guess everything I do for the next few weeks will involve both of us."

Ernie returned a knowing look. "Don't worry about it, Wes. Besides, it'll be just like old times. We can hang out together." He smiled. "I'm just here to help, you know. Let's try to make the best of it for your father's sake."

Wes nodded. "You're right, Ernie. Thanks," he said, turning to go to his bedroom.

●

Shawna half carried, half dragged her nylon suitcase across the wet Shasta Commons parking lot toward home. It was warm, humid, and overcast in Redding. The last drops of a midafternoon thundershower dotted the puddles on the asphalt.

She was exhausted from the weekend conference, having stayed up well past midnight every night talking and laughing with Terilyn and the other delegates from Reagan High School. But she was very glad to be home. Her brain was overloaded with thoughts and questions and conflicts from her two days in San Francisco. At times during the general sessions and seminars, everything she heard and experienced seemed so logical and exciting. At other times, Shawna wondered if she were the only sane person at the conference.

Where had all this stuff about tolerance and individual values and equal truth and equal lifestyles come from? Not to mention the big interest in ancient religious beliefs and practices. And what did it all mean? Shawna was careful to play along and keep her doubts to herself. To call into question verities clearly unimpeachable to others would have been an act of social suicide. But Shawna had come away confused, especially about the topics Ms. Carmona and Terilyn and the other girls seemed so sure about.

It was time to talk to Mom. Shawna had made the determination in the van on the way home as the other passengers dozed. She would not tell Mom everything, such as Ms. Carmona being involved in reading horoscopes or her strange beliefs about spirituality and higher powers. Nor would she tell her about the discussions she often had with Terilyn regarding tolerance and truth and spirituality. Shawna would talk about the issues in general and see what her mother said. If she liked what she heard, fine. If not, she could blow it off and believe whatever she wanted.

"Mom, I'm home." Shawna dropped her bag and jacket inside the door and listened for a response. Muffled electronic sounds of laser cannons, dogfighting planes, and exploding bombs down the hall told her that Collin was already home from his weekend with the Manns. Shawna wrinkled her nose. She had been looking forward to her mother's undivided attention.

Shawna found Stevie in the office sitting at the keyboard as expected. She had the phone tucked into her shoulder talking to someone about campaign business while tinkering with an advertising bid sheet on the computer. It was an all-too-familiar pose to Shawna these days.

Seeing her enter, Stevie smiled and waved hello without missing a word of the conversation. Shawna flopped into the side chair as her mother flashed a "be with you in just a minute" signal. Shawna kicked off her Nikes, picked at her nails, surveyed the walls, and waited. Her mother talked on about schedules and meetings. After five minutes, Shawna trudged back to the front door to retrieve her bag. She dumped the dirty clothes in the utility room and put the rest of her things away. Returning to the office, she received an "almost finished" hand signal. *This is stupid, Mom,* Shawna grumbled to herself. *It's Sunday. It's supposed to be family day. Can't you talk to these people later?*

Finally her mother tapped off the phone. "How was it?" she said, swiveling toward her.

Shawna flopped into the side chair for the second time. "OK," she said, wondering how to bring up the topics of the conference.

"Did you have a good time with Terilyn?"

"Yeah."

"What about the conference? Did you enjoy it? Did you get anything out of it?"

It was the perfect opportunity, Shawna thought. "They talked a lot about being tolerant of other people," she answered tentatively, testing the water.

"Being tolerant, that's good, honey," her mom said, turning back to the monitor for a second to move some figures around with the mouse.

Shawna blinked with surprise. "You think tolerance is good?"

Before Stevie could respond, Collin burst into the room. He acknowledged his sister with the briefest of glances. "Mom, I got to level X-fifteen," he chirped excitedly. "I still have six planes left in my squadron. I think I can get to X-sixteen next."

"Wonderful, sweetheart," Stevie said with pride, even though Shawna knew her mother was clueless about what Collin meant.

"You've got to see this, Mom," he said, grabbing Stevie by

the hand, adding as an afterthought, "You too, Shawna."
Shawna began to fume inside at the interruption.

"In a minute, Collin," Stevie said. "I'm hearing about
Shawna's trip to San Francisco."

"But, Mom," he whined, "my squadron is in hover mode. I
only have sixty seconds or I'll lose my level."

"You go ahead, honey. I'll be there in a minute."

Tired and irritated, Shawna gave him a little nudge toward
the door. "Yeah, give us a minute, toad boy."

"You don't have to hit me," Collin snapped angrily.

Shawna snapped back, "I didn't hit you." She suspected that
Collin was just as unhappy as she was about having to share
Mom's precious free time.

Collin left the room in a huff. Shawna picked up where she
left off. "I didn't think you would approve of tolerance."

"If you mean accepting people where they are, of course I
approve. That's what the Bible teaches. Jesus loves everybody
just the same, and so should we."

That's what Shawna had thought. It was the lifestyle part
that puzzled her. She said, "But what about—"

The telephone cut her off in midsentence. "Hold that
thought, honey," Stevie said. "I've been waiting for this call for
an hour. I'll just be a couple of minutes. Why don't you see
how your brother is doing on level twenty-five or whatever."
Then she tapped the phone on, swiveled back to the monitor,
and launched into a conversation.

It was a polite, well-meaning brush-off, Shawna thought,
but it was still a brush-off. And today she was in no mood to
come in second to a brother or an advertising deal or the first
governor of North California. She had finally ratcheted up her
courage to explore this confusing topic with her mother. It
was the kind of heart-to-heart conversation her mother always
said she welcomed. *So much for mother-daughter intimacy,*
Shawna thought, sighing softly.

She picked up her shoes quietly and left the office, head
down. After grabbing a can of pop from the fridge, she slipped
back into her Nikes and left for Terilyn's apartment without
leaving a note.

270

31

Sunday
October 10

IT WAS a little chilly and breezy for a meeting atop the houseboat, but this was Senator Daniel Bellardi's favorite retreat, a
quiet haven in the midst of a heated, stressful campaign. So his
key staff sat on the deck wearing long pants and jackets turned
up at the collar. In contrast to the many elegant gourmet meals
served in this setting by Matthew and Lucy Denherder, today's
lunch was barely a snack: make-your-own deli sandwiches,
store-bought coleslaw, potato chips by the handful, paper
plates and napkins, canned drinks or hot coffee. The caretakers'
services had not been needed today so they had not been summoned; food was the last thing on Senator Bellardi's mind. The
debates were finally over. It was time to take stock and regroup

for the final charge. Election day was just over three weeks away.

"All right, Robert, let's have it," Bellardi said, yielding the floor to his campaign director. Stevie watched the senator step back and sink into a deck chair. Dressed casually in faded jeans, polo, and windbreaker, he looked weary and haggard. Without the television makeup, which had made him look so robust during the debates, he appeared anemic. He wore the emotional weight of the campaign like a heavy cloak.

What had been predicted to be a cakewalk to the governor's office had turned into a dogfight with the well-financed, well-coached folksinger, Juanita Dunsmuir. Repeated threats and sporadic violent attacks from an elusive terrorist had lined his face with concern and pushed his wife to the brink of an emotional breakdown. Adding to Bellardi's burden, a recent discovery hinted that stress and fear were not the only causes of Patricia's difficulties. Robert Johnstone had told Stevie privately that Patricia had been diagnosed with early-stage Alzheimer's. Senator Bellardi had sworn his inner circle to secrecy and strictly forbade the medical findings from being released until after the election. In public, he remained the picture of confidence and enthusiasm, Stevie had noted. But at times like these she wondered if he would be able to hold it together until the election.

Today Stevie felt the same way about herself. The last three weeks had taken a toll. No amount of sleep seemed to lift the constant physical and mental fatigue—as if she had any time for extra sleep. Having been away from the kids so much, life at home was a shambles. Collin seemed cranky all the time, and Shawna, who spent far too much time at Terilyn's, barely spoke to her. Meals together were a rarity. Discipline had gone out the window. *It will be worth it when Governor Bellardi begins his first term,* she continually reminded herself.

Work was also a struggle. Stevie had sacrificed another client to the hectic campaign schedule, and the rest of her advertising work was slap-dash-pathetic, actually. It would take her well into the next year to regain the momentum she had lost. Other important activities had gone by the boards as well. Her personal devotions had been reduced to a thirty-second morning prayer, and regular church attendance was only a memory.

She had the social life of a convent-confined nun. The words *It will be worth it when Governor Bellardi begins his first term* had become more of a desperate prayer than a statement of confidence.

For the first time since Dougie's death, Stevie found herself tempted to take tranquilizers again. She felt the need for something to serve as a buffer between her and the grinding, incessant pressure of the debate team and the fax bulletins, something to quiet the gnawing guilt over her failures at home and work. Then, of course, there was the constant anxiety fueled by AntiCrist's threats against her candidate, his wife, and particularly his son, the Dougie she was trying to do right by this time. She tried not to allow herself even to think about Jon and that felon he had welcomed into her house, but the fear of what could happen nagged at her more than she liked to admit. The temptation to get a prescription for just enough tranquilizers to get her safely past the election was strong, but so far she had been able to resist it.

Robert Johnstone had been a big part of the reason she had resisted. His very presence seemed to exude a strength that infused Stevie with a resolve to see this trying time through—minus tranquilizers—one day at a time. And with each of those passing days, the attraction between Robert and Stevie grew. Where once she felt uncomfortable when he was near, now she found herself missing him when he was not.

Robert Johnstone stood before the small group huddled together on a collection of deck chairs. He was armed with the results of polls taken at the close of the previous night's final debate session at Humboldt State University in Eureka. Stevie sat near the back of the group, her lightweight parka zipped tightly against the cool breeze. She was not a member of Senator Bellardi's top staff, but Robert had urged her to come to the debriefing since she had been such an integral member of the debate team. He had also made a point of her not driving out to the lake alone, but rather riding out with him "so we can at least have a few moments together before and after the meeting." Again, she was flattered at being included in the senator's inner circle and pleased that Robert wanted her there for personal reasons. But here she was spending another three hours away from the kids, having just returned from Eureka late last night. She had promised them a movie and dinner out after their weekend apart. She resolved to make good on that promise as soon as she got home that afternoon.

Robert was the only member of the Bellardi team who seemed unfazed by the pressures of the campaign. He had maintained his summer tan and always appeared fit, impeccably groomed, and well rested, though Stevie suspected that he survived on about five hours of sleep nightly. Above all, his commitment to Daniel Bellardi and North California was unwaveringly positive. He was the anchor of the campaign—and was quickly becoming her anchor as well.

As she watched him make his presentation, Stevie realized again how disturbingly attractive Robert was. She reminded herself that she was not in a good frame of mind to think about a serious relationship with a man, but neither did she possess the resolve to prevent it. She had seen Robert almost every day for the past three weeks. On many days they had spent several hours together, although usually in the company of other staff. The looks—and occasionally the words—that passed between them assured Stevie that her attraction to Robert was more than reciprocated, but he had never behaved toward her in anything but a gentlemanly manner. In fact, with the stress and pressure of the campaign, Robert had told her very candidly that, although he wanted very much to take her out to dinner again, he felt it best to wait until after the election when both of them would be able to focus their time and energy on something other than the campaign. Stevie was in absolute agreement, but at times it was difficult to think of Robert Johnstone only as her boss.

"The latest polls indicate that we've come through the debates well," Robert was saying. "We've gained additional support, and Ms. Dunsmuir's base has declined slightly."

"What are the numbers exactly, Robert?" interrupted Ethan Worrell. As head of the debate team, Ethan clearly had a stake in the post-debate figures.

"If the election were held today," Robert answered, "Senator Bellardi would collect 48 percent of the vote and Ms. Dunsmuir would collect 41 percent." The figures were greeted with a ripple of applause. Daniel Bellardi continued to sit impassively.

"Eleven percent still undecided?" Ethan probed.

"That's correct," Robert said. "In effect, our gains were cross-overs. We're up 2 percent, Dunsmuir is down 2 percent. In reality, perhaps we won a few thousand undecideds and a few thousand of her supporters bailed out to middle ground. It's difficult to tell."

"And it doesn't really matter," media secretary Price Whitten threw in. "We still have some convincing to do." A hum of agreement followed.

Robert continued with the demographics. "The population centers along the I-5 corridor, the former Fourth Senate District served by the senator, are still solidly with us. Ironically, the highest concentration both of Dunsmuir people and undecideds are in the First and Second Districts along the coast and in the rural eastern counties."

"Where the marijuana grows full and free," someone threw in. There was a smattering of laughter. Neither Robert nor Daniel cracked a smile.

Robert ran through specific numbers to substantiate his general statement. Then he said, "Simply and plainly, ladies and gentlemen, this means that the senator will spend the last three weeks of the campaign stumping the coast along Highway 101 and blitzing a few key rural communities. It will be an intense, high-visibility, high-touch sweep of Juanita Dunsmuir's strongholds."

"And high *vulnerability*, it seems to me," Mike Bragan commented. Everyone knew what he meant. The entire campaign staff had spent the last three weeks on the ragged edge anticipating AntiCrist's next attack.

Robert nodded his understanding of Mike's comment. "The senator and I discussed this concern in detail this morning. We are prepared to go ahead with the tour because, since the fire at the ranch, there have been only two printed threats from AntiCrist and no attacks. He may be incapable of carrying out further actions because he lacks the intelligence and/or the resources. And we like to believe that our upgraded security has successfully prevented him from acting again." Robert nodded toward the two men stationed fore and aft on the top deck as he continued. "In addition to the team constantly assigned to the senator, Mrs. Bellardi and Wes are well taken care of. In spite of any possible danger, the senator and I have agreed that we're ready to move into high gear and push on to victory. We trust that you're all ready to run with us."

Stevie nodded her head enthusiastically along with everyone else on deck. Even though she was not an official member of the senator's staff, she was accepted by most as if she were. And even though Stevie's primary job on the team had been completed with the conclusion of the debates, Robert had asked her to stay on through the election. It had been Senator Bellardi's wish too, he had said. "Having worked with us on the inside," Robert assured her, "there are many areas where your communication skills will prove invaluable—if you don't mind being a utility player."

No, she did not mind being a utility player, because she desperately needed this campaign to succeed. She had already invested—*squandered* might be more accurate, she realized—too much already not to go the distance. Three more weeks could not make things much worse at home than they already were. Furthermore, she was committed to get melancholy, morose Wes Bellardi through the process. Although he had fully recovered from his cold, Stevie could tell his heart was not fully in the campaign. She knew he was concerned about his mother, and she was sure he wanted to be back at school, even though he had not actually said as much. And even though Wes had a deep personal regard for security cop Ernie Cruz, he obviously did not enjoy wearing him like a shawl. But Stevie cared deeply for this young man and was bound and determined to help Wes fulfill his assignment. She had assured him that, together, they would complete the last three issues of the fax bulletins and see the campaign through to its victorious end.

Wes would thank her someday, she knew, for encouraging and tutoring him. Right now she would be happy just to see a spark of enthusiasm or excitement from the young man. But whenever she was tempted to throw in the towel on Wes, she seemed to hear Dougie challenging her: "Hang in there, Mom. He's just like me. He needs you." No way could she ignore such a plea.

If all this were not reason enough to stay with the campaign, there was Robert. Robert was the prototypical North

California man: committed, sensitive, principled. *His good looks and devastating smile don't hurt any, either,* she thought, smiling to herself as she relived their brief ride together to the lake a couple of hours earlier. *We even have the same taste in music,* she mused. *How refreshing to ride in a car with someone who appreciates classical sounds instead of that country twang that Jon's always listening to.* As hard as she tried not to, she could not help but wonder what direction their relationship would take—and how far it would go—once the election was over.

As much as Ernie Cruz liked young Wes Bellardi and was committed to his protection, serving as his bodyguard was downright boring. Other than what he had to do to fulfill his obligations to his father's campaign, the kid stuck pretty much close to home, sleeping, reading, or watching TV. But Ernie had been appointed as his shadow, and he took his responsibility seriously. On weekdays Ernie drove Wes to headquarters, taking a different route into town each day for security's sake. Then he sat around the office for a few hours until the senator's son had completed his tasks. From there it was back to the ranch. Ernie knew from experience that Wes was a poor conversationalist so, beyond a few jovial amenities, Ernie left the boy alone and spent his own time reading his favorite Louis L'Amour westerns. It was amazing how much reading you could get done in three weeks when there was nothing else to do, he realized.

Weekends were tough. Wes tried every possible excuse to skip the debates, but they seldom worked. His father expected him to be in attendance, "particularly since your mother can't be there. We must present a strong family unit." Wes had grudgingly agreed, and Ernie had accompanied him. Thankfully, to date, there had been no problems, no attacks, and no need for Ernie to test his mettle at defending his longtime friend's only son.

Daniel Bellardi had encouraged Ernie to take a couple days off each week, leaving Wes in the care of other officers. But Ernie took his responsibility seriously. Having sent Carmen off to her sister's in Colorado until after the election, he took up temporary residence in one of the Bellardis' guest rooms. Boring job or not, Ernie would do his part to get his former classmate elected governor of North California.

Today had been a typical Sunday for Ernie: Eat a delectable breakfast prepared by Elena, read the Sunday paper, channel check between several morning football games, eat lunch, channel check between the afternoon games. Wes, greatly relieved at not being included in the top-level meeting on his father's houseboat, had taken full advantage of his morning off and slept in, not coming out for breakfast until almost noon. After a brief exchange of pleasantries with Ernie, Wes had taken a mug of coffee and plunked down on the couch to watch TV with his bodyguard.

Ernie made periodic tours of the house and checked in often by radio with his squad of security guards positioned outside. He could put up with the boredom for three more weeks as long as it meant that Wes Bellardi made it through the election without further incident.

Ernie had just come in from one of his checks around the house and had rejoined Wes, who was watching a news show during football halftime and drinking his third cup of coffee. "Hey, look at that," Ernie said, gesturing toward the television. "The latest polls are out. We're pulling farther ahead of the marijuana queen."

They watched the figures scroll across the screen. The off-camera political analyst interpreting the data stopped just short of projecting a win for Senator Bellardi.

"It's looking pretty good for your dad," Ernie added. "Apparently the debates woke up some people about what's wrong with legalized drugs and mercy killing and gays being coddled like a minority group."

Wes did not move from his position on the couch. "I don't know, Ernie," he said. "Eleven percent still undecided. It's too close to call."

Ernie shook his head. *With all the advantages Wes enjoys, he can sure can be negative sometimes,* he mused. *The kid will probably find something to worry or gripe about even if the senator wins by a landslide.*

Shawna and Terilyn sat side-by-side in deck chairs, bundled in jackets and watching the lights from the apartment buildings shimmer on the water. The temperature was rapidly dropping toward tonight's predicted low of forty degrees, so the Shasta Commons pool area was deserted except for the two girls.

Shawna was still confused about all the things she had heard at the conference in San Francisco, but she was not ready to accept totally what Terilyn and the others obviously already had. With her mother too busy even to answer her questions, Shawna desperately wished for someone objective to talk to. For the time being she had decided simply to enjoy her friendships with Terilyn and the other dwarfs without making a commitment on her beliefs one way or the other.

Terilyn broke a long silence. "How was the movie?"

Shawna shrugged in the darkness and answered without enthusiasm, "OK, I guess."

"Did you and your mom talk?"

"Yeah," Shawna answered with sarcasm in her voice. "She asked if I wanted popcorn and I said yes."

Terilyn laughed quietly. Shawna had kept her informed about the distance between her and her mother.

"Where's your mom *tonight?*" The meaning of Terilyn's question was clear by her emphasis: "Your mom is busy *every* night. What is it this time?"

"She's home in front of the computer doing campaign stuff."

"I thought her job was over after the debates."

"She still writes faxes and stuff," Shawna said, the disgust and disappointment obvious in her tone. "And her boyfriend keeps asking her to do more. Like a dope she keeps saying yes."

"Boyfriend?" Terilyn turned toward her in the darkness. "What boyfriend?"

"That guy Johnstone, the campaign manager."

"Robert Johnstone? I've seen him on TV. He's kinda cute— for an old guy."

"Yeah. I think he's got a thing for Mom. He's always calling her about something. I hate it."

"I know what you mean," Terilyn answered. "I hate it when my mom gets a new boyfriend." They sat in silence for several more moments.

"TV says Bellardi's going to win," Terilyn said.

"You couldn't tell by my mom. She's worried that Juanita will win and North California will go down the toilet."

"You know what'll happen if Bellardi becomes governor?"

"What?"

"Ms. Carmona and teachers like her who try to teach us how to think for ourselves will have to leave North California. Bellardi won't allow them to teach here and 'pollute' our minds."

Shawna thought for a moment. "That's intolerant," she said finally, thinking that's what Terilyn expected her to say.

"Shawna," Terilyn exclaimed, "I think you're getting it!"

"Getting what?"

"The idea about tolerance. You know, all people are equal, all lifestyles are equal, all truths are equal."

Shawna paused. "Yeah, I get it—at least most of it."

"What's not to get? When you start firing people because you don't like their lifestyle or their religious beliefs or whatever, you're treating them unequally. You're intolerant. In fact, that's what Juanita Dunsmuir says about your mom's boss: 'A vote for Dan Bellardi is a vote of intolerance.'"

Shawna did not want to talk about it anymore. For one thing, she was back to the same question that had nagged at her in San Francisco: Why was Adolf Hitler wrong and the Allied forces right? Following that train of thought, if all lifestyles and beliefs are equal, as Ms. Carmona insisted, then the Nazis should have been allowed to live out what they believed. If all religious beliefs and truths are equal, then Christians should be allowed to believe that lifestyles condemned in the Bible are wrong. If homosexuals are to be praised for their lifestyle, then straights should be praised for believing homosexuality is wrong. If everyone should have the right to choose, then pro-lifers have the right to believe that abortion is wrong. And yet she knew that Ms. Carmona—and Terilyn, of course—would not agree with those statements. Their logic regarding tolerance still sounded screwy to Shawna, but she did not want to embarrass herself by bringing it up.

For another thing, she did not like where Terilyn's train of thought was leading. Terilyn believed in tolerance for everyone—everyone, that is, except those she considered "narrow-minded," people like Shawna's parents and the people at Shawna's church. Therefore Terilyn wanted Juanita Dunsmuir to win the election. Shawna's mother worked for Senator Bellardi. If the senator won, as most people expected him to, then maybe, along with teachers like Ms. Carmona, Terilyn and her mother and the other dwarfs would leave North California. Shawna was not ready for that, and she surely did not want to bring up the possibility.

After a long silence, Shawna stood to leave. "I better go in," she said. "It's getting cold."

"Yeah," Terilyn agreed. "Summer is definitely over."

Stevie was already deeply asleep when the phone rang at ten-fifteen. She did not even try to sound fully awake. "Yes?"

"I'm sorry if I woke you, Stephanie."

The fog began to clear. "Robert?"

"I know you must be exhausted," he said. "It was a long day. I'll only take a minute."

"It's all right," she assured him. "Really. I'm fine."

"Good," he answered, his voice gentle but concerned. "Because I'm afraid we have a small emergency."

Stevie pulled herself up on one elbow. Her thoughts immediately went to Senator Bellardi and then to his son. "What is it?"

"It's Price Whitten."

"What happened?"

"Appendicitis. Came on him this afternoon. He's in surgery right now."

Had she been fully awake, Stevie might have anticipated the purpose of Robert's call. Instead, she just felt sorry for the senator's media secretary.

"He may be out of action for a week or more," Robert explained. "And I'd like for you to step in for him while he's down—you know, talk to the media for us, keep our positive image alive. What do you think? You've seen how Price operates, and I know you could do it." He paused, then went on. "Will you think about it, Stephanie? Sleep on it? I'll call you in the morning and you can let me know then. Would that be all right?"

Stevie wondered if she could be dreaming. *Take over for Price Whitten? Talk to the TV people? Deliver statements at press conferences? Not me. I'm just a volunteer. This can't be real.*

But the voice in her dream pressed her for a response. "Stephanie?"

If it was only a dream, then it did not matter what she said. Besides, her heart was racing, and she was not sure if it was out of excitement at being asked to fill in for Price or at the prospect of working even more closely with Robert. Either way, Stevie threw caution to the wind. "You don't have to wait until morning to get my answer, Robert. I'll be glad to step in for Price, if you think I can do it."

Stevie could hear the smile in Robert's voice. "I know you can," he answered, his voice especially warm. "And I'll be right by your side every step of the way."

32

Monday
October 11

JON DID NOT try to lose, but he obviously did not try to win as
hard as Ben did. The slight twenty-year-old, who continually
reeked of cigarette smoke, beat his citizen sponsor for the first
time in their nightly games of driveway one-on-one. The kid
did not exult when his game-winning jump shot dropped
through the hoop. Ben was still too macho to display such
childish emotions, Jon knew. Instead, the kid simply grabbed
the ball on the first bounce and banked it in again for good
measure. But a subtle display of pride and satisfaction was evident: chin up, shoulders back, the confident toss of his head, a
slight swagger in his step. Jon guessed that Ben Hernandez had

experienced few triumphs during his lifetime that he could boast about in public.

Jon threw out his hand. "Nice game, Ben." The kid accepted the handshake but said nothing. "Dinner's on me," Jon said. "Where do you want to eat?"

Ben grabbed a towel and wiped the sweat from his face, but not before Jon detected a spontaneous grin of pleasure tugging at the boy's lips. "My choice?" he said, still fighting the smile.

"Your choice. You deserve it."

The kid thought for a moment. "Bear Pit."

"Great choice. I could go for some ribs myself. Let's get cleaned up."

Jon enjoyed watching Ben put away a platter of baby-backs and a basket of fries. Since moving in with Jon, the kid had begun to fill out his clothes a bit. Because Ben was not wearing gang attire—a strict rule of his probation—no one would guess by looking at him that he was an ex-con. And the more he looked like a college student instead of a thug, the more he reminded Jon of Dougie.

Signs of improvement notwithstanding, Ben Hernandez was far from being out of the woods. Living without parental discipline most of his life, he struggled with authority figures. Ben clashed early and often with his welding instructor, a former military man with a "my way or the highway" approach to teaching. Jon had already negotiated a couple of major truces between the two headstrong men. In his worst nightmares, Jon saw Ben finally snap under the pressure and blast the instructor's face with his acetylene torch.

Ben also balked at Jon's authority at times. "This is stupid, you're a jerk, I'm gone," the kid would threaten when Jon made him get up on time for school or insisted that he smoke his cigarettes outside. Ben's fits of rebellion were liberally punctuated with profanity.

Whenever Ben's hackles rose, Jon prayed fervently and kept a steady hand on the tiller. "You can walk if you want to, Ben; it's your decision," he would say calmly. "But here's what will happen if you choose to leave the program." Listing the consequences of probation violation usually provoked more snarling before Ben finally backed off. When he did, Jon lavished him with affirmation for good judgment, and life returned to a reasonable peace.

At the other end of the scale from the occasional head butts were times like this, Jon thought as he gnawed the last shreds of meat from the bones on his plate. Ben was not much of a conversationalist—another area Jon had been working on. But basketball and eating, two of Ben's favorite pastimes, had become a strong point of connection for them. Jon guessed that if Ben was ever vulnerable to serious conversation about life and God, it would be on the court or at the dinner table. He was about to attempt a conversation with Ben when the young man surprised him with a question of his own.

"They're paying you to do this, right?" Ben asked, as he dragged a couple of french fries through a mound of catsup.

"Do what?"

Ben shoved the fries into his mouth but kept his eyes on his plate. "You know, be my P.O."

"I'm not your parole officer. Roger Ramirez is your parole officer. I'm just a citizen sponsor."

"You both have a leash around my neck," Ben said, glancing up for just a moment. "What's the difference?"

Jon laughed at the leash comment. "Being a P.O. is a full-time job. You need college training for that. A citizen sponsor is a volunteer."

"But they still pay you money, right?"

Jon shook his head. "No, Ben, volunteers don't get paid."

Ben stiffened slightly. "You're lying, man. I've seen your paychecks in the mailbox."

Jon shook his head again. "That's not a paycheck. The county sends me a little money each month to help with your expenses—you know, food, electricity, stuff like that."

Ben looked up. "How little?"

"Very little," Jon said, chuckling. "We just ate a good chunk of this month's check." Jon decided not to mention that it actually cost him money each month to be Ben's citizen sponsor.

Ben stayed busy with the french fries for several moments. Jon cleaned a couple of rib bones, interested to see where the kid was headed.

"If you get no money, why do you do it?"

Jon couldn't believe the open door. If he had ever been presented with a teachable moment, this was it. "Couple of reasons," he began, controlling his excitement. "For one thing, nobody else seemed to be available, and I was. It seemed kind of selfish to have a couple of empty bedrooms when somebody like you needed one."

Ben pushed fries around in the basket, continuing to avoid eye contact.

Jon hesitated on his second point. He had not yet talked to Ben about Dougie. "Also, I had a son who died as a teenager a few years ago. He would be close to your age."

Ben looked up. "The guy in the pictures at home?"

"Yeah, the older one."

Ben went back to the fries. "What was his name?"

"Douglas. We called him Dougie."

"How'd he die?"

Jon drew a long silent breath. "Drug overdose."

"On purpose? I mean, was it suicide?"

Jon winced inside. "Depends on how you look at it, I guess. I don't think he killed himself on purpose, but he took the drugs on purpose, and the drugs killed him."

Ben nodded. His rap sheet included minor drug violations, and Jon wondered how close to the edge Ben had come during some of his dark escapades. Thank God, the kid was drug tested regularly while on probation and had stayed clean—so far.

Jon continued, "I guess by helping you I'm trying to make up for failing Dougie." A knot swelled in his throat as he spoke the words. He had not admitted his sense of failure to many people. It seemed odd to be telling Ben—odd but right.

Ben nodded. Then he lifted his gaze as high as Jon's plate, perhaps his best attempt at eye contact. "A lot of people like me need a place to live. Why me?"

Jon shrugged and tried to answer as honestly as he could. "I'm not sure, Ben. It wasn't like I specifically requested you. I just agreed to be a sponsor, and they assigned you to me." He paused before going on. "But I don't really believe it's an accident or just chance that I got you instead of someone else. I . . . I believe it was meant to be."

This time Ben's eyes met his. "You mean God, don't you?"

Jon nodded.

"My *abuela*—my grandma—used to talk to me about God," he said, lowering his eyes again. "She took me to Mass every week. I really liked going to church when I was a kid, even though a lot of my friends told me there was no such thing as God. When my abuela died, I decided they were right. At least, I tried to believe it. Sometimes I'm not so sure. Sometimes it's like I can still hear my abuela telling me about Jesus and heaven. . . ."

His voice trailed off, and Jon waited. When Ben spoke again, his voice was thick. "Do you think she was right?" he asked. "I mean, that there really is a God and a heaven?"

"Yes," Jon said. "I believe your grandmother was right. There really is a God, and there really is a heaven."

Jon waited again. This time, when Ben raised his head, his dark eyes glistened with tears. He made no attempt to brush them away.

"Do you think she's there . . . in heaven?"

Jon nodded. "I'm sure she is," he answered. "And . . . I'm sure my Dougie is too."

Ben looked surprised. "Somebody who died from drugs? In heaven?"

Jon was fighting tears himself. "Maybe I have to believe that to be able to live with what happened," he said. "But I know that Dougie had a close relationship with Jesus when he was little. Even when he got into his rebellious period, there were times when he would talk about God. In fact . . ." He took a deep breath. "After Dougie died we found drug paraphernalia and other things that, had we searched and found them earlier, would have tipped us off to how serious his problems were. But . . . we didn't, so . . . Anyway, we found a diary, too. Dougie really liked to write, and apparently he only expressed his innermost thoughts and feelings on paper. It was hard to read it and realize how much he'd been hurting before he died, and how blind we were to his pain. But throughout the pages we found him crying out to God for help, pouring out his heart to the only one he seemed able to trust. Just before he died he had written out a prayer asking for God's forgiveness. I have to believe that God heard that prayer and that our Dougie is safe with him now."

287

Ben continued to look into Jon's eyes. "So," he said finally, "you think God can even forgive something as bad as drugs."

"Definitely. God not only can but does. He's much more anxious to forgive us than we are to ask him for it. And there's nothing—absolutely nothing—that he won't forgive."

When Ben dropped his eyes again, Jon sensed that the conversation had gone as far as it was going to at the moment. But he was more than pleased at the progress that had been made—for both of them.

Stevie was exhausted from a severely stressful day. She had arrived at campaign headquarters at seven-thirty in the morning to be briefed on her new role. By agreeing to step in for Price Whitten for a week or two, she was automatically on the traveling team with the senator's entourage, which was to leave Redding the next morning and be gone for several days. The entire first half of her day had been spent on her duties as interim media secretary, while the afternoon had been spent at home lining up child care and doing the kids' laundry. Then it was back to the office for more meetings. By eight o'clock that evening she was at the end of her strength.

"Why don't you go home and get some rest?" Robert asked, leaning over her desk. "You look exhausted."

"I am," she agreed, smiling her thanks. "I'm on my way."

Robert returned the smile. "Good. We want you rested and refreshed for the trip."

"What about you? How late are you going to stay?"

"As long as it takes to complete the senator's three-week itinerary," he said, still smiling. "But whether I make it home tonight or not, I'll be here when you arrive in the morning."

Driving home through a misty drizzle, Stevie lamented leaving the kids again. Thankfully, Collin was always welcome to stay with the Manns, and he enjoyed being with his good friend and schoolmate Brett. Terilyn's mother had agreed to take Shawna in, although Stevie still did not like the idea, knowing so little about Terilyn's mother. But she was out of options and out of time. *Only three more weeks, kids. Please hang in there for three more weeks. Things will get instantly better after the election.*

Stevie dialed Wes Bellardi's personal number as she drove.

Being on the road for much of the next three weeks, Stevie would direct Wes's work on the fax bulletins by telephone, with Rhoda Carrier serving as the on-site prod. Stevie had spoken briefly to Wes at the office earlier in the day, but she felt he needed one more pep talk before she left.

"Hello?"

Stevie put on her cheery voice. "Hello, yourself. How are you doing?"

"'Bout the same, I guess."

"What time did you head home today? I didn't see you leave."

"Three o'clock, maybe two-thirty."

"I'll bet you got a good start on the bulletins," Stevie said in her most positive tone.

"Not bad. I got the stuff you left about the debate results. I think I can get it all in. I should have a rough ready for you by Wednesday."

"Good," Stevie said, quietly elated at glimmers of initiative.

They talked through the contents of the *Prayer Fax* and *Fax-O-Gram* until Stevie was satisfied that he had sufficient direction. Then she added what she hoped would be additional motivation. "This is the big push, Wes. In just three weeks your father will be governor-elect of North California, and we can all take a little vacation. You've done a great job. When this is all over, I'm taking you out for a big steak dinner—or whatever you want."

"Thanks, Stephanie. You've been good to work with. Really, you've been very kind to me."

Stevie was surprised at the uncharacteristic compliment, though it was offered in Wes's typical sad-sack tone. "Hey, save the speeches for a few more weeks," she said, laughing. She turned into the Shasta Commons parking lot. "Got to go, Wes. I have to pack for the trip."

"When do you leave?"

"Tomorrow morning after my first press conference. Wish me luck. I'll talk to you later in the week."

"Good luck, Stephanie, and . . . thanks again. For everything."

Stevie tapped off the phone, shaking her head. How she wished Wes could find a little joy in life—a little excitement or enthusiasm for something—anything. She sighed. She wasn't about to give up on him now. He was a great kid with unlimited potential, and she was going to do everything in her power to help him realize that.

33

Tuesday
October 12

"GOOD MORNING, ladies and gentlemen. I'm Stephanie Van Horne, and I will be serving as Senator Bellardi's media secretary during Mr. Whitten's recovery from an appendectomy. Price Whitten wanted me to assure you that he was indeed sick from appendicitis, not sick of you. He said, 'If they don't believe you, tell them I'll send over my diseased appendix in a jar as proof.'"

The opening provoked a good laugh from the media corps assembled in the ballroom of the Red Lion Hotel, which was what Stevie intended. Price had encouraged her to break the ice with humor, and it had worked. The laugh also helped Stevie relax a tad. She had awakened at four that morning and never got back to sleep. Her heart was racing and her nervous stomach seemed to be doing handsprings up and down her throat. She had addressed many groups of colleagues and clients over the years, so she was no stranger to public speaking. But the anticipation of standing in front of local and national media spiked her anxiety to a new high.

What Stevie *knew* and how she *felt* had been in conflict all morning. She wore her most attractive suit, and her curly brown hair had fallen into place well today, so she *knew* she looked good. But standing before a fleet of cameras, she *felt* extremely unattractive. Stevie had learned well the intricacies of Senator Bellardi's philosophy and platform, so she *knew* she could speak confidently and field questions adequately when she had to. But glancing at the bank of microphones recording her every breath, she *felt* like a political dunce.

Outwardly Stevie appeared poised and confident. Inside she second-guessed herself continually. *Why did I agree to do this? How foolish of Senator Bellardi and Robert to ask me. How foolish of me to accept. I should walk away right now.* But reality was upon her. She had started the press conference, so she could not run away and hide until she finished it.

"Thank you for coming," Stevie continued, trying to make friendly contact with every eye in the room. "As you all know, Senator Bellardi leaves Redding today by private coach for a three-week tour. We are confident that the momentum gained during the recently completed debates will continue to build as the senator takes his message of what is right for North California to more than two dozen pivotal communities between now and election day. This morning Senator Bellardi will make a few remarks and then answer a limited number of questions. Ladies and gentlemen, Senator Daniel Bellardi."

Stevie yielded the lectern to Senator Bellardi and took her place behind him next to Robert. "Excellent job," Robert said, loudly enough for her ears only. Stevie did not respond. She stood erect with her eyes trained on Senator Bellardi and a pleasant smile on her face, just as she had been trained. The staff was always to appear attentive and pleased when the senator spoke. Stevie hoped her facade covered the severe case of nervousness causing the muscles in her legs to quiver as she stood. She also prayed she would remember to keep her hands in place and not run them through her hair as she often did when she felt stressed.

Senator Bellardi delivered the short version of his now-familiar message of hope for the people of North California: The only way to save this new state from the moral duplicity and depravity eroding the rest of America is to return to the traditional values of the Judeo-Christian community. The senator renewed his pledge to do what was right for North California by working tirelessly to establish high moral standards as the basis for law and community life. Stevie marveled at the candidate's energetic, charismatic public persona, a marked contrast to his often drained and brooding appearance in private.

As the question-and-answer session began, Stevie stepped away from Robert and moved closer to the senator, taking a position slightly behind his left shoulder. Her job now was to help conclude the press conference at the appropriate moment. Senator Bellardi was good at interacting with the media. But sometimes he didn't know when to quit, and sometimes he preferred to debate and defend where it was more prudent to back off.

As long as the conference was going well—meaning the senator had room to say what should be said—Stevie would not interrupt. But after fifteen to twenty minutes, or if the questions became redundant or potentially damaging, she was to touch the senator lightly on the elbow. The prearranged signal meant, "This may be a good time to wrap it up. If you agree, say your thank-yous and good-byes, then I will dismiss the crowd while you make a beeline for the bus." Maintaining her attentive posture, Stevie worried that nervous perspiration would soak through her expensive suit at any moment.

The first several questions were about "tabloid issues," as the senator's staff referred to them privately. Why is Mrs. Bellardi not campaigning with you? Is there any truth to the rumor that she is seriously ill? Has the campaign negatively affected your marriage? Do you expect AntiCrist to strike again? Are you afraid for yourself and your family? Have you considered withdrawing from the race in view of these threats? These questions arose in some form at virtually every question-and-answer session with the candidate.

Bellardi responded to each question with a concise, purposely vague answer assuring that everything was fine and that the campaign would continue to victory. The senator's top staff had these responses memorized. Stevie was confident that she could have fielded the questions adequately.

The first issue-related question came from a local TV news anchor. "Senator Bellardi, throughout the debates Juanita Dunsmuir repeatedly labeled you heartless and cruel for your position against homosexuality, abortion, assisted suicide, and so on. She stated that your Judeo-Christian views are more exclusive than inclusive, more judgmental than forgiving, and as such, not really Christian at all. How do you justify your hard-line stand in light of the Christian's duty to exercise compassion and forgiveness?"

Senator Bellardi nodded. "Good question, Robin. I take a hard stand against homosexuality, abortion, assisted suicide, and other immoral behavior for the same reason the California Highway Patrol takes a hard stand against people driving 110 miles per hour on Interstate 5: Somebody will get hurt if we don't say no. Imagine for a moment, Robin, that you and your children are out for a leisurely drive on I-5. A red Corvette races past a CHP officer at 110, and the officer does nothing. Then the reckless driver crashes into your car, killing your children. You confront the officer angrily for not enforcing the speed law.

"How would you feel, Robin, if the officer said, 'Have a little compassion. After all, the guy can't help it. He was born to speed. His lifestyle is to drive recklessly. You can't impose your values on him. You just have to learn to stay out of his way.' I daresay that you might be sorely tempted to violate the law yourself at that moment."

Stevie had not heard the senator's poignant illustration before, wondering if he had made it up on the spot. She knew exactly where he was going with it.

Bellardi swept the crowd of media people with his gaze. "Ladies and gentlemen, I have nothing personally against the homosexual. But when his or her promiscuous lifestyle influences a child to question his God-given sexual orientation or causes someone to be infected with a deadly virus, someone has to say no. I'm not without compassion, but my compassion is for the victims and potential victims of this individual's aberrant lifestyle.

"Furthermore, I have nothing personally against the woman who finds herself inconveniently pregnant. But when that woman terminates another human life in order to rid herself of the inconvenience, someone has to say no. My compassion goes out to the innocent children who are mercilessly sacrificed in such circumstances."

Bellardi offered two more pithy examples in his characteristically passionate style. Stevie could not imagine the point being driven home more forcefully.

The senator returned his gaze to the anchor who had posed the question. "So you see, Robin, I take a hard line because someone has to do what's right for North California. Compassion should be reserved for those who try to do the right thing but fail. Forgiveness is for those who fail to do the right thing but repent. And for those who ignore what is right in order to pursue a lifestyle that is harmful to others, someone must hold a hard line. That's what North California is all about. That's what Dan Bellardi is all about."

The media continued to hack away at Senator Bellardi's conservative platform and policies, just as Juanita Dunsmuir had done in the debates. With every knotty question, the senator displayed the mettle that had carried him through the debates and enlarged his lead in the polls. And with every answer, Stevie relaxed a little. She was in the presence of a master. It did not really matter how nice she looked or how cool she appeared at the lectern, she realized. Daniel Bellardi was God's man of the hour for North California; she was never more convinced. Stevie had a lot of reasons to dread spending the next three weeks away from home and business while touring North California in a bus. But at this moment she was really looking forward to it.

The long trip to Susanville in Senator Bellardi's monstrous, plush coach was actually fun. After a short meeting to review assignments for the afternoon and evening appearances, the senator retired to his private compartment in the rear to rest.

The other passengers—Stevie, Robert, Mike Bragan, a couple of trusty "gofers," and the senator's two bodyguards—sat around the table eating lunch and laughing about travel horrors eliminated by living on a bus: lost luggage, canceled flights, insipid airplane cuisine, rental cars that smelled of cigarette smoke. The unspoken excitement of impending victory flowed around them like the silent air from the air-conditioning ducts.

Drinking in her surroundings, Stevie flashed back to the unusual and life-changing turn her life had taken in only six months. From the immorality and terror of Los Angeles to the positive moral climate of North California. From the despair and grief of a son seduced by the culture to the bright hope of a secure and nurturing environment for Shawna and Collin. From anonymity as a self-employed advertising consultant to the inner circle of North California's soon-to-be first governor. Momentarily awash with gratitude, Stevie breathed a silent thank-you to God. She wondered if she was finally beginning to see the fulfillment of God's promise in Jeremiah 29:11: *"For I know the plans I have for you," says the Lord. "They are plans for good and not for disaster, to give you a future and a hope."*

Plans for good and not for disaster . . . a future and a hope. Stevie smiled. The exhilarating ride from the basement to the penthouse would soon be over. She was not a career politician, nor did she want to be. For all the time she had spent around Daniel Bellardi, the senator was not her friend or confidant. She knew through Robert that he appreciated her efforts, but aside from a friendly greeting now and then, he had spoken to her directly only a few times. She sometimes wondered if he would remember her name without Robert's coaching. For all she had contributed, in three weeks she would be just another name on Governor Bellardi's extensive list of loyal supporters.

Having played a small but time-consuming role in establishing the moral haven of North California, Stevie's primary commitment would revert to being a working mother. Thinking of her children now, she remembered her commitment to check in on Wes Bellardi daily. Even after the campaign she would stay in contact with this young man, whose personality seemed dominated by his father's seldom-seen brooding side. Wes deserved Stevie's ongoing maternal attention, just as Dougie would if he were still here.

Stevie excused herself to make the phone call from the conference room on the bus. Somebody suggested they all play a game of hearts. "Deal me in," Stevie called over her shoulder. She had not played hearts in years, but she knew Robert would be involved in the game. The prospect of getting to know him better over the next several days excited her. *This is going to be a fun trip,* she thought, smiling to herself.

Ernie's eyes snapped open in the darkness. The digital clock glowed 2:44, and Ernie had been sleeping soundly. Had a noise awakened him—a thump, footsteps, muffled voices? Or had it been another dream of someone coming after Wes Bellardi? Ernie could not remember, but something had jarred him awake.

He reached for his radio and spoke in a low tone. "Everything all right out there, Jerry?"

A crackle of static, then, "Everything is fine, Ernie. Quiet as a tomb out here. What are you doing awake?"

"I don't know. Something woke me up. I'll take a look around inside and let you know."

"Roger."

Ernie slipped into the jeans he kept by the bed, grabbed his gun and radio, and quietly left the guest bedroom. He moved like a shadow through the central area of the house: living room, family room, dining room, kitchen, office, library. All were dark and unoccupied. He slipped in and out of the Bellardis' vacant suite and another unoccupied bedroom. Everything seemed normal and undisturbed.

Finally he reached Wes's room. The door was closed, but light seeped from inside at the carpet line. Ear to the door, he heard nothing. He tapped on the door and opened it slowly. "Wes, it's Ernie. Just checking on you." He waited to be invited in but heard nothing, not even the rustling of sheets or the sound of breathing. He spoke louder. "Wes, it's Ernie. Are you all right?" Nothing. Realizing he might have to apologize later for the intrusion, he stepped fully into the room.

Ernie took in the scene in a single glance. The bed was empty. The mattress hung half off the box spring, and the sheets were torn and scattered over the floor. The bedside lamp, still illuminated, was on the floor where it apparently had fallen. Items from the bureau and nightstand littered the floor. Wes Bellardi was gone.

Ernie was on the radio in an instant. "Jerry, have you seen Wes tonight? Has he been outside?"

"Negative, Ernie. No action out here tonight at all. What's the—"

"Have any of you guys seen Wes?" Ernie asked the rest of the men surrounding the house. The same response came back from six other masculine voices: "Negative."

"What's up, Ernie?" Jerry called through the radio.

Ernie could hardly form the words. "The kid's not in his room. He's not in the house, at least that I could see. Jerry, get in here on the double to help me look. The rest of you guys stay sharp."

"Roger."

Concern seized Ernie as he moved to the bed for a closer look. He brushed his hand over the top of the mattress. It was cool, no evidence of body warmth. He looked closely at the ragged sheets. Part of the top sheet appeared to have been torn into strips. Having been in law enforcement and security work for almost forty years, Ernie's investigative mind supplied an answer. *Bonds to tie wrists and ankles.* He noticed small dark spots and smears on the rumpled fitted sheet. *Dried blood.* On the pillowcase the smears were formed into a distinct block: A. *AntiCrist.*

Then another dark word leaped into his mind, a deduction from the cursory examination of the scene: *Kidnapping.* It was followed by a logical argument: *Impossible. Kidnappers couldn't get in and out of the house without being seen—not unless they somehow got in and haven't yet escaped.*

When Jerry arrived, the two of them slipped down the hall to the only room Ernie had not checked. With revolvers drawn, they called Elena out of her room. She emerged alone and frightened to the point of tears, having seen and heard nothing. After calling the county sheriff's department for backup, Ernie was on the radio to his men outside. "We have a possible kidnapping in here, but the kidnappers and the victim may still be on the scene. Close in on the house from all sides and stay alert. Jerry and I are going to sweep the inside."

298

Guns at the ready, the two officers moved cautiously from room to room, turning on lights and checking in closets, under beds, and behind furniture. Six county patrol cars arrived in time to head up the search of the crawl space, attic, garage, and outbuildings. Within an hour, over fifty uniformed and plain-clothes officers and four search dogs were present to comb the property with floodlamps. The kid had disappeared without a trace.

At daybreak, Ernie returned to the house and collapsed in the family room, disheartened. For the second time in a month he had failed to protect Wes from attack. For the second time in a month he had betrayed the trust of his old friend Daniel Bellardi. Only this time his failure might prove fatal to the reclusive only son of the future governor. Ernie knew by now that someone had informed the senator of the tragedy, and sometime this morning he would have to face him and give account. He had done the best he knew how, but his best was not good enough. Someone had stolen the senator's son right out from under Ernie's nose. He had no idea what he was going to say to his friend.

The house swarmed with officers, and Ernie was no longer needed. He found a quiet corner and wept.

34
Wednesday
October 13

HAD ROBERT not been there to steady her, Stevie would have rented a car and left Susanville to search for Wes on her own. It was a knee-jerk reaction to the shocking news, but Robert quickly convinced her that the best way for her to help Wes was to stay on the job. So Stevie found herself about to preside over a second media conference in as many days. Only this time the meeting was unscheduled, and Senator Bellardi was absent, having left town by helicopter at six o'clock that morning to meet with investigators at the ranch.

It had been four hours since the news of Wes's disappearance had awakened Stevie and the others sleeping on the bus. The senator and his bodyguards, who always spent the night in a hotel room when the bus was on the road, had been called by the county sheriff at five. By the time Bellardi and his men lifted off in the helicopter, Stevie, Robert, and Mike Bragan were dressed and on the phones to Redding gathering information.

Stevie was numb with shock, but she had not yet shed a tear over the tragedy. There was no time to cry; there was work to be done. The senator's son had ostensibly been abducted by the terrorist AntiCrist. Although no note was found at the scene and no message had been received at Bellardi's office, the staff expected the demand to be the same: Quit the campaign. Hope of keeping the disappearance from the media had long since died. Several reporters with police scanners had arrived at the ranch shortly after security chief Ernie Cruz had called in county officers. A statement had to be prepared and a press conference hastily organized in the lobby of the senator's hotel. Stevie had to hold it together, so she did. She even found herself wondering whether she would be able to shed many tears for Wes, having grieved so deeply for his predecessor, Dougie.

The smile was absent that morning as Stevie stepped to the microphones. Nor did a cheery "good morning" seem appropriate. She simply began reading the statement she and Robert had polished. "Sometime between ten o'clock last night and two-thirty this morning, Wes Bellardi, twenty-year-old son of Senator and Mrs. Daniel Bellardi, disappeared from the family ranch in the Palo Cedro area east of Redding. His whereabouts are unknown at this hour. Senator Bellardi left Susanville for the ranch at six o'clock this morning by helicopter.

"Preliminary investigation at the scene indicates the possibility of foul play. So far, no—" A sudden and very inconvenient swell of emotion stopped the words in Stevie's throat. She continued to stare at the printed statement on the lectern, but her mind's eye had been diverted by the image of her firstborn son lying gray-white and still on the emergency room gurney. For the first time it occurred to her that Wes might not only be missing but dead. At this very moment he might be lying somewhere lifeless, his creative mind and budding potential stilled forever. *O God, not Wes, too,* she begged silently.

Clearing her throat and steeling herself against the rising flood of emotions, Stevie continued. "So far, no message or

302

demands have been received from a possible abductor. Detectives from the Redding Police Department, Shasta County Sheriff's Department, California Highway Patrol, and the FBI are conducting a thorough investigation of the scene. Senator Bellardi is confident that the perpetrators will be quickly apprehended and that his son will be returned to him unharmed."

Stevie was ambivalent about the next paragraph of the statement. She understood where the senator and Robert were coming from, but the words seemed to ring cold and uncaring. She had said as much to Robert as he dictated the lines to her. He said the voters must be assured that Bellardi would not allow this tragedy to divert him from his commitment to North California.

"Senator Bellardi fully intends to continue with the campaign during the investigation and the search for his son. Should the disappearance of Wes Bellardi prove to be an act of terrorism intended to dissuade the senator from his mission, it will not succeed. Senator Bellardi will not allow his commitment to the people of North California to be thwarted by unconscionable thugs. He will continue to fight for what's right for North California as he seeks the return of his son."

Stevie was tempted to add an impromptu paragraph to soften the "damn the torpedoes, full speed ahead" feel of the statement. *Senator Bellardi also has a message for his son: "Wes, wherever you are, please know that your mother and I love you and miss you. Getting you back safe and sound is our first priority. All my resources and influence are at the disposal of those who are looking for you right now. We will not rest until you are back home with us."*

As much as Stevie felt an addition was needed, it was not her place to put words in the senator's mouth. That was Robert's expertise, and he had framed the content of the statement. Perhaps she could convince him to add a dash of compassion in future statements as the search continued. She could not imagine going on with life as usual if either Shawna or Collin turned up missing.

Most of the questions from the media focused on the "gory details" of the supposed abduction. Were there signs of forced entry? Was there blood at the scene? Did Wes Bellardi have any known enemies? Were drugs involved in any way? Each mention of possible violent injury or death to Wes inflicted another blow to Stevie's already burdened heart. Yet she continued to hold it together.

Stevie responded to each question in clipped generalities as she had been instructed. Every answer was a slightly different version of the only things she could safely say: It's too soon to discuss the details of the investigation; Law enforcement officials are following up every lead and clue; We will let you know when more information becomes available.

At the conclusion of the press conference, Stevie could not get back to the bus soon enough. Suddenly it was all too much. She felt totally overwhelmed. In the beginning, all she had hoped to do was stuff envelopes to help Senator Daniel Bellardi become governor so she could promise a safe and happy future to her children. She was not built to deal with deadlines and press conferences and being away from home. And she certainly had not been prepared for mad bombers and arsonists and kidnappers and possibly killers.

Entering the bus, Stevie hurried to her tiny sleeping compartment and locked herself inside just before the dam burst. She sat on the bed and cried hard and long for several minutes. She cried for herself, for Shawna and Collin, for her dead son, and for Wes. But tears were not enough. She had to talk to someone. Robert, she knew, would have no free time for the rest of the day. Without pausing to evaluate the impulse, she picked up her cellular phone and dialed Jon's work number.

Ernie Cruz's meeting at the ranch with Dan Bellardi had been brief and surprisingly positive. Without giving his old friend a chance to explain, Bellardi said, "Ernie, I don't blame you for this. I know you did everything humanly possible to prevent it. We're dealing with ruthless, hardened criminals. But they won't get the better of us. Rest assured, we'll find them and punish them to the full extent of the law." Then he was off to meet with the police before being ferried back to Susanville by helicopter.

It was consolation and absolution Ernie neither expected nor felt he deserved. Wes's baffling disappearance had occurred during his watch, and that meant he was responsible whether the senator believed it or not. Ernie knew of only one course of action: Work more diligently to find Wes than he had to protect him. Even if the search eventually failed, even if the kid turned up dead somewhere, Ernie could not live with himself if he did not make every effort to reunite his friend with his only child.

Ernie was only slightly comforted to learn that the investigative team on site was as stumped as he was to determine how, when, and with whom Wes had left the property. They had found no clues, no suspicious footprints, and no trail of blood. The search dogs proved to be no help because Wes's scent was everywhere inside the house and nowhere outside.

Known by sight to most of the officers combing the ranch for clues, Ernie was free to go almost wherever he pleased. So he began his own intensive reexamination of the scene, beginning from the center and working outward. The supposed crime scene, Wes's bedroom, was off-limits to Ernie as investigators pored over it inch by inch looking for fingerprints, lint, strands of hair—anything that might provide a clue to Wes's disappearance. So, with the sheriff's permission, Ernie began in the other bedrooms. He methodically worked through each room, including Elena's, since the distraught housekeeper had gone to stay with a friend for a few days at Senator Bellardi's encouragement.

Ernie moved furniture and opened drawers and closets to examine every individual item in each room. He searched under beds and crawled over the carpet, looking and feeling and smelling for anything. From the bedrooms he moved out to the library, the study, the family room, the living room, and the kitchen. He found nothing.

He entered the crawl space under the house through a tiny doorway low on the garage wall. Wriggling on elbows and knees over dusty plastic sheeting, he looked everywhere with his flashlight, checking heating and air-conditioning ducts, screened vents to the outside, every corner and crevice. Again, nothing.

A fold-down ladder in the ceiling of the laundry room accessed the spacious attic. Hunched down to avoid bumping his head on the studs, Ernie made his way around dozens of dusty storage cartons, shining his flashlight into every corner.

The plywood floor creaked as he made his way to the east wing and then back again to the west.

It was late afternoon by the time Ernie concluded his first thorough search of the house—except for Wes's bedroom. He was still no closer to understanding the mystery than when he started. Having been awake since two-thirty that morning, he was dog tired. But he could not rest now. There were outbuildings to check: a gardening shed, a pump house for the well, a barn housing a tractor and an old pickup. Ernie thought he could finish them before dark.

Tomorrow and the next day he would walk the property, trying to discover how someone could get in and get Wes out without being seen. By all rights it was impossible; there was no place to hide out there. Ernie knew he was not the smartest guy in Shasta County—after all, somebody had carried off the senator's son without his knowing it. He did not know how it had happened, and so far nobody else did either. Somebody had joked that the only way the kid could have left the ranch was to have been beamed up to a spaceship right through the roof of the house. The real explanation was more down-to-earth than that, Ernie knew. And he was determined to find it or wear himself out trying.

Jon's nylon suitcase was packed and stowed behind the seat of the truck when he picked Ben up at Pierce College at four. The kid saw the bag and questioned Jon with a look. "I have to go away for a while, maybe a couple of weeks," Jon said.

Ben eyed him suspiciously but said nothing, just as Jon expected. Driving back to the house, he continued with the explanation he had been rehearsing in his mind. "You know that my ex and kids live in Redding." Ben gave a single nod and Jon went on. "Well, she's kind of stressed right now, so I need to go up and help her out with the kids for a while. I've made arrangements with Ramirez for you to stay at the group home. They'll make sure you get to school. It's only temporary till I get back; you don't even have to move all your stuff over. I'm sorry I couldn't tell you about this sooner; it just came up today."

Ben studied the floor of the truck, processing. Finally he said, "You quit your job, man?"

"No, I just took some personal time off. I told them three weeks. It may not be that long."

Ben was silent again, then said, "I've never been to North Cal."

Jon knew what he was hinting at. "I'd take you with me if I could, Ben. But you can't leave the state while on parole. Besides, you need to stay with your welding so you can get your certificate. Then you'll get a job and be rolling in money so we can eat at Bear Pit every night."

Ben did not even smile at the joke. Jon took his obvious disappointment as a backdoor compliment. Maybe it meant the kid felt at home with Jon and did not want him to leave. Jon had prayed throughout the afternoon that Ben's disappointment would not lead him to undo all the progress he had made since being released into Jon's care.

Parole officer Roger Ramirez arrived at the house fifteen minutes after Jon and Ben got home. Half an hour later the kid was at the door with suitcase in hand. Jon apologized again for his sudden departure, then stuck out his hand. "I'll call you, Ben. And I'll be back in three weeks, max. Hang in there."

Ben followed through with the handshake, though his heart did not seem to be in it. "Good luck, man," he said softly.

Watching them drive away, Jon considered Ben's parting comment something of a milestone. In his own halting way, Ben had wished him well; he had initiated a giving act. Up to this point, Ben had been strictly a taker, and not a very gracious one at that. Jon hoped the little spark of progress would not die out during his time away.

Leaving the L.A. basin on Interstate 5, Jon tried not to think about what he was doing, because it was not very practical. Taking off work for three weeks—two of those weeks without pay—was a step backwards financially. And living away from home for three weeks was going to be very expensive. Shuffling Ben off to the group home just when the two of them seemed to be clicking did not seem very smart either. Had Jon evaluated this trip strictly from an economical and practical standpoint, he had plenty of reason to turn around and go home.

It did not make sense to go to Redding, but he had to go. He knew it as soon as he had hung up from talking to Stevie almost eight hours earlier. She had not asked him to come or even hinted that she wanted him to come. She had cried softly as she vented her stress, her fear for Wes Bellardi's life, and her concern about being away from the children. When Jon asked if she would be OK, opening the door for her to say, "I could use some moral support, and the kids need you here," she had instead insisted, "Yes, I'm fine. I just needed to talk. Thanks for listening. I'm sorry I bothered you."

An hour after saying good-bye to Stevie, Jon had cleared his calendar and secured three weeks of personal time off from his superintendent. By noon he had made arrangements for Ben, and by one he was on his way home to stop the mail and the newspaper.

Racing northward on the freeway, he considered some of the logistics. He could stay at the apartment and be with the kids while Stevie was on the road. On the few days she was home, he could move to the motel. He had worried about Stevie's safety since the terrorist had begun to make good on his threats. The abduction of Bellardi's son enlarged his concern. He knew he could not talk Stevie out of finishing the campaign, but he felt better about being in Redding in case . . . well, just in case.

When should he call and let Stevie know he was coming? Jon had not figured that part out yet. And he had no idea what her reaction to his uninvited, unplanned visit might be. He would stop for gas in Stockton in about four hours. He could call then or wait until morning to call from some flea-bag motel north of Sacramento. He would just have to play that by ear.

35
Thursday
October 28

SINCE THE TOUR began, Stevie had slept very well in her compartment aboard the luxury coach as it sped along the highway each night. Sheer exhaustion was the greatest contributor to her easy adjustment. After the high-energy, eighteen-hour days, Stevie could have fallen asleep on the bare floor of a boxcar thundering down the track. Another contributor was the fact that Jon was now in Redding. Knowing that Shawna and Collin were sleeping in their own beds and that Jon was supervising their daily activities lifted a large worry from her mind.

But this night Stevie could not sleep. It was two o'clock, and the bus was somewhere between Yuba City and Ukiah. She was physically exhausted as usual, but her eyes were wide open. Other concerns were heavy on her mind tonight.

The last two weeks seemed a blur, the days having flown by. Every day a different city or town, but every day the same routine. The romance of working in Bellardi's gubernatorial campaign had been reduced to a daily grind. Up by six for breakfast and the daily game plan with Senator Bellardi, Robert, and the team. Then back-to-back-to-back rallies, speeches, handshaking, and baby-kissing at senior citizen centers, schools, day-care facilities, union halls, factories, farms, shopping malls, baseball games. Stevie had learned to force down a hearty breakfast each morning because she seldom saw hot food again or had five minutes to eat it until the team was back in the bus at night.

Clamoring crowds were waiting wherever they went. After the first few days, the people all looked alike and asked the same kinds of questions. Stevie was amazed that Senator Bellardi could dispense the same basic information day after day and yet tailor it to each audience to keep it fresh. She had learned to do the same with the media people. She had also learned from the senator how to give the answers she wanted to give, whether or not they answered the questions asked, while stating them so graciously that no one was offended. She recited the party line a dozen times a day in a dozen different ways.

The kidnapping situation had also become disturbingly commonplace to those on the tour. AntiCrist had indeed claimed responsibility for the abduction four days after Wes Bellardi's disappearance. Another computer fax had arrived at campaign headquarters. The note, replete with poor spelling and grammar, simply read, "Abanden the campain for your sons sake. AntiCrist."

But Daniel Bellardi would not abandon the campaign. He stayed on the road except for periodic helicopter hops to Redding to meet with local police and the FBI. Having turned up nothing in two weeks, they had little to tell the senator. After each briefing, Bellardi returned to the campaign just as driven and passionate as before. In the meantime, Mrs. Bellardi remained in Redwood City under a physician's care. Wes's job at headquarters had been taken over by Rhoda Carrier and another volunteer. The ranch had been temporarily closed up, the security staff on the property disbanded, and Elena given a month's paid vacation.

Stevie had difficulty accepting the senator's seemingly light regard for his son's safety. True, she had sacrificed time with and attention to her children to get Bellardi elected, but he appeared ready to sacrifice his son's life. It was one thing not to cower under the threats of terrorism in general. It was quite another to say to someone already holding your child hostage, "I will not quit the campaign no matter what you do." Had Senator Bellardi even considered for a moment postponing his bid for governor in order to get his son back? Had he considered offering a ransom? If so, Stevie was unaware of it. Could Bellardi justify sacrificing his only son to save the people of North California? Such an act was appropriate for God, but Stevie was not convinced that a mortal father—even such a godly man as Daniel Bellardi—could or should be so selfless.

Yet the campaign continued, and the senator remained focused on the issues instead of his missing son. Stevie had been instructed to keep the media fully informed of the latest developments in the search for young Bellardi while prohibiting all questions about Wes or the ongoing investigation. Every morning's breakfast meeting began with prayer, and Wes's safety and release were uppermost among the petitions. But once the bus door opened and the daily rush commenced, it was as if Wes Bellardi did not exist. Even Stevie found herself going several hours at a time without thinking of him. Then the mention of his name in a crowd brought a momentary pang of sadness, which was quickly swept away in the frantic whirlpool of activity. Stevie's nightly prayers for Wes were sometimes overwhelmed by exhaustion before she was finished. She often felt guilty for becoming so calloused to such a tragedy. But the daily madness continued.

In the midst of it all, Robert was her rock. As busy as he was and as conscientious and devoted to his job, he managed every day to find a few moments to pull Stevie aside and check on her well-being. Was she all right? Did she need anything? Was there anything at all that he could do for her? Had she spoken with Shawna or Collin? Were they all right? His con-

311

cern was a soothing balm to her tired, aching heart, and she had told him as much.

But this day's chilling development had kept her awake well into the night and moved her to prayers with tears. Another note from AntiCrist had arrived at campaign headquarters that day, only the second communication since Wes had disappeared. When Stevie returned to the bus at nine-thirty that evening, a copy of the original was waiting in the fax tray. The team had been informed about the note by telephone earlier in the day, but seeing the message with her own eyes brought a new chill to Stevie's spine. It read, "Hallaween will be terminel for your son if you dont quit NOW!"

Senator Bellardi seemed to have been affected by the blatant threat. He had Mike Bragan reschedule an early afternoon gathering for later in the day, then he retreated to his compartment on the bus for two hours. Had he used the time of solitude to pray, to rest, to memorize a speech, or to make a deal with God: his soul in exchange for North California *and* his son's life? Stevie had no way of knowing. But when he emerged after his retreat, the senator was back to the business at hand as if nothing had changed, which meant that Stevie and the team were back to full speed again.

During the hours she should have been sleeping, Stevie's mind was besieged by a collage of horrifying images. As much as she resisted them, flashbacks to Dougie's overdose and death occupied her consciousness like a gallery of photographs dragged up from a dungeon in her soul. Interspersed with the memories were grotesque imaginings of the fate awaiting Wes. Every new scene of Dougie forced a groan from Stevie's aching heart. Every unbidden view into Wes's possible future drew an audible cry for God's mercy. "Deliver him from evil, dear God. Deliver him from evil." The heavy hum of ten huge tires over the pavement helped to muffle the sound. Stevie kept praying until she slid into a fitful sleep.

312

Ernie was in the attic again. He had gone through it—as he had every square inch of every room in the house—several times. And yet, there had to be something he had missed. There had to be.

No one had asked Ernie to give up the key to the Bellardi house, so he just kept it and kept quiet. He knew Dan would not mind. He also conveniently remembered the codes for the security system. The sheriff's department still cruised the ranch regularly, but since the place was empty and electronically protected, no live security guards were needed. It occurred to Ernie fleetingly that if the system had been armed the night of the kidnapping, Wes might still be around. With a live security team on duty each night, no one had seen a need to crank up the alarm.

Step by step, he worked his way slowly around stacks of cartons toward the east wing of the attic by the light of his flashlight. And then he saw it. A loose panel of plywood on the floor near the eaves. *How could I have missed it?* he thought, his heart racing with excitement. *I've looked here half a dozen times.* He cautioned himself not to get carried away, even as he searched with his flashlight for something to use to pry open the board. *It may be nothing,* he told himself. *Just a loose board. It doesn't necessarily mean anything. Who knows what I may find? Maybe nothing. Or maybe . . .*

He refused to finish the thought. Spotting a flathead screwdriver on the floor, he used it as a crowbar, yanking on the board with his free hand. The board came up easily—*too easily,* Ernie thought.

Setting down the flashlight, he grabbed a corner of the panel and lifted it up. He was immediately assaulted by a putrid odor. "Geez, smells like an outhouse," Ernie groaned aloud.

Picking up the flashlight to take a look, he steeled himself for what he might find in the foul-smelling hole in the attic floor. He directed the beam into the open space, which was surprisingly large, then released a slow breath. The hideout was empty, but the wallboard between the studs appeared water-stained. There also appeared to be smaller dark stains on the studs and wallboard. Setting the panel aside, Ernie dropped to his haunches and stared at the illuminated space for several seconds. The stains appeared fresh. Blood, maybe? Urine?

Ernie continued to study the scene without knowing what he was looking for. He hated to admit that he was not a detective. And he hated to admit that someone like AntiCrist, who could not even spell his own pseudonym, could get through his security and leave no traces. He was either a genius with a mental block when it came to spelling, or he was an incredibly lucky dumb guy. But perhaps the hole in the attic would provide an answer. Ernie did not know what it all meant, but it had to mean something. The only way to find out *what* it meant was to call in the pros.

36

Friday
October 29

SHAWNA AND TERILYN took their usual seats in a far corner of the food court. They ate lunch together almost every day at school. Sometimes Josie and Alexis joined them; other times they went off campus together during lunch break.

"Your dad is stupid. I mean *ultra* stupid," Terilyn stated emphatically. "That gang guy is just setting him up to waste him and steal all his stuff."

Shawna ate her sub sandwich and said nothing. She wished she had never told her friend about the ex-con staying with her dad. Terilyn imagined that almost everyone in L.A. was a gang member or a serial killer. And since she never knew her own dad, Terilyn thought all dads were wimps or crooks or both.

Shawna's dad had not done anything stupid; at least Shawna did not think so. Instead, she was secretly proud of him for helping this guy, whoever he was. It made her feel like her dad was a hero in some way.

After Terilyn's little speech, Shawna decided not to mention how much she enjoyed having her dad at home. Her friend would probably find something else to criticize. On the practical side of having a live-in dad, Shawna felt good about being in her own apartment instead of sleeping over at Terilyn's. Dad was not the greatest cook in the world, but at least he had something hot and edible ready for them at five-thirty every evening. And he was a champ about driving her and Collin to school, picking them up, doing the laundry, and keeping the place tidy. It was like living with Mom before she got involved in the campaign.

But there was more to Shawna's contentment than having Dad around as cook, chauffeur, and maid. He sat down and talked to her—like telling her all about his jail visit with Eugene Hackett and how it had led up to his becoming a citizen volunteer to Ben Hernández. He asked about her classes and offered to help with homework. He popped popcorn and watched TV with the two of them. The rules were still the rules with Dad, but he seemed so relaxed and happy to be with his children, and that helped Shawna relax and enjoy being with him.

Furthermore, Shawna was glad to be home because she felt a little smothered being around her best friend day and night. Terilyn was loyal, witty, and fun, but she had taken advantage of the live-in situation by getting a little pushy about her tolerance and spiritual views. Shawna liked Terilyn and she was interested in what she had to say, but she needed space and time to decide for herself if Terilyn's ideas were something she could buy into wholeheartedly. Shawna was still confused about all the things she had heard at the conference, even though on the surface they all sounded good.

When Shawna did not respond to the stupid-dad comment, Terilyn changed the subject. "We have to decide on our costumes for the Halloween party or there won't be any good ideas left."

The Young Women's Leadership Club at school held an annual Halloween party, and Shawna had heard it was a rather eerie celebration of different religious beliefs and ancient occultic practices. The dwarfs were thrilled at the prospect of being exposed to "deeper" religious thoughts and practices than they had experienced before.

Shawna was not sure she wanted to go, but it was difficult to turn down Terilyn and her other friends from the club. Besides, Ms. Carmona would be attending and had offered to read everyone's horoscope, as well as help those who were interested get in touch with their "spirit guides." Shawna had never had her horoscope read before, and she did not have a clue who or what her spirit guide was. She had always assumed it was God's Spirit, since that is what she had been taught in church and Sunday school all her life. But when she mentioned that to the dwarfs, they had laughed so hard that Shawna decided to keep further questions on the subject to herself. She would just have to wait and learn all about it at the party.

"So, what about our costumes?" Terilyn asked. "Any ideas?"

Shawna shrugged. "I don't know. I could go as Snow White, I guess."

Terilyn groaned. "Oh, sure. You go looking beautiful and the rest of us go as some ugly dwarfs. No thanks."

Shawna smiled. Her friend had a point. "What's everybody else wearing?" she asked.

"I heard Ms. Carmona is coming as a witch," Terilyn answered, her eyes shining with excitement. "In fact, I heard it's not just a costume."

"What do you mean?"

"I mean," Terilyn explained, her voice lowered to a whisper, "that Ms. Carmona really is a witch."

"No way!" Shawna was shocked. "There's no such thing . . . is there?"

"Sure there is. Witches have been around forever. Don't you remember what we learned at the conference about ancient religions?"

"Well, sure, but . . ." Shawna hesitated. It was one thing to learn that some people considered witches and their beliefs and practices to be a true religion, but it was something else to actually know somebody who really was one. "Are you sure?"

Terilyn smiled wickedly, her eyes still shining. "Who can be sure about anything? But I heard that at the party she's going to cast a spell on the Bellardi campaign."

Shawna's jaw slacked. "Cast a spell? Are you joking?"

"No, I'm not joking. That's what witches do, you know. And after she puts the devil's hex on Senator Bellardi Sunday night, he's sure to lose."

The passing bell rang, and Shawna was relieved that lunch period was over. She did not want to talk about the Halloween party anymore. In fact, she was less sure than ever that she wanted to go.

"You don't want Bellardi to lose?" Terilyn asked.

Shawna quickly backpedaled. "I didn't say that. I just don't like talking about all that other stuff, like witches and spells."

Terilyn blew an exasperated sigh. "I'm sure, Shawna. Just when I think you're ready to leave the religious dark ages you go and say something like that. It's a new day, Snowy. Tap into all the powers available to you. Don't let your brain get in the way of your true feelings. Go with what works for you. You've come so far since I met you. Don't give up now."

Shawna avoided eye contact and did not answer. She stood, slung the book bag over her shoulder, and gathered up her lunch trash, quite ready to go to class. There was something about what Terilyn said that sounded so good, so true, so desirable. And yet, lately, Shawna had begun to see another side of her friend that seemed so dark and dangerous, a side that reminded Shawna of Destiny Fortugno. She did not want to lose Terilyn for a friend, but Shawna feared that if she kept up the friendship she might end up doing something she did not want to do.

"Good afternoon, ladies and gentlemen. I want to recap for you as briefly as possible two recent developments in the disappearance of Wes Bellardi. I wish I could say more, but we know very little. So, as usual, Mr. Whitten and I will only entertain questions related to the campaign itself, not the investigation. Thank you for your cooperation."

Stevie felt supremely confident in her media secretary role. Remaining upbeat and approachable but firm as Price Whitten had instructed her, she had earned the respect of the correspondents traveling with the Bellardi campaign. That was the reason Price and Robert had decided late yesterday to let her continue as cosecretary through election day. It was too late in the push to change personnel. Continuity would best be served if the recuperated Whitten and his temporary replacement finished the campaign together. Stevie was flattered at the vote of confidence and relieved that in six days it would all be over.

"On Monday morning, another fax was received from the alleged abductor, AntiCrist. You have all seen the text of the note. We regard it as a clear death threat against young Wes. But Senator Bellardi's resolve continues strong. He will not allow his commitment to North California or its glorious future to be controlled by hatred. The senator is supremely confident that the FBI and local agencies will discover the identity of the perpetrator, bring him to justice, and return Wes Bellardi to his parents alive and unharmed."

Stevie felt like a phony. She related the senator's conviction as if it were her own, just as she was expected to do. Yet she continued to question the senator's seemingly heartless position. Wes's life might be hanging by a thread at this very moment, yet the senator seemed no more disturbed than if his dog were lost.

"Senator Bellardi was greatly encouraged yesterday when the Shasta County Sheriff notified him of a development in the investigation. Recent evidence suggests that the victim may have been secretly concealed in the attic of the Bellardi home for a day or more after the abduction. Crime experts are conducting tests in a fairly sizable compartment found under a loose attic floorboard. Law enforcement officials are hopeful that this discovery will lead directly to Wes Bellardi and his captors. That is all we are prepared to say at this time about the disappearance."

Stevie agonized privately over this odd turn of events. Small amounts of blood found in the attic were determined to be from Wes Bellardi. The fact that Wes's blood had been spilled both in his bed and in the attic hovered oppressively and constantly over her soul. Adding to the burden, police had no explanation for the most recent discovery. Theories ranged from the macabre to the ridiculous. One FBI agent

319

suggested that the victim was first drugged and hidden in the attic, then murdered, dismembered, and carried out in a couple of suitcases after the house closed down. Another agent suggested that, if the abduction had been carried out by only one person, the attic compartment could possibly have hidden both Wes and his abductor until the house was empty and escape possible. A sheriff's deputy suggested that Wes had not been abducted at all, that he was playing a cruel game of hide-and-seek. A psychic unofficially consulted by the sheriff's department claimed that Wes was the victim of a time-travel experiment from a future century.

For all their theories, investigators seemed no closer to finding Wes, and the consequences of AntiCrist's Halloween ultimatum drew nearer by the minute. Stevie could hardly keep her mind on her work. And yet, paradoxically, the demands of her work kept her from drowning in her concern.

Stevie pressed on determinedly. "In the Bellardi camp, today is V-minus-four. We are only four days from a great victory in North California. Senator Bellardi will now update you on the progress of the campaign and answer a few questions."

The senator took the lectern. He was more reserved in manner and quieter in tone than on previous appearances, but his passion for victory in North California was undimmed. Stevie assumed her mannequinlike pose beside Robert to listen. *V-minus-four is catchy and clever, Senator, but what about AntiCrist and D-minus-two?* she questioned silently. *In two days your son may be dead. What if the police fail to find him by Halloween? Is your passion for North California greater than your passion for your son?* All the while the campaign smile remained frozen on her face.

The conditions were perfect for asking the question. Collin was at soccer practice, and Shawna and Jon were home alone in the living room folding clothes. Still, it took her several minutes to work up the nerve. "Dad," she said finally, "do you think tolerance is good?"

"What kind of tolerance are you talking about?" Jon asked, adding to a stack of Collin's clean, folded T-shirts.

"The new kind," Shawna answered, wondering if he needed

more of a definition. She knew that Ms. Carmona would probably classify her father as a fundamentalist bigot, hopelessly locked into the outdated and traditional view of tolerance. But Shawna suspected that he knew more about tolerance than her horoscope-reading faculty advisor.

"The kind Juanita Dunsmuir promotes and Daniel Bellardi is against?" Jon asked.

"Yeah."

Jon rubbed his forehead. "Is this a loaded question? I mean, do you already have an opinion you want me to agree with, or are you really interested in what I think?"

"I want your opinion about tolerance," Shawna said, "because . . . well, I'm confused about mine."

Jon nodded and remained thoughtfully silent until he had folded another shirt. "Let's make sure we're talking about the same brand of tolerance. How does Ms. Dunsmuir and her kind define it?"

Sometimes Shawna wished her father were a firefighter, a lawyer, an architect, or even a cop. Teachers never gave straight answers; they always had to involve the student in the topic.

She sighed and tried to remember the definition Ms. Carmona gave at the conference in San Francisco. "Everything is equal. All people are equal. All beliefs are equal. All lifestyles are equal. Nobody can say, 'My beliefs are better than yours.' Nobody can say, 'The way I live is right, the way you live is wrong.'" Then she waited, expecting her father to mentally grade her response.

"As compared to *traditional* tolerance," Jon added, "which agrees that all *people* are created equal, but that some *beliefs* are valid and some are not, that some *lifestyles* are right and some are wrong."

"Yeah, I guess."

Jon was silent again. Then, to Shawna's surprise, he began with a statement instead of another question. "All right, you asked for my opinion, I'll give it to you straight out. I have a problem with the new tolerance because the basic assumption behind it is faulty. Do you know what tolerance is based upon?"

Shawna answered truthfully, "No, Dad, I'm not real clear on that."

Thankfully, her dad did not make fun of her ignorance. "The basic assumption behind tolerance," he said, "is that there are no moral absolutes. To these people, right and wrong are a matter of personal opinion, not a code of principles established by God that applies to everyone everywhere all the time. That's why they say all beliefs and lifestyles are equal, because they don't accept a hierarchy of values that differentiates between beliefs and lifestyles."

Shawna suddenly felt engulfed in a tidal wave of jargon. "Oh," she said meekly.

Jon laughed. "Sorry, sweetheart. I didn't mean to sound like a philosophy professor. But to understand the new tolerance, you have to understand its bottom line: Everyone decides what's right and wrong for himself, because there's no such thing as absolute right and absolute wrong. Are you with me?"

The explanation helped clear some of the fog. "Yeah, I think so."

Jon continued. "OK, now for the big question: Is right and wrong a matter of personal opinion, or is it objective—something decided outside of ourselves?"

This was the very question Shawna had been struggling with. She knew what Ms. Carmona would answer: Truth is relative; don't let other people make the rules for you; do what you feel is right. But then she would say that people who live according to the moral standards in the Bible were "fundamentalist bigots." She was tolerant of people who were tolerant like her, but she was not tolerant of the intolerant. It did not make sense.

Her dad already said he had a problem with the tolerance bottom line, so she could guess the answer to his "big question." But she remained quiet to let him give it, which he did in great detail. The words flew at Shawna faster than she could catch them. But her dad's stand on the subject was clear: Truth is absolute, based on the Bible, coming from God's nature and character. Right and wrong is not something we decide but something God decides. Though she did not grasp it, Shawna sensed that her dad was telling the truth. In fact, she was touched as much by his sincerity as his conviction. His answer brought a subtle but much needed quiet to her soul.

"Thanks, Dad," she said. "That really helps. I'm sure glad I have you to talk to."

"You're welcome, honey." Jon paused as he laid another folded T-shirt on Collin's laundry pile. "I'm glad I could be here for you. You must miss having your mom around to talk to."

Shawna bit her lip. "Yeah, I really do. Either she's gone all the time or, when she is here, she's too busy with clients or campaign business or that Robert guy to talk to me."

Jon frowned. "What Robert guy? Who's Robert?"

Uh oh, Shawna thought, feeling her face flush. *I really opened my big mouth this time.* She tried to look surprised. "Robert? Oh, Robert. Yeah, well, he's just this guy that . . . I mean, he's some guy in the campaign with Mom. Well, not with Mom, I didn't mean that. It's just—"

"Are you talking about Robert Johnstone?" Jon asked, the surprise on his face obviously not contrived. "That tall, good-looking guy that your mom stands next to during the senator's press conferences?"

Shawna just nodded.

"I've seen them on TV together," Jon went on. "Isn't he the senator's campaign manager?"

Shawna shrugged. "I . . . I guess so."

Jon moved the stack of clothes he had been working on and sat down on the couch. Shawna wished he would say something. Then she wished he would not. She did not want to answer anymore questions about Robert.

"Are they . . . seeing each other?" Jon asked finally, his voice barely above a whisper.

"I . . . well . . ." Shawna swallowed, wishing above all else that she could take back her mention of Robert. But of course she could not. Why, oh why, had she let it slip about Robert and her mom?

Jon held up his hand before she could say anything else. "Never mind," he said. "You don't have to answer that. I don't want to put you in the middle of this situation. Besides, it's really none of my business." He smiled up at her, but Shawna knew he was not smiling inside. "Let's just drop it," he said, reaching once again for the pile of laundry. "We've got work to do, right?"

Shawna nodded, willing the lump in her throat to dissolve so she could speak. "Right," she said, then clamped her mouth shut. She was not about to risk saying the wrong thing again.

37

Saturday
October 30

IT WAS JUST before two the following afternoon when Stevie
dragged her bags through the door. She had not expected to
be home this soon. The team had planned to stay in Yuba City
until early afternoon and ride the bus directly to the Redding
Convention Center for the last high-visibility rally of the campaign. But following the senior citizens' breakfast meeting,
Senator Bellardi abruptly canceled the rest of his stops for the
day, complaining of fatigue. So the entire entourage sped back
to Redding so the senator could rest up for the rally. Stevie
could not have been more pleased at the decision; she was
exhausted.

Relieved to find the apartment empty, Stevie jotted a quick

note asking not to be disturbed and left it on the dining room table. Then she retreated to her bedroom and locked the door. In five minutes she was submerged in a hot bath, fighting tears, as tense muscles and emotions slowly relaxed. *You can make it till Tuesday,* she coached herself. *You have to make it till Tuesday!*

After a long bath, she dressed, with every intention of unpacking, doing laundry, and preparing a nice dinner for Jon and the children before leaving for the Convention Center, but the bed drew her down before she could lift a suitcase. Catching the faint scent of Jon's cologne on the pillow, Stevie again felt humbled at what her ex-husband had done over the last three weeks. Her last conscious thought was one she would not entertain had she the strength to dismiss it: *What kind of a woman would let a man like Jon get away?*

When she finally emerged from the bedroom two hours later, Jon was stretched out on the sofa, channel surfing. Seeing her, he sat up quickly as if he had been caught loafing on the job. "Sorry I didn't get the sheets washed and your room straightened up," he explained. "I thought I had time this afternoon."

Stevie sank into a chair, dismissing the inconvenience with a shake of her head. "Don't worry about it. I should have warned you." She explained her earlier-than-planned arrival, then asked, "Where are the kids?"

"Collin's down at the condos' rec center entertaining himself in the video game room. Shawna's at Terilyn's—of course. They're working on their costumes for the big Halloween party." He paused and raised an eyebrow questioningly. "I'm surprised you're allowing her to go."

Stevie sighed. She knew what Jon was trying to say. She had always been so adamant about Christians not celebrating Halloween. Jon had, on occasion, hinted that he felt she was a bit legalistic about that sort of thing, but she had stood strong—until now. "I know," she said. "I'm really not crazy about the idea. It's just that . . . well, I've been gone so much and I . . . I don't know. I guess I just didn't have the time or energy to say no and reinforce it."

Jon nodded and tapped the TV remote. The golf tournament

disappeared, leaving the monitor blank. "Will you be going to the rally tonight?" he asked.

"Oh, yes," she said, eyebrows lifted for emphasis. "I'm definitely expected at the rally."

"I suppose . . . everyone . . . involved in the campaign will be there?"

"Of course. We've all invested too much in this thing to miss something as major as this."

"You don't sound very excited about it."

Stevie's sigh was louder this time. She was too tired to put on a front. "I'm worn out. This has been an ordeal for me in more ways than one."

"I've seen you on TV a few times. You look and sound like a pro, like you know what you're doing and . . . enjoying it."

"I *have* to look and sound that way, Jon. But sometimes I wonder how I got myself into this."

"You did it for the kids, remember?"

"Yes, I did it for the kids, but I only planned to stuff envelopes or register voters. I never planned to be Senator Bellardi's media secretary."

Jon was silent for a moment. Then he said, "Well, there must be some sort of perks to keep you so involved."

Stevie frowned. What was Jon getting at? Did she detect a hint of sarcasm in his voice? She opened her mouth to ask, but Jon interrupted her.

"At least it looks like your man is going to win. You must be happy about that."

"Sure," Stevie answered, then shrugged. "I'm glad he's going to win, but at what cost?"

"You mean his son and the 'Halloween ultimatum,' as the press calls it?"

Stevie looked away, not wanting to think about it. Finally she said, "Senator Bellardi won't walk away, Jon. He won't give in to the threats. He doesn't even seem greatly bothered by them. If this AntiCrist idiot means what he says, the governor-elect and his poor wife will bury their only child before . . ." A wave of helplessness and grief swelled in her throat.

After a respectful silence, Jon asked, "Do you know the senator's son well?"

"As a matter of fact, I do." Wondering why she had considered it important to keep it from him before, Stevie told the whole story of her four-month involvement with Wes Bellardi. She was proud of herself for holding together emotionally through it all, even when relating her concern for his life.

"So you have a Dougie project too," Jon summarized softly when she was through.

Stevie reflected on the comment, once again fighting tears. "Why am I doing it, Jon?" It was a question she had asked herself repeatedly since Wes had come into her life. "Why is either of us doing it? Me with Wes, you with Ben. Do we have some driving inner need to get this part right so we can move on in life? Have we taken on these two young men as a sub-conscious act of penance? Is God giving us a second chance to show that he forgives us for what happened to Dougie?"

Jon shook his head slowly. "I don't know. I've considered all those answers. Maybe Dougie had nothing at all to do with it. Maybe it's just a big coincidence. Ben and Wes both needed somebody, and we happened to be available. We each did what we felt was right, and something good has come of it."

"Not much good has come Wes's way since I met him," Stevie said soberly. "He's as closed and hard to reach as Dougie ever was. And now he's . . . gone."

"The kidnapping wasn't your fault, Steve. Don't blame yourself for something you can't control."

"But if he dies—"

"That's not your fault, either," Jon interrupted forcefully. "Your feelings for him and your attempts to help him are wonderful. Having had a similar experience, I identify with your concern. God forbid that Wes gets hurt at all. But whether he lives or dies, you are not to blame for it any more than you are for what happened to Dougie."

Stevie was shocked breathless by Jon's last words. Jon dropped his gaze, obviously realizing what he had just said.

Stevie was not about to let the comment pass. "That's not what I remember, Jon. According to you, I *was* to blame for what happened to Dougie." In all fairness, she knew she had also dumped a lot of blame and guilt on Jon, but she assumed he would remind her of that momentarily, so she refrained from mentioning it herself.

The atmosphere was suddenly arctic cold and still. For all

328

the warming in their relationship over the past six months,
the issue of blame had remained untouched between Jon and
Stevie.

"I've been thinking a lot about that," Jon began tentatively.
"Especially these last three weeks. I knew I would have to say
something sooner or later. I guess now is as good a time as
any."

Stevie knew she did not have the emotional energy for this.
Whatever Jon was going to say, it sounded major, and she was
sure it would bring out the tears she had been holding back all
afternoon. If she allowed herself to start crying now, she felt as
if she would never be able to stop. She was tempted to scream,
"No, Jon! I'm already up to my tear ducts in gut-wrenching
inner conflicts. You'll have to take a number and talk to me
after the election." But she restrained herself, knowing that,
tears or not, she must hear Jon out. She owed him at least that
much for three weeks of volunteer child care. Furthermore,
this opportunity to clear the air, ill-timed as it was, might
never come again.

Jon continued haltingly. "I've come to realize that some of
the things I said after Dougie died were . . . were very unfair
and unkind. I was devastated by what happened—as you were.
So I guess I had to find . . . to find a reason for what happened.
I was too proud to shoulder any blame. Since I couldn't allow
Dougie's death to be my fault, it . . . well, I had to make it your
fault."

Jon was obviously laboring both to maintain eye contact
and to keep his words flowing. He seemed like a nervous
schoolboy presenting an oral report before he was fully prepared. Stevie could tell he had spent time thinking about his
speech. Now, called upon to say his piece sooner than
expected, she knew he was doing his best.

Stevie bit her lip and her chin trembled involuntarily.

"But that's just the point," Jon continued. "We can't do anything now about what we failed to do back then. I was . . . I
was wrong to blame you for what happened. It wasn't your
fault." Jon also seemed on the verge of tears, but he pressed on
determinedly. "I'm sorry, Steve. I'm sorry for hurting you in so
many ways. Will you please forgive me?"

Stevie began to cry. She was gripped as much by dark conviction as by the sheer release provoked by the sudden, sincere apology. Jon's missiles of blame were not the only weapons fired in the days and weeks after Dougie's death. The verbal and emotional firefight had been mutual, and many of the hurtful words she had launched at him still loomed ugly in her memory. Stevie had never apologized for her part simply because Jon had never apologized to her. She realized now how childish her reasoning had been. Her excuse had just evaporated in a moment's time.

"Of course I forgive you," she managed to say. "And please, will you forgive me, too?"

Their eyes locked and Jon nodded, yet neither spoke. There seemed to be nothing more to say at the moment. It was if they had just crossed a line, not only of forgiveness but of mutual understanding. As different as they were and as different as their approaches to parenting might be, Stevie suddenly saw how those differences might have been used to complement one another, rather than allowing them to drive a wedge between them. She was about to ask him if he sensed the same thing she was feeling in this regard when her thoughts were interrupted by the ringing phone.

Stevie was not sure if she was relieved or annoyed at the interruption. She pulled her eyes from Jon's, cleared her throat, and reached over to grab the phone on the end table beside her chair. "Hello?"

"Stephanie?" The concern in Robert's voice was immediate and obvious. "Stephanie, are you all right?"

Stevie took a deep breath. "Robert, hello. Yes, of course, I'm all right. I'm fine. Just a little tired, that's all."

"I can imagine. I hope I didn't get you at a bad time."

Stevie glanced at Jon. He was still looking at her, but immediately averted his eyes. "No, this isn't a bad time, Robert. This is fine, really. What's up? Is there something new about Wes?"

"Afraid not," Robert answered. "I was just calling to see if you wanted me to pick you up for the rally tonight. We could catch a late dinner afterward if you feel up to it."

"Dinner? Oh, I don't know. I . . ."

"You don't have to decide now. I'll just swing by and pick you up so you can relax on the way over, and then you can let me know how you feel later. Either way, I'll get you home safe and sound, I promise."

Stevie could hear the smile in his voice. She could see his gray eyes, warm and concerned, yet hopeful at her response. Stevie managed a slight smile. "Sure," she answered. "That would be great. Thanks."

Ernie Cruz had spent another several hours at the Bellardi ranch, as he had nearly every day that week. With the Halloween ultimatum ticking down to its final hours, Ernie felt constrained to do everything he could to avert whatever AntiCrist had planned for young Wes Bellardi. His numerous methodical searches inside the house had turned up nothing more since the discovery of the loose floorboard and the hidden compartment in the attic. He was inclined to agree with the FBI that the kidnapper had performed his deed without leaving a trace. Even a thorough examination of the attic's hiding place had led them nowhere.

So for the last two days, Ernie had concentrated on the grounds around the house. He had patiently examined the flowerbeds, the vegetable garden, the large, lush lawn surrounding the house, and the mown fields stretching to the white rail fence at the highway. It was a needle-in-a-haystack effort, Ernie knew. The task was exacerbated by the fact that he did not know if the "needle" he was searching for—a telltale footprint or matchbook cover or cigarette butt or piece of lint or scrap of paper or whatever—even existed. But he kept looking because it was the only way he knew how to help.

Almost ready to head home for dinner, Ernie decided to take one last look inside the barn behind the house. He had searched the large corrugated metal building with the county officers the night of Wes's disappearance, later with FBI agents, and twice by himself since the house was closed up. There was not much to see, so Ernie had not been back in over a week. The Bellardis had ceased any semblance of farming on the property and sold off most of the equipment several years earlier. Since then the cavernous structure had housed an assortment of garden tools, a riding tractor/mower/snowplow, and a beat-up 1962 GMC pickup. As large as it was, the barn could be searched in minutes because it was mostly empty space.

Ernie unlocked the large padlock and swung both tall door panels wide open to allow the retreating sunlight to flood in. He shined his flashlight in the darker corners and rafters, behind the garden tools, and under the tractor without seeing anything extraordinary. About to snap the padlock closed, Ernie was arrested by a curious thought. He quickly pulled the lock from the hasp and swung the doors open again. Surveying the barn, he could not believe what he had overlooked. By searching the cracks and corners of the barn, he had almost missed a possible clue right in front of him. Being so intent to find *something,* he almost missed *nothing.*

Ernie pulled the cellular phone from the pocket of his jacket and hurriedly dialed the Shasta County sheriff's personal number. The call went to voice mail as expected, but he knew that the sheriff checked his mailbox several times a day, even on weekends. "Sal, this is Ernie Cruz. Something I thought you might want to know about and pass on to the feds. I'm standing inside the barn behind the Bellardi house. Remember the old beater pickup they keep in here, the one with a shell with the windows busted out? Well, it's gone."

When Robert dropped Stevie off at home after the rally, it was almost eleven. Thoroughly fatigued, she had declined Robert's invitation to stop somewhere for a quick bite to eat, but enjoyed their ride together nonetheless. It was so much more relaxing to lean back and let Robert drive, his soothing voice a balm for Stevie's jangled nerves. *Later,* she told herself. *After the election is over, then Robert and I can talk about things like going out to dinner and . . .* Her thoughts trailed off. What else would they discuss? Where would their relationship go once they had the time to nurture and develop it? How serious a relationship was she ready or willing to pursue at this juncture in her life? It was one of many questions she was too tired to think about that night.

Shawna and Collin were already in bed, and Jon had moved his things back to his motel room. Stevie wished Jon had come back before she left for the rally. She had planned to offer him the Hide-A-Bed for his last few nights before returning to L.A.

on Wednesday, but she had not had the opportunity. Now that he was already back in his room at the Quiet-Nite Motel, it would seem inappropriate to invite him to return.

She wondered if she and Jon might still manage to find some time before he went back home to finish the discussion they had started. As painful as their discussion had been, the words of forgiveness had been liberating and cathartic. Yet there was so much still left unsaid.

Stevie climbed into bed feeling as if a great weight had been lifted from her shoulders. It was not so much what Jon had said, though his surprising confession had moved her deeply. It was that she had confessed her own fault and found forgiveness.

She glanced at the illuminated numbers on the clock radio: 12:16 A.M. Suddenly another weight settled down upon her as she realized that, twenty-four hours from now, the fate of Wes Bellardi would likely be known. Where was he now? Would the FBI find him before AntiCrist fulfilled his morbid vow? Would Senator Bellardi relent at the last minute and pull out of the race to save his son? Remembering a story from the Bible, Stevie prayed that time would stand still long enough for Wes to survive Halloween.

38

Sunday
October 31

NOBODY KNEW how long the GMC had been missing from the
Bellardis' barn or where it had gone or who had taken it. The
house had been closed up for almost two weeks with the electronic surveillance system armed. The pole barn had been
securely padlocked, but it had no alarm system. County deputies patrolled the property regularly and made sure that doors
and windows on all buildings were secure. But officers were
not required to enter the house or the outbuildings during
their rounds. Someone had obviously slipped in between
patrols, removed the truck from the barn, locked the padlock
behind him, and driven off.

Ernie Cruz arrived at the ranch just after six-thirty in the morning to find a dozen FBI agents and county detectives swarming over the barn. Ernie was a little embarrassed for County Sheriff Salvatore Corrales and the feds. It was bad enough that the truck was stolen from a secure, patrolled location, but it was even worse that no one on the kidnap task force even knew the vehicle was missing. Ernie also empathized with his brothers in the law enforcement fraternity. Someone—perhaps the same someone who had made the truck disappear—had stolen a much more valuable prize right out from under his nose.

"Are they finding anything?" Ernie asked as he approached his friend Sal, who stood watching the endeavor.

"They didn't find anything the first or second time through," Sal said. "No fingerprints on the lock, no unusual footprints around the barn—except yours of course. Like you said, there's nothing to suggest that the truck was even stolen—except that it's missing, and no one among the senator's family or friends or campaign people has it."

"You told Dan?" Ernie said.

"Dolores left a message with Johnstone last night to see if Dan loaned it out to someone or had the shop come get it. Answer came back no. The truck should be right here in the barn."

Ernie thought for a moment. "Anybody ask the Denherders about it—the people who take care of the houseboat?"

"Couldn't locate them. Johnstone says he thinks they're on vacation till after the election. Locked up the houseboat at Bridge Bay and went to New Zealand or somewhere."

Ernie raised his eyebrows. "Really? Seems odd."

"What?"

"Oh, nothing," Ernie answered with a shrug. "Just thinking out loud." Then he asked, "You think this truck thing is connected to the kidnapping?"

"Come on, Ernie," the sheriff chastised good-naturedly. "Do you think somebody is going to break into the Bellardi place and steal a beater pickup just to turn a few bucks? Of course it has something to do with the kidnapping. Maybe the bad guy needed wheels to haul the body away. We don't know yet."

Ernie winced at the thought and kept watching the Feds

work. "Where are the TV people?" he probed, even though he had a good idea why the place had not been overrun by uplink trucks and nosy TV anchors.

The sheriff confirmed his suspicion. "Didn't tell them about it. Kept the information off the police radios. No use adding insult to injury by letting them blab our oversight to the whole country."

Ernie nodded. "They'll find out sooner or later, Sal. One fly will sniff out this tidbit of garbage and tell the whole swarm."

"Oh, I know that, Ernie. I just hope we find the truck—and Dan's kid—first."

"Everybody's looking, right?"

Sal nodded. "Chippies, county cops, everybody. A sixty-two Jimmy with expired tags won't get far. But I also notified South Cal, Oregon, Washington, Nevada, and Utah just in case."

Ernie surveyed the cloud-choked canopy above, which had virtually canceled a glorious dawn and promised serious rain by midmorning. The weather emulated his own somber mood. "Well, we're likely to know something about Wes by this time tomorrow. I just hope it's not as bad as AntiCrist wants us to think."

Sal agreed, then excused himself to join the search.

Ernie had scoured the Bellardi ranch for more than two weeks. His efforts had finally paid off inside the pole barn, but Wes Bellardi was still gone. The husky Latino security cop was not about to give up at the eleventh hour, but he no longer expected the ranch to be the best source of clues. So he climbed into his black Dodge Ram pickup and left the ranch to conduct his own personal search for the GMC pickup.

By the time Ernie Cruz arrived at Shasta Lake, his hunch was turning into a clear suspicion. Why had he not thought of this earlier? It seemed so obvious now. Someone close enough to the Bellardis to know the layout of their home and property, even while harboring a secret resentment over the senator's success. Someone who was around often enough to be privy to the Bellardi family's comings and goings, yet not so often that his presence would make him an obvious suspect. Someone just smart enough to appear dumb and steer the investigation off in all the wrong directions.

He pulled up in front of Matthew and Lucy Denherders' mobile home. The carport was empty, and it did not appear that anyone was inside. But as Ernie made his way out back, he found exactly what he was looking for. Parked directly behind the mobile home, out of sight of anyone passing by on the street, was the missing pickup.

A couple of quick peeks inside the mobile home's windows confirmed his first impression that no one was there. A few knocks on the doors of the surrounding mobile homes raised only one person—an elderly lady who said she had not seen anyone around the Denherders' place in some time. She also said she heard that Lucy had gone to New Zealand to visit her sister; she assumed Matthew had gone with her. Ernie was about to expand his door-to-door search-and-inquiry mission in and around the small mobile home park when he stopped himself in his tracks. His heart raced as he realized instinctively where Matthew Denherder was. If his suspicions were right, he had also just figured out who AntiCrist was and where he was hiding Wes.

It did not take Ernie long to make his way down to the boat launch area, which was deserted at the moment. Ernie reasoned that the serious anglers had already launched their boats and disappeared into the many arms and fingers of Shasta Lake. Others would arrive at the lake if and when the temperature bested sixty degrees. Most water-skiers and jet skiers would likely stay indoors today.

Bridge Bay Resort was approaching hibernation stage for the winter. Most of the rental ski boats and fishing boats had already been dry docked, but Ernie managed to secure a small skiff to rent for the day. He knew he was going to need it when the man at the rental office confirmed that he had just seen the Bellardis' houseboat leave the docks less than ten minutes earlier. Although the man had not gotten a close look at the person steering the sixty-four foot craft, he just assumed it was Matthew Denherder. Who else could it be? After all, the houseboat's captain had sounded the Bellardis' customary farewell—two shorts, a long, and another short— on the air horn, as it glided past the no-wake buoy toward the towering interstate bridge.

Ernie took off, anxious to catch up to the houseboat but knowing he must be cautious so as not to tip his hand. Besides, even with 30,000 acres of surface and 370 miles of shoreline, Shasta Lake could not have swallowed up the Bellardi craft yet. Ernie was leaving the docks only a few minutes behind the boat, and with so few other boats out on the lake, it should not be too difficult to track it down.

Ernie was right. Within twenty minutes he had the houseboat in his sights. He only wished he had brought a cellular phone and some binoculars. Hanging back at a safe distance, he could make out the slight figure of a man, dressed in dark clothing, steering the boat farther out into the lake.

Where are you going, Matthew Denherder? Or should I call you AntiCrist? Ernie swallowed hard, fighting tears. *Where are you taking Wes? What are you planning to do to him? And how do I stop you before it's too late?*

Stevie assumed her customary place on the platform as Senator Bellardi addressed an after-church rally at the small Yreka shopping center. The team had left Redding early that morning in time for the senator to attend a community-wide church service in this I-5 community near the Oregon border. Following the rally, the bus would head south for a furious series of whistle-stops along the I-5 corridor, concluding with a rally in Williams, near the South California state line. It was the final day of campaigning on the road. The senator would spend Monday in Redding doing live TV interviews. Tuesday was election day, the moment of truth.

At the urging of his top staff, Senator Bellardi sounded two themes in his talk, a talk that would be repeated at every stop. First, he expressed profound gratitude for the encouragement and support of the people of North California since his son's abduction. Cards, letters, E-mail, and voice mail had poured in encouraging Bellardi to stand his ground against the terrorist's demands. Prayer vigils for the safe return of Wes Bellardi were ongoing in numerous communities across the state. In his thanks, Bellardi reaffirmed his commitment to stand firm to the end.

Second, the senator took advantage of the holiday to woo

the large block of undecided voters in the state. "Our nation and neighboring states have accepted and even encouraged a Halloween existence. Hatred, violence, terror, killing, perversion, indecency, lawlessness, and falsehood go unchallenged in their streets, in their schools, in their clinics, and in their homes. On Tuesday, God-fearing, law-abiding citizens all over North California will say an emphatic no to the monsters who intend to take over our state as well: the abortionists, the mercy killers, the drug lords, the pornographers. I invite you to join us in banishing these horrors of Halloween forever and make North California a place where the beauty and values of Easter, Thanksgiving, and Christmas are a way of daily life."

Stevie smiled and applauded with the enthusiastic crowd, but her heart was not in it. With Price Whitten in charge of the emceeing today, she felt more like a hood ornament than an assistant media secretary. Furthermore, her thoughts wandered far from the busy campaign day yet ahead.

She went back and forth with herself over the big talk with Jon. One moment she cautiously questioned the possibility of reconciliation—though it had never come up in their discussion. Jon's humility and vulnerability had fanned deeply buried embers of respect and admiration for him. The next moment she was convinced that the emotional confrontation promised nothing about the future. Jon was still Jon. He had his life in Los Angeles, and she had her life here. The air was clearer between them, but life would go on.

Besides, she had yet to see or talk with Jon since their lengthy conversation the previous day. He had walked out without offering a word of explanation while she was on the phone with Robert. Had he left simply to afford her privacy while she was on the phone? If so, why had he not returned after a reasonable amount of time? Or did it have something to do with the fact that the person on the other end of the line was Robert Johnstone? Could Jon possibly suspect her relationship with Robert? Was it jealousy that had motivated Jon's hasty exit?

Ridiculous, she told herself. *How could Jon possibly know how I feel about Robert? I'm not even sure myself!* Yet she could not deny that, whatever those feelings might be, they were

340

strong—and she was going to have to come to terms with them very soon. The prospect both frightened and excited her.

With the end of the campaign trail clearly in sight, the rest of Stevie's life stood in desperate need of triage. Her business was dying for lack of attention. Her children probably thought she had abandoned them. And she had not seen the inside of a church or read her Bible in weeks. She would cast her ballot on Tuesday, then go straight home and get to work. The to-do lists were already forming in her brain.

Constantly at the fringes of her thoughts was the steady, ominous, almost audible ticking of the clock. Wes Bellardi's time was running out. Somewhere at this moment, the despicable creature identified only as AntiCrist awaited his final move. Unless God miraculously intervened, an innocent lamb would be sacrificed as the new governor of North California ascended his throne. Jon had insisted that Wes's fate was not her responsibility. Her head knew he was right, but the pall remained heavy in her heart. As she boarded the bus for the quick hop to Weed, the only words she could find to pray were, *Spare him, spare him, God. Please, spare him!*

The houseboat was anchored in a remote cove several miles from the main channel of Shasta Lake, not far from the shoreline. From Ernie's vantage point he could see nothing more than the location of the boat. To risk getting any closer would be to risk being seen by AntiCrist, possibly precipitating disaster for Wes.

As Ernie hunkered down under the small canvas covering of his boat, bobbing up and down on the choppy lake, the only sound he could hear was the continuous splattering of raindrops on the canvas and deck. The storm had pulled a shade on sunset just as it had muted the sunrise. By four-thirty it was nearly dark outside. The day would soon be over—and Wes Bellardi's time would run out.

Ernie could no longer sit there doing nothing. He had to get back to shore and call for assistance as quickly as possible. If AntiCrist held true to his threats, then Wes was presumably safe until midnight. Ernie could only pray that the houseboat would stay where it was until he could get back with help.

39

Sunday
October 31

SHAWNA DID NOT really know what to expect. It was the first "real" Halloween party she had ever been allowed to attend. Her mother had always said that Christians should not celebrate Halloween and even restricted the types of costumes she and Dougie and Collin could wear for Halloween parties in their school classrooms. The dwarfs had convinced Shawna that they should all go as vampires, unanimously voting her the most realistic looking vampire because of her height. At the moment, however, she would have been happy to be wearing a clown or ballerina costume—something her mother would approve of—and to be dunking for apples in the safety of an elementary school classroom. Shawna felt anything but safe in this ominous gathering tonight.

Although there seemed to be more girls than boys, there were several mixed couples in attendance. Most seemed to be of high school age or slightly older; many Shawna did not recognize. But almost all had an "otherworldly" appearance about them, as if they expected at any moment to be transported into another dimension. Shawna suspected that much of what Terilyn referred to as the "spiritual experiences" people might experience tonight could be directly linked to the heavy smell of alcohol and marijuana that seemed to linger over many of the partygoers—including the so-called adult chaperones.

Even the party games were unlike any Shawna had ever played: mind-reading games, tarot-card games, horoscope readings. She eluded being roped in on most of them by excusing herself to get punch or go to the bathroom. But worse than the games was the eerie feeling in the air. There seemed to be nowhere to go to escape it.

"Hey, what's wrong with you, Snowy?" Terilyn asked, her painted white face and heavy black eyeliner adding to the creepy feeling of the party. "Isn't this what we've been looking forward to for weeks? You haven't even had Ms. Carmona read your horoscope yet. Get with it, girl! You're missing out on all the fun."

Shawna glanced toward the front of the room where Ms. Carmona was offering her specialized services. Josie and Alexis were standing in line behind a young couple who were holding hands, quietly waiting their turn. The girl seated on the floor at the long, low coffee table opposite Ms. Carmona seemed enthralled with what the frighteningly realistic-looking witch was telling her.

"Maybe . . . later," Shawna said. "There's a line right now."

Terilyn laughed. "Of course there's a line. How often do we get a chance to have our horoscope read by a real live witch? Come on, Snowy. Don't wuss out on me."

Shawna shook her head. "Not right now. You go ahead. Maybe I'll come over later."

Terilyn's displeasure was obvious. "Fine. You just sit here and sip your punch by yourself. I'm going where the action is." She turned on her heel and flounced off to join Josie and

Alexis, leaving Shawna standing where she had been much of the evening—beside the punch bowl.

Maybe this would be a good time to leave, Shawna thought, glancing around the room. *If I just had some way to get home. . . .*

"Sit down on the floor, everybody," Ms. Carmona suddenly yelled above the din. Shawna looked over to where, just a moment earlier, her faculty advisor had been sitting with her enraptured devotee. The girl was gone, and those who had been standing in line were dispersing. Ms. Carmona was waving her arms to get everyone's attention, her long black gown billowing out around her.

"Sit down," she repeated, a sinister smile making her overdone makeup look even more grotesque. "It's time to get serious and make contact with the greater powers." The partygoers squealed with delight and noisily jostled for good seats in front of the coffee table. Shawna purposely took a place at the back of the group, provoking another scowl from Terilyn, who had managed to squeeze in right up front.

"Come on, Snowy," Terilyn mouthed, beckoning Shawna with a wave. "Up here." Shawna shook her head and Terilyn turned away, her disgust evident.

Someone had placed a large tub of water in the center of the table. Shawna was pretty sure it was not for apple-bobbing, but she could not even begin to imagine its purpose. On either side of the tub were candles of all descriptions. Ms. Carmona lit them as the guests settled into their places. Someone else turned out the lights.

"I'm going to cast a major spell tonight, my little goblins," Ms. Carmona began in her best witch's voice. "We're going to put the hex on that fundamentalist bigot candidate for governor and turn him into a cross-eyed toad." She produced a fiendish cackle, while applause and cheers rose from the crowd. "But there's enough magic in the room for everybody tonight. So who would you like to put the hex on? Make a wish for good or evil, and the powers will make it so. Who's going to be first?"

The girl in front of Shawna spoke up. "My physics teacher is a beast, and I want the powers to send her to Uranus," she said in a spiteful tone.

"Yes, old Mrs. Wiggins to Uranus," another girl chipped in.

345

The crowd cheered agreement. Several others got into the spirit, wishing ill on teachers, rivals, and even parents. The comments were crude and hateful. The guests jeered and hissed each name mentioned. Shawna could not believe her ears.

"All right, all right," Ms. Carmona called above the clamor. "That's enough mayhem for one spell. Let's call on those whose powers can make these things happen."

This is getting too weird for me, Shawna thought. *As soon as this witch act is over, I'm outta here—ride or no ride!*

Attention focused on Ms. Carmona again as she began her incantations. The weird sounds and lewd gyrations turned Shawna's blood cold. Several of the guests, including Terilyn, began rolling their heads and moaning, as if in a trance. If this was only a charade produced by a "part-time" witch, Shawna never wanted to see the real thing.

Ms. Carmona began chanting in a hideous voice, "Prince of darkness, hosts from hell, accept our gift, empower our spell." Others joined in, and the pitch and volume rose. Shawna cringed as the chant neared a crescendo. Then she saw the "gift." From the shadows behind Ms. Carmona, another one of the adult chaperones produced a squirming black kitten, eyes ablaze with fear. In one continuous motion, Ms. Carmona grabbed the kitten and thrust the terrified animal into the air with both hands, then plunged it into the tub of water and held it there.

"No!" Shawna's scream was lost in the raucous, blood-chilling chant. She leaped to her feet as if launched by a coil spring. Scrabbling over the swooning guests in front of her, she frantically threw herself at the coffee table, sending tub, water, candles, and the surprised Ms. Carmona flying. Somehow the soggy, sputtering kitten was in her arms. Shawna stumbled through the dark chaos to the door, burst outside into the rain, and ran. Unable to distinguish deliverance from danger, the kitten howled and clawed at her. But Shawna held on and kept running, her tears mixing with the rain that poured down her face.

There was no levity in the Bellardi coach on the long drive back to Redding. Even the sense of relief at the end of the campaign trail was lost in unanimous concern for Wes Bellardi and uncertainty over his fate.

Stevie sat at the table in silence with Robert, Price Whitten, Coleman King, and Mike Bragan as the coach rumbled northward. Daniel Bellardi and his bodyguards were spending the night near the southern border of the new state at the plush ranch of an old friend. Patricia had been flown to the ranch from Redwood City late that evening. Together the couple would await news about their son and pray for his safe release.

Finding courage to broach the topic that had plagued her since Wes disappeared, Stevie said, "Is it really worth it?" Looking up from their coffee mugs, the men gave her their attention. "I mean, if you had to choose between your child and the governor's seat, would you do as Senator Bellardi has done?"

Robert answered immediately. "Absolutely. Granted, it would be extremely difficult, as it has been for the senator. But he made the right decision. Don't you agree?"

The other men appeared to be less sure, and said nothing.

Stevie pressed the issue. "Robert, you're talking about literally sacrificing your child for a political office."

"No, Stephanie, not an office," Robert interjected, his voice warm but adamant. "A cause, an ideal, a truth. And truth outvalues human life. That's why our young men and women join the armed services and volunteer for combat." His voice dropped a notch. "If young Wes dies at the hand of this terrorist—God forbid—his death ranks up there with those who died defending America's freedom."

"But Wes didn't volunteer for combat, Robert," Stevie argued. "He didn't even volunteer for his father's campaign. He was drafted, pressed into service. He should be at Berkeley right now working on his literature degree."

Robert's eyes were sympathetic, but he did not waver. "Draftees die in combat too," he said. "So do civilians. It goes with the territory."

347

Stevie shook her head. "I don't see how you can say that. I'm talking about a person here, someone I care about very much."

Robert reached over and covered her hand with his. It was the first time he had extended such a personal physical gesture to her, particularly in public. "I care about Wes too," he said, speaking to her in a way that made her feel as if everyone else had disappeared. "But there are millions of people across this state and around this country to consider. If we compromise our campaign to save one life, the terrorist wins and everything that's right for North California and America is lost. I don't mean to sound blasé about it, Stephanie, really. But the solution to this dilemma comes down to a simple matter of priorities: the sacrifice of one to save many. The senator understands this. The fact that the one being sacrificed is close to all of us doesn't diminish the validity of this priority."

"Just a minute, you two," interrupted Coleman King, the senator's policy advisor and the elder statesman of the campaign. "To paraphrase Mark Twain, the report of Wes Bellardi's death is greatly exaggerated. As far as we know, he's still alive. That's what everybody's been praying for. Perhaps the death threat was a ploy, a bluff. This AntiCrist nut could be all blow and no go, and his scare tactic didn't work. Wes could be free and heading for home right now. Let's keep thinking positively and not borrow trouble."

Stevie was only slightly comforted. "You're right, Cole," she said with a sigh. "I guess I'm seeing the glass half empty. Let's hope for some good news when we get back to the office." Slowly she withdrew her hand from Robert's, then stood and took her empty mug to the sink. She had a sleeping compartment to pack up before the bus arrived in Redding.

Robert caught her in the passageway. "I don't want to leave the discussion hanging, Stephanie. Are you OK with what I said? I mean, do you understand what I was trying to say about the priority of the cause, the value of the many over the few—even when it involves someone we both care for a great deal?"

Stevie studied the strength in his face and the sincerity in his eyes. Behind this attractive facade was an astute mind of a master political strategist. Stevie wondered if she was looking at the campaign director of not only Governor Bellardi but possibly U.S. Senator Bellardi or President Bellardi. If anyone could get Dan Bellardi to the White House, Robert Johnstone could.

"I think so," she answered softly, fighting an urge to ask him to hold her, to impart to her some of his strength and assurance. She forced a smile. "I just pray, in this case, that there's room in God's plan for the many *and* the one." Then, before she could yield to her urge to touch him, she stepped inside her compartment and closed the door.

Stevie clearly understood the principle of sacrificing one to save many. A soldier smothers a hand grenade with his body to save his patrol. Thousands of soldiers die so that millions of citizens may live in freedom. But she was still not sure Wes Bellardi fit in the category of a sacrifice. It was one of many things she wanted to talk in detail to Robert about once the campaign was over. Strangely enough, she realized she wanted to talk to Jon about it as well.

Shawna ran through the rain until she could run no more, then slowed to a fast walk. It was at least another mile to Shasta Commons. Her lungs ached, and her knee, which she must have banged on the tub or coffee table in her flight from the party, throbbed. She stayed to the backstreets in case Terilyn or anyone else from the party was trying to find her. The neighborhood trick-or-treaters had long since been put to bed. Shawna was on the streets alone.

Wet and cold, she had stripped down to her shorts and tank top to wrap the kitten in her long black vampire dress. The animal was docile now in its captor's gentle embrace. Shasta Commons did not allow animals and Shawna did not really want a cat for a pet, but a sense of kinship with her fellow escapee was growing. They had both been severely traumatized and lived to tell about it.

And Shawna had decided she *would* tell about it. She would tell her father the whole story as soon as she got home—if he was still at the apartment. And she would tell her mother the whole story as soon as she saw her—if she would listen. *I did it again,* she would say. *I let my friends lead me into stuff I shouldn't be in.* She would come clean about everything: the party, the spell and sacrifice, Ms. Carmona and the conference in San Francisco, the secrecy about Terilyn's interest in other religions and their practices, even her own confusion and temptation on those issues.

And when she had told all, she would tell her mom and dad a thing or two about North California. It does not matter where you live or who the governor is or what the laws are, she had decided. Kids are going to do what they want. And if kids can get into drugs and spells and animal sacrifices and who-knows-what-else, adults can get into that much and worse. The problem is not the place; the problem is the people.

At exactly 11:59 P.M., AntiCrist faxed his last message. As with previous communications, he had overridden caller I.D. on the computer's fax program so his message could not be traced.

Draining his vodka glass for the third time, he poured one final drink before setting to work on the final stage of his plan. The senator had disregarded his ultimatum; there was only one recourse. It was not what he wanted to do; in fact, it was something he dreaded. But Senator Bellardi had left him no choice.

The bomb was crude, but it would serve its purpose. Once it was lit he would have just enough time to clear the boat and head for shore. AntiCrist had not succeeded in getting the senator to give up his bid for governor in order to save his son; all that was left now was to make sure that Daniel Bellardi spent the rest of his life regretting his decision.

40

Monday
November 1

"I'M SURE this is the one," Ernie said into the mike of his head-set, his face pressed against the darkened window. "At least . . . I think it is." He sighed and shook his head. "This lake is loaded with tentacles, and it's so hard to see from up here. We've got to find that boat, Chuck. We've got to."

It was shortly after midnight, and the Sheriff's search-and-rescue helicopter was cruising just below the rain-laden clouds over every back inlet they could find in the area where Ernie had last seen the Bellardis' houseboat. He had flown with Captain Chuck LaChappelle a number of times before retiring from the CHP. Ernie could not have been more pleased, after returning to shore and calling for help, to find that Chuck would be the search pilot. Ernie had been so sure he could direct the chopper right back to the houseboat. Now he was becoming increasingly frustrated at his inability to do so. A flash of light in the corner of his eye caught his attention.

"What was that? Was it lightning?" Ernie pointed between the pilot and copilot to where he had seen the flash.

"No way, Ernie. It's bad enough flying in this soup at night. If there was a chance of lightning in this storm, you never would have got me up here."

Ernie felt completely safe. Chuck knew the lake and its many arms like he knew the names of his six children. Copilot Jeff Butler had been his partner during scores of rescues in the Shasta Lake region. "Then what was it?" Ernie asked.

"Something on the ground—or on the water," came Butler's reply through the earphones. "Not far from here. Probably up toward Doddle's Creek. Could be a searchlight, or . . ."

Ernie finished the sentence for him. "Or an explosion."

"Could be."

"Get us there, Chuck," Ernie urged. "Get us there fast."

The captain angled the chopper toward the flash, dropped toward the surface of the water, and opened up the throttle. The craft banked around rocky slopes following the ever-narrowing ribbon of water, illuminated by the craft's powerful search beam.

"There!" Ernie said excitedly, pointing ahead. "Light on the water. Something burning."

In seconds they were over the scene at about eighty feet. Chuck pulled the chopper into a tight circle as the copilot swept the surface with the multimillion candlepower search-light. Looking almost straight down from the back window, Ernie mouthed a prayer. Motion sickness never bothered him, but the circling motion combined with the dreadful sight suddenly made him feel nauseated. *We're too late,* he thought.

The charred skeleton of a houseboat listed in the water at about forty-five degrees, small flames feeding on what used to be wood paneling, furniture, and appliances. Most of the top deck was peeled away and floating beside the boat in three large sections, still attached by twisted ribbons of metal. Debris, some of it still burning, littered the surface for a radius of three hundred feet. Some chunks of metal and wood had reached the nearest shoreline.

"I see a victim," the copilot announced, training the light on a small island of debris about sixty feet from the shoreline. "Looks like the only one. Let's take a closer look." Chuck broke off the circle and began to descend slowly.

Ernie could see nothing in the splash of light but shreds of metal tangled around shattered strips of paneling and a section of a pontoon. *If there's only one victim, who is it?* Ernie worried. *If it's Wes, where's Matthew? Did he manage to escape and make it to shore already?*

Then Ernie saw a head, shoulders, and one arm protruding from the mass. The head and exposed limb were dipping in and out of the water as the floating island of junk rocked on the surface. The body was not moving. *Oh, dear God, we* are *too late.*

Chuck's solemn voice came through the headset. "Hope that's not our boy, Ernie. Looks like a fatal to me. If the blast didn't kill him, he probably drowned. But we have to go find out."

In less than a minute, Deputy Jeff Butler had looped his leg and arm into a sling and was descending on a cable from the side door of the helicopter. Ernie leaned out the open door to watch. The heavy prop wash, exacerbated by the glare of the light on the spray of water and smoke, screened most of his view. The chopper lurched slightly as Butler dropped into the water to examine the body. The sling dangled wildly in the agitated wind.

Ernie could see the copilot treading water next to the ark made of debris, but he could not make out what was happening. Then Butler looked to the pilot and gave a hand signal.

Chuck's voice came through the headset. "Jeff says the victim is alive, Ernie—barely. I'm bringing up the cable so you can attach the basket. Let's get him out of here. I'll notify the ER at St. Vincent's."

In minutes, Butler had the victim loaded into the basket, wrapped in a blanket, and strapped for transport. Ernie's job was to swing the portable stretcher into the tiny cargo area, then reattach the sling and send it down for Butler. The body was completely covered when the basket reached the doorway. Ernie quickly maneuvered it into the bay, detached it, and sent the sling down for the copilot.

As Butler ascended, Ernie reached back and pulled the blanket back, revealing the victim's face to the dim cabin lights. At first he thought the victim was African-American, then realized with a shudder that he was looking at charred flesh.

"Who is it?" Chuck asked.

Ernie shook his head. "Can't tell. I need more light."

Chuck passed him a flashlight as the copilot boarded the chopper and shut the door. The pilot banked the chopper toward the main channel of the lake and accelerated. Ernie directed the light into the grotesque face of the unconscious victim. Recognition rocked Ernie like a blow to the stomach. "Let's roll, Chuck," he said soberly. "It's the senator's son."

"That was the FBI agent monitoring communications at campaign headquarters," Robert Johnstone reported as he tapped off the phone shortly after midnight. Stevie and the other passengers aboard the coach, which was nearing the Redding city limits, anxiously gathered around.

"He said they received a message just a few minutes ago from AntiCrist," Robert explained. "All it said was, 'Time's up. Your son is dead. Enjoy your rain as king. AntiCrist.'"

Stevie gasped. "Oh, Robert, do you think it's true?"

"They can't be absolutely sure until they find a body, Stephanie," he answered, his voice shaking slightly. "But he says the message looks like . . . like all the others, right down to the bad spelling." He took a deep breath. "I'm afraid I'll have to . . . notify the senator."

The others nodded their agreement as shock and grief threatened to settle down upon them like a shroud. Stevie, however, chose not to believe it—either that the note was genuine or that Wes Bellardi was indeed dead. In a few hours, she told herself, he will walk into campaign headquarters and wonder what all the fuss was about. He will explain that he was away at Berkeley visiting friends for a few weeks and just forgot to tell anybody he was going. Classic mind-in-the-clouds Wes. That was what Stevie decided to believe until proven wrong.

Shortly after the coach arrived at campaign headquarters in the middle of the rainy night, Stevie was proven wrong. Robert received the call from the hospital on his personal phone as the team ferried boxes of campaign supplies from the bus into the office.

"Wes has been found," he announced gravely to the team. Stevie held her breath and braced herself for the worst. "A houseboat exploded out on the lake, and Wes was in it. He's alive, but he suffered burns, internal injuries, and head injuries. The police airlifted him to St. Vincent's. He's headed into surgery right now, hanging by a thread. I'll call the senator again. You folks can go home or go to the hospital, whatever you need to do."

Stevie let the tears roll, but she determined not to fall apart. She would be of no use to Wes or Senator Bellardi or anyone else by indulging in a breakdown now. Nor would any purpose be served by obeying the urge to drop everything and race to the hospital as she had the night she heard about Dougie. For her own sanity, she had to make sense of this whole debacle herself, which meant she must remain in control. So as the rest of the team filed out bearing their own burden of emotions, Stevie calmly loaded her suitcase and briefcase into the Cherokee. Robert offered her a ride, but she declined, feeling the need to think things through alone. On the way to the hospital, she stopped at an all-night donut shop for a large coffee. She sensed it would be a long night.

By the time Stevie arrived at St. Vincent's, Price Whitten had enlisted the Redding police to cordon off the surgery wing because of the growing swarm of media. He promised no statement and would answer no questions until morning at the earliest. All details of the explosion and recovery of the victim, including the fact that the houseboat belonged to Senator Bellardi, were withheld. First reports from the scene merely stated that Senator Bellardi's son was critically injured in an alleged assassination attempt by the terrorist AntiCrist, who was still at large.

Inside the surgery wing, little more was known. Wes, who remained comatose, was bleeding internally. Shock and serious burns made him a risk for surgery, but he would surely die if they did not get inside and stop the bleeding. Senator and Mrs. Bellardi would not arrive by helicopter for an hour or more. The Sheriff's Department and FBI continued searching the site of the explosion to learn what more they could about AntiCrist. So far, no other victims had been found. Anti-Crist had more than likely swum the short distance to shore and disappeared. There was nothing to do now but wait and pray.

A husky, graying Latino man, bowed and contemplative, sat apart from the small group of Bellardi staffers in the waiting room. Stevie recognized the man from her visits to the Bellardi ranch. "Mr. Cruz?" she said, approaching him. Seeing a tear-stained face turn to her, she said, "I'm sorry, I didn't mean to bother you," and began respectfully retreating.

"No, it's all right. I'm fine," Ernie said, standing and wiping his face dry with a handkerchief.

"I'm Stephanie Van Horne," she said, extending her hand. "We met at the ranch a couple of times. I'm with the senator's campaign."

"Yes, I remember," he said, shaking her hand.

"Did I hear someone say you're the one who found Wes at the lake?"

Ernie shrugged and nodded. "It's a long story, but I was aboard the search-and-rescue helicopter, searching the coves and inlets for the boat where we believed Wes was being held captive. We saw a flash of light in the rain and . . . there he was."

Stevie expected him to say more, but he remained quiet. "You're a friend of the Bellardis as well as their security chief, as I recall," she said.

"Yes, Dan and I go all the way back to high school."

"Then you know Wes pretty well."

Ernie nodded. "My boy and Wes practically grew up together. He's kind of like a nephew to me. How well do you know him?"

356

"We met in July, and I worked closely with him in the com-munications department of the campaign." Originally, that was all she intended to say, but instead she found herself pouring out the whole story to someone she sensed knew the real Wes as she did, not simply Wes Bellardi the senator's son. She told about Wes's uncanny resemblance to Dougie, which meant she had to tell Dougie's tragic story, including the sense of failure and the redemption she experienced mentoring Wes.

Ernie Cruz responded in kind. He described the last two and a half weeks as a living hell, having failed his friends Dan and Patricia by allowing Wes to be kidnapped. He detailed the days and nights of searching the ranch inch by inch for something with which to redeem himself.

"But your diligence paid off," Stevie interjected. "Had you not kept looking for clues you might not have gone to the lake, and Wes might not have had a chance. At least he's alive right now."

Ernie studied the woman's face thoughtfully for a moment. Then he leaned closer and spoke with the obvious intent of secrecy. "I need to tell you something about Wes. It's something that's been nagging at me for a while, but I just couldn't pin it down. When I discovered the truck missing it occurred to me that possibly the Denherders, the Bellardis' caretakers, had borrowed it for some reason. But then I was told they were on vacation—out of the country, as a matter of fact. That seemed rather odd to me, as close as they're supposed to be to the senator and all. You'd think they'd stick around for the election."

Stevie frowned. "Now that you mention it," she said, "I remember seeing them the morning of the bombing at campaign headquarters. I didn't know who they were, of course, but Wes told me. He seemed surprised to see them there." She paused. "You don't think they could have had anything to do with any of this, do you?"

Ernie shook his head. "No. Not now, anyway. I did earlier, though. In fact, that's what led me out to the lake in the first place. I was trying to remember everything I'd ever heard about their relationship with the Bellardis, and I wondered if maybe there was some hidden resentment on the Denherders' part. You know, Dan being so successful and all, Matthew Denherder having to leave his job because of his health, then ending up working for the Bellardis as more or less a hired servant. Maybe Denherder felt he was living off charity or something and the resentment grew. And he would certainly have had access to any information needed to plan an attack on Bellardi."

Stevie nodded. "Makes sense," she said. "But you say that now you don't think the Denherders are involved?"

"No. After I got out to the lake and found the pickup parked behind the Denherders' place, I was sure Matthew Denherder was AntiCrist. According to one of the neighbors, they were supposed to be in New Zealand visiting Lucy's sister, but I just wasn't buying it. I figured Lucy might be in New Zealand, but not Matthew. And when I found out that the Bellardis' houseboat had left the docks only a short time earlier, I was sure Matthew Denherder had taken Wes out on the boat to await his midnight deadline and then finish him off. In fact, right up until about an hour ago, I was absolutely positive that Denherder was AntiCrist."

Stevie frowned. "What changed your mind?"

"I tracked down Lucy Denherder's sister's name and phone number in New Zealand and called them. Not only is Lucy there visiting, so is Matthew. I spoke to him."

"But I don't understand . . ." Stevie's voice trailed off. None of this was making any sense. If Matthew Denherder was not AntiCrist, then who could it possibly be? It seemed that, other than having finally found Wes, they knew no more than they had when this AntiCrist thing first started.

"I don't know if there's any way to understand," Ernie said, his face drawn with fatigue. "With all my heart, I wish I were wrong. But I know I'm not. You see, something has been nagging me about Wes for several weeks now, but it wasn't until I spoke with Matthew Denherder in New Zealand that it all began to come into focus. I suppose I should have figured it out when I saw Wes burned and bleeding in the chopper but . . . well, I guess maybe I just didn't want to believe it."

He leaned closer and lowered his voice. "The problem is, I don't know if I can tell anyone. I can still hardly accept it myself. But after what you've told me tonight, I think you'll understand."

Stevie wondered if she was getting in over her head. Having bared her soul to the kind, fatherly security officer, she felt obligated to let him do the same. "What is it?" she said.

Ernie studied her a moment longer, as if reevaluating his decision to tell her. Finally, lowering his voice to a whisper, he said, "They're out at the lake searching for another victim right now— AntiCrist. They're also searching the shoreline near the explosion, thinking he probably got away. But they're not going to find him—not in the water, not on the shore, not anywhere— because . . . because Wes Bellardi is AntiCrist."

358

41

Monday
November 1

HEARING THOSE WORDS—"Wes Bellardi is AntiCrist"—Stevie's opinion of Ernie Cruz changed instantly and dramatically. One moment he was a wise, tenacious ex-cop, loyal friend of the Bellardis, and a sudden soul mate on the topic of Wes Bellardi. The next moment he was an escapee from the St. Vincent's psych ward, on a par with someone who claimed that the president of the United States was an alien infiltrator from another galaxy. Believing that Wes Bellardi could be the terrorist plaguing his own father's campaign was flat-out crazy. Stating such a ludicrous idea at a time like this was downright cruel.

The shock must have registered on her face, because Ernie

touched her hand gently and said, "I know this sounds very, very bizarre. But you know how intelligent Wes is, and you also know how closed he is, almost secretive. I believe there's a whole world inside that brainy head of his that we know nothing about. Unfortunately, there's a dark side to this hidden world. Please, let me explain."

Stevie did not want to hear it, any more than she had wanted to hear that her son, whom she knew infinitely better than Wes Bellardi, had died of a drug overdose. Drugs could not be a part of her son's world, she had thought, until she was confronted with the truth. Truth is good. Truth is right. But the truth sometimes hurts, and Stevie did not want to be hurt again.

As much as she wanted to flee, Stevie sat and listened. Ernie laid out the evidence, working from the present to the past. Each statement was like a painful slap on the face.

The houseboat that exploded belonged to the Bellardis. Yes, Matthew Denherder would be the first suspect at that point but, as Ernie had explained, he had since spoken to Matthew in New Zealand. In fact, they had been there for almost two weeks.

"But I saw them at campaign headquarters the morning of the bombing," Stevie protested, desperately grasping at straws. "Wes thought it was strange they were there and—"

"A lot of people were there," Ernie interrupted. "They could very well have heard the news on the radio or a police scanner. Who knows? Anyway, they're not even in the country now. There's no way they could have been involved in any of this."

"But you said Matthew resented the Bellardis. What about that?"

Ernie shook his head. "I didn't say he resented the Bellardis. I said it was a possibility. I was looking for something, anything, to tie him to Wes's kidnapping."

"All right," Stevie said. "So maybe it wasn't Matthew Denherder. But that doesn't mean it was Wes. It could be any one of a dozen kooks out there who doesn't want to see Bellardi become governor of North California. It could even be someone from Juanita Dunsmuir's campaign, couldn't it?"

Again, Ernie shook his head. "I wish I could believe that, I really do. And, of course, that was one of our first thoughts from the very beginning. But the FBI just hasn't come up with any possible suspects connected with the Dunsmuir camp, especially anyone who would have access to the Bellardis' houseboat. Not only did Wes have that access, he knew how to pilot the boat, and he knew the air horn signal that would quiet any suspicion in the marina. He also has a slight build, the same as Matthew Denherder, which is another reason I thought Matthew was AntiCrist when I saw him in the distance on the houseboat. The explosion occurred about an hour after he faxed AntiCrist's last message to the office."

By this time Stevie could think of nothing more to say. The evidence against Wes was mounting, but she simply could not believe what she was hearing. Ernie went on to explain that Wes also had keys to the GMC pickup and the barn. Trash in the cab of the pickup suggested that Wes could have hidden out in the barn for several days after the ranch was closed down. Then he had access to the house at night for food. He also could send AntiCrist messages from there.

What Ernie Cruz was trying to get Stevie to believe was that Wes had, in effect, kidnapped himself. He messed up his room and spread around a little blood from a self-induced cut. Then he hid in the floor of the attic, which was stocked with a little water and food. That was how the mysterious kidnapper got in and out of the house undetected. He was in the house all along, staying there until the house was closed down. Anti-Crist's message arrived several days after the kidnapping, when Wes could finally exit the attic and get to his portable computer.

The terrorist attacks against the campaign were Wes's work also. He slipped out his bedroom window and firebombed his parents' home while the security guards were rotating locations. Then he jumped back into bed and pretended to be asleep. He also firebombed headquarters and shot up the place with a deer rifle and long-range scope. "I'm the one who taught him how to use a rifle," Ernie added remorsefully.

Grasping for one final reason to discount Ernie's incredible scenario, Stevie protested, "Wes is just a kid—a university literature student, a promising writer. He's not a mad bomber or a political terrorist. He didn't even care about the campaign. It was all I could do to keep him on task."

"You're talking about the Wes you and I know. I'm talking about the Wes who, up until now, was known only to Wes. This AntiCrist stuff all came out of the dark side of his head, a side we didn't know existed."

Stevie kept looking for cracks in the story. "How could a twenty-year-old kid fool the police and the FBI for so long?"

"For one thing, he's very smart. For another, he was very lucky. If I had discovered the hiding place in the attic or gone back to the barn sooner, I might have found him. Or if we had discovered one day earlier that the pickup was missing, we might have found Wes hiding at the marina. Sooner or later, his luck would have run out." Glancing toward the closed doors to the operating rooms, he added with a sigh, "Perhaps it already has."

Stevie could hardly bring herself to say the words, but she had to ask. "Are you saying that . . . that Wes, pretending to be a political terrorist, tried to get his father to quit the campaign? And then, when the senator didn't comply, he . . . Wes tried to . . . kill himself?"

"I think that's what I'm saying," Ernie answered. "At least, that's what it looks like right now. Unless. . . ."

"Unless what?"

"Unless it was an accident. Not the explosion, but . . . Wes being caught in it. Maybe he thought he could escape in time and something went wrong."

"I don't understand," Stevie said. "What would be the point of blowing up the houseboat? And why would Wes—if he really is AntiCrist—send a message saying Wes was dead if he wasn't planning to . . . to commit suicide?"

"This is all just guesswork," Ernie answered, his eyes mirroring Stevie's confusion. "I don't really have any answers for you. But I've been sitting here asking myself the same questions you're asking. I guess because I don't want to believe that he was trying to kill himself, I'm trying to come up with something else. The only thing I can think of is that maybe Wes was going to disappear—for a time, for good, I don't know—to make his dad think he was dead, to punish him for not caring enough about him to withdraw from the race." Ernie sighed and shook his head. "I don't know, Stephanie. I just don't know. But I was really hoping you might. You're the one who's been working with him for the past few months. How has he been acting? What has he been talking about? Is there anything—anything at all—that you can think of that might explain some of this?"

Stevie suddenly felt very tired. This was not why she had come to the hospital. She wished she could rewind the last ten minutes, back to the moment she recognized Ernie sitting alone in a corner of the waiting room. She would not talk to him. She would not listen to his story. She would find her own quiet corner in which to sit and grieve and pray for Wes Bellardi.

Instead, in deference to Ernie's sincerity, she said, "That's just it. Wes doesn't talk; he keeps to himself. For the life of me, I haven't been able to get past his hard outer shell. Like a lot of writers, Wes seems to express himself on paper more easily than face to face."

Ernie nodded. "I don't know much about writers," he said. "But that sounds like Wes."

They were silent for a moment, then Stevie asked, "So, have you heard anything more about his condition since you got here?"

"Afraid not," Ernie answered. "I don't really expect to for quite a while. I'm just sitting here waiting because . . . because I don't know what else to do."

Stevie nodded in agreement. "You're probably right," she said. "In fact, if you don't think we'll have any news for a while, I think I'll head home and check on my kids. I'll be back in an hour or so." She fished in her purse for a piece of scrap paper and a pen. "Here's my cellular number," she said, scribbling it down. "Will you call me if you hear anything before I get back?"

"Sure," Ernie said, folding the paper and stuffing it in his shirt pocket. "But in the meantime, if you talk to anyone, please don't tell them what I've confided to you. I don't want to upset Dan and Patricia. And if Wes . . . doesn't make it, then, well . . . perhaps they don't ever need to know. It may be just as well for all concerned if AntiCrist dies with him."

Stevie swallowed the lump in her throat. "Don't worry, Mr. Cruz. I won't breathe a word. And thank you for trusting me with your concern." She meant it about remaining silent. Ernie's theory, though arguably believable, was still conjecture and purely circumstantial. She was not about to discuss it with anyone until she determined it to be fully true. With all her heart she prayed that something would turn up to prove him wrong.

Stevie avoided the media by exiting the hospital through the day-surgery wing. She hurried through the rain to the Cherokee and locked herself inside, willing herself not to cry. She needed to hold herself together until this thing was over—no matter what the end result.

She put the key in the ignition and was about to start the engine and head for home when she remembered she had not checked her E-mail for several hours. She could wait until she got home but, since she had the computer with her, she might as well do it now.

Retrieving the computer from the backseat, she booted up and jacked into the communication port on the dash. She glanced at her list of incoming mail. Nothing that could not wait until later, except . . . Wait, what was this? She recognized Wes's E-mail address. The date and time listed on the letter was October 31, 11:15 P.M. The caption under SUBJECT read "Can You Keep a Secret, Stephanie?" Desperately trying to control her trembling hands, she opened the letter. As she did so, she remembered her words to Ernie about writers having trouble verbalizing their feelings. *Maybe the answers we're looking for are in here,* Stevie thought. She took a deep breath and, as rain continued to pelt the roof and run down the windows in rivulets, she began to read.

Dear Ms. Van Horne—Stephanie: I'm kidding about the secret. I've had a little bit to drink tonight—actually more than just a little bit. Must be the vodka turning me into a comedian. By the time you get this, it won't matter what you know or who you tell. My little game will all be over.

What can I say? First, you need to know that none of this was your fault. You didn't know what was going on in my head. You busted your tail trying to cultivate me as a writer—and friend. I know I didn't show it, but your attempts at friendship did not go unnoticed—including the free lunches. Thanks.

Second, since you were square with me, you deserve to know what's going on. If you want to tell anybody, that's your business, I don't care. I just don't care about anything anymore.

So how do I say what I want to say? I guess I just say it. I'm going to blow myself to kingdom come tonight because I'm a scared little gay boy who can't come out of the closet. Let me define my terms.

Gay, *as in homosexual. That's right, your protégé, Wes Bellardi, is (or was, by now) an avowed, practicing homosexual. Surprised? I'll bet you are.*

Scared, *as in scared of AIDS. Several of my friends already have it, and three of them have died. One of those three was my lover at one time. (Sorry if that ruffles your conservative Judeo-Christian feathers.) So far I haven't tested positive, but every time I get a sniffle, I wonder. It's a horrible way to die, Stephanie. Believe me, I know. I've watched it happen—close up and personal.*

Closet, *as in hiding place for almost three years. Closet may also be translated dungeon, prison, outer Mongolia, or wherever the soon-to-be-crowned king of North California will send people like me during his reign.*

Here's the way it is, Stephanie. I suspected I was gay back in high school. When I got to Berkeley, I was sure of it. Was I born this way? I honestly don't know. I just never felt right about myself until I changed how I thought about my "orientation."

But I have a major problem: How does a gay boy tell his straight, conservative father that he's gay—especially when that straight, conservative father is busy running for king of a straight, conservative state? Major, major problem: After the election, the new king intends to put gay boys like me in their place: out. Talk about a hindrance to open, honest, father-son communication!

So how does a scared gay boy win the love and understanding and (dare I say it?) blessing of his father? It can't happen, especially if the father becomes king. But if the father is somehow convinced by a mad, illiterate political terrorist not to become king—Well, I think you get the idea.

My dad is a remarkable man, Stephanie, and I love him like any adoring son would. Unfortunately for me, I came along when his career and political ambition were a bit higher up the priority list than a little snot-nosed heir. (In case you didn't know it, Dad was forty-one when I was born.) You probably thought we were the perfect family, but Dad and I never "bonded" (if that term is still in vogue). Is that why I'm gay? Who knows? Who really cares?

The rest, as they say, can be seen on the eleven o'clock news. I tried to change Dad's mind about being king. (I thought the Anti-

365

Crist plot turned out to be some of my best fiction. I had no idea it would work so well. You can use the idea for a novel if you like.) But, as always, the kingdom is more important than one little intro-verted kid. So I'll just step out of the way and let the king be king. Who knows? Maybe when I'm gone he'll realize how much he loved me. Or maybe not.

Well, I'm nearly out of vodka, and the bewitching hour approaches. So I'd better quit rambling and get on with the dra-matic climax of my story—even though I had really hoped for a dif-ferent ending. You're a nice lady. I hope you find many young writers to mentor. Sorry it didn't work for me.

Your friend, Wes

Stevie could withstand the surging emotional tide no longer. She set the computer aside and let the tears flow.

42

Monday
November 1

JON DROVE into St. Vincent's parking lot at two-thirty in the morning, barely fifteen minutes after Stevie woke him at the Quiet-Nite Motel with her phone call. While she waited for him to arrive, a large gray sedan delivered Senator and Mrs. Bellardi to the hospital entrance. Stevie remained in her car and watched the bodyguards burrow into the crush of media to escort the couple inside.

Jon pulled his Ranger up to the driver's side of the Grand Cherokee. The rain had nearly stopped. He transferred from his car to Stevie's and closed the door.

Stevie had composed herself, and her eyes were dry. She handed the computer to Jon, feeling only a little embarrassed about getting him out of bed in the middle of the night. But after reading Wes's letter, she knew she needed to talk with Jon before going any further. Because Jon had expected her home that night, he had gone back to the motel after getting the kids to bed. Stevie was relieved that she had not had to call the house to speak with him and risk waking the kids. On the telephone, she had explained the tragedy, related her conversation with Ernie Cruz, and summarized Wes's message. Jon insisted on coming over, something she had hoped he would do.

Jon read the letter without a word, then set the computer on the console between them. "Tell me what you're thinking about all this," he said, gesturing to the text still on the monitor.

Stevie gazed through the rain-beaded windshield. When she finally answered, she spoke softly. "I'm devastated about Wes. I had no idea he was so messed up inside. It's like losing Dougie all over again."

"We haven't lost him yet, Steve," Jon said. "He's still alive."

"But from the sounds of this letter he doesn't want to be. Wes gave up, Jon. How can he survive without a will to live? What does he have to look forward to?"

Jon did not respond.

"I'm really disappointed in Senator Bellardi," Stevie continued. "I thought he and Wes had a good relationship. Here's the champion of family values in America, and he's too busy for his own son. He sounds like any deadbeat dad who puts a career ahead of his kids. What kind of message does that send to the people of North California: 'Do as I say, not as I do'?"

"Maybe it's not as bad as Wes makes it out to be," Jon offered. "Like we tell the kids, you have to hear both sides of the story."

"Well, I've seen a little of the senator's side these last three weeks," Stevie countered. "It bothers me greatly that he seemed so unaffected by Wes's disappearance. I understand the importance of the campaign, but there are more important things in life than elections."

Jon's voice was soft when he responded. "It's interesting you would say that, Steve, because I heard almost the same words just a couple of hours ago—from our daughter."

Stevie turned to him with a questioning look. "Shawna? What do you mean?"

"I don't want to add to your burden," Jon began, "but you need to hear this before you see Shawna again." Jon described his late-night conversation with a very soaked, very distraught fourteen-year-old cuddling a wide-eyed black kitten. Stevie bit her lip as Jon related Shawna's feelings of abandonment in the midst of her mother's busyness with the campaign. She covered her face as he told about their daughter's search for acceptance among members of the "Young Women's Leadership Club." She cringed at the description of the Halloween party. Though Jon related the words without condemnation or blame, the harsh reality of Shawna's pain cut into Stevie deeply. Waves of conviction and remorse prompted another outflow of tears.

"Shawna said she tried to talk to you, but you were always too busy," Jon concluded. "But, as I said earlier, there are two sides to every story. Is she blowing things out of proportion?"

Stevie dabbed at her eyes and nose with a tissue. She was tempted to respond to Jon just as she had repeatedly rationalized to herself when putting the campaign ahead of the kids: *I'm doing it for them. I'm committed to making North California a haven against the world's version of tolerance. As soon as Senator Bellardi wins the election, everything will get back to normal for the kids and me.* Instead she said, "No, she's not exaggerating. I have a lot of making up to do."

Jon glanced toward the hospital. "Maybe Senator Bellardi feels the same way right now. Maybe this tragedy will serve as a wake-up call for him."

"I truly hope so," Stevie said.

After another space of silence, Jon gestured toward Wes's letter on the computer and asked, "So what are you going to do about this?"

Stevie sighed resignedly. "I have to talk to Senator Bellardi."

"What will you tell him?"

"Everything. Wes needs him now more than ever. The senator has an opportunity to make things right. That's more than we had with Dougie. And he has a responsibility to tell the people of North California what happened. After all, they've stood behind him with their prayers over the last three weeks. Senator Bellardi must know the truth, Jon, and he must share it with his constituents." She took a deep breath. "I'll . . . tell him right now."

"Do you want me to go in with you?"

Stevie pondered the offer for a moment. "I appreciate that, but I'll be all right. I'm more concerned that someone is at the apartment when the kids wake up, just in case I don't get home—although I'm hoping to sometime before the night's over."

"No problem. I'll go over there now and sack out on the Hide-A-Bed."

"Thank you, Jon, very much. I'm so glad you're here."

Jon smiled, then stepped out of the Cherokee and drove off into the light drizzle.

Stevie activated the print command on the computer, sending the text of Wes's letter to the fax/printer mounted in the dash of the Jeep. She made two copies: one for Senator and Mrs. Bellardi and one for Ernie Cruz.

After sneaking past the media to the surgery floor, Stevie set out to find the Bellardis and wait for an opportunity to speak to them. A hospital security guard stopped her at the doors to the surgery ward, where a small knot of concerned staffers were huddled. Seeing her through the window, Robert Johnstone signaled to the guard to let her enter.

"He's still in surgery," Robert said. "He's in severe shock due to extensive burns. Usually they try to stabilize the patient with IV fluids and electrolytes before surgery. But the stomach cavity was filled with blood, so they had to go in right away. So far they've found a ruptured spleen and lacerated liver. They almost lost him."

"What about—head injuries?" This concern had been primary when Stevie thought about Wes's physical condition. She wanted to talk to him again, assure him that she was still his friend.

"There seems to be some damage, but it's too early to tell if he'll be permanently affected. They're more concerned about his vital organs at the moment."

"Where's the senator?"

"They have a small room down the hall. The medical staff is updating them every ten to fifteen minutes."

Stevie had planned to inform Robert about the letter as

soon as she talked to the Bellardis. It occurred to her now
that he might know best how to break the news to them.
"Robert, I have something very important to show you,
something Senator and Mrs. Bellardi must know about Wes's
. . . accident. I think the hospital medical staff should be
informed too. May we speak privately?"

Robert ushered Stevie into a vacant room. "I found this in
my E-mail box less than an hour ago," Stevie said, handing
him the letter. Robert took it and read it through without speaking. Stevie stood by quietly, appreciating that the campaign
director, still wearing his suit coat and tie, looked as professional and competent—and handsome—as always.

Robert's eyes were moist when he looked up. "I'm so glad
you brought this to my attention, Stephanie. It seems almost
too bizarre to be true. This must have been quite a shock to
you."

Stevie nodded, then opened her mouth to say she intended
to show the letter to the senator and his wife and to notify the
medical staff of the possibility that Wes might have AIDS, but
Robert spoke first.

"Here's what I'd like you to do, Stephanie," he said, guiding
her toward the door with a gentle hand on her elbow. "Go
home and get some sleep; you must be exhausted. I'll keep the
letter and discuss it with the senator when it seems appropriate."

"I don't mind staying, Robert," Stevie said, suddenly feeling
left out of the loop. "I'd like to be here when you talk to him,
especially since Wes sent the letter to me."

Robert continued moving her slowly toward the exit. "I understand. But it could be several hours, after Wes is safely out of surgery, before I have the opportunity to discuss it with him. Price
and I need you back here in the morning to help us handle the
media."

"Sure, I can be back here at six if you like."

"Seven is soon enough. Try to get a little sleep." He smiled
down at her. "Please, Stephanie."

Stevie summoned a return smile. "I suppose you're right.
And I'll try, but I do want to be here when the senator makes
his statement."

"We won't do anything without you," Robert said. "The senator's main concern is getting Wes through surgery. Then we can talk about what else must be said and done."

Stevie paused. "But what about the possibility of Wes having AIDS? Shouldn't the doctors be informed that he might be HIV-positive?"

"Of course," Robert agreed. "I'll take care of it. Now you just go on home and get some rest."

Stevie resisted the thought of leaving the hospital, but she knew Robert was right. She would be of little help to him or the senator if she did not get at least a couple hours of sleep.

Robert stopped her well short of the security guard, gently taking her arms and turning her toward him. "Stephanie," he said, his voice soft but adamant, "it's imperative that we keep this information confidential for now. Not a word to the media, nor to the rest of the staff, not even to our families. Are we in agreement on this?"

The order was too late to include Jon, of course, but Stevie could guarantee his discretion—without telling Robert about it. This also meant she could not show the letter to Ernie Cruz as she had planned. As it was, the security chief knew more than most people already, and he would know everything soon enough. "Yes, I agree," she said.

Robert nodded, gazed into her eyes a moment longer, then leaned down and kissed her gently on the forehead. The next thing she knew he had turned and was retreating down the hall. The letter was still clutched in his hand, while her forehead burned with the memory of his lips.

Stevie was home by three-thirty. She tiptoed past Jon, who was already sleeping soundly on the Hide-A-Bed. Once in her room with the door closed, she set her alarm for six, relieved that Jon was there to get the kids up for school when she left for the hospital. Later that day, she had decided, she would sit down with Shawna after school and have the first of many long-overdue, heart-to-heart, mother-and-daughter talks. By then Wes's story would be public knowledge, as would Senator Bellardi's renewed commitment to his son. What a positive beginning for election eve in North California.

Stevie dropped off before she could remind herself that she had too much on her mind to sleep.

43

Monday
November 1

STEVIE WAS BACK at St. Vincent's a few minutes before seven, feeling less than put together after only a couple hours of rest. Even her most flattering suit did not fully compensate for the hasty hair treatment her early schedule allowed. But she had decided to live with it.

The first person she found on the surgery floor was Price Whitten. "Wes came out of surgery about twenty minutes ago," he informed her. "He'll be in recovery for at least an hour. The next crisis is to keep the burns from getting infected. He's still a long way from being out of the woods."

The fact that Wes was out of surgery boosted Stevie's spirits a notch. "How are the Bellardis doing?" she said.

"As well as can be expected. They left for the ranch while the surgeons were closing. The senator is holding together well, but Patricia seems pretty shaky. She's losing a little more ground to Alzheimer's every day."

"Sad," Stevie said. Then, "So what's the game plan, Price?" It was the question Senator Bellardi's staff had discussed every morning of the campaign. It meant, "Where is the senator going today, what is he planning to say, and how can we help make it happen?" Stevie had a keen interest in Price's reply; his answer would reveal if Robert had divulged to him the contents of Wes's letter.

"The senator will rest until eleven and be back here for a press conference at noon, down in the main lobby. Then we'll proceed with the original afternoon schedule—the in-studio TV interviews."

Sounds like you're in the dark like everyone else, Stevie thought, watching his eyes. She tested him with another question: "What's the bottom line of the senator's statement?"

"I don't know," Price said, shrugging. "Robert and the senator hammered it out while I caught a few winks."

You are *in the dark. Robert meant what he said about telling no one.* "Where is Robert? I need to get my marching orders for the day." *More correctly, I need to know how Senator Bellardi and his campaign manager are planning to present the truth to the people of North California.*

"Ten minutes ago he was heading down to the cafeteria for something to eat."

"Basement?"

"Right."

Stevie found Robert at a table drinking coffee with two physicians. When he saw her, the campaign manger quickly excused himself and found an empty table for them. He appeared to have been waiting for her. "Would you like something to eat? Bagel? Coffee?" he asked, seating her.

"Just a cup of tea, thanks."

Robert returned in two minutes with a mug, a small pot of hot water, and a selection of tea bags. Stevie was impressed with the service. "Have you been upstairs already?" Robert inquired.

"Yes. Price told me that Wes is in recovery. That's encouraging." She dropped a tea bag in the mug and added hot water, leaving the tea to steep.

"I got a glimpse of him through the window," Robert said. "His face, torso, and arms are completely covered with that white antiseptic salve."

"They have to stop the infection."

Robert nodded. "They were able to patch up his vital organs, but infection can be just as lethal. He's not out of danger yet."

Stevie nodded, anxious to get to the point of her visit. "So how did the senator take the news in the letter?"

Robert focused on the steaming, dark brown solution in Stevie's mug for several seconds. "He was . . . concerned."

Stevie was stunned. "Concerned? That's all? He finds out that Wes is gay, that there's a possibility that he could have or develop AIDS, that he plotted the whole AntiCrist thing, that the explosion was an attempted suicide, and he's no more than 'concerned'?"

Robert's eyes never left the mug of tea. "I'm sure it affected him deeply. He just didn't say much."

Stevie pondered the response. "No wonder Wes had trouble getting through to his father," she said. When Robert said nothing further, Stevie went on. "Price told me about the game plan for today, but he didn't know anything about Senator Bellardi's statement. You apparently haven't told him anything about the letter."

"We agreed to keep this confidential," Robert said, lifting his eyes but lowering his voice. "You haven't talked to anyone, have you?"

Stevie saw a spark of humor in the question. "Robert, since I left you three hours ago, I haven't even *seen* anyone—outside of my family, and they were asleep." Then she was quickly back to the point. "What is the senator going to say about the letter today?"

Robert locked onto her eyes without blinking. "Nothing."

Stevie gripped his eyes with equal strength. "What do you mean, 'nothing'?"

"The senator will explain that Wes was critically injured in the blast, and that he is on the road to recovery from his many injuries. He will thank the people of North California for their prayers and thank those responsible for Wes's rescue.

But he will say nothing about the contents of Wes's letter to you."

Stevie held the answer in front of her, turning it one way and then the other, looking for a meaning other than that which was starkly apparent to her. "Are you saying that Senator Bellardi won't even mention the fact that Wes was behind the AntiCrist plot?"

Robert still had not blinked. "Not at this time."

"'Not at this time,' meaning . . . ?"

His voice was a little softer now, but just as firm. "Meaning just what I said. Not at this time."

The picture was painfully clear, and Stevie felt her face flush warm with indignation. "Not at this time, meaning not until after the election. Is that what you're saying?"

Robert nodded, his lips pressed tightly together.

"In other words, the senator is purposely withholding the full story until after the polls are closed. To reveal Wes's involvement in his own disappearance would also be to risk having people find out that he's gay, and all of that might negatively affect the election. Bellardi won't admit his failure as a loving father because he knows some people might pull their votes."

Robert studied her face before answering in a gentle voice. "Let me say it a different way, Stephanie. Today the senator will tell the people of North California all they need to know at this time, namely, that Wes is alive and safe. In the days ahead they will be further informed on a need-to-know basis."

Stevie could not let it go at that. "What about AntiCrist? What will the senator say when the media ask him about the search for AntiCrist?"

"He will say the search is continuing, which it is."

"But the authorities will eventually discover that Wes is the culprit."

"We'll cross that bridge when we come to it."

"After the election, you mean."

"Most likely after the election, yes."

Stevie glared at him. "Robert, that's not right. It's against everything we stand for. The senator must tell the whole story. The people need to know the truth."

"And they will," he said. "We'll tell the whole story—eventually, as it becomes . . . necessary."

"Who is 'we'? Was this the senator's decision or yours?"

Robert hesitated, then took a deep breath. "The senator and I decided jointly."

"On your recommendation?"

"Yes," he answered, his voice barely above a whisper. "It was my recommendation, but the senator concurred fully." His gaze softened, his eyes pleading with her for understanding. "Stephanie, we're not even sure that Wes wrote that letter. It could have been AntiCrist trying to throw us off the trail."

"Of course it was Wes's letter," Stevie insisted. "After all, he had my E-mail address. And he talked about our friendship. I know it was him."

"But we're not absolutely sure," Robert repeated. "We can't rush in and implicate Wes until we know all the facts; it wouldn't be fair to him, and it might hamper the investigation. It could take several days to piece all the evidence together. And besides, anyone who really wanted to could get your E-mail address."

She knew he was right about the address, but that did not change what she already believed to be the truth. "Don't you think I wanted to believe all this was part of AntiCrist's scheme, that Wes had nothing to do with it? But, Robert, we have to face the truth. We have to deal with the truth, and the sooner the better. To withhold the truth—all of it—is the same as perpetrating a lie. When the people of North California finally find out about Wes—and they will—they're going to ask, 'When did you know he was gay? When did you know he was the terrorist? When did you know he was starving for his father's love?' What will you tell them then, Robert? What will Daniel Bellardi say to his faithful constituents then?"

"He will tell them that he didn't want to act irresponsibly by running ahead of the police investigation, stating things as facts when they were still suppositions," Robert explained. "The people will understand that."

"I don't think so," Stevie argued. "I'll tell you what I think they'll say. They'll say, 'You lied to us, Governor Bellardi. You promised to do what's right for North California, and you lied to us.' And they'll be right. If the senator doesn't tell the whole truth and publicly own up to his failures with Wes, they'll have every right to disbelieve everything else he says. And they'll have every right to impeach him for his lack of integrity."

"If they find out," Robert said softly.

Stevie weighed the words. "You're talking cover-up."

"No, I'm saying that we must be certain of the complete truth before we say anything."

Stevie ran her fingers through her hair, considering his words, then shook her head. "Call it what you want, Robert. It's still a bald-faced cover-up and you know it. It's not right. The senator must be completely transparent about this entire fiasco."

"I agree," Robert said. "But not prematurely. If he makes announcements before we know them to be factual, then our vision for North California could be lost forever." He reached over and covered her hand with his. His eyes bore into hers, pleading with her to understand. "Is that what you want, Stephanie? You came to North California six months ago because you wanted your children to grow up in a safe, loving, Christian environment. No drug pushers harassing them outside the school yard, no homosexuals recruiting them in the classroom, no pedophiles luring them into their cars, no thugs driving by your house blazing away with automatic weapons. You wanted to put a stop to this new brand of tolerance, the insidious idea that right and wrong are a matter of personal opinion. You wanted to help establish the first state in the union since the eighteenth century to be governed by Christian principles. This is your dream, remember?"

For a moment, as she gazed into his eyes and felt the warmth of his hand on hers, she struggled to remember something . . . anything. Had she really believed that moving five hundred miles north to a new and different location could protect her children? Had she believed the move, coupled with her sacrificial involvement with Bellardi's campaign and the mentoring of his only child, could somehow absolve her of her guilt over Dougie's death? Could she truly have believed, even for a moment, that the determined, dedicated man sitting in front of her could ever be a permanent part of her life?

"For I know the plans I have for you," says the Lord. *"They are plans for good and not for disaster, to give you a future and a hope."* The words from Jeremiah 29:11 suddenly returned to her with

a clarity she had never seen before. Of course God's plans for her were good. Of course he wanted to give her a future and a hope. But she would never realize those plans by running away. The only way those plans would be fulfilled was by running *to* God, finding safety in his love.

Robert was speaking again. Stevie shook her head to clear her thoughts. "We're only one day away from fulfilling your dream, Stephanie. *Only one day.* Are you ready to forfeit that dream by disclosing an unconfirmed fact that will not only hurt the senator and his family, but disillusion those who have supported him so faithfully?"

His eyes were as concerned and sincere as Stevie had ever seen them, but they had somehow lost their charm. Even the touch of his hand had turned cold. It was suddenly much easier to speak objectively to Robert. "This 'unconfirmed fact' happens to be someone I care about very much," she said, her voice calm but confident. "You're not sweeping a detail under the rug, you're sweeping a person under the rug. What happens to Wes in all this? Will the senator buy his silence too? Will he force his gay son back into the closet and hide him there indefinitely? And if Wes should develop AIDS, what then? When death comes, will the senator cover up the truth again, saying he died of pneumonia or some rare jungle disease?

"And in the meantime, Robert, what kind of life does Wes have? Does the senator forbid him to go back to college, to pursue his education and his literary interests for fear of his son's lifestyle being exposed? If he contracts or develops AIDS, does he isolate him like a leper? Keep him locked up at the ranch? Force him to live a lie for the rest of his life? And will the senator make amends for ignoring his son when he needed a father so desperately? Will he finally try to make up for his insensitivity to Wes all these years? Or will he still be too busy?"

"You're talking as if the police have already confirmed Wes to be AntiCrist. They haven't, Stephanie," Robert countered. "And besides, we have to think of the children of North California. Think how many of them—including your own—will be saved from drugs, from homosexuality, from child pornography, from assault—"

"The sacrifice of the one for the many," Stevie cut in, reminding Robert of his own words.

Robert pressed his lips together again. "Maybe so," he said. "The sacrifice of the one for the many. After all, Jesus said, 'Greater love hath no man than this, that a man lay down his life for his friends.'"

Stevie closed her eyes. "Don't," she whispered, pulling her hand away. "Don't quote Scripture to justify this. Wes Bellardi is *not* laying down his life; Senator Bellardi is *taking* it." She opened her eyes and looked at him, willing him to understand. "It's an abortion, Robert, don't you see? Senator Bellardi is aborting his twenty-year-old son. And I will not be a part of it."

44

Monday
November 1

DRIVING STRAIGHT HOME, Stevie awakened Jon for the second time in the last six hours. He had obviously crashed on the sofa again after taking Shawna and Collin to school, but he seemed eager, once awake, to hear what Stevie had to say. Pacing the living room floor, she recounted the details of her conversation with Robert Johnstone, practically reciting the exchange verbatim. Then she threw herself into the chair opposite the sofa, drained by the emotional diatribe and discouraged by the shattering of her dreams.

Jon listened and maintained eye contact but said nothing. When she finished, he went to the kitchen. Stevie could hear him puttering around, putting something in the microwave and then loading the dishwasher while the microwave hummed. Soon he returned to the living room with two cups of tea, placing one on the small table next to Stevie's chair. Then he was back to the sofa, seemingly ready to hear more.

Stevie, however, had nothing more to say. Up until recently, she had regarded her time in North California as the most significant period of her life, despite the pressures on family and career. Yet in the last few hours, those six months were devalued to dirt in her estimation, a half year wasted. Jon had cautioned her about what she was getting into. He had every right to bring those comments to her remembrance now. She probably deserved it. But she hoped he had something more comforting to say.

After several moments of silence, Jon spoke. "A few months ago, sitting right here, I made a statement I've regretted ever since. We were talking—actually, I guess we were arguing— about Daniel Bellardi's beliefs. I said something like, 'If I lived in North California, I would probably vote for Juanita Dunsmuir.' It was a thoughtless way to make my point. Remember?"

Stevie nodded. She remembered all right. The searing words had smoldered in her consciousness for weeks.

"I was being sarcastic, of course," Jon continued. "I really couldn't vote for Juanita Dunsmuir and her brand of tolerance with a clear conscience. I admire Bellardi's dogged commitment to Judeo-Christian values and his vision for North California. But there's something missing in his approach to righting the wrongs of society. It bothered me then, and it bothers me now. I think it ran across your grain, too."

The aroma of the lemon tea reached Stevie, comforting her. She lifted her cup and sipped. She also sensed needed strength coming through Jon's words.

He continued. "When I think of someone acting justly, like the Bible talks about, I think of Senator Bellardi. I believe he sincerely wants to do what's right under God for North California. But that verse about doing justly in the sixth chapter of Micah has two other requirements: to love mercy and to walk humbly with God. The senator has a plan for bringing the hammer down on abortion, drugs, homosexuality, and the tolerance movement. But does he have any mercy for the women who have had abortions or for drug addicts or homosexuals or any of the other people caught up in the tolerance lie? Does he care about helping these people do right, or does he just want to punish them or kick them out of his state for doing wrong?"

The two questions rumbled through Stevie like an earthquake, rattling some of her own views about lawbreakers. "Mercy," she said softly. "Like you've shown to your young charge, Ben Hernandez." The mental image of her ex-husband taking in the ex-con had remained vivid.

"I'm not trying to put the spotlight on me," Jon responded. "But Ben has been God's instrument to teach me something about mercy, real love, and humility. And it started with Eugene Hackett. I definitely wanted justice for the pain and fear Eugene caused you and for the damage he did to the house. But I had no compassion for him as a person until God prompted me first to forgive him. It was as a result of that visit to Eugene that I found myself volunteering as a citizen sponsor."

"I really admire you for that, Jon," Stevie said.

"You've done the same with Wes Bellardi," Jon countered.

"Except Wes is not an ex-con with a rap sheet. Wes was easy to love. Ben would be a challenge for anyone."

"But if what you tell me is true, Wes is also a criminal. He could be arrested for destruction of private property. People could have been hurt in the firebombing and the rifle assault on Bellardi's building. What's more, he's a homosexual. So what's the difference between him and Ben?"

"The difference," Stevie asserted, "is that I didn't know these things about Wes when I took him on as a project."

"But you still care about him now; you still want to help him, don't you, even though you know the truth about him?"

"Yes, I care about him very much."

Jon leaned forward in the sofa. "That's mercy, Steve," he said with emphasis. "That's genuine love. You love him despite his faults. You know he'll have to atone for anything wrong he's done, but you want to help him get through it. He's blessed to have a friend like you."

383

"And Ben is blessed to have a friend like you," Stevie said.

Jon did not respond to the compliment. "This vital quality is missing when I look at Dan Bellardi," he said. "He knows how to act justly, but he has a lot to learn about expressing mercy and compassion, beginning in his own home. He may be a champion for what's right, but he seems incapable of humbling himself when he's wrong. He knows how to deal with crime, but he doesn't know how to deal with the criminal.

"Juanita Dunsmuir and her kind are just the opposite: high scores in their view of mercy, low scores in justice. The new tolerance says, 'Everybody is OK, everybody has a right to their beliefs—gays, abortionists, suicide doctors, even sex offenders.' But by making all values and lifestyles equal, they don't know when to say, 'No, that's wrong.' That's not love as God defines it.

"I don't believe someone from either extreme will make a good governor. North California needs a leader who will do the right thing *and* do the loving, merciful thing, and do them both in humility toward God."

Stevie sighed. "I really thought Senator Bellardi was the one."

Jon paused, then said, "Maybe he is."

Stevie flashed him a puzzled look. "What do you mean?"

"He hasn't made the statement yet."

"What statement?"

"The statement he's scheduled to make at noon. You know, the cover-up statement Johnstone told you about."

It took a few seconds for Stevie's sleep-deprived brain to catch up with his logic. "You mean, there's still time for someone to convince him—or at least try to convince him—to come clean."

"Exactly."

In a few seconds more, she had caught up to him fully. "And you think I'm the one to do the convincing."

Jon nodded. "The senator knows you and trusts you. You're in the inner circle of his campaign."

"He doesn't really know me, Jon. I'm just another gear in the machine."

"But he must realize by now that you're an important part of his son's life. I think he'll listen to you."

"Maybe," she said. "But what am I supposed to say to make sure he follows through? 'Tell the world about Wes or I'll spill the whole story'—would that work?"

Jon verbalized what they both knew. "You can't make him do anything, Steve. And blackmailing him won't change his heart. But the truth spoken respectfully, lovingly, and humbly just might."

Stevie stood and began to pace again, instantly anxious at the prospect of confronting the senator. "I already said my piece to Robert. I thought I was done."

"I'm not saying you have to do this. It's up to you."

"That's just the point. I know you're right. I'm the one who received Wes's E-mail. I'm the one who should talk to his father." After a few more strides, she turned to face him. "Will you go with me?"

Jon stood. "No, I think I would be a distraction. It's better if you go by yourself."

Stevie grimaced at the thought, but she knew he was right.

"One more thing," Jon continued. "If it's all right with you, I'd like to pray for you right now. And I'll keep praying until you call me at the motel and tell me how it went."

Stevie smiled and nodded, then reached out to join her hands with his. As they stood together in the middle of the living room, Jon prayed the most beautiful, courage-building prayer Stevie had ever heard. Even after he had finished praying and gone back to the motel to gather his things, the warmth of his hands and his words still lingered.

Stevie arrived at the ranch just before eleven. She was surprised to find Ernie Cruz in uniform at the security gate. "The senator has asked not to be disturbed," he explained. "I hope you understand."

"What I have to say to him relates to what you brought up last night. It has nothing to do with you, and I won't bring you into the discussion at all. But I'm sure he'll see me if you let him know I'm here." Stevie felt almost dishonest not telling Ernie about the letter, but she had given Robert her word, and she intended to keep it.

Ernie stepped to his truck and called the house on the radio. A minute later he returned and waved her through, wishing her good luck.

Stevie was not exactly sure what she would say to the senator. She had been alone for two hours after Jon left, but she had not used that time to frame a speech. Instead, she puttered around the apartment asking God to give her the right attitude. She felt very confident, as if Jon's prayers had enveloped her with peace.

She harbored no anger toward the man she was about to confront, nor did she fear his response. Instead, Stevie saw herself as the bearer of great good. Daniel Bellardi was not a villain; he was a good man who would hear her out. What he did with the gift she presented to him was his business. She was doing the right thing, and she would do so with all the love and humility God would provide.

Stevie was ushered immediately into the senator's study by a bodyguard who regarded her suspiciously. It occurred to her that the visit had been given last-minute, top-priority clearance. She was tempted to revel in a sudden, heady sense of importance. Senator Bellardi had no choice but to see her. What she knew—better yet, what she could tell—could possibly spell the difference between victory and defeat the next day. But she dismissed the temptation and consciously focused on a higher purpose for her visit.

Bellardi sat at his large walnut desk as Stevie entered the room. The bodyguard closed the door, leaving the two of them alone. The senator stood. "Good morning, Stephanie," he said coolly, motioning toward a leather chair facing his desk. The long hours and many miles of the campaign had stooped his posture, but he was still an imposing figure.

A sudden wave of anxiety challenged her confidence as she approached the desk. "Thank you, sir, but I prefer to stand," she said, hoping her legs would hold her up. "I'll only take a moment of your time." The senator nodded, then sat down.

Stevie breathed a prayer and began. "Senator Bellardi, I moved my children from Los Angeles to Redding six months ago because I believed in your vision for North California. I volunteered to assist in your campaign and accepted every opportunity to serve for the same reason. It has been an honor and a privilege for me to play a small role in the propagation of your dreams and goals for my family and the people of this state. Your vision has become my vision."

Bellardi shifted in his high-backed leather chair. Stevie thought she detected a glimmer of surprise on his face, as if a compliment was the last thing he expected from her today.

"As I stand here today, sir, I still believe in that vision. I believe in everything we've done to make North California a safe, decent, moral place in which to raise a family. But I've come to realize that we've left something very important undone. And I greatly fear that all the good we've done is about to be nullified by the vital good we haven't done. Our dream for North California is on the precipice of becoming a nightmare. If you allow the dream to die, my dream and the dreams of hundreds of thousands of North Californians also die."

Stevie talked about her admiration for Wes and his writing talent and related her shock at the contents of his letter. She expressed her disbelief upon hearing the senator's decision to sweep the affair under the rug. She shared fresh insights about justice, mercy, and humility, confessing her own shortsightedness to fight for the right thing while overlooking the importance of love and mercy for people in the wrong. Bellardi listened impassively, occasionally glancing at his watch.

"Senator, about two and a half years ago I lost a son. He would be about Wes's age now if he had survived. Your son reminds me of Dougie in so many ways. I'm sure that's why I enjoyed being involved with him. But Dougie had a dark side too. He got in with the wrong crowd at school. He started experimenting with drugs and, unfortunately, my husband and I didn't see the warning signs. By the time we found out, it was too late. He died of a drug overdose. Not a day goes by that I don't wish I could turn back the clock to help him and love him through those dark days."

Stevie bit her lip, wishing she did not have to say the next words. But it was right to say them, so she pressed on. "I also discovered only hours ago that I almost did the same thing to my fourteen-year-old daughter, Shawna. Right here in North California, in the name of the dream you and I share for this state, I've been neglecting her. I've been so busy trying to do what's right that I forgot to spend time showing her that I love her." Stevie held her breath to control a swell of emotion.

"Dougie's gone, but thank God I have a second chance with Shawna. You have a second chance too, sir. Wes has his own set of problems, but at least he's alive. He needs a father who will love him, forgive him, and encourage him to do what's right with the rest of his life. And I think North California needs that kind of governor."

Bellardi rose from his chair, signaling the end of the meeting. "Thank you for your concern," he said, backing her toward the door. Stevie had heard him say those words dozens of times to pushy supporters telling him how to run his campaign. He sounded no more sincere now than he had then. She knew she was getting the standard brush-off. She was barely out the door before it closed firmly in her face. The bodyguard instantly appeared to whisk her out to the car.

Sitting behind the wheel, Stevie sensed clouds of discouragement rolling over her. *Did he hear anything I said? Did he care at all, or is he hopelessly blind and calloused to mercy and compassion? Did I just waste another fifteen minutes of my life after having thrown six months into the garbage?*

Driving out to the road, she criticized herself for being too direct in her approach, calcifying the senator's resolve to ignore his son. Then she criticized herself for not being direct enough. By the time she reached the end of the driveway, Stevie had pulled herself back to center. *I went to the man, and I said what I should have said,* she assured herself. *I'm not responsible for how he responds.* Having dealt with the discouragement, she was now filled with a profound sadness for Senator Bellardi. She drove past Ernie Cruz with a benign wave and turned the Cherokee toward St. Vincent's Hospital.

45

Monday
November 1

JON PACED the small motel room, waiting for the call. His mind
swirled with thoughts and emotions. He felt caught between
two worlds. He had promised to stay in Redding until after the
election to take care of the kids, and he certainly could not
back down on that promise now. Besides, he enjoyed being
with Shawna and Collin and did not really want to leave them
at all. At the same time, he was truly looking forward to getting back home. He was anxious to see Ben again and get their
relationship back on track, as well as wanting to return to
work. But he could not even focus on going back to L.A. until
things were at least somewhat settled here. As it was, he could
not concentrate on anything except waiting to hear from

Stevie that Wes was finally out of the woods and that her conversation with Senator Bellardi had gone well.

Of course, in between pacing and staring at the phone, willing it to ring, he continued to pray for Stevie, as he had promised he would do. He had not said anything to her, but he was
also praying that, if there ever had been—or still was—anything
romantic between Stevie and Robert Johnstone, that too would
be resolved. As many times as he had tried to convince himself
that, as Stevie's ex-husband, he had no business being jealous of
her interest in another man, it simply had not worked. He *was*
jealous. And he could no longer deny the reason.

Jon was still in love with Stevie—maybe more now than he
had ever been. Because now he saw things so much more
clearly. It was not Dougie's death that had driven them apart; it
was their lack of understanding of their differences. God had
meant those differences to complement each other, but they
had allowed them to divide and destroy. Their discussion earlier
that morning about justice and mercy and love had solidified
that understanding in Jon's mind.

Steve, he thought silently, *I understand now. I really do. You
only wanted to do what was right for our children. You wanted to
protect them by teaching them about justice. And you wanted me to
help you. Together we could have done that. But I let you down. You
wanted me to take a firmer stand, especially with Dougie, but I was
so caught up in being his "buddy" that I failed him as a father.
That's what made you so vulnerable to getting involved in Senator
Bellardi's campaign. I know I've asked for your forgiveness and
you've given it, but . . . can we ever find our way back together? Is
it too late for us to be a family again?*

He switched gears then, turning his words back to prayers
for Stevie, rather than thoughts *toward* her. But even as he
prayed, he anxiously kept his ears tuned for the ring that
would signal her call.

390

Members of the media choked the hospital's main entrance
preparing for the senator's press conference, so Stevie slipped
in through the emergency entrance. Reaching the critical care
unit, she discovered that everyone from the senator's staff had
left for the lobby, with the conference scheduled to begin in fif-

teen minutes. On her way into town, Stevie had decided not to attend the conference or even watch it on TV. She could not bear to see the senator make his final appeal to the voters of North California while tacitly denying the truth and rejecting his son. She would spend the next little while with her friend, Wes Bellardi. Then she would go home to her children.

Moving purposefully, Stevie found Wes's room and entered. Thankfully, no one tried to stop her. The sight nearly caused her to turn around and run. The bed was shrouded in a clear plastic tent intended to shield the patient's exposed wounds from germs. Half a dozen tubes and wires ran from a collection of monitors and receptacles to the still form lying on the bed. From what Stevie could see of him, most of Wes's hair was gone. Much of his head, torso, and limbs were slathered in antiseptic cream, just as Robert had described earlier. Only his midsection was draped with a sheet. Signs of a fresh abdominal incision and sutures were visible where a corner of the sheet was turned back.

Stevie forced herself to look at the sedated patient long enough to confirm that it was Wes. Then she drew a chair close to the bed, sat down, and lowered her gaze. For several moments she listened to the soft music of the electronic signals around her and the *whish* of life-giving oxygen inside the tent. Despite Wes's grave condition and the dismal prospects for his future, Stevie was filled with awe at the sanctity and significance of this one human life.

In a soft whisper, she told Wes everything that had happened to him in the last twelve frantic hours, events he would not remember. She would tell about something, then wait, as if giving Wes time to process the words and to respond. She knew he could not hear her, but the approach seemed more like a conversation to Stevie.

The wall clock swept slowly past noon. Stevie tried not to think about what was happening in the lobby. She talked to Wes about Ernie Cruz, the angel God sent to Shasta Lake just at the right moment. She told him about the journey his E-mail letter had taken, from her computer to Robert Johnstone to the senator. She warned him that life with his father might not be any easier than before. Then she assured him that God loved him and that his life, as long as it lasted and as difficult as it might be, was a treasure to be guarded.

Stevie had just begun to talk to Wes about Shawna when someone stepped softly into the room. Stevie turned, expecting to find a nurse or doctor entering to check on the patient. Instead she looked up into the face of Daniel Bellardi. As usual, he was smartly dressed in suit and tie.

She stood quickly. "Senator?"

The expression on his face was one Stevie had never seen before. While trying to maintain his customary aplomb, he appeared bewildered and unsure of himself.

Stevie checked the clock. It was exactly 12:15 P.M. "Senator, the press conference," she said, puzzled.

"I . . . postponed it," he said, looking past her to the bed, "until four o'clock."

Stevie did not know what to say. She suddenly felt like an intruder. She moved to step past the senator and leave the room.

"Wait, Stephanie," Bellardi said, grasping her arm gently. "Please stay."

Stevie stopped in her tracks. She glanced past the senator and out the door. Robert Johnstone stood twenty feet down the hall, arms folded, chin on his chest, his eyes closed as he leaned against a wall. She wondered how long it had been since he had slept. She wondered, too, when she looked at him now, why all she could think of was the warmth and strength she had felt when Jon held her hands and prayed for her.

"I've been thinking about what you said this morning," Bellardi said, bringing her back to the present. "I'd like to speak with you again, if you have a few minutes."

Stephanie's heart seemed to bolt into a sprint. "Yes, sir, of course."

The senator nodded. "But first, if you don't mind, I'd like to spend a little time . . ." His voice cracked and tears formed at the corners of his eyes. "I'd like to spend a little time with my son."

Stevie quickly backed out of the room, pulling the door closed. As she did so, she could hear Senator Daniel Bellardi sobbing. She walked down the hall, past Robert, to look for a quiet place. She had a phone call to make.

PART FOUR

winter

46

Thursday
December 23

SHAWNA PULLED the ski cap down over her ears and gave each of her mittens a firm tug. Then she lifted a large box packed with her things and trudged toward the front door. Collin hailed her as she passed his bedroom door. "Can you carry one of my boxes on top of yours, Shawna?"

"For the five-zillionth time, no!" Shawna called back without breaking stride. "I pack my boxes, you pack yours. I carry my boxes, you carry yours."

"But it's snowing outside," Collin whined at her.

"You have mittens and a cap just like I do, Collin," Shawna answered without sympathy. "You have to carry your own boxes to the truck."

Shawna opened the front door while balancing one side of the box on her knee. She backed outside, then closed the door the same way. The icy wind stung her face. What Collin called "snowing" was only a light dusting. The wind swept most of it off the walkways.

Hurrying to the U-Haul truck, she lifted her box to the floor of the cargo area and pushed it inside. A couple of rented college guys in the apartment complex had loaded the furniture and heavy boxes earlier in the morning, under the watchful eye of Shawna's mother. Shawna and Collin had been instructed to cart the smaller boxes and odds and ends to the truck while their mom finished cleaning the apartment. The truck was to be packed up and ready to leave by noon.

Shawna was almost back to the apartment when she saw the figure huddled in the doorway of the laundry room, watching her. Terilyn was bundled in an oversized ski jacket with the hood up. Shawna hunched her shoulders against the wind and walked over to her. The two girls had not talked since Halloween night. "Hi, Terilyn."

"Hi." Terilyn's body language suggested that she preferred to remain unnoticed.

"We're leaving today," Shawna said.

"Yeah, I see that. Back to L.A?"

"Right. I guess you got my message. I left a gazillion of them on your machine."

"I heard them."

"I wrote you a couple of letters too."

"Yeah, I saw them."

"But you never called back or answered your door when I came over. And you won't even look at me at school."

Terilyn shook her head. "What's the use? You ran out on me at the party and embarrassed me in front of everyone there. You don't come to the leadership meetings anymore. We live in two different worlds."

"Yeah, I guess we do. I've changed my mind about a lot of things since the party. But I still want to talk to you."

"Why?"

"Because you're my friend, Terilyn. I don't agree with you about a lot of things, but I still care about you."

"That's an intolerant statement, Shawna. You should know that by now."

Shawna smiled. She was not intimidated by Terilyn's subtle accusation. "Like I explained in one of my letters, I've renewed my commitment to Christ since we last talked. I've chosen to live my life by the principles in God's Word. The Bible doesn't tell us to be tolerant; it tells us to be loving. Part of loving others is warning them about things that God says are wrong."

"There are millions of people in this country who don't believe everything the Bible says, including me," Terilyn stated.

"I know, but I still want to be your friend. If I write to you, will you write back?"

Terilyn seemed surprised. "You really want to write to me?"

"Sure. I like to keep in touch with my friends."

"Are you going to preach at me in your letters?" Terilyn asked with half a smile.

Shawna laughed. "No. All I'm going to do is be your friend."

After a tentative good-bye hug, Terilyn turned and jogged toward her apartment. Shawna said another prayer for her friend as she watched her go.

Stevie locked the cab of the U-Haul and snapped a padlock on the pull-down rear door. Leaving the truck in front of the apartment, Stevie and the kids took the Cherokee to the manager's office to drop off the apartment keys. Then they set out on a sixteen-mile drive into the country.

"We're not very dressed up for a Christmas party, Mom," Collin protested. Excited to get on the road in the U-Haul, he had been looking for a way to get out of their last social event in Redding.

"It's not exactly a party, honey," Stevie said. "We've been invited to stop in for a glass of eggnog and to say good-bye. Besides, they know this is moving day for us. They're not expecting us to dress up."

"Why do we have to go?"

"We don't *have* to go, honey," Stevie explained. "I *want* to go because these people are special to me."

Collin continued his whining. "But I don't want to go. I don't even know them. Why do *I* have to go?"

"Because we were all invited," Stevie said firmly. "We won't stay very long."

"This is going to be boring," Collin threatened. "I hate egg-nog."

"There will probably be candy there," Shawna said, tempting her brother.

"Candy? What kind of candy?"

"Maybe fudge and candy canes. Maybe Christmas cookies, too, and Christmas punch. It's all there just waiting for some nice little boy to come over and enjoy it all."

Collin was entranced. "Fudge isn't boring, that's for sure," he said dreamily. "Maybe we can stay longer than a few minutes." Stevie and Shawna laughed.

Driving into the Bellardi ranch, Stevie flashed back to the many times she had traveled this driveway during the campaign. Unpleasant memories of stress and personality conflicts on Bellardi's team had already begun to soften, enhancing the memories of camaraderie, mutual commitment to a cause, and work well done. She was relieved that the active political phase of her life was over. But she was still pleased it had been a part of her life.

Looking as elegant and refined as ever, Patricia Bellardi welcomed them at the door. "Stephanie, we've been expecting you," she beamed. "And the children are with you. How wonderful. Please come in and have some treats." The sounds of holiday music and cheery conversation from inside the house were equally inviting.

Stevie was relieved to find Mrs. Bellardi lucid and conversational. There were other days, she had heard, that the senator's wife wandered through the house not knowing who she was or where she was. Advancing Alzheimer's played its cruel tricks on the lovely lady every day. Stevie sympathized with her family.

As Patricia guided the children toward the refreshment table, Stevie found Robert Johnstone, overcoat slung over his arm, waiting for her near the entry. Stevie greeted him with a pleasant smile and a businesslike handshake. "I'm just on my way out," he explained, slipping into his coat. "I have a ton of work to do. But I had to stay long enough to see you one more time and . . . to say good-bye."

"I'm glad you did. I was hoping you'd be here."

Robert's voice fell to the level of a private conversation. "I'm not much for speeches; that's your gift. But I didn't want you to leave Redding without knowing how much I appreciate and . . . care for you." He smiled warmly. "I admire you, Stephanie, for your strong convictions and the courage to live them out, even when the heat is on."

Stevie returned his smile. "Thank you, Robert. You've been a . . . good friend. I've learned a lot from you."

"Not as much as I've learned from you," Robert insisted. "Thank you for your wisdom and sensitivity." His smile quavered slightly, but he held steady. "All the best to you and the family," he said, reaching for the door. Then, with a cheery "Merry Christmas and good-bye," he was gone.

"Good-bye," she said softly, but the door was already closed. She turned back to the party.

"Stephanie." Senator Bellardi stood waiting under the broad arch leading to the living room. The suit coat had been replaced by a V-neck sweater in conservative gray, but the tie was in place as always. The smile of welcome was warm and genuine.

Stevie extended her hand. "Merry Christmas, Senator."

Bellardi took her hand, then pulled her into a fatherly embrace. "Merry Christmas to you. I'm so glad you decided to come by."

Collin appeared at his mother's side holding a half-eaten chunk of fudge on a Christmas napkin. He looked up at the senator and spoke with bold, boyish innocence. "Are you the governor now?"

Bellardi, still smiling broadly, shook his head. "No, young man, I'm not the governor now."

Collin frowned his disappointment. "Mom said you're governor of North California."

"I said he is governor-*elect* of North California," Stevie clarified. "He was elected in November. He actually takes office in January."

"Just *barely* elected," the senator added, still smiling. "But a slim majority of the people in this state have asked me to serve, so I will serve."

Indeed, after the senator's surprising and emotional statement on the eve of the election, the vote was much closer than originally projected. The people of North California were horrified to learn that there was such a gulf between young Wes and his father that the boy had resorted to terrorism in an attempt to get his attention. Furthermore, the senator did not castigate his son, but instead tearfully apologized *to* him and *for* him in front of a national television audience. Fallout from the eleventh-hour political bombshell was a vote swing that erased all but half a percent of the senator's lead. He was declared the winner by the slimmest of margins—and that only after a recount.

Elena appeared in the living room with a tray of eggnog. Stevie took a glass. Collin turned up his nose and left for another pass at the dessert table. "How are the preparations coming along for the new administration?" Stevie asked the governor-elect.

"Very well, thank you. Robert is working extremely hard to get us ready for the inauguration—too hard, in fact. He'll probably miss Christmas."

Stevie nodded. That sounded like Robert. "So I suppose your team is already busy working on legislation."

"Yes. But thanks to you, we're now much more sensitive to the people for whom the laws are written. We'll strive for morality and justice in North California without forgetting to be compassionate and merciful. I will be forever grateful that you helped me see that important balance."

Feeling a little embarrassed at the compliment, Stevie changed the subject. "What about your appointments— cabinet and staff?"

"Proceeding well. Robert, of course, will be my chief of staff, but I still have several vacancies." Bellardi leaned a little closer. "It's not too late to reconsider, Stephanie. I need people like you working alongside me, people with character and strength of conviction."

Stevie smiled. The governor-elect had telephoned her four times in the last six weeks trying to convince her to accept a staff position. She felt flattered and appreciated, but each time she politely declined.

"Thank you, sir. As I've said before, it would be an honor to serve with you, but God is leading us in another direction right now. I believe North California is an ideal environment for Christian families. But not everyone can move here. And not everyone *should* move here. Believers in New York City, Chicago, Los Angeles, and other places around the country must live out the values of justice, mercy, and humility wherever they are, even if it is a more hostile environment. As much as we love North California, I think the Van Hornes are needed in L.A."

Another wave of arriving guests separated Stevie from her host, permitting her to migrate through the living room toward the family room. She exchanged holiday greetings and received best wishes and farewells from several former coworkers on the Bellardi staff: Coleman King, Price Whitten, Rhoda Carrier, Eden Hunter-Upshaw, and members of the debate team. When she could locate them, Stevie corralled Shawna and Collin long enough to introduce them.

Finally she found the person to whom she least wanted to say good-bye. Wes Bellardi was sitting on the leather sofa in the family room, still appearing thin and fragile, but growing stronger every day. He was sufficiently healed from his life-saving abdominal surgery, but burns had left him badly scarred. He wore a soft knit cap over his skull where as yet little hair had grown back. But thankfully he still tested negative for HIV.

Stevie had visited Wes at least three times a week since the Halloween night blast. As soon as he had been well enough to talk, he had told Stevie the details of that Halloween night. His original plan was to escape from the boat before the explosion and swim to shore. Unfortunately, he drank too much vodka and lost his balance on the slippery boat deck just after lighting the fuse. Wes had planned to disappear for a while, hiding out as long as he could in the gay community at Berkeley, allowing his father to believe he was dead. He had thought that surely then, as his family grieved for him, he would finally experience his father's love, even if it was from afar. Stevie—and Senator Bellardi—had been extremely relieved to know that Wes had not intentionally tried to kill himself. It made working through all of Wes's other problems—including the legal aspects, which had yet to be fully resolved—a bit easier.

Until recently, Wes came home from the hospital only one day a week. Just the previous day, however, his parents had brought him home for good. Stevie wondered if that accounted to some degree for Mrs. Bellardi's positive mental state today.

Stevie sat down beside Wes and touched his bony, blemished hand. "Hi," she said.

Wes turned toward her and smiled. "My favorite person," he said. "Even if you are a hard taskmaster."

Stevie smiled back at him. "Was I really that hard on you?"

"Absolutely," Wes answered, his smile widening. "And I needed it. I did some of my best writing under your watchful eye. Have you ever thought about becoming a professional mentor?"

She leaned close to him and whispered, "Too dangerous. I'm looking to get into something easier—lion taming, maybe."

Wes laughed out loud. Stevie's heart warmed to hear it. She knew he was getting better.

"I guess you'll be leaving for Los Angeles today," Wes said, the smile fading from his eyes. "I'll miss you."

Stevie swallowed the lump in her throat. "I'll miss you too." As she gazed at her young protégé, she recalled the long hours they had spent together in the hospital as Wes fought through his pain to question her about faith and forgiveness. Once again she had to fight tears as she remembered his sweet, simple prayer of repentance and commitment to God.

Wes reached inside his new red Christmas sweater—an early present from Stevie—and pulled out an envelope. "Here," he said, holding it out to her. "I have a present for you."

"A present for me? How thoughtful." Stevie opened the envelope and pulled out a single sheet of paper. On it was scrawled a simple poem, one that expressed gratitude and appreciation—and hope. Because of Wes's still scarred hands, the penmanship was shaky, but the message was clear.

"Thank you, Wes," she whispered, the tears she had been fighting finally spilling over onto her cheeks. "I couldn't have wished for a nicer gift."

"You told me I was a good writer," he said, displaying a scar-twisted smile.

"My favorite writer in the whole world," Stevie said, brushing the wetness from her face.

The voice of Dan Bellardi rose above the conversation in the room. "I know she's here somewhere," he said, weaving between the guests. Then, seeing Stevie, he said, "Here she is."

Stevie rose just as Jon appeared, making his way through the crowd with Shawna and Collin hanging adoringly on each arm. Stevie welcomed him with an embrace and a kiss on the cheek. "You finally made it," she said, unable to conceal her joy. "How was your flight?"

"Bumpy," Jon replied. "But at least it's over."

Stevie suddenly realized they were the center of attention. It was up to her to handle the introductions. "Everybody, this is Jon Van Horne, Shawna and Collin's father. He just arrived from L.A. to drive the truck down for us. We decided that the best thing for our family at this time is to be together in L.A., where Jon works as a school counselor." Stevie's mouth curled into an impish grin. "And for those who are too nice to ask, Jon and I are . . . dating again."

Spontaneous applause erupted. Jon and Stevie blushed.

Jon spoke up, "And I would like to introduce my traveling companion." He turned to the dark-haired young man behind him, who seemed overwhelmed by the roomful of strangers. "This is my friend and roommate from Los Angeles, Ben Hernandez. He just experienced his first ride on a turboprop puddle jumper. And he's going to keep us company on Interstate 5." Several people around Ben welcomed him with a handshake.

As general conversation resumed, Jon formally introduced Ben to Stevie, Shawna, and Collin. Then Stevie pulled Ben close to the sofa. "Ben, I would like you to meet a dear friend of ours, Wes Bellardi." She smiled. "You two have more in common than you might think."

"Hey, man," Ben said, sticking out his hand, seemingly unfazed by Wes's appearance.

Wes reached up and took Ben's hand. "Hello, Ben. I'm happy to know you."

As the two young men talked and Shawna and Collin wandered toward the punch bowl, Jon pulled Stevie aside. "When would you like to leave?"

"I hate to leave Wes, but I know we need to get on the road. So let's start saying our good-byes and moving toward the door."

Jon took both her hands in his. Their eyes met and held. For a moment they were alone in the room. "Steve, I've been waiting to say these three words for a very long time." Then he pulled her closer and kissed her lightly on the lips. "Let's go home."

Passing on the Truth to Our Next Generation

The "Right From Wrong" message, available in numerous formats, provides a blueprint for countering the culture and rebuilding the crumbling foundations of our families.

Read It and Embrace a New Way of Thinking

The Right From Wrong Book for Adults

Right From Wrong - What You Need to Know to Help Youth Make Right Choices
by Josh McDowell & Bob Hostetler

Our youth no longer live in a culture that teaches an objective standard of right and wrong. Truth has become a matter of taste. Morality has been replaced by individual preference. And today's youth have been affected. Fifty-seven percent (57%) of our churched youth cannot state that an objective standard of right and wrong even exists!

As the centerpiece of the "Right From Wrong" Campaign, this life-changing book provides you with a biblical, yet practical, blueprint for passing on core Christian values to the next generation.

Right From Wrong, Trade Paper Book
ISBN 0-8499-3604-7

The Truth Slayers Book for Youth

The Truth Slayers - The Battle of Right From Wrong
by Josh McDowell & Bob Hostetler

This book–directed to youth–is written in the popular NovelPlus format and combines the fascinating story of Brittney Marsh, Philip Milford and Jason Withers and the consequences of their wrong choices with Josh McDowell's insights for young adults in sections called "The Inside Story."

The Truth Slayers conveys the critical "Right From Wrong" message that challenges you to rely on God's word as the absolute standard of truth in making right choices.

The Truth Slayers, Trade Paper Book
ISBN 0-8499-3662-4

103 Questions Book for Children

103 Questions Children Ask About Right From Wrong
Introduction by Josh McDowell

"How does a person really know what is right or wrong?" "How does God decide what's wrong?" "If lying is wrong, why did God let some people in the Bible tell lies?" "What is a conscience and where does it come from?" These and 99 other questions are what kids ages 6-10 are asking. The *103 Questions* book equips parents to answer the tough questions kids ask about right from wrong and provides an easy-to-understand book a child will read and enjoy.

103 Questions, Trade Paper Book
ISBN 0-8423-4595-7

Hear It and Adopt a New Way of Teaching

The Right From Wrong Audio for Adults
What You Need to Know to Help Youth Make Right Choices
by Josh McDowell

What is truth? In three powerful and persuasive talks based on the book *Right From Wrong*, Josh McDowell provides you, your family, and the church with a sound, thorough, biblical, and workable method to clearly understand and defend the truth. Josh explains how to identify absolutes and shows you how to teach youth to determine what is absolutely right from wrong.

Right From Wrong, Audio–104 min.
ISBN 0-8499-6195-5

The Right From Wrong Musicals for Youth
The Truth Works Musical by Dennis and Nan Allen
The Truth Slayers Musical by Steven V. Taylor and Matt Tullos

The *Truth Slayers* Musical for junior high and high school students is based on the *Truth Slayers* book. The *Truth Works* Musical for children is based on the *Truth Works* Workbook. As youth and children perform these musicals to their peers and families, it provides a unique opportunity to tell of the life-changing message of Right From Wrong.

Each musical includes complete leader's instructions, songbook of all music used, dramatic script, and accompanying soundtrack on cassette or compact disc.

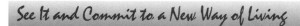

See It and Commit to a New Way of Living

Video Series to Adults

Truth Matters for You and Tomorrow's Generation
Five-part Video Series featuring Josh McDowell

Josh McDowell is at his best in this hard-hitting series that goes beyond surface answers and quick fixes to tackle the real crisis of truth. You will discover the reason for this crisis, and more importantly, how to get you and your family back on track. This series is directed to the entire adult community and is excellent for building momentum in your church to address the loss of values within the family.

This series includes five video sessions, a comprehensive Leader's Guide including samplers from the five "Right From Wrong" Workbooks, the *Right From Wrong* book, the *Truth Slayers* book, and a 8-minute promotional video tape to motivate adults to go through the series.

Truth Matters, Adult Video Series
ISBN 0-8499-8587-0

Video Series to Youth

Setting Youth Free to Make Right Choices
Five-part Video Series featuring Josh McDowell

Through captivating video illustrations, dynamic teaching sessions, and creative group interaction, this series presents students with convincing evidence that right moral choices must be based on a standard outside of themselves. This powerful course equips your students with the understanding of what is right from what is wrong.

The series includes five video sessions, Leader's Guide with reproducible handout including samplers from the five "Right From Wrong" Workbooks, and the *Truth Slayers* book.

Setting Youth Free to Make Right Choices, Youth Video Series
ISBN 0-8499-8585-4

Practice It and Make Living the Truth a Habit

Workbook for Adults
Truth Matters for You and Tomorrow's Generation
Workbook by Josh McDowell with Leader's Guide

The "Truth Matters" Workbook includes 35 daily activities that help you to instill within your children and youth such biblical values as honesty, love, and sexual purity. By taking just 25 - 30 minutes each day, you will discover a fresh and effective way to teach your family how to make right choices—even in tough situations.

The "Truth Matters" Workbook is designed to be used in eight adult group sessions that encourage interaction and support building. The five daily activities between each group meeting will help you and your family make right choices a habit.

Truth Matters, Member's Workbook ISBN 0-8054-9834-6
Truth Matters, Leader's Guide ISBN 0-8054-9833-8

Workbook for College Students
Out of the Moral Maze
by Josh McDowell with Leader's Instructions

Students entering college face a culture that has lost its belief in absolutes. In today's society, truth is a matter of taste; morality of individual preference. "Out of the Moral Maze" will provide any truth-seeking collegiate with a sound moral guidance system based on God and His Word as the determining factor for making right moral choices.

Out of the Moral Maze, Member's Workbook with
Leader's Instructions
ISBN 0-8054-9832-X

Workbook for Junior High and High School Students

Setting You Free to Make Right Choices
by Josh McDowell with Leader's Guide

With a Bible-based emphasis, this Workbook creatively and systematically teaches your students how to determine right from wrong in their everyday lives–specifically applying the decision-making process to moral questions about lying, cheating, getting even, and premarital sex.

Through eight youth group meetings followed each week with five daily exercises of 20-25 minutes per day, your teenagers will be challenged to develop a life-long habit of making right moral choices.

Setting You Free to Make Right Choices, Member's Workbook
ISBN 0-8054-9828-1
Setting You Free to Make Right Choices, Leader's Guide
ISBN 0-8054-9829-X

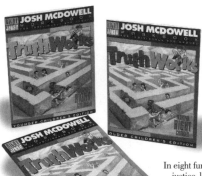

Workbook for Children

Truth Works - Making Right Choices
by Josh McDowell with Leader's Guide

To pass on the truth and reclaim a generation, we must teach God's truth when our children's minds and hearts are young and pliable. Creatively developed, "Truth Works" is two workbooks, one directed to younger children grades 1 - 3 and one to older children grades 4 - 6.

In eight fun-filled group sessions, your children will discover why such truths as honesty, justice, love, purity, self-control, mercy, and respect work to their best interests and how four simple steps will help them to make right moral choices an everyday habit.

Truth Works, Younger Children's Workbook ISBN 0-8054-9831-1
Truth Works, Older Children's Workbook ISBN 0-8054-9830-3
Truth Works, Leader's Guide ISBN 0-8054-9827-3